Praise for *Buffalo Jump Blues*

"McCafferty's wryly bantering characters are irresistible, his humor tangy, and his lyricism potent as he matches escalating action with intriguing disquisition. . . . A sharply ironic and suspenseful tale surreptitiously veined with profound insights into love, friendship, cultural collisions, and dire conflicts over wildlife and land, the sacred and the profitable."   —*Booklist* (starred review)

"Absorbing . . . [An] entertaining tale."   —*Publishers Weekly*

"With wry humor, Montana PI Sean Stranahan negotiates the territory between tradition and public interest with native rights in a mystery filled with characters we city folks don't meet often enough."
—*Minneapolis Star Tribune*

"Explosive, gripping, and not to be missed. Keith McCafferty gets the West just right with its cast of individualistic characters, stunning backdrops, and a past that breaks through in violent and unexpected ways. *Buffalo Jump Blues* is an impressive crime novel, and McCafferty is an impressive writer."

—Margaret Coel, *New York Times* bestselling author of
The Man Who Fell from the Sky and *Winter's Child*

"Keith McCafferty understands that there is much more to a riveting mystery than what is commonly found in the typical whodunit. He also knows that a rousing good tale can often shine a light on important matters that deserve our attention. In *Buffalo Jump Blues*, McCafferty does that and more as he takes us into the heart of Big Sky Country, a place he knows and loves, and treats us to a tightly crafted tale packed with quirky, captivating characters—mostly good, some just plain mean, and several who are simply murderous—and weaves an adventure that leaves you wanting more. He writes with heart and command of the story that sparkles on every page."

—Michael McGarrity, *New York Times* bestselling author of *Backlands*

"*Buffalo Jump Blues* is an evocative portrayal of the West, as rugged as it is fragile, and the centuries-old conflicts that still haunt the land and the people. McCafferty nails the delicate balance between humor and heft in a genuine way as he skillfully weaves together history and a present day mystery through an eclectic, endearing cast of characters. You will be thinking about this book long after you read the last page."

—P. J. Tracy, *New York Times* bestselling author of *Off the Grid*

"McCafferty has an ear and eye for character, language, history, politics, and murder, all of which come together in this strikingly original novel, which plays the past and present conflicts of American Indian life with and against a very contemporary story of identity, corruption, and murder that grabs the reader on the first page and never lets go."

—Jonathan Santlofer, bestselling author of *The Death Artist*

"Rich in history, local color, and unique characters."

—*Kirkus Reviews* (starred review)

A PENGUIN MYSTERY

BUFFALO JUMP BLUES

Keith McCafferty is the survival and outdoor skills editor of *Field & Stream*, and is the author of *The Royal Wulff Murders*, *The Gray Ghost Murders* (recommended by Oprah's Book Club), *Dead Man's Fancy*, and *Crazy Mountain Kiss*, which won the Western Writers of America 2016 Spur Award for Best Western Contemporary Novel. Winner of the Traver Award for angling literature, Keith is a two-time National Magazine Awards finalist. He lives with his wife, cat, and, as a wild bird rescue volunteer, various feathered friends, in Bozeman, Montana.

keithmccafferty.com

BUFFALO JUMP BLUES

Keith McCafferty

—A SEAN STRANAHAN MYSTERY—

PENGUIN BOOKS

PENGUIN BOOKS
An imprint of Penguin Random House LLC
375 Hudson Street
New York, New York 10014
penguin.com

First published in the United States of America by Viking,
an imprint of Penguin Random House LLC, 2016
Published in Penguin Books 2017

ISBN 9780525429593 (hardcover)
ISBN 9780143128878 (paperback)
ISBN 9780698406353 (ebook)

Printed in the United States of America
3   5   7   9   10   8   6   4   2

Set in Warnock Pro
Designed by Alissa Rose Theodor

For the Great Gutkoski

Behold, my brothers, the spring has come. . . . Every seed is awakened and so is all animal life. It is through this mysterious power that we too have our being and we therefore yield to our neighbors, even our animal neighbors, the same right as ourselves, to inhabit this land.

—Chief Sitting Bull, Hunkpapa Lakota Sioux

When the last buffalo falls on the plains I will hunt mice, for I am a hunter and I must have my freedom.

—Chief Joseph, Nez Perce

Acknowledgments

Writing about a subject that is as complicated and politically charged as bison is no small undertaking. I needed considerable help, and foremost want to thank Joe Gutkoski, founder of the Yellowstone Buffalo Foundation, for his historical perspective on bison and his passionate work on their behalf. For patiently answering my questions, I thank Matt Skoglund, the Rocky Mountain director of the Natural Resources Defense Council, the noted environmental journalist Todd Wilkinson, Montana State Representative Mike Phillips, Bonnie Lynn, and Glen Hockett, president of the Gallatin Wildlife Association. Particular thanks to Arnie Dood, bison biologist and formerly the threatened species coordinator for Montana Fish, Wildlife & Parks.

For reading early drafts and offering input from a Native American viewpoint I thank Marsha Small, the Montana tribal outreach associate for the National Wildlife Federation and a member of the Northern Cheyenne tribe. I also owe a debt of gratitude to Robin Heide from the Chippewa Cree tribe, formerly a resident of the Blackfeet Reservation, where parts of the book are set.

Over the course of my research, I attended public meetings about bison management, where I benefited from the perspective of local ranchers, as well as officials from Yellowstone National Park, the Montana Department of Livestock, and other organizations.

It's safe to say that not all of those I interviewed, on or off the record, agree with the views extended by some of the characters on the page, and I would stress that characters depicted as representatives of state agencies do not speak for those organizations. *Buffalo Jump Blues* is a work of fiction, for which I bear all responsibility.

Perhaps the least expected but most cherished rewards of becoming an author is developing friendships with readers. Andie Ray was a very special reader, and a kind, gracious, funny, and beautiful woman who met me with her husband last summer. She was loved by many, and she is missed by this writer.

Finally, I'd like to thank Susie and Tori Laher, Amanda Hardin, Claire Barley, Erin Deleissegues, and Mellanie Stordahl, for their smiles.

CHAPTER ONE

Kettle of Blood

"I suppose a gun would be too much to ask for."

Harold Little Feather stared across the river. A small group of gawkers, two fishing guides and the couples who were their clients, gathered at his back. Moaning sounds emanating from the tree and willow tangle at the base of the cliffs were spaced farther apart now, just in the thirty minutes since he'd driven up from Ennis. He'd been sitting down to breakfast when he got the call. His day off, a date to meet Martha and cast a fly in the braids of the Madison, hence unarmed.

"I mean, this being Montana and all, land of free men and open carry, I'd think somebody would be packin'."

If Martha was here she'd have her Ruger, day off or not. Strapping up was part of her a.m. ritual, like turning Goldie out for a run while she steeped her tea, running a ChapStick across her lips and looking at her face critically in the mirror before squaring her hat. On nights when Harold slept over he'd step up behind her, bring his big hands to her face, chestnut against white, lift the corners of her mouth so she saw herself smile.

"I got a two-two."

Harold turned around. He'd heard the crunch of gravel a few minutes before as another truck pulled up. It was Peachy Morris hauling his ClackaCraft, the one with the pink ribbon on the hull to show his support for breast cancer research, though anyone who knew Peachy knew the only breast research he was interested in was the hands-on kind. The lanky fishing guide crinkled up his eyes, a *What do we have here?* look on his face. Harold's glance took in Peachy's clients, a tall, sandy-haired man he recognized as a member of the Madison River Liars and Fly Tiers Club, though he had forgotten the name, and a small girl who looked maybe seven.

"And what's your name?" Harold asked the girl.

The girl hid her face behind a wing of straw-colored hair. *It's because I'm Indian,* he thought. When she'd boldly pronounced her armament, he'd been facing away from her.

The sandy-haired man extended his hand. "Robin Hurt Cowdry. We've met."

"Sure. You're from Zimbabwe, you import the African artifacts."

"Botswana," the man corrected. "Mugabe redistributed my keister all the way to Botswana. This is Doris, my niece." And to the girl, "Mind your manners."

She shyly faced Harold. "You can have my two-two," she said, "but it's back at the house."

"I might need something bigger than that," Harold said. His eyes turned to the cliffs as the moaning picked up in volume.

"Sounds like a bloody pride of lions," Cowdry said.

Harold's nod was half an inch. "It's bison. Guy on the Tenderfoot Creek game range saw them on the escarpment last night, maybe a part of the herd that came out of Yellowstone onto the Hebgen Plateau, reported it to Fish, Wildlife, and Parks this morning. A guide putting in heard the ruckus"—Harold jerked his head to indicate the group standing at the boat ramp—"so he called the county and here I am with my hands in my pockets."

"So you figure they fell over the cliffs?" Peachy Morris was tugging on his rowing gloves. "Fourth of July. All that racket down in the valley, people setting off fireworks. They could have panicked."

"That's what I'm thinking."

"Then let me see what I can come up with."

Harold crossed his arms against the bite of morning chill, caught the girl staring at his tattoos, the weasel tracks hunting around his left upper biceps, the hooves of elk following each other around his right.

"Are you an Indian?" she said, pushing the hair out of her face. "I've never seen an Indian."

"Absolutely," Harold said.

"I saw a Zulu warrior dance. They're fiercer than you."

"That's because I didn't put on my paint this morning."

Peachy was back, handing over a revolver in a leather holster.

"It's a .454 Casull. The loads are just snake shot, but there's some hard cast rounds floating around in my boat bag. Shoot through thirty inches of wet phone books."

The girl's eyes widened. "Jah, you could right donner them with that. Couldn't he, Uncle Robin?"

"Speak American, Dorry," Cowdry said.

Morris produced five hard cast loads with the comment that they might not be enough. "How many you think there are?" he said.

"Sounds like a few." Harold tipped out the cylinder to eject the snake loads and fed in the full-power rounds. He turned to Cowdry. "I left a message with the sheriff. She comes, she'll have donuts. Tell her to save me one of the glazed. Make sure your niece gets one."

He raised his chin to the guide. "Peachy, you think you could row me across?"

He spoke briefly to the group who'd been standing on the bank, telling them to wait until he'd crossed before launching and to stay in their boats until they were through the cliffs. He left them stringing fly rods and pushed off with Peachy at the oars of the driftboat, making for a backwater on the far bank.

"You want me to come with you?" Peachy dropped the anchor.

"No, I got it."

Harold ran his eyes to the tops of the cliffs, which were known as the Palisades and stood sentinel for a solid mile over the river's west bank. The moaning sounds were louder here and sounded more like growling, though the reverberation on the rock walls made them hard to place. He drew the Casull from the holster to double-check the loads. "I won't be needing this," he said, and tossed the holster to Peachy. He started hiking up the bank, holding the heavy handgun at his side.

The first buffalo was dead, a jagged edge of cannon bone sticking through the skin of its foreleg, its bowels evacuated, its enormous eye glazed over. A cow, fingers of shaggy winter coat hanging off it like brown moss. The cow had rolled after falling off the cliff, carving a wide swale through the brush. Twenty yards farther up, where willows choked the river bottom, was a second cow. Its cavernous rib cage expanded, then collapsed like an accordion. With each exhalation, a ragged gurgling sound blew bubbles in the blood covering its nose and mouth. Its eye followed Harold as he walked around it, but it lacked the strength to turn its head. Harold clenched his jaw. He extended his right arm and shot it in the back of its skull.

At the shot, Harold's arm jerked up and back, spinning him halfway around. He brought the barrel down out of recoil, feeling a sharp pain in his shoulder from the wrenching of his arm. Jesus, the thing was a cannon. His ears ringing, he sat down beside the dead bison. The roaring of other bison had become an undertone, dull and muted from the concussion. Eventually the underwater sensation subsided and the sounds of the dying animals came back.

Harold tucked his braid under the back of his shirt and fought through brush. He climbed until he reached the base of the cliffs, which was scree rock and sagebrush studded about with giant slabs of stone that had broken away from the cliff face. The rattling, guttural sighs seemed to surround him. He found another dead cow and then three bison still clinging to life, two of them lying down, one on its knees, feebly pushing its short horns against the withers of one of the fallen animals. Harold tore strips from his bandana and wadded them into his ears. He looked away for a few moments, putting off the inevitable. Then he grasped the rubberized grips of the revolver with both hands, extending his arms, and shot the bison that was on its knees. It rolled over and was still. He moved a few feet, sat down, and shot the next one, and then the third. The great heads rocked with the impacts and the moaning stopped.

Harold got to his feet. He pulled the cotton out of his ears. Except for the river running, he heard nothing, and the relative silence seemed oppressive. That must be the lot, he thought. He had gone a long way inside himself to find that still place where the hunter went when he killed, had gone so far as to regard the bison as "it" rather than he or she, something no Indian would do without conscious decision for they were his brothers, his sisters, and only now did he take in a bigger picture. Harold was Blackfeet, his people were buffalo people, nomads who had followed the herds until there were no more herds to follow. For thousands of years his ancestors had driven bison over cliffs similar to those above him. In fact, Harold thought, it was entirely likely that they had driven bison over these very cliffs, for this had been a Blackfeet hunting ground and the cliffs formed what was called a *pishkun* in the tribal language, a "deep blood kettle." But that was before the white man came with his seeds and his cattle, before the Sharps rifles spoke and the Sun Dances held on the reservation became only ceremony.

Harold squatted on his heels, facing the river. He watched the occasional car pass by on the highway, a quarter mile to the east. If you lifted your eyes it was Eden as his grandfather's grandfathers had seen it, the mountains uncolored by time. The irony of what he had done, killing the first bison to have returned to these ancient hunting grounds in one hundred and fifty years, was not lost on him, and the tears that hung on the high bones of his cheeks were the tears of his people. He ignored them as a white, boxy-looking vehicle slowed and turned onto the access road. That would be Martha's Cherokee. Well, he'd better get back across and give her the news.

The slope he'd climbed earlier was choked with willow and alder, and he looked for an easier route down to the river. To his right the gradient eased, and he'd descended a few yards when he saw the bushes above him bulging and heard a sound like rocks clashing. The head of a bison emerged from the brush, strings of bloody mucus hanging from its nostrils. It was striking its hooves against the stone scree, pawing it. The bison was thirty feet away and it came in a stumbling charge. A bull, its great hump standing taller than Harold's head, coming on three good legs, one rear leg flopping. Harold cocked the hammer on the last round in the Casull and held his fire. Twenty feet, ten, the bison's head dropping to toss him with its thick, incurved horns. Harold brought the muzzle level with its forehead and pulled the trigger, then jumped to the side as the bull fell heavily, its nose plowing into the scree. For a moment it lay still. Then, slowly, it began to slide down the hill. It picked up speed, rolled over once, and came to rest against the trunk of a limber pine tree.

Harold had felt the earth shake as the bison fell, and now he couldn't feel his feet underneath him. Where he'd been standing, blood painted the stones. He worked his way down to where the beast lay dead, into the envelope of its heavy odor, into their collective past. The underwater sensation was back and he shook his head. Such a magnificent animal. Such a waste of life.

That's when he heard the bleating. It was not loud, but higher-pitched than the moaning he'd heard earlier. He knew it must be a calf. He thought about going back to the landing, waiting for Martha, borrowing her .357 to finish it off.

No, do it now. Get it over with. He reached for the bone-handled knife on his hip.

CHAPTER TWO

Facts of Nature

Martha Ettinger stood on the riverbank, looking across to the cliffs where she'd heard the last shot.

"That's all he had with him, five rounds," Robin Cowdry said.

Martha placed her hands on her hips and drummed the grips of her revolver. Harold should have waited for her, but if he'd waited, he wouldn't be Harold.

"I can't hear anything," she said.

"He must have got them all."

Martha shook her head. This was going to make news. Bison were a hot-button issue in Montana, had been ever since the herds started migrating out of Yellowstone Park more than two decades before, hazed back by cowboys and helicopters, or shot after crossing the border. To a degree the animals were pawns in a controversy that went beyond animal control and was in fact cultural warfare, everyone in on the act, from the cattle ranchers who couldn't say the word "bison" without spitting to buffalo hippies who'd take a bullet for them, from Native Americans who wanted to bring herds back to the reservations to the urban electorate who'd like to see them roam freely on public lands. Even the governor was caught between the rock that was the livestock industry and the hard place that was public sentiment for this icon of the West that only a century ago had stood at the brink of extinction.

"Harold thought this was part of that Hebgen herd," Cowdry said. "The ones that came out of the park."

"Mmm."

He might as well have been talking to a river stone.

"Here they come," Martha said.

She'd seen the skiff pull out of the cove, Peachy hard at the oars. Harold wasn't sitting in the bow seat from which a fisherman would cast, but looked to be kneeling on the boat's bottom. Caught in the current, the skiff swept downriver at an angle, Peachy working it into the near bank some forty yards below the landing. He hopped out in his waders, taking the bow line to haul it upstream. Harold stayed where he was, Martha now seeing that he was bending over and his head was down. She felt a flutter in her blood and subconsciously brought two fingers to the artery in her throat.

"What's that in the bottom of the boat?" Cowdry had pulled on his waders and was stepping into the river to help Peachy with the skiff. The girl, Dorry, stepped up beside Martha and reached for her hand. Her mouth was white with powdered sugar from the donut Martha had given her.

"Look," she said. "Look." She let go of Martha's hand and jumped on a rock to gain a higher vantage. "Look, Sheriff, he's got a buffalo!"

Harold had stepped out of the boat into thigh-deep water, his back to the bank. When he turned around, the bison calf was bleating against his chest. The veins on his biceps stood out from the strain of lifting it. He sloshed to shore and stepped onto the bank.

Martha started to speak, but there was something behind Harold's half smile that gave her pause.

"Did that snakebit calf pull through?" he said. He set the bison down so that the girl could pet it with her sticky fingers.

Martha gave him a look. "No, I gave her mouth-to-nose until Jeff Svenson showed, but she was too far gone."

"What happened to the carcass?"

"Skinned and hanging. Why, do you want some veal? Personally, I'm a little put off by meat pumped with poison."

"When did this happen?"

"Last night." *Last night when you didn't come over.* That part went unsaid.

Martha caught the amused look Peachy Morris was giving them. The last time Peachy had heard Martha talking with Harold about something and what they were really talking about was something else, he'd told them to get a room.

She looked hard at the fishing guide. He rolled up a stick of gum and put it in his mouth, wiped the grin off his face.

"What did you do with the skin?" Harold asked.

The shoe dropped as Martha shook her head.

"Hun-ah," she said. "It isn't going to happen."

Harold knelt down beside the little red bison, which had quieted down while the girl had her arm around it, but was now bleating incessantly.

"Hey, little fella," Harold said. He lifted his eyes to Martha, who mouthed the word "No."

"Meet your new mother," Harold said.

————

It took some finagling. You couldn't just put a bison into the bed of a truck unattended. Somebody would have to hold it while the other drove, and Harold took the honor, climbing into the bed. After introducing the bison to the Angus cow that had lost her calf, presuming that went smoothly and there was no guarantee it would, they'd drive back to pick up the Cherokee, which Peachy Morris and Robin Cowdry agreed to shuttle downriver to Ennis after their float.

Martha looked at the girl, sitting under a frayed straw hat on the stern seat of the skiff. They'd had to pry her arms from the bison's neck and tears had tracked down her cheeks, beading up on top of her sunscreen. But she'd bucked up when Martha told her she could visit the calf, a lie of a certain color.

"Don't let her play with the siren," Martha said, as she pushed the driftboat off the ramp. "You know how birds attack a boat when you hit the siren."

"I won't let her touch it." Peachy pulled at the oars, winking at Martha, going along.

"And remember the ejector seat. Whatever you do, don't touch the red button."

Peachy curled his fingers underneath the rowing platform. "It's right under my thumb here."

"Ejector seat!" the girl said. Her eyes grew big. "You don't have no ejector seat. Do you?"

"Pitch you right into the water if you don't behave," Peachy said.

"Nah. He doesn't have an ejector seat, does he, Uncle Robin?"

Martha waved good-bye as the driftboat swept away down the river, Robin Cowdry already false casting his fly line.

She turned back to the truck. Harold had climbed into the bed and was sitting with his arms around the little bison. "Ejector seat, huh? I didn't know you were so good with kids."

"You forget I raised two of them."

Harold jabbed his chin, a *Look over my shoulder* gesture. "I knew we waited around, they'd finally show," he said.

"Who?"

"Drake. I can smell him from here."

Martha looked up the access road. Harold was right. A truck was coming, it rattled down the grade, a horse-and-cattle emblem identifying as a DOL vehicle—Montana Department of Livestock.

"Harold, this doesn't have to get personal."

"Maybe if your eyes are blue."

"Well, my eyes are blue, so just let me do the talking. Okay?"

It was Drake, Francis Lucien Drake, though everyone just called him Drake. He stepped out of the truck in parts, everything about him big, pushing his hat back on a high forehead, hitching his jeans, shaking his head when he saw the bison calf. He stuck a hand-rolled cigarette into the corner of his mouth and worked it without lighting it.

"You cavorting with livestock now, Harold? Getting yourself some of that barn candy?" A smile on his face, or rather a deliberate pulling back of his lips, exposing tombstone teeth stained by nicotine. He had a whorl of creases in his chin that constantly shifted, as if worms churned under the stubble.

Another man, shorter, swarthy, had climbed from the cab. He kicked caked mud from his boots against a big truck tire with a dragon-tooth tread. Carhartts head to cuff, old cracked boots. A gunfighter mustache gone salt-and-pepper. Martha knew him, had to wait a second to recall the name.

"Calvin," she said.

"Sheriff."

She made the introduction to Harold, who knew Calvin Barr only by his reputation as a wolfer for Animal Damage Control. Barr spoke out of the side of his mouth to say hello, his eyebrows, wiry and black, running together as he frowned at the calf. He came forward in a bowlegged walk and rubbed the head of the bison.

"Little red bull calf," he said. His voice had sandpaper in it.

"I see somebody's been crawling the stock of his rifle," Harold said.

"You'd think I learned the lesson." Barr tapped the upper arch of his right orbital bone, where dozens of half-moon scars, caused by the steel rim of a rifle scope, showed white through a forest of eyebrow hair.

"What kind of gun recoils so hard the scope cuts you?"

"Forty-five ninety Sharps original with a Malcolm's six-power. But it's my own durned fault. If I kept my cheek back where it belongs, the scope wouldn't jump back far enough to kiss me."

Martha had led Drake away from the truck. Harold could see them standing by the river, Martha with her hands on her hips, Drake shaking his head.

"Just so we're clear," Harold said. "He points the finger, you pull the trigger?"

Barr tilted his head as if considering. "That would be the job description," he said.

"I heard the wolf lovers called you Killer Barr."

The man nodded. "That wasn't fair. I made it my business to know if I was shooting a guilty party. A lot of livestock deaths are blamed on predators when it's rancher neglect, blue tongue . . ." He shrugged. "Teeth don't have a thing to do with it sometimes."

"No, it wasn't fair. You're just a man caught in the middle, doing his job. My problem's with the law that has you do it. 'Bout an hour ago I shot five bison that fell off the cliff. That's where I found this little fella. Don't know how he survived the fall."

"Must have fallen on top of one of the others, reduced the impact."

"Maybe."

"Had to be hard, what you did."

"Shooting them was an act of mercy. Seeing them suffer, that was hard. How many have you killed?"

"Bison?" The man took the question seriously, ran his eyebrows together as he considered. "I'd say three hundred plus since I contracted to DOL. They stray out of the park, out of the buffer zone, I get the call."

"You ever think about not answering the phone?"

Barr seemed to think about that question, too. "There's a way I look at it," he said. "If it isn't me, then they get somebody else. Then maybe the bullets don't go where they're supposed to and somebody has to clean up the mess, like you did yonder."

"You're the reluctant executioner who makes sure the job is done humanely."

"Buffalo take a lot of killing." Barr rubbed the hairy back of his hand against the bison calf's forehead.

"Those bison this morning," Harold prompted. "If they hadn't fallen off the cliff, you were going to kill them anyway, am I right?"

"I won't lie to you. As soon as they crossed onto the public land, the department had the green light."

"You'd have shot this calf along with the rest."

"That's the policy. You want to get all of them. You don't want to leave one that has the unacceptable behavior ingrained, because it will lead others back to the same place."

"Unweaned calf do that?"

"It's policy to cull them all."

"'Cull.' That's an interesting word. I saw some cowboys cull a herd of thirty up out of Gardiner once, enough blood to cover a football field. One cow was dragging her guts on the ground, little calf like this one following her."

The calf was bawling again and Harold rubbed its head.

"What are you thinking to do?" Barr said.

"Sheriff has a cow lost its calf. We'll wrap this little guy in the skin and hope she accepts him."

Barr nodded. "I heard of that being done, but never heard of it take. Worth a shot. I say good luck to you."

Martha and Drake were coming back, Drake making a tisking sound with his tongue as he shook his head.

"Harold, you know I can't let you have that calf."

"Not my calf to give. This is a wild, free-ranging bison," Harold said.

"There ain't no such animal, no sir."

"Times are changing, Drake. The buffalo are coming back, just like the wolf did. It's people like you the clock's ticking down on."

"You're wrong about that, but that's not the issue. This calf hasn't gone through quarantine and it could be spreading disease to cattle."

"You mean brucellosis. That's bullshit and you know it."

"My job is to remove bison that have strayed beyond the zone of tolerance, which this herd clearly had. Plus you're violating state law pertaining to possession of wildlife."

Harold looked at Martha, who didn't return his glance. He looked at Barr, who had stepped away from the truck. It had become an old-fashioned western, two men in a dusty street.

"'Pertaining,' huh? You must have learned a new word, Drake."

Drake pulled at his cigarette. "We'll wait until you're gone to do our duty, that makes a difference to you."

"No, I'll be taking him with me."

The man nodded, showed his teeth in a gray smile, as if that was the response he'd expected.

"Then I'll have to write you up to the supervisor. Someone will be knocking. Probably be me."

"We'll have the TV crew on call. World can see you for what you are. Tell you what, though, it comes to that, I'll rub your smile in buffalo manure for the camera. Rest of your life, first thing people will think when they see your face is how an Indian stuffed your mouth with shit."

Drake stared at him, his eyes squinted up in folds of flesh. The worms in his chin crawled and crawled. He spat the butt and ground it under his heel.

"We're done here, Calvin. Let's go before I do something I regret."

"Anytime, anywhere," Harold said.

Drake took a half step forward to find Ettinger blocking the way.

"You want to do something about this, go through your channels," she said to Drake. "But once the calf is on private property, you'll have to get a court order to have it removed."

"Not according to interagency statute, not if I deem it an imminent threat to livestock or property." He shrugged. "But maybe I won't have to take him. Sometimes, animals just disappear. It's a fact of nature."

"Anything happens to this calf," Harold said, "you'll answer to me."

"Is that a threat?" He was looking at Ettinger. "This man has threatened physical violence upon my person and all I'm doing is trying to execute my job. I want it duly noted."

"Not a threat." Harold rearranged his grip on the struggling bison calf. "Like you said, Drake, some things are just a fact of nature."

CHAPTER THREE

The Trout Tails Bar and Grill

Every July 7, as far back as he remembered, Sean Stranahan had gone fishing. The rivers changed, the spots on the flanks of the trout changed with the species, but the ritual at water's edge was the same. He'd pull the rod his father had milled from Tonkin bamboo from its sock, drink in the scent of tung oil, joint the nickel silver ferrules, and string a double-tapered silk fly line through the guides. The fly box, an old polished pewter Wheatley with spring clips, held three dozen flies, all that remained from his father's vise. His father had tied them with mechanic's hands—thick, blunt fingers with remote nerve endings—and the flies were crude by modern standards. They were traditional wet fly patterns, the oldest tied on vintage blind-eyed hooks, but they had been catching trout since before Sean was born. This year he chose a #12 Gold-Ribbed Hare's Ear and knotted it to a 3X monofilament tippet. The tippet was one size too heavy for the fly, but, having only a handful of his father's creations left, Sean didn't want to chance the leader being broken on a sizable fish.

The water eddying around his wader belt was his favorite stretch of the Madison River, only a short walk upstream from the log cabin owned by the Madison River Liars and Fly Tiers Club. Sean was an honorary member of the club; his dog, Choti, pacing the bank as she watched him cast, was a more or less permanent one during the summer months. Patrick Willoughby, the club's president, had affected mock disappointment when Sean declined his offer to fish with him after dinner.

"My dear boy, you cut me to the quick," he'd said, and shaken his head, his round-rimmed glasses and moon face lending him the look of a professorial owl. But he had not pressed the matter. He'd only asked if Sean would return in time to accompany the club members to the bar later.

Sean had said that was up to the trout.

It was still up to the trout an hour after he'd started casting. He'd clipped off the Hare's Ear, replaced it with a Leadwing Coachman, lost faith in the Coachman, and was swinging a somber pattern called a Dusty Miller when the line stopped, a trout into the air at the sting of the hook. The fish pulled away to midriver and wrapped the line around an exposed boulder. It hung there, the line throbbing while Sean lied to himself, telling himself there was still hope. As a last recourse, he threw slack into the line, hoping to fool the fish into thinking the pressure was from the opposite direction and coax it into swimming back around the rock. It didn't. Something had to give, and it was the knot that gave.

Sean reeled in the slack line, feeling a hollowness in his chest that had less to do with losing the fish than the fly.

"Sorry, Pop," he said.

He thought about tying on another fly. He couldn't recall a time when he hadn't caught at least one trout on his father's birthday, and he knew that if he fished into the enveloping darkness, he still had a very good chance. But not catching was fishing, too, as his dad would have been the first to remind him. It was the angler's song in minor key.

Sean started back toward the cabin, Choti following, the rod balanced on his shoulder with the tip backward, like a boy in a Rockwell painting. Water had always been his window to the past, and as he walked along the fisherman's path his mind turned to an earlier trail, one that wound through a swamp along Michigan's Au Sable River. Twilight gloom had gathered in the arms of the cedars. His father took his hand as they crossed the deep part, a trout against the far bank rising like a metronome to mayflies that spread their wings on the surface, crucifix offerings to the trout. The line whistled. The trout took, walloped its tail with a hollow smacking sound and then went deep as his father handed Sean the rod, that throbbing pull the only drug he'd ever need. When he curled his fingers under the gills to carry the trout back to camp, lightning bugs burned their lanterns under one willow, then the next, a string of winking lights to show the way.

Such recollections came less often now. They rusted away with the passing of the years, like the old hooks on the flies his father had tied.

"You have the look of a man who's been somewhere else," Patrick Willoughby said, peeling his waders off on the stoop of the porch.

———

The Trout Tails Bar and Grill, "Tits and Tails" as the locals called it, was or rather had been one of those unzoned, wood-slat, metal-roofed Bud-and-burger bars that change ownership as often as the anglers who inhabit them change trout streams. Since Stranahan's move to Montana four years previously, it had been called the Bear Claw Bar and Grill, the Last Cast Saloon, and After the Hatch, each establishment succumbing to the fiscal limitations of a three-month season.

Its latest incarnation was a nod to the Sip 'n Dip Lounge, the Great Falls mermaid bar that had been christened by *GQ* magazine as the country's best watering hole. Sean had dropped into the Sip 'n Dip once while fishing the Missouri River and been surprised to discover that the real attraction wasn't the women flipping their tails behind glass, but Piano Pat Spoonheim, a great-grandmother who played a triple-decker keyboard and had been talking her way through old standards at the same bench for more than fifty years.

Trout Tails, built on a high bank of the Madison opposite its confluence with the West Fork, sported an electric sign wrested from pink-and-aqua neon tubes that operated on a timing mechanism, so that a mermaid's tail appeared to flip back and forth as you passed through the door. Inside was Margaritaville North—crab traps suspended from a bamboo ceiling, a neon parrot advertising Budweiser beer, globe lights reflecting cheeks blushed by alcohol, a goldfish bowl for tips on the top of a battered baby grand. Sean arrived a few minutes behind the other club members and found Pat Willoughby already ensconced at a corner table, along with Kenneth Winston, a hairstylist from Baton Rouge, Louisiana, who supported his trout jones by teaching white hairdressers how to barber black men's hair.

"You need a trim," Winston said as Sean sat down. "I know you're going for the lumbersexual look, but still, a lady likes a little grooming."

"I need better luck is all. That's my first fishless night in a long time."

"What you need, my dear fellow," Willoughby said, "is a pint of Slow Elk Oatmeal Stout and a deluxe blue cheese bison burger, on me of course, though I'm still smarting from your snub."

"Today's my father's birthday. I like to make a few casts for him. I'm sorry for not telling you earlier."

"Perfectly understandable."

Willoughby nodded to the waitress, and when the beers came, they toasted to Sean's father.

"Still no one to play the piano?" Sean said.

Winston raised a pair of sculpted eyebrows. "You're in a mermaid bar and you're worried about the piano player?"

"Actually, I heard they might be getting someone from New Orleans," Willoughby said.

"Oh?"

Sean had had an affair of the soul, the body, too, though perhaps not the heart, with a piano bar singer from Mississippi shortly after he'd moved to Montana. The singer, who went by Velvet Lafayette and whose real name was Vareda Beaudreux, had read the etched letters on the ripple glass of his art studio at the Bridger Mountain Cultural Center—*Private Investigations*—taken the sign literally, and hired him to find her brother, and then her brother's killer, when the man wound up drowned with a Royal Wulff trout fly hooked in his lower lip. No, it couldn't be her. Vareda had disappeared back into the Delta country from which she had come, but then she had mentioned singing in New Orleans once.

"You wouldn't have caught the name?" he asked Willoughby.

"No, it was just something the Queen of the Waters said in passing."

"Ah, queen of my heart," Winston said.

"I believe the body part to which you refer lies somewhere south of the heart," Willoughby corrected.

When Sean had entered the bar, the seven-thousand-gallon tank was empty, the mermaids who took turns taking dips changing shifts. Besides the Queen of the Waters—a copper blonde with Botticelli curls who had been coaxed from South Florida, where she swam with reef fish as a surprise treat for the patrons of a glass-bottomed boat—the mermaids included the Parmachene Belle and the Chippewa Nymph. All had taken their names from fishing flies, and with the exception of the Queen, who was seeing Sean's best friend, Sam Meslik, Sean knew more about the histories of the fly patterns than of the women who assumed their names.

Hearing a splash, he turned his head to see the Parmachene Belle enter the tank, trailing a fizz of bubbles. Her hair was platinum with dyed red streaks and her long white tail was scarlet-banded, the color combination of the trout fly. A muscular swimmer, she backflipped, bubbles blowing out of her nose, her candy-cane tail flowing. Sean turned his attention back to his burger and the table's conversation, which was about the bison falling off the cliffs, the Palisades being only a few miles downriver from the clubhouse and even closer to the bar. Robin Cowdry had broken the news, which thanks to Peachy Morris was up and down the valley in the span of a day. Sean's sympathy for the buffalo already being voiced by those at the table, he nodded along, and when his eyes returned to the glass, the Parmachene Belle had kicked to the front of the tank, where she stared incuriously at the patrons of the bar, who stared back as if they were observing an orangutan in a zoo. When a man raised his camera, she beckoned him closer with the waving hands of a belly dancer.

Sean felt his phone buzzing in his pants pocket—a surprise as this part of the valley was usually a dead spot for reception—and walked outside to take the call. It was Katie Sparrow, the search dog handler who worked as a backcountry ranger in Yellowstone Park.

"Is dickhead one word or two?" she said by way of hello.

"Uh, one, I think."

"'Cause I'm writing a text, and it starts, 'Dear Dickhead, where were you last night when you said you'd help me bake dog biscuits?'"

Sean had been afraid that's where the conversation was heading. "I'm sorry, Katie. I didn't know it was a date."

"What did you think it was?"

"Uh, more of a suggestion. I was just tired. It was a long day on the water and I didn't want to make the drive when I was half asleep."

"Really? I'm not just your strumpet, some piece of low-hanging fruit like a kumquat. You just take a bite whenever you feel like it?"

"Do you even know what a kumquat is?"

"Don't change the subject." Then: "Do you?"

"No," Sean admitted. "I don't know what a strumpet is, either."

"Where are you now?"

He told her. Silence.

"I got a tail, too." There was a forlorn note in her voice.

This was the Katie Sparrow that Sean had come to know over the past few weeks, bold and chipper one moment, small and alone the next.

"You're still in love with Martha, aren't you? You want to be faithful even though she's taken up with Harold again."

Sean didn't have an answer.

"I knew it. I guess I'm not one who can throw the first stone, though."

Finally he said, "Tell me about the tail."

"It's the one I wore to the Sheriff's Ball. The puma costume."

"I remember." He hesitated. "If I come over, will you show it to me?"

"If I can find it. I think it's in a drawer or something."

By the time he closed the phone and returned to the bar, Willoughby had paid the bill and he and Ken Winston were standing up to go.

"We're fishing streamers at five a.m. sharp," Willoughby said. "Pursuit of the mythical ten-pound brown."

Winston's skeptical eyebrows meant that remained to be seen.

"You *are* bunking with us, Sean." Willoughby gave him his peering-over-his-glasses look. "You *will* accompany us on this most hearty of endeavors."

"I don't think so."

"Elaborate," Winston said.

"No," Stranahan said.

Mischief danced in Winston's eyes. Very white teeth in a knowing smile.

"It was a wrong number," Sean said.

"Uh-huh. Five-minute wrong number."

"Oh, leave the poor boy alone, Ken," Willoughby said. "Can't you see he's hit a rough patch? A little R and R is quite in order and it just leaves more fish for us."

Sean finished his beer standing and followed them out the door. They said their good-byes and he stood a minute, lifting his eyes to the sky. A sickle moon, a few stars, too early for the diamond glitter of a Montana midnight.

"Are you looking for any one in particular?"

He turned to see a woman standing on the porch of the bar. She brought a cigarette to her lips, making a brief cherry circle.

"Tobacco is one of the four sacred medicines," she said, waving the cigarette. She had long hair that created a shadow, making it hard to see her face. "So which one?"

"It's the star of Pegasus, Beta Pegasi. There." He pointed to a bright star that dimmed, then grew bright again.

"I know most of the Native American constellations. I'm not sure they have that one." She puffed at the cigarette.

"You shouldn't be doing that to your lungs, medicine or not."

"But I don't inhale. I just smoke for the therapeutic aspect."

He crossed the few yards that separated them and shook her hand. "I'm Sean," he said.

"Ida." She leaned back against the rail of the porch, hooking the heel of one boot over the toe of the other.

In the glow of the neon tubes, Sean could make out the sprinkle of freckles across her cheekbones and the bridge of her nose. Level eyes. Chestnut-colored hair. Her posture was utterly relaxed and unselfconscious, though an oversize jean jacket hid the contours of her body.

"Why that star?" she said.

"A woman I know believes her daughter's spirit resides in it, because it pulses like a heart. Something to do with the heating and cooling of the gases."

"That's a very Indian thing to believe."

"She is Indian, a little."

They looked at the sky.

"I'm a quarter white on my mother's side," she said. "We're from Rocky Boy. Chippewa Cree."

"What brought you here?"

"MSU. I had a basketball scholarship. Things happened and I wound up back on the reservation. Then I was out of state awhile." She waved the cigarette. "Nomadic people and all that. Now I'm back in school, or will be fall semester."

"How did you end up in a fish tank?"

"Ah, so you know my secret."

"It's my powers of deduction. You weren't at any of the tables and you're smoking beside a service entrance. And I know who the Parmachene Belle and the Queen of the Waters are, and you don't look like kitchen help, so that leaves the Chippewa Nymph. Besides, your eyes are bloodshot. I'm guessing that's an occupational hazard."

"Aren't you a smart fellow?"

"I'm a private detective."

"Really?"

"Sort of."

She brought the cigarette to her lips and exhaled. "The Queen's the real attraction. Cal only hired me because I could fit into a tail he bought on eBay."

"Pays the tuition, huh?"

She shrugged. "The hourly's so-so, but we get fifty dollars for walking down the bank and posing with the fishermen."

"I didn't know about that."

"Yeah. If a guy wants a picture of himself holding a mermaid while he's standing in the river with his fly rod, like 'Look what I caught,' it's fifty dollars and tips. I made five hundred on the Fourth, being passed around like a trout."

"What's Montana coming to, huh?"

She smiled. "So are you going to watch me swim? I'm in the tank in twenty minutes."

"I would, but I have to be somewhere else. Perhaps tomorrow night?"

"I don't work tomorrow."

"Then it's my loss. I've never had a date with a mermaid before."

"Who said it was a date?"

"I stand corrected."

"Smoke with me," she said, holding the cigarette out to him.

Sean puffed.

"Coward." She took the cigarette back and flicked the ash with a fingernail. The silence between them was comfortable.

"Bad timing," Sean said. He smiled back at her. He hadn't flirted with a woman in a long time. Ida seemed genuine and he was beginning to regret telling Katie that he'd come over.

"I've got to go wriggle into my tail. It was nice meeting you."

"What's your last name, Ida?"

"Evening Star."

"Like Venus?"

"No, Venus is a planet. It's just called the Evening Star."

"Ah. So that's why you asked me earlier about the stars."

"No, I was just making conversation."

"I showed you mine, show me yours. Is it out tonight?"

"Maybe if I knew you better."

"Are you?"

"Going to know you better? I don't know."

She ground the cigarette out on the rail, and thirty minutes later Sean was knocking on the door of the Forest Service lease cabin outside West Yellowstone, where Katie Sparrow lived. Her Class III search dog, a shepherd named Lothar, checked him out by running his nose from cuffs to crotch, then gave his okay by trotting back to his dog bed. Katie raised on her tiptoes to kiss him. She'd streaked whiskers on her cheeks with eye liner and was wearing the puma costume with the tail held into a curl with fishing line.

"Would you care to see my lair?" she said.

———

He awoke to scrambling feet as Lothar jumped down from the bed and stood under the window, beating his tail against the nightstand. Outside, floating on a chill wind, Sean could hear the faint howling of wolves. Katie stirred in her sleep and he thought of waking her. She loved to hear wolves. It was why she left the windows cracked, even in winter.

"Katie," he said. She was naked under a flannel sheet and he drew a finger down her spine.

"What is it?"

"Wolves."

She sat up. In the moonlight spilling through the window, Sean could make out the tattoo of a cracked heart on the swell of Katie's left breast. On the first night Sean had spent with her, he had kissed the tattoo and felt her body stiffen. "No, please don't do that," she said. Nor was he permitted to kiss the beauty spot under her right collarbone because Colin, her fiancé whom she'd lost in an avalanche, had always kissed it, and, like the heart, it was reserved for the memory of his lips. In other ways she was sexually freer than any woman Sean had known, even if she had yet to show him the sex move she'd joked about patenting.

"You aren't ready for it," she'd told him. And added, "Maybe next time."

That had been three or four next times ago, and it summed up their relationship. He could aspire to her sex move, but there was skin he couldn't kiss, a level of intimacy beyond which he could not pass. And if he was being honest, it was the same with him, though without the physical boundaries. He and Katie were temporary harbor, ships throwing lines to each other in a wine-dark sea.

He smiled at the image in his mind of a wine sea.

"Whatcha thinking?" she said.

"Nothing."

"You always do that when we're together. It's like you're somewhere else."

The wolves howled, saving Sean from coming up with a lie.

"That's the Cougar Pack," Katie said. "They made a kill up on Gneiss Creek three days ago. Now they're hunting again." Sean felt her fingers interlace with his as she spoke. She squeezed his hand. "Come on, let's make love, we can howl with them if we're quick."

They weren't quick, but by then it didn't matter.

CHAPTER FOUR

A Light for Someone Else

"I haven't slept in a barn since Two Dot," Martha said.

Beside her, Harold stirred. Martha shone her flashlight, picking out pieces of straw clinging to his braid.

"Stop that."

"I'm going to have to yank this one," she said.

"Okay, okay, I'm up. What happened in Two Dot?"

"I was a bad girl."

"You? Martha Ettinger?"

She acted like she hadn't heard.

"How's the little guy holding up?"

"Good, I think," Martha said. "She let him nurse about an hour ago and he's lying down. I think we can relax now. The skin seems to have worked."

They had laced the skin of the dead calf around the bison calf, securing it with baling twine and duct taping the cord anywhere they thought it might chafe. The result was a very odd-looking animal, and the first time the calf had tried to butt up under the cow, she had stepped away, her eyes wide with alarm. He'd tried again, and again she'd stepped away, but on the third attempt she'd accepted him and he'd nursed at her swollen udders. It had taken all of twenty minutes.

Twelve hours later, the last seven spent on the straw in the barn, the question was no longer if, but "what now?"

"I'm going to lose my job over this," Martha said, putting voice to what she'd been thinking all night long.

"And I won't?"

"Drake had a point. What we're doing is against the law."

"Only if he pushes the issue."

"Oh, he's going to push it."

"He'd risk being disgraced on the camera. I meant what I said. He knows I meant it."

"It doesn't matter what *he* decides to do. Use your brain, Harold. It's what *we* did. Too many people know already for us to have any chance of keeping a lid on this."

"Then we'll take it as it comes. Public opinion's going to be on our side."

"That and five grand will buy us a bail bond."

"You're wrong there, Martha. We'd be released on our own recognizance."

That brought her smile up in spite of herself. She let out a sigh, then shook her head. "Come on in the house," she said. "Let's have some tea and I'll call Rosco and see where we stand. Things are never so bleak once the sun is up."

But the sun was two hours from being up and the house was dark, the only light a soft yellow haze cast by the porch bulb, which had been left on all night. Harold was right by her side and yet not there at all as she walked toward that light, remembering other nights she had left it on, hoping that Sean Stranahan would see the glow when he walked his dog along the gravel road, up from the tipi where he lived.

There had been a time, a year ago now, when the light served as a signal that he was welcome to come in and help her work the picture puzzle spread out on the ponderosa pine slab that served as her desk. One puzzle piece would lead to another, one kiss to the next, and they would be lost to one another's touch, and then lost further. There had been that time. Then Martha had ended it for fear of it ending, getting out when the hurt wouldn't go as deep. All last winter the porch light had been out, last spring, too. She'd only switched it back on after her son's visit in June, when circumstances had brought

Sean and Martha together again. David, her son, had found the big brother in Sean that he had looked in vain for in his own brother, and Martha had softened, admitting to herself how much she cared. And so the light had gone back on, but Sean had either not seen it or ignored it. For four nights she'd left the light on, waiting for his knock. She had almost given up when she heard the rap at the door, had swallowed the last of her chamomile tea and sought the pulse in her neck with two fingers, willing herself to be calm. *What will I say?* she thought. *Will I simply fall into his arms and all is forgiven?* She had opened the door. It was Harold, come to borrow her horse trailer because his needed rewiring.

"Harold," she said.

"Who were you expecting?"

And she'd flung herself at him, Harold with whom she'd had a short-lived affair a few years before, Harold who had left her to go back to his ex-wife in Browning, Harold who had then left his ex-wife because he said he was tired of talking her off a ledge, which was a joke because there weren't any buildings tall enough to have ledges on an Indian reservation. *That Harold,* with whom Martha had no real future and knew it. But there he was, and here he was now, and she reached for his hand as they walked toward the light meant for somebody else.

———

Over the phone line, Martha could hear Rosco Needermire sigh.

"Martha, Martha, Martha," the county prosecutor said.

"You don't sound like you're happy I helped you get elected," she said.

He said he'd get back to her.

"Well?" Harold said.

"The gist is I'm a cooked goose two ways till Sunday. Number one, state law does give Drake the license to remove bison from private property if they are deemed a threat to livestock. No surprise there."

"You're talking brucellosis. That's—"

"Bullshit. So you've said. But law's law. The fact is, he can legally take the bison *without* a warrant. Rosco says about all I can do is fall back on delaying tactics. I can apply for quarantine status and say that I'll raise the calf away from contact from any livestock except for the cow. But there's a lot of hoops to jump through. Anyway, he'll see if there's any way the rules can be bent, considering the circumstances. The fact that the calf's in my possession is to my advantage, that and the bad publicity the DOL would get for pressing the matter. So he thinks Drake will want to make the department look responsible and go the warrant route, which gives me a little time."

Harold was shaking his head. "Needermire still wear a *Jaws* undershirt when he goes to trial? 'Cause for a man who thinks he's a shark he doesn't have many teeth."

"Harold, there's only so much he can do. You've got to calm down about this."

"You're just as upset as I am."

"Yes, I am."

"Something's been nagging at me, Martha."

"What's that?"

"Why?"

"Why what?"

"Why did they go over that cliff? My grandfather had this old juniper bow backed with sinew, said his grandfather had used it to finish off buffalo after they drove them off the cliffs. I didn't know whether to believe him, because the people had horses by then and nobody used pishkuns once they could run buffalo on horses."

"You mean a buffalo jump?" Martha said. "You're thinking somebody drove them over the cliff?"

"I don't think it was suicide."

"There were fireworks. It scared them, you said it yourself."

"I know. It's the plausible explanation. Still, I'd like to talk to that range manager up at Tenderfoot Creek who made the call, find out what he actually saw."

"Harold, this isn't a crime scene."

"Then I'll do it on my own time."

"No, I can give you some line on this. A couple days. See what you can find."

He nodded. "I'll go back this morning. I want to see how they're handling the recovery. The ones I finished off won't have spoiled, but they're going to have to work fast."

"Don't get into it with Drake. That's not my advice. That's an order."

"Order, Martha?"

"Whatever you want to call it."

———

He didn't get into it with Drake. Drake wasn't there, nor was his trigger man, Calvin Barr. Who was there was John Rain in His Face from the Fort Peck Reservation. He was the head of a team of seven other Indians, mostly Assiniboine and Sioux, though one man was Blackfeet, like Harold. They were representatives of the Intertribal Buffalo Council who supervised treaty rights, sanctioned by Montana Fish, Wildlife, and Parks, to hunt bison that strayed beyond the buffer zone outside Yellowstone National Park.

Rain in His Face said they'd boned out the meat from the five bison Harold had finished off and that it had been driven overnight to a meatpacking facility in Fort Peck. This morning they were salvaging hides and skulls from another six that had been dead too long and had spoiled and bloated in the sun. The parts of the carcasses they had no use for would be hauled to the landfill, though he was squabbling with the DOL over who had the honor.

"So that's eleven," Harold said. "I guess I missed a few of the dead ones."

"Fifteen thousand pounds, give or take," Rain in His Face said. "A lot of waste." He was well over six feet, with a broad chest and stomach, a wide nose, and deeply pockmarked cheeks. Blood from the biceps down, his shirt stained with gore.

"Let me ask you, John, how do you suppose they went over the cliff like that?"

"I don't know. Those guys from DOL didn't tell me shit. The range manager was here earlier. Said he saw them above the cliffs night before last. Not your standard-issue department man. Struck me as a bit on the mad side. But white people, huh?" He shrugged. "Why, do you know something I don't?"

"No."

"Then what's your involvement? This doesn't sound like a police matter."

"Same question I've asked myself. But there's a question of jurisdiction because the game range is a hodgepodge of land ownership— Forest Service, Bureau of Land Management, state, private, it's all mixed up. If the herd was on federal or state land, then the Department of Livestock had the right to shoot them. More complicated if they were on private property. Then they'd have to haze them onto public land before they could lower the boom. *I think.* The law's a bit confused. But the real reason I was first to the scene is because I was close by and a fishing guide called the sheriff's line. He'd heard the racket and didn't know whether to put in at the landing or not. So there was a public safety issue involved."

"I see."

"What I'd like to know is why. I thought of wolves, we have a couple packs in the Gravellys, what's your take on that?"

"I doubt it." Rain in His Face shook his head. "Buffalo fend off wolf attacks by presenting a unified front. Seen it time and again. Herd stands its ground to protect the small ones. If they run, the calves get caught."

"So if it wasn't wolves, what was it?"

"Could be lightning strike. I've seen buffalo stampede from thunder and lightning."

"What about fireworks?"

"Maybe." Rain in His Face shook his head. "This was back in the day, I'd say my people herded them over the edge, or yours. First thing I told myself when we got here is this is a perfect place for a drive. I climbed to the top earlier and you even got a dip in the land before the cliffs. Like a ski jump. They'd never know they were going over until their hooves were in the air."

While they were talking, the crew had been shuttling back and forth across the river, using a battered johnboat to ferry the heavy hides that they'd stripped from the carcasses. Clouds of flies made a halo over each human head and the boat itself was enveloped in a fog of insects. The scent was powerful and dark, with a tang of turning meat. Harold realized that Rain in His Face was the least bloody of the workers. Three of the men had been smart enough to save their shirts and were bare-chested.

"Gives you an appreciation for our ancestors," Rain in His Face said. "We were born too late, you and me."

"I know what you mean," Harold said. "We have the meat but we lost the hunt."

Rain in His Face called the crew over. The Blackfeet man turned out to be a distant cousin of Harold's, not surprising given the complexity of the family trees. But Harold didn't know him, he didn't know any of these men, and the bond of heritage only went so far. He was a badge to them, *the man,* if less so than a white man would be. Harold asked if they'd seen anything unusual during the recovery work. Nobody spoke up. He made a joke about knowing he was among brothers by the condition of the vehicles parked at the river access, wondering if there was a working turn signal in the lot. That got a laugh. Indians were nothing if not self-deprecating. But the laugh was on the polite side. He wasn't learning much and the men wanted to get going.

After the two trucks had driven away, Harold pulled on his waders to cross the river, trying to prepare himself for the bones and the gut piles. The dew point had risen and fingers of midmorning fog lingered among the ghosts of the dead. It wouldn't be so bad once the sun rose higher in the sky. Still, he hesitated. He was remembering what Rain in His Face had said about the game range manager.

Not your standard-issue department man. Struck me as a bit on the mad side.

Harold decided the cliffs could wait. If nothing else, paying the manager a visit would eat an hour or two, give the day a little time to put the spirits to bed.

CHAPTER FIVE

A Man of Numbers

Theodore Thackery had a wheezy voice, a hard handshake, and that kind of bull-in-the-china-shop vigor that made you think of Theodore Roosevelt, once you'd heard his first name. He stood amid a scattering of quarter-round splits, stripped to his undershirt under a pegged sun, barrel-chested, sweating healthily, his thick biceps burned pink, swinging a double-bitted ax with a long handle. Harold thought he belonged to that bygone era of men who carved a living from the West with sharp edges, Swede saws, and buffalo rifles—men in that first wave of settlers who didn't let a bit of weather deter them and spelled the end of the wolves with their traps, the end of the bison with their bullets, and the end of Indian life as Harold's ancestors had known it.

Yes, he'd been the one to see the bison, seen them directly from his porch as he was getting ready to drive into town on an errand. Reported it first thing next morning. About an hour before dark, make that nine p.m. No doubt a splinter group from the herd that had taken refuge on a private ranch in the Hebgen Valley.

Harold asked how many he had observed.

"Sixteen. Seven cows, six with calf, three bulls. Yes sir." When he nodded, his jowls shook. "Heard about what happened. You did what had to be done, I commend you for your prompt action."

Harold nodded. "Only eleven went over the cliff. We can't account for the other five."

"Nor can I. I only saw them the once."

Harold wanted to know exactly where they were when he'd seen them. Thackery stuck the ax in the chopping block and got a metal clipboard from his GMC pickup. The clipboard held several dozen copies of the same topographic map and he thumbed back a couple pages, explaining that the maps were for counting animals on the game range. He tapped the three red circles penned onto the map. The circles represented the locations in which he'd seen bison, and inside each circle he'd penned the number of animals observed in the spotting scope. Thackery said the cows and calves were in the biggest of the circles. The two smaller circles located the three bulls that were satellites of the main herd. All the bison were well up on the escarpment, the rising slope of open country above the cliffs.

"What's this mean?" Harold pointed to a blue circle at a much lower elevation, close to the cliff tops. The circle had a "2" in it and enclosed a question mark.

"I thought I saw a single down there, then I thought maybe two, but by the time I had the scope focused they were gone. Blue circle is a maybe."

Harold nodded to himself. Something was tugging at the periphery of his thought. "So Theodore—"

"Thack."

"Thack, was there anything unusual about the bison you saw?"

"You mean except for the fact they were there to begin with? The answer to that is no. They were grazing, milling a little. Most of the little red ones were lying down." He shrugged. "Just being buffalo."

Harold wondered out loud where the survivors had gone.

Thackery said he'd driven the entire game range with the quad but hadn't found any of them. He planned to drive down to the Avery Ranch in the Hebgen Valley where the herd had been in residence to see if the group had returned to it. It was twelve miles to the south, but twelve miles to bison wasn't a long distance.

"How would you know they were the same bison?"

"Head count. That herd had forty-four bison. You subtract the sixteen, that's twenty-eight. You add back the five survivors, that's thirty-three. If I go down there and count thirty-three bison, that accounts for both the dead and the return. Now, if the numbers match, first thing I'd do is look for a cow with a broken horn, 'cause one of the ones I saw had a broken horn. I talked to the Intertribal agent doing the recovery and he said none of the ones that went over the cliff had a broken horn. So I'd know for sure then the number wasn't inflated due to other buffalo migrating out of the park." Thackery nodded. His jowls seconded his conclusion.

Harold admired the man's thoroughness to detail and told him so.

"Numbers always tell the story," he said. He had walked back to the yard, or rather he had charged without running, thick legs pumping, and pried the ax out of the chopping block.

"Huh!" he exclaimed loudly, and the round spilt in two. "Huh," he said again, and there were two more pieces. He paused, leaned on the ax handle, and looked directly into Harold's eyes.

"I've spent half my adult life counting wildlife," he said, "trying to figure out what the numbers say about population trends, range quality, effects of predation. It's part of the science of wildlife conservation. But bison, now that's a different story. The only number that matters is one. One bison on state or federal property is one too many to the cattlemen. The reason given for not allowing bison to roam on public land is brucellosis. Bison are a carrier and brucellosis makes cows abort their calves. You know all this."

"I do."

"Here's something you probably also know." Thackery's eyes were alight with his passion. "What number am I thinking of when somebody asks me how many times bison have transmitted brucellosis to cattle in the state of Montana."

"Zero," Harold said.

"You have my point. We're fighting a bison war over a disease that bison do not transmit. That's what I call a hypocrisy. And here's how absurd the state's argument is. Say that bison did transmit the disease. If that was the case, the only possible vectors of that disease would be pregnant cow bison. Why? Because brucellosis is transferred to cattle by cattle licking fetal afterbirth. Bull bison, heifer calves, cows that have already calved—no way they can transmit the disease. Biologically impossible. So that bull calf you found at the cliffs, it poses no danger whatsoever to livestock. Yet the state persists in perpetuating the myth that all bison pose a risk of disease. It's ludicrous."

He shook his head. "If the livestock industry was really worried about disease, they would be worried about elk. Elk not only carry brucellosis, they are much more likely than bison to transmit the disease, because they mix with cattle on public and private lands at the same time cow elk are giving birth. But is anyone calling for elk to be quarantined or hazed back into Yellowstone Park? Shot on sight if they stray beyond arbitrary lines on a map?"

"No," Harold said.

"Why do you suppose that is?"

"They bring in hunters."

"That's right. And hunters bring in dollars. Elk hunting's a three-hundred-million-dollar business in Montana. If bison hunting garnered even a fraction of that, you can bet we'd be a bit more accommodating when it came to where they could set a hoof."

He leaned forward, looked at Harold with his brow furrowed, his head cocked to the side.

"I'm a plainspoken man, Harold. More than that, I'm a man who believes wildlife management should be driven by the science, not by the politics. But science doesn't matter to the state of Montana, or to Yellowstone National Park, whose hands are equally bloody. When you work for a state agency, believing in science and speaking your mind is a combination that will get you fired every time."

"Then how do you manage to keep your job?"

"I didn't. Didn't you know that?" He took a step back.

Harold shook his head.

"I was demoted last year. I was the FWP coordinator for forming the interagency bison management plan, but apparently they were afraid I might insert a few words of sense into the document. I was given the choice of staying on here as a statistician. I can keep counting animals so long as I don't try to tell anyone what the numbers mean. I would have been fired outright if they hadn't been worried that I'd go to the press and make a stink. This way they can bury me in the boonies where there's no one to talk to but the animals."

He jerked his chin, his jowls shook, and the light that had burned so brightly in his eyes dimmed. It took two seconds and Harold was looking at a different Theodore Thackery.

"You better go now before I get back up on my high horse," Thackery said in a quiet voice. "I usually reserve my bluster for my better acquaintances."

He stood another block and pulled the ax from the wood.

"I should touch up this blade. You have a very good day, and I thank you again for putting down those bison. I won't abide a man who lets an animal suffer."

They shook hands and Harold saw that Thackery's jaw trembled with his emotion.

"I mean to go over there where you saw that herd and have a look around," Harold said. "You're welcome to come with me. Another set of eyes might help."

"I'd do that, certainly I would, wasn't for this damned malaria. You can't stand the light, that's one of the first symptoms of recurrence. I take it easy, I might stave it off."

"How does a range manager in Montana come down with malaria?"

"You've heard of Doctors Without Borders? In my thirties I was a biologist without borders, trying to atone for the selfishness of my youth. I helped native people start fish farms in places like Sri Lanka until I got bit by the wrong mosquito. But I thank you for the invitation. Not a lot of people request the pleasure of my company these days."

"I understand," Harold said. But he didn't. If Thackery was worried about exerting, about bright conditions, what was he doing chopping wood under the eye of the sun?

A minute later he said good-bye to Thackery's back and heard the "huh" as the blade split the block. People weren't always your notion of what they'd be, and Harold had liked the man more than he'd expected to. But even before he'd put the truck into gear, his mind changed directions to focus on the tableau of open land above the cliffs, where a question mark had been circled in blue ink.

CHAPTER SIX

Echoes of the Fallen

The first rock cairn was a hundred yards above the tops of the cliffs, which Harold had gained easily if painfully through a rift choked with thornbushes. From the top, the land rose in a gentle roll to the base of the mountain range, relatively open ground, the rocky soil grown up in fescue, bearded wheatgrass, and fragrant tangles of sage. This was where Thackery had seen the bison, and turning to face north, Harold could just make out the tiny box of the game ranger's cabin. Raising his binoculars, he caught a glint from that direction and wondered if it was Thackery looking back at him through the same spotting scope with which he'd observed the herd. If so, it was a natural behavior, and Harold dismissed any possible significance. He sat back on his heels, plucked a stem of grass, and ran his thumbnail to remove the seeds. He stuck the stem between two lower teeth and picked thorns from his arms, licking the thin lines of blood like a cat, as he considered the cairn. It wasn't actually a cairn that he was looking at, he concluded. Rather, a cairn was what it had been before being dismantled, for the rocks were scattered over several square yards.

Walking in expanding circles, Harold found where each stone had been pried from the earth. One of the depressions was more than one hundred feet away. Someone had gathered the rocks at no little discomfort, for they were heavy, a few more than half buried, and it would have taken serious effort to pry them up and carry them. He could see the circle of flattened grass where they had been stacked together. Why had the cairn then been dismantled and the rocks either tossed or rolled aside? Harold had to think that someone had not wanted other people to know about it.

Now that he knew what to look for, it didn't take long to find the remains of other cairns. The first he'd found was one of a pair set some seventy yards apart, with another pair some distance down the slope, set a little closer together, and yet a third pair no more than forty yards apart and not too far above the tops of the cliffs. Standing above the topmost pair of cairns, Harold's eyes drew imaginary lines through the cairns from top to bottom. The two lines formed a funnel.

Harold felt a shiver in his bloodstream. The cairns confirmed what he'd suspected even before talking with John Rain in His Face. The herd's panic had not been caused by predators. Nor had it been caused by fireworks or lightning strike. It had been triggered by men, by hunters engaged in a reenactment of an ancient ritual.

From his vantage he could picture it, the drivers starting the bison's flight between lanes formed by the cairns, their scent drifting down to disturb the herd, the hunters behind the rocks standing and whooping to keep strays from breaking out on the flanks, the thunder of the hooves, then the bones cracking as they plunged over the cliffs, their impacts echoes of the fallen from centuries past.

But why? And why this place? And why leave the wounded to die? Harold's ancestors would have finished them off with spears and arrows while women immediately went to work stripping the skins. They would make bowls from the head caps, spoons from horns, tobacco pouches from bladders, fill the empty stomachs with food and place hot rocks inside to boil stews. No part of the animal would have been wasted.

A patch of color that contrasted with the summer grasses caught his eye, and Harold, curious, walked over for a closer look. It was a badger hole. The escarpment was full of badger holes, but this was the only one he'd seen that had been recently dug, the light-colored earth excavated by powerful forearms and claws. The badger had been Harold's grandfather's totem animal and Harold admired its courage and ferocity. He smiled, then the smile was gone and he squatted for a closer look.

The partial print of a boot was clearly visible in the overturned earth. It was a heel mark, made by a sole with an air-bob tread. Air bobs were fragile compared to Vibram-type soles, and Harold noted a space in the print where one of the bobs had torn off and didn't register. He placed a finger against the edge of the track. The nap or grain of the soil that stood on end when the heel came down, making a crisply outlined imprint, had begun to crumble inward, softening the outline. Harold estimated the track to be two days old, which put it in the time frame for the buffalo drive. Of course it could have been made by someone unassociated with the hunt, but Harold thought the odds of that were slim. He photographed the print with his cell phone and made a few measurements, penning the width and length on a dollar bill and marking the position of the missing air bob. Then he picked another stem of grass as his eyes focused inward.

It would have been no small undertaking getting the hunters to the area. The execution of the drive would have demanded planning and organization, not to mention that the men would need prior knowledge that the herd was on the escarpment. Improbably, all of this had happened within a mile of the highway that ran the length of the Madison Valley. Yet no one, with the exception of Theodore Thackery, had reported seeing anything.

Harold itched at an old scab on his elbow. He had climbed far above the lip of the cliffs and wondered if he could get a bar on his cell phone, and if so, if he should call Martha. She wouldn't want to be left out of the loop if he was right about the pishkun, and it would help get him back into her good graces, their relationship always seeming to be tested, at least in a professional sense.

He got through and without going into detail told her why she might want to meet him at the boat landing at the Palisades. He listened to her objection, which was expected and only halfhearted.

"I know you're the sheriff," he told her. "But I'm not so sure you have anything better to do . . . An hour, then."

He saw his face reflected in the blank screen of the phone and gave a wry smile before holstering it. He hiked down the slope toward the top of the cliffs, thinking that he had the answer to the question marks in those blue circles on the map.

————

Martha Ettinger crooked two fingers and itched them along the line of her jaw.

"Pishkun, huh?" She stepped down from the Jeep Cherokee and looked up at the cliffs. "And you have a gut feeling something bad happened."

"There's a reason why they didn't finish off the buffalo," Harold said. "I'll show you when we get across."

"If that's the way you want to play it, then let's wader up."

She refused Harold's offer of his hand as they began to cross the river, but had to cave when they reached a braid where the current swirled deeper. They got past the tricky part and slogged to the bank to peel off their waders. Above them, the slope rose sharply before reaching the base of the cliffs, the layered rock appearing to glow in the low eye of the sun. Harold led her upriver, Martha wrinkling her nose at the stench of the gut piles. He raised his binoculars, nodded to himself, and handed the glasses over.

"When I talked to Thackery," he said, "I started thinking about something my grandfather told me about running the buffalo, that in a big drive there would be hunters wearing buffalo robes stationed at the top of the cliffs. The idea was that they would bleat like calves, and the cows would hear them and try to round up the strays. That way, you could get the herd moving in the right direction before the drivers started pushing them from above. The hunters at the lower end were called runners. Once the herd panicked and the stampede was on, their job was to run ahead of the buffalo, lead them right up to the lip, and then at the last second throw themselves behind rocks or take cover in cracks in the cliff. That's what I think Thackery saw. What he thought were two buffalo separated from the main herd were the runners working into position, wearing robes so that from a distance they looked like buffalo. Do you follow me?"

"I'm still looking for what it is I'm supposed to be seeing."

"Focus about four feet down from the lip, what looks like a spike. And a couple feet below it, another. There's a line of them. They're climbing pitons, if I'm not mistaken. You drive them into cracks in the rock and attach carabiners to the holes to pass your rope through, to anchor you when you're climbing."

"I don't need you to tell me what a piton is. Yeah, I got 'em. They blend into the rock color."

"That's why we didn't spot them before. Okay, now look twenty feet to the right. There's a second line of pitons. I'm thinking there were two runners and this is how they avoided being trampled. They tied ropes onto rocks on the top and threaded them through the carabiners, so they could lower down, pull themselves into the underhang where they'd be safe from the buffalo falling."

"You think this or you know it?"

"I found the two rocks the ropes were tied to. There were fibers adhering to the surface. I think they'll check out."

"So your theory is that after the buffalo fell, the runners would climb the rest of the way to the bottom, retrieve their bows and arrows or whatever other weapons they'd stashed there, and dust off any animals that were still alive."

"I think that was the intention."

Martha nodded as she lowered the glasses. "So why didn't they?" she said. "Finish them off."

"Something went wrong. It made them lose their appetite for it."

"What's that hangy thingy on the third piton on the left side?"

"That's the reason they lost their appetite."

———

On top of the cliffs, Harold showed Martha the rocks. The coarse fibers of nylon showed plainly where friction had shaved them from the ropes—purple and red fibers adhered to one rock, yellow and blue to another. He edged to the lip of the cliff and peered down at the line of pitons, Martha hanging back.

"I got a thing about heights," she said.

"That's okay. Just get down on your stomach and crawl to the edge here. I'll hold your legs."

Her "All right" wasn't enthusiastic, but she elbowed up to the lip and peered down at the pitons.

It looked like a dead snake more than anything else, and she uttered, "Sweet Mother of Mary," as the realization of what it could be occurred to her. But it wasn't until Harold managed to pass a loop of cord over the end that dangled from the piton, cinch it tight, and pull it up that her suspicion was confirmed.

He swung the purplish-gray coil out toward her. "You get a couple feet of intestine ripped out of your gut, you pretty much lose interest in hunting buffalo."

"Get that thing out of my face," she said.

Harold lowered the coil onto a bare rock.

Martha patted her pockets. "I didn't think to bring an evidence bag."

"My sister fixed me a ham sandwich. I could fold it into the bag. A little mustard wouldn't hurt it."

"Wilkerson would have a heart attack."

"CSIs only care if there's a crime committed."

"Is there?"

"That's the question. Want to hear the theory I came up with while I waited for you to drive up here?"

"No, Harold."

"No?"

"No means yes. It's called irony. Jesus, you're as clueless as Walt."

"Look who got up on the wrong side of the bed."

Yes, and all by myself because you were already up and brewing tea, she could have said, and almost did before catching herself.

"Well, the first thing is he fell, odds are," Harold said. "You've got hooves sounding behind you, the earth shaking, shit happens. The hunters may have only spotted the bison a few hours before, so you have to figure there wasn't a lot of practice involved. They got the pitons in place, tied off the ropes, and that may have been about it. So one of the runners miscalculates, he gets stuck on the piton. After that it would be damned difficult to climb back up, and I don't think he did, because there'd be bloodstains on the rocks here. So he either fell or managed to lower himself the rest of the way to the bottom with the rope."

"You think he could still be alive?" Martha shook her head.

"It's not impossible. Remember that bow hunter who fell out of his stand at Headwaters and got caught on one of those climbing steps you screw into the tree? He pulled a ribbon of intestine out of his abdomen ten feet to the ground, climbed back *up* to the stand to unhook himself, then stuffed some mud and leaves to hold it in place while he drove himself to the hospital.

"No, I think that one would have stayed with me."

"Maybe you were on vacation. Anyway, one way to find out."

"We should have called in Katie and her dog."

"Not necessary. Man dragging his innards is going to leave a trail you can follow with a head cold."

———

The blood on the apron of scree below the cliffs had dried to a rusty color. Darker globules pooled between rocks were still soft in the middle. Blood rubies, Harold called them. Wordlessly, for Harold never spoke on trail, they followed a very light splattering of blood drops shaped like tears, the tails pointing to direction of travel. Harold had picked up a stick and tapped at the ground ahead of him, indicating bloodstains on grass stems and the occasional snotlike streak of something livery. The trail led through a tangle of brush where the man had evidently fallen, smears of blood painting the ground and the brush smashed down as if a pig had wallowed. From this point the blood trail turned to contour the slope into a stand of limber pines, the blood drops overlapping each other to form a thin, intermittent stream.

Martha, three steps behind, walked up to tap Harold's shoulder. "How's he still on his feet?"

Harold frowned as Martha blushed inwardly at the extraneous nature of the question. *Shut up,* she told herself. *Just shut up.*

They were now well out of the zone where the bison had fallen, the trail leading into an area that nobody had bothered to search. Martha had a sinking sensation she'd felt on other searches, when you knew in your heart it was time to call in the cadaver dogs. Ahead was a great slab of rock shaped like a grand piano with its lid propped open. A spruce cone had fallen into a crack in the rock and grown into a small sapling shaped like a Christmas tree. A smear of blood showed where the man had crawled along the base of this rock, past the tree, until he reached the overhang on the far side, where his spirit had mercifully departed his body.

Martha dropped her chin into one hand as she squatted to peer down at the body. The man was dressed in dark, bloodstained jeans, tennis shoes, and a mustard-colored long-sleeved shirt. He wore a ratty piece of bison robe cut like a vest, hair side out, with buttons made from bits of wood. Before dying he had curled into a fetal position with his arms wrapped around his knees. His eyes had gone from glassy to opaque and had begun to shrink back into his skull.

"He's an Indian," Martha said.

CHAPTER SEVEN

The Chippewa Nymph

Sean Stranahan had been renting an art studio at the Bridger Mountain Cultural Center since the day he'd arrived in town. The rent was ridiculously cheap, but the manager had balked. She already rented to a dozen artists and had an eye toward diversity. Put on the spot, Sean told her he was a licensed private detective who'd worked for a law firm in Boston, the only lie being the tense, his license having expired. But it had the desired effect and he'd got the room. Hence the discreet *Private Investigations* etched into the rippled glass door pane, underneath BLUE RIBBON WATERCOLORS, though he wasn't strictly tied to the medium. The capital letters paid the rent, that and seasonal work as a fly fishing guide on Sam Meslik's outfitter's license. The scripted letters were what got him into trouble.

Hearing steps in the hallway, he raised his eyes from the half-completed oil on the easel. He took a masculine pride in knowing who was passing down the hall by the cadence of the footsteps on the travertine tiles. He didn't know these footsteps. Nor did he recognize the rap at his door.

"Come in," he said.

Sean paused with his brush raised as Ida Evening Star opened the door. She closed it behind her and leaned back the way she'd leaned against the porch rail at the bar. But the easy silence of the night before wasn't as easy this time around.

"You aren't wearing your tail," he said.

"I don't work today. I told you that."

"So you did."

"You really are a private detective. I wasn't sure last night." She nodded to herself. "Men will say anything, you know, anything at all."

"Honesty is one of my more dependable virtues. Please, have a chair."

But she was running her eyes around the room, taking in the paintings on the walls. "This one," she said, pointing to a watercolor of a serpentine river, white pelicans painting their reflections at the point of an island, "I think I know this place."

"That's the Missouri River near the Dearborn junction."

"Eagle Rock," she said.

"That's right. How do you know it?" Sean stood his brush in a Mason jar of spirits and scrubbed his stained fingers on a turpentined towel.

"Oh," she said at length. "It's on the way from here to there."

"Here to where?"

"Browning. I lived there when I was a girl."

"That's the Blackfeet Reservation. I thought you were from Rocky Boy."

"There, too. My father worked for Indian Services. We moved from one rez to another. Blackfeet, Flathead, Northern Cheyenne, Crow. Finally back to Rocky Boy. I'm not from anywhere, really. My family was Little Shell Chippewa. We were called the landless Indians."

"How did you find me?"

"Molly Linklatter. She's the Queen of the Waters."

"Ah, Sam Meslik."

She nodded and finally took up his offer for a chair, but not before he ran his eyes up and down. She was wearing a jersey top and tight-fitting black jeans that revealed the outline of what looked like a folding knife in the right front pocket. Open-toed leather sandals. Her hair was gathered in a ponytail and looked dull, in stark contrast to the fiery hues of her eyes.

"It's called heterochromia," she said, anticipating his question. "Actually, I have heterochromia iridis, which means the irises are different colors, and I have central heterochromia, too, which means each eye is more than one color. You see it in dogs more than people."

"I have a Sheltie with mismatched eyes, one brown, one blue. Yours are . . ."

He looked closely. The left eye had a narrow gold ring around the pupil, radiating to a wide green band. The right had a dark brown ring like a starburst that bled into a band of purple.

"My mother told me my left eye was my white eye, that her side of the family, the Little Shell Chippewa, had interbred with French fur trappers and the clan was identifiable by their green eyes. She said my right eye was my Indian eye. Then I learned that it could be because of an injury when I was little. I accused her of dropping me on my head, but she didn't remember that. But then there were chunks of our life she didn't remember."

"She drank?"

"My family was the opposite of the stereotype. My father got drunk exactly once in his life. But I hardly ever remember my mother sober."

A lull came over the room, a silence in the wake of her confession.

"Is that a knife in your pocket or are you happy to see me?" Sean said. He offered an encouraging smile.

She fished the knife from her pocket. "Don't you know that Indians always carry knives, Mr. Stranahan?"

"Call me Sean."

"Sean. May I?" She opened the knife one-handed and flipped it. It turned over twice, the point burying into the wood of the desk. The blade vibrated, then stood still between them. She leaned back in the chair, fingering a wayward strand of hair. She looked critically at it. The tips were tinted an insect green.

"Chlorine?"

She nodded. "About once a week I put color on the ends and treat it with a cream that's used to condition horses' manes. Otherwise, people would think I was punk."

"I doubt that."

"The worst are the headaches. Every night, the water runs out of my ears onto the pillow. And my eyes burn. I could wear goggles, but who wants to look at a mermaid wearing goggles? It's the same reason I don't wear a nose clamp."

"Sacrifice for your art and you shall be rewarded."

She gave him a sideways look.

"It's something my mother said when I told her I wanted to be a painter. I think she got it from someone famous. My father didn't agree."

"You're a very good one."

"Thank you. I'm a better artist than I am a detective. Or fishing guide. Though I've spent the past few years being a relative failure at all three endeavors. Tell me something, was it just a coincidence we were both looking at the sky last night?"

"What was it you said when I asked if you were really a detective? 'Sort of.' Well, that's my answer—'sort of.' Sam pointed you out when I was with Molly. It was like, 'That guy over there, the disreputable-looking one with the black man, I taught him all I know and he's still a fuckup.' You know how Sam talks."

Sean had to laugh. "That I do, but the disreputable part is the pot calling the kettle black. For the record."

"Anyway, it was in the bar about a week ago. He was going to introduce us, but something came up. And when you walked out on the porch it was dark, and it was dark when I'd seen you before, so I wasn't sure until you came over. I thought, 'Ah, here's the guy I wanted to ask a question.' I was going to ask you then, but you had to be someplace else and I had to swim."

"And I thought I'd cast a spell over an attractive woman." Sean smiled. "A mayfly nymph at that."

"I've seen those things. They don't look very appetizing."

"They are to a trout. That black man you saw is Kenneth Winston. The Chippewa Nymph is his creation. Ken is one of the best fly tiers in the world. We call him Hot Hands."

"I should feel honored, I suppose."

Sean smiled. "See, this is you getting to know me better. That's so that the next time I see you, you'll point out the star you're named for." He mimed rolling up his sleeves and placed his palms on the table. "What can I do for you, Ida?"

She would either get to the point now or back away from it, and Sean found that despite the encouragement in his voice, which was simply his nature, he didn't care one way or the other.

His apathy, though "apathy" was not an adequate word for the pall that cast over him, was a reflection of just how much the past couple months had changed him. The last time he'd countersigned one of his standard contracts, he'd ended up buried in a grave of horse remains. A man had died and Sean had been the one who made him die. He'd managed to live half a lifetime without killing anyone, and the next half, provided he had one, he'd live with the fact that he had. That and Martha turning out the light had darkened his outlook on life, and he'd followed his despair into a hole of self-pity protected by irony, and with only minor assistance from the traditional, mood-altering suspects.

As his mind drifted, Ida was speaking. He held up a finger. "You were in the tank and saw who? When did this happen? Start over."

"Well, that's just it," she said. "It was last Thursday and I'm not sure what I saw. The people behind the bar are kind of a blur, and I'm not like Molly or Jessica, I don't go up against the glass and flirt with the men.

"A modest mermaid."

"It's being duplicitous, I'm aware of it. I'm flipping my tail and here I am casting judgment."

Sean smiled. Despite his current state of indifference, he liked Ida Evening Star and had been intrigued from the start. Any attractive woman who could flick a folder open one-handed was his kind of trouble. He knew he'd say yes to whatever she asked of him and perhaps that's what he needed, a job, a paying one so he'd have to pay attention, something to drag him out of the doldrums.

"So who was it you thought you saw?"

"Someone from a long time ago, from Browning."

"When you were a girl."

"We moved there when I was eight. We left on my twelfth birthday."

"Go on."

"There was a boy who lived with his aunt. They called him John Running Boy, because he ran everywhere. He had a corduroy shirt that was his father's and he wore it almost every day. When he ran, the shirttail waved behind him like a flag. He had a crush on me."

"Did you have a crush on him?"

The light behind her eyes changed, seemed to draw inward to a pinprick of intensity as she paged back through the years.

"No. Not at first. He was a year younger, and that's a difference when you're a kid, and I was half a head taller, but later, he . . . grew on me. I guess that's a way to put it. He's the first boy I ever kissed. We were sitting on a swing set and his face got serious and he kissed me. I'll never forget it."

"What happened?"

"We moved. My father got assigned to the Flathead Reservation and it was a couple hundred miles. Kids are cats. They move on where people feed them, they only look back for a little while."

"And you never saw him again?"

She shook her head. "Not until last week."

"Ida . . ." Sean hesitated. "This John Running Boy, how old would he be now?"

"I'm twenty-six, so he would be twenty-five."

"And he looks Indian?"

"He's full-blood Blackfeet."

"Do you know why I'm asking?"

"I know about the body they found at the cliffs yesterday, if that's what you mean. It was in the newspaper this morning."

"Okay . . ."

"It isn't him." Her voice was firm.

"You said you couldn't see clearly through the glass and he would be what, ten years older than the last time you saw him?"

"Twelve."

"Then how can you be sure the man you saw wasn't the one who died?"

"Because the man who came into the bar last week was there again last night, about an hour after you left." She leaned back in the chair. *So there.*

"You saw him last night?"

"No. But Vic did, and he saw him last week, too, the first time he came in. It was the same person."

"Bartender Vic?"

She nodded.

"What is it you want me to do, Ida?"

"I want you to find him. I can pay you."

Sean's face was skeptical. "You'd probably be wasting your money. Say I do find him. He may not be the man you saw in the bar. Do you want to open up that chapter of your life all over again?"

"But I do know it was him. It's only my eyes that can't be certain."

Sean waited for her explanation. She seemed to make up her mind and stood from the chair. Reaching her left hand into the pocket of her jeans, she pulled out an arrowhead and placed it on the desk. The head was small and shiny black, no more than an inch long.

"It's a bird point," Ida said.

Sean fingered it, the rippled edge carefully, for it was very sharp. He knew next to nothing about arrowheads but nodded his appreciation. "What's it chipped from?" he asked. "This looks too dark to be flint."

"The secondary process is called pressure flaking, where you push the tool against the stone instead of striking it. That's what makes the serrations. It's obsidian. That night, after I swam, I was going to go look for the man in the bar, but he was gone by the time

I changed. Vic handed me this. He said the man had told him to give it to me."

"That's all he said?"

"That's all, just to give it to me."

"And you think John Running Boy made this."

She nodded. "He learned flint napping from a man whose name I can't remember, an Indian with a white name. Anyway, this man lived up the lane from the trailer where John lived with his aunt. Even when he was seven, he napped beautiful points. Sometimes he'd give me one. I had a collection in a goldfish bowl."

"Do you still have them?"

"Not the ones in the bowl. When the goldfish died, my mother got in one of her moods about cleaning things out and she dumped the bowl into the trash. She said she didn't know the points were in there, but she did. She never liked John. She said he stunk like an Indian."

"But she was mostly Indian herself. Right?"

"She didn't mean how he smelled. She meant his circumstances, living with his aunt in a trailer. John was just a village dog to her, running with his shirttail flapping. She wanted me to do better than him."

"So you don't have any of his arrowheads except this one, which a man who reminded you of him gave to someone to give to you."

"But I do have another one. I have one here, see?"

She fingered a thin oval chain from under her shirt and lifted it over her head. The arrowhead was small and dark, with a silver base cap soldered to a ring to hang it from the chain. She placed it beside the one on the desk. "No two arrowheads can be exactly alike, but as you see, these are very close."

Sean nodded.

"He gave this one to me the night before we moved. He had two of them and let me choose. He'd keep the other one. They were like engagement rings. I had the cap made a few years ago."

"You talked about marriage and you were twelve?"

"We were in love." She said it as a fact.

"And you were still in love when you had the cap made?"

"Not really. It's a piece of nostalgia now, something that grounds me in my past. I lost my mother a few years ago, it was a complicated relationship, and my father, he's out of the picture."

"I'm sorry."

She shook her head. "No, there's nothing to be sorry about. But people change. I don't know who John is now, if he still carries a torch or has some kind of fixation on me."

Sean leaned back, cupping his hands behind his head and kneading his skull. It was a habit he'd picked up from Martha Ettinger, who said it got the blood moving and made her smarter. It had never had that effect for him, but it made him look like he was thinking, in any case.

"Will you find him for me?"

"You had me at 'duplicitous.' But why not try yourself first? Can you still get in touch with the aunt, or maybe the man who taught him how to make the arrowheads? There must be people around who knew him."

"You're trying to talk yourself out of a job."

"I told you—"

"I know. Honesty is one of your more dependable virtues."

Her face became serious. "I haven't decided, that's the thing. If I really *do* want to see him again. But still, I'd like to find out why he was in the bar, why he left before I could speak to him, why he came back. Something to give me an idea what his intentions are. It makes me feel vulnerable not to know."

Sean brought his hands forward and interlaced his fingers. He said, "Here's what I'm going to do. I'll have you sign a standard contract. But I'm going to cut my daily in half because I don't want to be responsible for you dropping out of school. If I can't get any traction by this weekend, we'll reconsider. No, don't argue. I'm not patronizing you, and when you see the rate, you're still going to wince and I'm still going to make money. But you might not have to drop any classes to ease your mind."

"You'll drive up there? It's almost to Canada."

"If I need to. But he was seen in the valley, so I'll ask around here first. You found me through Sam, you said."

She nodded.

"Does he know you were coming into Bridger to see me?"

"No. That night he pointed you out to me in the bar, he talked about a couple scrapes you two got into. He pulled his shirt out and showed me where he'd taken a bullet for you."

"Not exactly, but that's Sam for you."

"He told me what you did, about the studio . . . this other business. He said you were going through a rough time. I think he had the idea of hooking us up."

"That's Sam for you, too. The reason I ask is that there might be a time when I want to bring him into our confidence. Actually, that will be today. Sam knows everyone in the valley. Is that going to be a problem?"

"I don't see why."

"Okay, let's go back to last Thursday. You said the man looked Indian. What does that mean? That his face was Indian, his hair in a braid?"

"His hair wasn't that long, maybe down to the top of his shoulders. His skin was darker than mine, but then I'm very light. It was more his posture that made me notice." She dropped her chin to her throat, crossed her arms over her chest. "Like this. He'd stand this way when he was around people like my father, authority figures. Present a shell when uneasy is what he really was."

"How was he dressed?"

"Jeans, I think. Some kind of shirt, long sleeves. Not tucked in. I remember that because it hung below his jacket and the jacket was short and didn't have sleeves."

"Like a vest."

She shrugged. "It was a dark color and looked bulky. Oversized. John always wore hand-me-downs, clothes that were too big for him. I think he had a cousin somewhere who was older. I know somebody sent packages of clothes to his aunt.

"Uh-huh." Sean picked up a pencil. He took down some personal information, her address, two phone numbers, a cell and a landline, the mention of which made him raise his eyes. In his experience, the only young people you could reach on landlines lived off the grid on ranches. She said the landlord of the trailer park where she stayed paid for a communal phone because cell reception was hit-and-miss. You could dial out on the landline and you could call that number, but unless someone walking by heard it ringing and that person was willing to walk down the road and knock on your door, you couldn't be reached. Which didn't surprise Sean. Unreliable communication was one cost of doing business in Montana. He initialed some changes on a contract and she signed on the line. She stood and pulled her knife from the wood and pocketed it, and was reaching for the arrowheads when Sean's hand stopped her.

"Let me have the one the bartender gave you, just for a couple days. I promise I'll return it."

He saw her reluctance.

"I promise."

She relented, nodding. She tucked the chain with the capped arrowhead under her shirt. "Good fishing," she said, turning to leave.

"What makes you think I'm going fishing?"

"Sam said you never go anywhere without getting your fly wet."

Sean laughed softly. "I suppose that's one way to put it. And the Blackfeet Reservation does have some very good lakes. But if I drive up there, I promise I won't play hooky on your dollar."

"Sam said that, too. He said you were trustworthy, that you were a man—how did he put it? Someone who would manage to step into shit even if there was only one horse in the pasture. I think he meant it as a compliment."

On that note she left, and Sean listened to her footsteps as they echoed down the hall. He'd know them the next time, for every other step was a little louder than the one that preceded it, hinting at a limp that he'd failed to notice. He opened the lower right-hand drawer of his desk and took out the bottle of George T. Stagg sixteen-year-old. Bourbon was one of his few indulgences, but one that he'd been indulging in more often. He looked at the bottle, then replaced it in the drawer without pulling the cork.

He picked up the arrowhead from the scarred desktop. Holding it between his right thumb and forefinger, he used the point to etch a small question mark into the wood.

CHAPTER EIGHT

A Mermaid, an Arrowhead, and True Love

Sam Meslik glanced up from the glass display case of fly reels as Sean walked into the fly shack. It was a shack. The wood sign with the burnt letters over the door proclaimed it—*Rainbow Sam's Fly Shack.*

Sam's booming voice filled the room. "If it isn't my fucking best buddy I never see anymore. What can I sell you today? No, don't tell me. You have the look of a man who needs this Bozeman Reel Company Vom Hofe design SC Classic. Handcrafted by lightly perspiring virgins. Fit for a fucking prince." He pawed a handsome fly reel with a perforated spool from the top shelf of the case. " 'Course you'd have to pay on the installment plan. Hard to go lump sum when you keep turning away jobs. I had four guide days for you last week, had to pawn them out. I know. You've been having issues." Sam scrolled quote marks with his fingers. "You know, you could talk to me. I'm not a fucking stranger. Come on"—he walked around the case—"let's hug it out."

Sean drank in a big breath after Sam released him, the big man smiling, showing the grooves in his teeth where the enamel had worn away from biting monofilament leader tippets.

"What brings you to my door, Kemosabe?"

"Indians. Or rather one Indian."

"That wouldn't be Ida Evening Star, would it? That's one comely young woman, and I was hoping you'd hit it off with her."

"It's not what you think." Sean told him what it was instead, the short version, as Sam shook his head.

"No, man. I wasn't in the bar that night. Thursday's Molly's night in dry dock. The Queen of the Waters was right here. We were just kicking back, maybe doing a few other things." He grinned his wolf's grin.

"She says he was there again last night, at the bar."

Sam shook his head. "Can't help you. I wasn't there then, either."

"Are you on the wagon?"

"I'm thinking about it. Let's leave it at that."

Sean faced his hands. *None of my business.* "Okay," he said, "what's your impression of Ida?"

"I thought you were eating dog biscuits and playing kissy face with Katie Sparrow."

"People know about Katie?"

"What part about 'Sam knows everything' don't you understand?"

"Ida," Sean persisted.

Sam shrugged. "I can't say I really know her. She doesn't seem to have many friends, except for Molly. It can be tough for Indians. You go off the reservation, go to school like she did, try to better yourself, there are people treat you like a deserter. Tell you to come back, 'keep it real.' You go back, keeping it real gets to be claustrophobic and you start looking outside the rez again. Back and forth, man, for a lot of young people it's back and forth."

"How would you be the expert?"

"Kuwait. I bunked with another medic. His Lakota name was Oda-kotah. Means 'friendship.' Said he was descended from Red Cloud his own self. We were like this." He held up two fingers. "And I was from me to the door when he got blowed up. Some guys, they don't want to get too close to a brother, 'cause maybe that guy's not around to-morrow, how it is over there. Not me. Best buds I ever had were bullet catchers, and he was best of the best. We talked about some deep shit. You figure you got a chance of modeling a body bag or coming home on the stumps minus your dick, you can get into some really deep shit with a brother. Shit, man, I miss you. Where the fuck did you go?"

"I'm right here."

"Well, I hope so. Hell, let's go fishing. Put the dogs in the truck, make it a Montana double date. I want you to try out this sculpin pattern I been tying with bison hair. I'm calling it the Buffalo Jump Blues account of what happened to that herd that went over the cliffs. Has a ring, huh? See if it fishes as well in the Big Hole as it does in the Madison."

"I'd like that, Sam, but first I need to find out who saw this guy, who he was hanging with, if anyone knows where he is. Think you might want to ask around? There wouldn't be a lot in it for you. Same cut as before, except I already halved my rate for her."

"And you're not interested, right? But yeah, Sam could do that. You're going to have to tell me about it, though. That 'I'd be betraying a confidence' shit, 'need to know' shit, that shit gets old."

Sean started to tell him the full version while Sam got two beers from the cooler. They sat on the porch in sling chairs regarding the river. Sam got up and got two more beers. So much for the wagon.

"That's an interesting story," he said.

"So what do you think. True love?"

Sam popped the cap and took half the can in one swallow. "Either that or the arrowhead's a warning that he's going to shoot one through her heart for leaving him when they were kids."

"What makes you say that?"

"Nothing. I just say things to be contrary, you know that."

"Speaking of love, how are things with Molly? I never really heard the whole story about how you met."

"Key West. It was back in March. I was setting up the guide business and she drove down to see about a job with a dive boat. Said she was getting tired of the glass-bottomed shindig in Largo. I racked up a game of eight-ball at the Parrot and she ran about half the table and asked me if I'd ever been kissed by a woman who could hold her breath for five minutes. I said, 'Why, do I need to sign a disclaimer?' Anyway, we wound up exploring some other kind of pockets and I told her to forget the dive boat, come to Montana instead. Told her a bar on the Madison was going to add a mermaid tank and she could be the star attraction. I must have been persuasive, 'cause here she is. No call, just a cab in the drive and a knock on the door. One suitcase with her clothes, another for her tail."

"And things are good?"

"I get a log like a redwood just hearing her voice, knowing she's the one to holler timber."

A rental Suburban lifted a cloud of dust coming up the drive and four anglers spilled out, one with comb tracks in his hair, another wearing a ponytail, and two who didn't look like they'd been good-looking in the first place and made no attempt to do so in their fifties. Sam put on his salesman's hat and ushered them inside to aerate their wallets. Sean finished his beer, knowing where to drink the next one.

———

Vic Barrows was a tatted-up iron pumper with enough ink under his skin to print the Sunday edition of the *Bridger Mountain Star*. He finished pouring a Cold Smoke Scotch Ale and cut the foam with a knife. He placed the pint in front of Stranahan and shrugged. "Stringy hair, living in his clothes 'cause I could smell him, a couple inches shorter than you. If he was a white guy, I'd say your normal local, minus the gut."

"Can you describe his face?"

Again the shrug. "Young guy. An Indian, you know. What was strange was the way he stared at her. I mean, everybody looks, that's why the girls are here, but he really stared." Barrows folded his arms like Mr. Clean and stared at Sean. "I don't think he blinked in half an hour."

"And as soon as Ida's shift finished, he left?"

"That's right. He handed me the arrowhead and split."

"What did he say?"

"'Please give this to Miss Evening Star.' Exact words. I said if he waited five minutes he could give it to her himself. He just walked out the door."

"And you saw this same guy again last night?"

"Yeah, he weaseled around for a minute or two and split. Like he was just checking to make sure it was her in the tank."

"Back to last Thursday. If you'd had your eyes closed, would you know it was an Indian speaking?"

"Now that you put it that way, no. I'd have thought he was an English teacher."

Sean couldn't tell if he was being serious or sarcastic. "A lot of customers take photos in here," he said.

"Are you asking?" The bartender didn't wait for an answer. "Sure they do. And video. It's okay with me if it goes up on YouTube. It spreads the word."

"And you get a lot of repeat customers."

"Come on, what do you think? Guys camping on the river, they come in every night they're here. Guides turn their clients on to us. Weekends, the place is packed."

"Do you have a piece of paper and a marking pen?"

"What for?"

"I'd like to leave a note on the door outside."

"I'd have to clear that with the owner."

"Where's the owner?"

"Carmel, California."

"Look, all I want to write is—"

"I'm bullshitting you. I'll get the paper, but I do want to see what you write."

He produced the paper and Sean pushed his note over for inspection.

If you took photos or video here last Thursday night, July 3rd, please call this number. We're trying to identify a patron who left something of sentimental value. Thank you.

"All right with you?"

The bartender nodded. "I'll get you the staple gun. I hope you find him and at the same time I don't, if you know what I mean. Guys who stare are never good news." He looked hard at Stranahan. "She's a nice kid, that Ida. I wouldn't want to see anything happen to her."

————

Martha Ettinger sat up abruptly when she heard the Land Cruiser pull into the drive, heard Sean's Sheltie bark her greeting as Goldie bolted out the double barn door.

For Christ sakes, why now?

"I must look like a witch," she said aloud. She heard the harsh scream of the resident barn owl as she ran her hands down her front, flicking her fingers at stray pieces of straw. Then: "Oh, hell with it," and splashed a smile on her face.

"Caught you," Sean said.

"Try being a mother again at forty-one," she said. "You'd be sleeping when you could, too."

He was backlit at the door, so she couldn't see if he was smiling. For some reason she always amused him, the bastard.

"I suppose you came to see him," she said. "Place has become a revolving door since the news broke. It's like that Indian guy we found doesn't even register. All anybody cares about is the buffalo calf. Where did you hear?"

"Horse's mouth once removed," Sean said. "Ken Winston heard it from Robin Cowdry."

"Humpff. Did you hear what went down with the DOL?"

He shook his head.

"No, I guess you wouldn't. Harold threatened to rub Drake's face in shit if he tries to take the calf."

"Really?"

"Oh yeah, they've got bad blood going back years, when there was the first talk about Indians wanting herds of their own. There was a public meeting where Drake made a joke about the 'bucks' who drove down to field dress a bull bison that the park rangers had shot, that they were half naked and only one of them had a knife and they walked around the bison three times and left, figuring the job was too big for them. It was bullshit—they were just waiting for the truck to arrive with the guy who had the permit from the state—but Drake said if Indians couldn't be trusted to properly process one bison, how could they be trusted with a herd? Harold waited outside for him and they almost came to blows."

"You think he'll follow through on his threat?"

"If I know Harold. So, you want to see the cause of all this trouble?"

She crooked a finger, leading him to a stall where the bison calf lay on his right side, the cow, a few feet away, on her left side.

"I heard about the trick with the hide," Sean said. "I guess it doesn't take a lot to fool a cow."

"No, the cow's not the problem. But the calf's developed a nervous condition and hasn't been putting on the weight he should. I think he's still traumatized by what happened. Anyway, there he is. You've seen him, now you can leave."

"Come on, Martha."

"No? How do you want me to act? As if nothing happened? Well, that's exactly what happened, nothing. I kept expecting you and you never came."

"What are you talking about?"

"I'm talking about after you took my son fishing last month. I turned the light on, on the porch. Four nights I left it on. Don't tell me you didn't see it."

"That was for me?"

"Who else would it be for?"

They looked at each other from a few feet away. Martha sighed, exhaling through her mouth. "I even put on the kinky boots you like, thinking maybe you'd figure it out through telepathy."

"I saw the light, Martha. And when I walked up the road there was Harold's truck, parked in front of your house."

Martha shook her head. She sat down on a hay bale and with her elbows on her thighs put her head in her hands. "That was the fourth night," she said quietly. "I'd given up on you."

"My dear, it seems we've been at cross-purposes."

"Don't go Rhett Butler on me."

Silence, then far away the hoot of an owl.

"I should have never made you see that movie. Oh, go away. Just go away."

"I didn't come here to see the buffalo."

"No? Why, then? You know something about the Indian? Because we could use the help. There wasn't a scrap of paper on the body, so he's over in the morgue with a J. D. tag on his toe."

"Not him, either. You said if I had trouble getting over what happened at the burial pit, you knew someone I might talk to. Well, I'm at that point. I can still see him jerking the hay hook in, only sometimes his face changes and it's somebody else. Somebody innocent. Someone I know. It's like a bad dream I can't shake and I'm killing the people closest to me night after night."

"Yes, of course. I'm glad you came to me. I mean it. We all need someone to talk to in this line of work. I'll set it up and give you a call."

"I got a job. I may be out of town a few days."

"Painting?"

"No, it's more the line of work you're talking about."

"What's it about?"

"A missing person. Someone saw a face from the past and wants me to find him for her."

"That sounds . . . uninteresting."

"It is, though. It's got a mermaid, it's got an arrowhead, maybe even true love."

"True love is a myth."

"So, how's it going with Harold, or shouldn't I ask?"

"It's going. It certainly isn't love. What about you and Katie Sparrow, or is that a rumor?"

"We're having . . . fun. I guess that's the word."

"She's only been throwing herself at you for the last three years."

"I finally caught her."

It was quiet in the barn.

"I guess your owl realized it was too early to hoot and went back to sleep," Sean said.

They walked into the twilight. It took a second try, but Martha managed to put a smile on her face. It faded as he drove out of sight.

CHAPTER NINE

Indian Directions

There was, predictably, a dog in the yard. White with brown patches, some terrier in it, no right rear leg and no surprise there, either. Three-legged dogs were as common as three-fingered men in Montana, the Blackfeet Indian reservation no exception. The dog had taken a keen interest in Stranahan's shoelaces and he was bending over to retie them when the door of the trailer opened. He'd planned on talking his way inside and knew right away it wasn't going to be easy.

Browning was a seven-hour drive from Bridger, and it had taken him another to find the trailer after reaching town. Ida Evening Star had no address, only what she called Indian directions—right where the road forks, left past the mailbox with a flag shaped like an upside-down rooster, down "I don't know, maybe a mile, you'll see a house with a chimney." What kind of chimney? "A tall one." She said the trailer would be about a quarter mile north of there on a dirt lane. It was white with a black band. There used to be a swing set in the yard.

There was no fork, the road had changed, he was climbing into aspen stands on the flanks of the Front Range before he had the sense to turn around.

He pulled over to talk to a man walking along the blacktop, not a house to be seen in either direction. "Black-and-white trailer?" The man itched at the back of one hand. "That's the old Campbell place, but there hasn't been anyone there for years. Just ghosts." Sean offered him a ride, which he declined. But the man told him where to go and was wrong, because the woman who stood in the doorway with her head thrown back and her arms crossed was no ghost.

Sean decided his only chance was to level with her and watched as she listened, not hiding her suspicion of him as a white man, or maybe as any man. She was younger than he'd expected the man's aunt to be—midthirties, heavyset, with a fleshy face with large pores and short black hair. She wore an oversize red sweatshirt with a Browning Indians logo.

"I don't know John Running Boy. I moved here last spring and you're talking stuff when I was in Cut Bank." And shut the door in his face.

Sean gave the dog a pat and the old swing in the yard a push, the rusty chains creaking. The one double-wide wood-slat seat looked like it would break if a bird perched on it. He walked back to his rig. People had been telling him he must have Indian blood since he was little, but apparently it wasn't enough to pass. He idled back the way he had come and looked at the house with the big chimney he'd driven by on the way in. Ida had told him that was where the man lived who'd taught John how to nap arrowheads. It was two-story with a checkerboard roof of missing shingles and looked deserted, a haunted house built on a little hill, though there was a vintage truck in the drive with a grille big enough to roast a pig. Sean climbed the two steps to a sagging porch, noticing an American flag in a flag holder. He knocked. No answer.

He walked back and placed a hand on the hood of the truck. It was warm, but then it was a warm day.

He heard the door open. A man appeared. He'd been quite tall once, but was now so stooped he had to lift his head, turtlelike, to see in front of him. He tapped his cane, stray yellow-gray hair falling over his shoulders and hanging in front of his face.

"What do you want? Are you from the registry?" His voice was strong but had a quaver to it.

Stranahan said he wasn't.

"They said they'd send someone to talk to me."

"It wasn't me. What does the registry want?" Stranahan had no idea what the registry was, but thought his chances for cooperation were better if he could keep the man talking.

"They're going to interview me for their war records before my soul passes into the spirit world." The man had managed to make it to the bottom step, where he lifted a hand to shield his face from the sun. "Nobody wants to come out and say I'll be dead and then it will be too late, so they pick their words accordingly."

"I'm here about someone you might have known a number of years ago. His name is John Running Boy. Or it was."

Sean advanced one stride but went no closer, out of courtesy, not wanting the man to have to crane his head farther to look up at him. The man's right forearm shook under the weight he placed on the cane.

"You'll come into my . . . house." He placed the stick as a pivot and turned around it.

Sean followed the tapping up the steps and inside, where he could see depressions in the floorboards worn by the cane's metal tip. It was like following an elk trail in the mountains that kept splitting off in different directions, a line of pockmarks leading to a living area, another branching into a kitchen, a third bending into a corridor.

The man stopped in the middle of the room to take a few breaths. "My wife made me put a crutch tip on my stick, but she's complaining from the other side now and I choose to ignore her voice. I like the sound it makes, it's company." He tapped the cane on the wood—*tap, tap, tap*—and directed himself toward the only chair in the room, a boxy recliner.

The house could have been any run-down dwelling in Montana, on reservation or off, with the exception of a built-in bookcase that took up most of one wall. Besides the reclining chair, the living area had a leather loveseat and a threadbare throw rug. A hair-rubbed cowhide was spread under a coffee table stained with coffee cup rings. A shed elk antler perched on the fireplace mantel, cobwebs stretching from one tine to the next. Above it was a photograph of a group of men in uniform, standing and kneeling. Sean waited to speak until the man sat down, an undertaking that took time.

"You were in the Army," Sean prompted.

"Eighty-first Infantry Division. I was a code talker." He pressed his hands on the coffee table and pushed himself up so that his back was nearly straight. Doing that added significantly to his stature. Though his eyes were smoky and there remained a minor trembling of his jaw, Sean was aware that he was in the presence of an impressive man.

The stick wavered as the man indicated one of the GIs in the photo. "I was nineteen, never been outside Montana."

"I thought the code talkers were Navajo," Sean said.

"Everybody thinks that, including most Indians, but there were Crow, Choctaw, Comanche, Kiowa, even Sioux. When I joined up in '44, they asked if I spoke Indian, and I said two different languages. See, I was Blackfeet, but my wife was Oglala Sioux, so I spoke some Lakota, and they had another guy who did, too, so I was recruited. I worked for a two-star general in the Pacific and helped pass messages back and forth with his chief of staff before the combat landing on Angaur Island. I'm proud to have served my country, even if my country failed to serve my people. You can sit down on the sofa." He tapped the love seat with the cane. "It's got a sag, but that's no nevermind to a young man like yourself."

Sean sat down.

"Melvin Campbell," the man said. "Bland name for an Indian, huh?" He put out a livered hand and Sean leaned forward and shook it. "I'd offer you coffee, but it takes some starch out of me just going to the door, so I'll ask you to get yourself a cup. It's on the counter."

"Would you like some?"

"I'd appreciate it. With about a tablespoon of that condensed milk on the top shelf of the refrigerator."

Sean went to make the coffee. He knew he'd be here awhile now, whether or not Melvin Campbell had anything to recall about John Running Boy. It was a function of being in the country where people talked to their dogs and their departed, where flesh-and-blood company, expected or not, was the highlight of the day. He returned with the coffee and watched Melvin Campbell's lips purse, fishlike, to explore the brim of the cup.

"John Running Boy," he said. He took a sip and set the cup down. "When he was little it was John Runs Away, the name his father gave him. I always thought that was ironic. It was the father who went away. His aunt Thelma died back in '08. I'm the one rented her the trailer."

"That's your property?"

"I don't think of it that way, but there's a piece of paper somewhere says that it is."

"The woman living there now isn't very cordial."

"No, she is not." Campbell laughed, a short "ha" that made a little spit. "Feel sorry about her dog, though. There was some kids from the high school got together to watch *Smoke Signals* and decided to drive all over the rez in reverse. A lot of fun, ha-ha. The dog was out to the mailbox and they hit it, I could hear it squeal from here. They were just whooping it up." He shook his head sadly. "There isn't a kid in these parts hasn't seen that movie five times."

Sean thought to steer him back on track. "I heard you taught John how to nap arrowheads."

"Yes. He was a fast learner, better than me in just one summer. Had the knack."

"Do you know where he went after his aunt died?"

"His mother took him back. When he was little, she shacked up with a no-account and they just fought all the time and she couldn't be bothered, so she sent the boy to his aunt's. She's got a place down in Heart Butte, came into an inheritance. Found Jesus. You ever been to Heart Butte?"

Sean said he hadn't.

"Flat like that." He held out his hand. "She's got one of those houses on the allotments by the sub agency."

"Is John still living with her?"

His eyes seemed to roam far away before settling their focus. "John, he used to come up here when he was in high school and would get a ride. Pretty rough-looking. You had to look a long time to find the boy I'd known in there. I remember he came in all beat up one time. He and some kids had driven into Great Falls and got fighting with white boys who insulted them, called them Mowgli. Hard to believe they were so ignorant they didn't know the difference between an India Indian and a Native American. I wanted him to enlist like I had, but one of the white boys was from the Malmstrom Air Force Base, so that soured him on the military. I could see he wasn't going anywhere, so I tried to interest him in Blackfeet history." He waved a hand toward the bookcase. "I urged him to go to Montana State and major in Native American studies."

"Did he?"

He shook his head. "No. I still see Judy once in a while when she comes to the supermarket."

"That's his mother?"

"Yes. Judith Crandall."

"When's the last time you saw her?"

"Back . . . been a while I guess. I want to say March, but it could have been February."

"And he was still with her then?"

He nodded. "They say Italian men live with their mothers until they're forty. We might give them a run for their lire."

"When's the last time you saw him?"

"It was after when I talked to his mother. Early May? He sat right where you are. The first time I saw him in years. He'd quit coming around and that Ford outside and I have an agreement. She'll keep on getting me from here to there long as it isn't any farther than

South Browning. Heart Butte's 'bout forty mile from here, might as well be Mars."

"Why did he come?"

"He wanted to borrow some books. He'd become interested in the history of our people. He looked good. Had a shirt buttoned all the way up, his hair was washed, he'd had some work done on his teeth. I encouraged him to take all the books he wanted, then bring them back and get some more. I had an ulterior motive, you see. Showing up after so much time passed, I wanted him to feel an obligation to come back. I wanted the company, but I also saw him as someone who could help me transcribe some notes I've written over the years, oral histories and so forth. I have the arthritis now that makes writing painful."

"What books did he take?"

"Biographies of the chiefs—Sitting Bull, Looking Glass, Joseph, Crowfoot. Histories of Plains Indians, tribal traditions, Native hunting traditions, American Indian Wars. A general overview. I made the selection for him." He nodded to himself. "I've seen it happen before. Kids grow up here, they're just weeds blowing in the wind. A lot of poverty, a lot of alcoholism and self-defeating behavior. No jobs. You get mad at the world and on the way to that your fellow man. It's no different than the urban poor in a city. Kids rebel against their fate by assuming an attitude of indifference Where you see no future in life, life has a reduced value. Like what happened to that dog. Those kids didn't even bother to stop and see if it was hurt."

The old man looked up at Stranahan.

"Something snaps inside the brain," he said. "It can be triggered by life-changing experience or just words someone says. They see a fire in somebody's eyes who has walked beyond the boundaries of life as they know it, and they realize they are part of a rich cultural history and want to tap back into it. The revelation exhilarates them. It gives them purpose and they turn around and help others see what they have seen."

As he listened, Sean had all but forgotten about the man's frailty, which was only noticeable in the shaking of the cup. He found that he was both surprised and unsurprised by Campbell's erudition and eloquence. Sean had knocked on a lot of doors, and the farther he was from centers of population, the more unexpected the result. It was one of the first things that struck him upon moving to Montana.

"Perhaps yours was the fire he saw that made the change," he said.

"I'd like to think so, but he met some other people. A few weeks after he got the books, I called his mother and she said he'd taken off with two white boys and another boy she said looked like deep rez. All that means is it's somebody she never saw before. I call them boys, but I suppose they were young men, like John. He told her he'd be back in a week, but it's been more than that and I worry about him."

"He didn't say where he was heading?"

"No, she asked me the same question. I'd like some more of that coffee if it isn't too much trouble."

As Sean made the coffee, he realized that Melvin Campbell had never asked him why he was there or who he represented. He brought the coffee back to the sitting room and made the playing field level, told him about Ida Evening Star, the old man listening without interruption. He produced the arrowhead from his pocket and Campbell took it in his fingertips, which were calloused and had yellowed nails.

Campbell nodded. "John liked bird points because they demanded a precise hand. Also our supply of obsidian would last longer." His eyes swam away for a moment. "I remember the girl," he said. "Her father worked for Indian Services and we were both involved with the Museum of the Plains Indian."

"Do you have any idea why John might have gone to the Madison Valley?"

"None whatsoever. But you're asking if he traveled there because he knew that's where he could find Ida Evening Star."

"The Hyalite County sheriff always tells me that there is no such thing as coincidence."

"Our people would agree. Nothing is attributed to accident. On the contrary, everything that happens is the result of a person's relationship with his environment. Our lives are guided by a sacred force symbolized by the sun." Melvin Campbell smiled, the creases in his skin drawing cracks across his face. "Or perhaps someone told him where to find her."

He counted back through the years, mouthing the numbers. "I have a set of journals upstairs, in case this place ever floods," he said. "Try 2001 and 2002."

He told Sean where to find the room, and a minute later Sean was back with four notebooks, one leather-bound and the others with cardboard covers. Each was dated with a span of months. Sean hadn't counted, but there must have been close to forty journals of different sizes in two cardboard boxes, dating back nearly thirty years.

"Before I got the arthritis," Campbell said, "I wrote almost every day." It took the shaking fingers a few minutes to find the appropriate journal and then the page. He placed a pencil as a bookmark and handed it over.

The photograph was black and white, held in place with pasted-on corners. It showed a boy and a girl sitting on a single wood-slat seat of a swing set. It was the swing set Stranahan had seen outside the trailer. The end that the boy sat on was lower and the girl had slid down so that she pressed against him. It was a blustery-looking day, the kids wearing tatty coats, the girl's hair feathering in the wind. Their smiles looked as unforced and as chaste as childhood dreams. Under the photo, scrawled in pen: *John Running Boy and Ida Evening Star. April 22, 2001.*

"Did you take this?"

Melvin Campbell shook his head. "A white woman named Peavey. She wrote histories of pioneer women and was a poet in the schools. I encouraged her to document Indian women's lives and she took a lot of pictures, but the project never got the funding. When John's aunt passed, I helped clean out the trailer and found this in a drawer with half a dozen others, all very similar. One of the pictures had gum stuck on the back, which made me think he'd put it up on a wall. I asked John if I could safekeep them for him. He just shrugged. He was at that age where a kid won't admit that anything matters."

"He never asked for it back?"

"No. But I gave him one."

"Was that the last time he visited you?"

"No, three or four years ago. You could see him thinking back to the time."

"Do you think he might have become fixated on her?"

"I think it would depend upon his circumstances, whether he had someone or was lonely. But he didn't confide in me that way."

"You said there were a few of these photos."

"You may borrow this one, if you wish. I do ask that you return it."

"I give you my word."

For the second time a smile ran fissures into his cheeks. "Your people have said that to our people before."

The day was into its decline by the time Stranahan reached the community of Heart Butte, sixty or so houses built around the old sub agency that doubled as a senior center and health clinic. The building was closed and all Stranahan had was a name, but he hadn't knocked on more than a half dozen doors before the name rang a bell. He was directed to a house where nobody was home. A woman with a heavy, attractive face one door down told him that Judy had driven to the Great Falls Clinic, where Carl was being treated for snakebite. Carl—it was just Carl, no elaboration—had cut the head off a prairie rattle-snake and wanted to see if it was true that the head could still bite, so he'd picked it up and got the answer he deserved—"Half dumb and some, ennit?" She had a very pretty smile.

Sean thanked the woman, who had no idea when Judy might return, and had walked halfway back to the Land Cruiser when a young man banged the screen door open and came up running.

"Hey, what you want with my mother, man?" His hair was crew cut and he wore a LeBron James basketball jersey that hung to his knees.

Sean said he was looking for John Running Boy.

"Running Boy, huh?" A flicker of smile. "He's always running with something. Used to say call him John Runs with Wolves. Could be Runs with Deer, could be buffalo. Always running, just can't settle on what with."

"Do you know where I can find him?"

A short laugh. "You see his car here?" He pointed to the next-door lot. "He's gone, man."

"A friend saw him in the Madison Valley. Do you know who he might know there?"

"No, that's like the United States or something." He ran a hand across the hood of Sean's Land Cruiser. "You could climb a mountain with this, huh?" Sean saw that he had a rat tail hanging over the back of his collar, with something white braided into it.

"I just use it to get from here to there. Look, here's the deal. A woman I know thought she saw John in a bar on the Madison River. They were sweethearts when they were kids, but he left the bar before she could talk to him. She wants to find him."

"Rekindle the flame."

"It's mostly to satisfy her curiosity."

He shook his head. "All I know is he was hanging with a couple of white dudes who were like brothers. Anyway, they looked like brothers. John said they would like pick stuff off of the other one, like you'd pick lice. Weird."

"Did he tell you what he was doing with them?"

"They were driving around, going to historical places on the rez. He said they were doing research."

"What kind of research?"

"He acted like it was a secret. But I know they were out to the pish-kun, the one up on the Two Medicine. My brother-in-law run them off. It's reservation land, but a guy who lives there and works with the archaeological people thinks he owns it."

"Who's your brother-in-law?"

"He's tribal police."

Sean thought about what Melvin Campbell had said about coincidence. And Martha Ettinger's comment about his case—*That sounds . . . uninteresting.* Well, at the mention of a buffalo jump, it had just got a whole lot more interesting.

"Was there another Indian with him, or just the two white boys?"

"Once there was an Indian, sat in the backseat like a statue. But I didn't know him."

As they spoke, a couple of other young men drifted up the street. They nodded to the man Sean was speaking to. "Whassup, Joseph?" And stood listening, one with his arms folded to pop out his biceps, and the other, his head shaved with a Mohawk stripe, bobbing like he was a fighter in the ring.

"What kind of a car does John drive?" Sean asked.

"A Fairlane. A genuine rez rocket." Joseph nodded. "Gets eight, maybe even ten miles to the gallon."

"What color?"

"Blue. It's old. Like with fins. But hey, you get tired, you don't need no motel. You crawl in back. Take a nice nap."

The man who had his arms crossed spit on the street. "John ain't got no money. He'd be on foot before he ever reached Choteau."

"Yeah," said the other man, whose head had stopped bobbing. "Maybe Letterman pick him up, give him a ride into town."

Sean thought it was time to extricate himself. He'd read a tone of aggression in the voices and could see how the situation might escalate.

"I better go," he said.

"You don't want to go, man. Where you want to go?" It was the man who'd made reference to David Letterman, the former talk show host who had a ranch up Deep Creek on the Front Range, common knowledge in the state.

"I was going to camp at Duck Lake," Sean said.

"Duck Lake? Get your ass eaten by a grizzly bear." The man who had his arms folded, folded them the other way. They were very strong-looking arms.

Sean glanced at Joseph, who saw his unease. "We're just bullshitting you," Joseph said. "Have dinner with us. Jerry's right. You don't want to camp at Duck Lake."

Sean ended up not only eating dinner with Joseph and his mother, whose name was Darleen, but also saying the grace and, after Darleen went to bed, staying up long into the night talking with Joseph on the front porch. He ended up spending the night on Joseph's couch, at his insistence. It wasn't the first time he'd been made aware of his assumptions toward those who were different from him, felt a tickle of fear in his blood that was unwarranted. Nor was it the only time an instant friendship had been kindled under the circumstances. An old brittle-whiskered tabby hopped up on the couch toward morning, its motor running in its throat, and the next time he opened his eyes he could smell cooking. Joseph came in and handed him a cup of coffee.

"Mom's making fry bread just for you. You tell her it's the best you ever had and you can carve your name on this couch, stay here anytime you pass through town."

Sean said that might be sooner rather than later.

"You my brah now. You open the door, you say, 'Hey, Cuz,' you don't never need to knock."

CHAPTER TEN

A Step at a Time

The Queen of the Waters flipped backwards in a languid circle. She came up to the glass, rolled over like a seal, then kicked her tail and swam up and out of sight.

"I stood up from this stool, I'd have to walk on three legs, know what I mean, Kemosabe?" Sam drained his bottle of Moose Drool and tapped the surface of the bar for another. "Any PMDs about?"

PMD was short for pale morning dun, a mayfly with translucent wings that resembled a hovering angel, if mayflies were angels and rivers were the dance floors of heaven. Sean had fished the Missouri River on his drive back from the reservation and nodded.

"Tough, though. You'd get one to come up, think you'd hit on the right pattern, then the next six fish would refuse it."

Sam grunted sympathetically. "That's the Mo for you. Like a woman who won't put out until you buy her roses and then says they're the wrong color."

"So, what is it you found out?"

"A guide I know says he saw a couple Indians with two white dudes at the Food Roundup in West Yellowstone. He says the white dudes were volunteers for the American Bison Crusade, the hippies who beat their drums and march down Main on the Fourth. They're the ones who film the hunters shooting buffalo so they can bleed the pockets of the bleeding hearts. Anyway, what was I saying?"

"I don't know, Sam, it's your story."

"Yeah, right. Thing is, my buddy knew these guys a little bit, because he floated their father a couple of times. The dad's a wig, has a summer cabin at the Cinnamon Creek Guest Ranch, rents it for like a month."

"So these white kids, they're brothers?"

"That's what I just said. Anyway, you said find an Indian, I found you one and threw in a spare."

Two Indians, Sean thought. That could mean something or nothing. But two Indians with two brothers involved with the American Bison Crusade, it was hard to think they weren't the same group that Joseph had seen on the reservation.

"What's the father's name?"

"Augustine Castilanos."

"Sounds like somebody out of a Greek *Godfather.*"

"Yeah, except the guy looks like he's part Japanese. The kids are like trust funders or, what's the word, those kids go to private schools and talk Latin?"

"Preppies?"

"Yeah. I think the old man's their stepfather and they got a different last name."

"You did good, Sam."

"I'm not done." Sam drained the bottle.

"Guess who's booked to float them for two days, starting day after tomorrow?" He thumped his chest with a stout forefinger. "Well, not me specifically, but the shop. And the man said two boats, so who knows, maybe he'll take the progeny with him." He smiled, exposing the grooves in his teeth. "I tie the fly on for you . . . I make the cast, I . . . Come on, help Sam out."

"You set the hook?"

"That's right. All you got to do is reel them in. Even a sorry-assed painter can reel in a fish."

Sean was absorbing the information when Sam said, "Ah, it's the Queen herself. Is she a swipe right, or is she a swipe right?"

Sean didn't have a clue what he was talking about, but he rose from the stool as she approached. Molly Linklatter possessed that combination of carriage and confidence, call it class, that made men dust off old-fashioned manners. She offered her hand and held his eyes one long second longer than necessary, during which she mentally added him to her legion of admirers, or so Sean imagined. He had met her only briefly once before, on that occasion, like the present one, after she climbed out of the aquarium with her hair dripping and no trace of makeup, but with her allure undiminished.

"Sam called you a swipe right. I assume that's a compliment."

"Oh, that Sam." She looked at Sam with affection, then abruptly walloped him on the upper arm with a straight right that made people turn their heads. She returned her attention to Sean, as Sam winced and rubbed his arm. "People post selfies and you can swipe right if you like the photo or left if you don't. If you swipe right on each other's pictures, then you can arrange a date. That's the ladylike way of saying it."

"So why did you hit him? General principles? I've hit him myself, it can make you feel good."

"A queen doesn't hook up."

They moved to a table, where she mollified Sam by kissing his cheek. Beers came for the men, an Orangina for Molly—they drank to salmonflies raining from the sky. Sean was unwinding from the drive sip by sip when the bartender told him a man at the bar wanted a word.

Sam lifted his eyebrows. Sean shrugged.

The Hawaiian shirt stretched across the broad back had a surf-board motif, though the man who turned on the stool to face him, longneck in his fist, looked like he'd be more at home attacking a plate of grits than catching a wave.

"I read the notice on the door," he said, and tapped the camera slung around his neck.

"Did you try to call? I've been out of cell range."

"No. This is the first I've been in since Thursday. That's the day the note said you're interested in."

"That's right. You took photos?"

He nodded. "You're free to look at the playback, but just to satisfy my curiosity, what's it about?"

"Someone saw someone they thought they knew, but then he disappeared. She'd like to find him."

"Blast from the past."

"Something like that. It's a confidential matter."

"So what are you, a private investigator?"

"Licensed," Sean said.

"No shit?" The man brought his head back an inch. He was impressed. "I was just joking."

"No shit."

The man took the camera from around his neck. "Just hit the left arrow to scroll back."

Sean bought the man one of the same he'd been having and started through the photos. The man Sean was looking for was standing a few feet behind the bar in half a dozen shots. Jeans, a shirt with the tail out, a dark-colored vest—the focus on the tank so the man was not in sharp focus, but close enough to the description Ida had given him. As the photographer was behind the man and both were facing the tank, Sean couldn't see a face.

"Your mystery man there?"

"Hard to tell. I saw that you took a video of the mermaid."

"Yeah, her." He pointed to Ida Evening Star, who was taking her turn in the tank. "Chippewa Nymph, my ass. The bull must have jumped the fence, because she's whiter than I am."

Sean ignored the crassness of the comment. "Do you just click on it to play it?"

"Yes, but I uploaded it into my iPhone. It's a bigger screen." He said the iPhone was on the charger in his SUV. Sean wondered why he hadn't said so in the first place.

The SUV, a 4Runner jacked so far up it was like mounting a horse, had a dead cigar in an ashtray and dice hanging from the rearview. It took the man, who'd got around to introducing himself as Taylor, only a minute or two to find the video. Sean watched it, the video starting with a tour of the bar and its tiki hut decor before fixing focus on the mermaid tank. Ida was swimming in a gold tail with red and blue spots inside gold circles that creased and uncreased with every undulation. She didn't possess the athleticism of the Parmachene Belle, nor the showy seduction of the Queen of the Waters, but she swam with languid grace and drew whistles from a couple men at the bar.

"She looks like a brown trout in spawning colors," Taylor offered.

Sean kept his eyes on the screen. Once Ida had become the focus, the camera turned to track her, and the man whom Sean was interested in was in and out of the left-hand side of the frame. He was facing away, but at one point two men approached the bar, and when one accidentally jostled against him to get a better view of the tank, the man turned his head briefly, nodding at the one who'd jostled him and not bothering to uncross his arms. His face was in profile for perhaps two seconds, but Indian all right. Whether it was John Running Boy was impossible to say. Ida would be the judge of that, and she would be drying off in a few minutes.

"Can you send this to my cell phone?" Sean asked.

"Pretty big file for that. For a private investigator you don't know much about technology." He shook his head mock disapprovingly, his double chin shaking. "Tell you what I can do. I can give you the camera card, then you can do anything with it you want."

"Don't you need it?"

"I bought an eight-gig two-pack and the photos on the card are already uploaded."

"How much was the two-pack?"

"Thirty-nine fifty. You buy me the porterhouse with Cajun fries and we're square."

"You can come up now."

The stairs to the top of the tank consisted of all-weather carpet strips glued to the steps of an aluminum extension ladder. Stranahan climbed up and peered over, where the Chippewa Nymph sat on a deck a few inches above the waterline.

"So this is where the magic happens," he said.

"Yeah, the magic. I'm not a mermaid, I'm an 'aquatic performer.' " Ida was working the tail off her legs and handed it to him, along with a six-pound weight belt used for ballast. The tail was heavy, some kind of vulcanized material with a slime.

"It's called Dragon Skin," she said. "It's silicone. They're like a thousand bucks, but this one was on eBay for two fifty. I thought Cal—he's the owner—was lending it to me, but when I got my first check he'd deducted it. I suppose I should have known how cheap he was when I saw that I'd have to climb a garden ladder."

Sean descended the ladder and steadied it for her. She asked him to turn around while she took off her top and bikini bottom and slipped into clothes.

"Feel better?" Sean said, when she said he could turn around.

"Lots better. The thermostat broke, so it's too cold in the tank tonight. Molly said her nipples got so hard she was afraid they'd break the clamshells. She can be pretty funny. Anyway, I just hope when the semester starts I'll still have my eyesight. Cal wanted me to do four sessions Saturday and I said no way. Even after two, your vision is so blurry it's hard to read a newspaper."

"That's too bad," Stranahan said, "because I have some photos to show you." He showed her the card chip.

"Did you go up to the reservation? Did you find him?"

"Yes and no. I just got back. Is there someplace private we can talk?"

———

Ida lived in a trailer court between the river and the Earthquake Inn, a few miles downstream from the dam at Quake Lake. Sean followed the taillights of her Tercel and found himself standing before a vintage Airstream with blue Christmas tree lights outlining the door and windows. A regiment of garden gnomes guarded tomato plants that were outgrowing their wire cages, three to either side of the door. Across the river, on the south bank, softer lights gleamed from a log mansion where a baker's dozen of Sean's riverscapes hung from the walls. Sean had once thrown a man into a pond on that property, it seemed a lifetime ago.

"The lights came with the trailer," Ida said. "The owner considers them festive."

"Makes you want to take a turn around a roller rink," Sean said. He looked up, another starry night, the moon thinned to a silver parenthesis. "You said when you knew me better, you'd tell me what star you were named for."

"The star I'm named for isn't in the sky. It's a birthmark, and I'd have to know you a lot better to show you that."

The trailer had eggshell-blue walls and a bolted-down Formica table. The table was chipped, the wood cabinets had warped so that the doors didn't properly close, and the coverings on the bench cushions looked like they had been worked on by the claws of a bobcat. Nonetheless, the place had a scrubbed feel to it.

"I'm one of those 'a place for everything and everything in its place' types. People like to read into that, but I think it's just a reaction to the chaos my mother was comfortable with."

"I'm not reading anything into anything."

Ida opened her laptop and Sean sat beside her as she slipped in the card. Their shoulders brushed, something Sean was acutely aware of. The heat of her skin was a palpable presence; he could hear the intake of each breath.

"This won't take a minute," she said. It didn't, though Sean wouldn't have minded if it had taken thirty.

He told her to click on the video segment, identified by the time marked on the lower right corner. They watched it through, then on second viewing paused it when the man turned his head. The cheek in profile was clean-shaven. A wing of black hair, parted in the middle, hung over the ear. As the man glanced at the person who had jostled him, he showed a slight downturn of his mouth under a straight aquiline nose.

"Good-looking man," Ida said. "But then John was a good-looking boy."

"You say that, but if he hadn't handed the bartender the arrowhead, could you be sure?"

She canted her head. "Like I said, it's his posture that makes me think of John. That and something I really can't put my finger on."

"Maybe this will help." Sean drew the photograph from his shirt pocket.

As she examined it, a sad smile drew the corners of her mouth. "I remember that day," she said. "John wanted me to sit to the left of him on the swing, so that he only saw my purple eye. He knew my mother called it my Indian eye, and he would study it like it had a secret to tell. A flock of wild turkeys came into the yard that morning."

She looked from the faded three-by-five to the computer screen. "It's him, you can almost tell just from the photo."

"It's him or you want it to be him?"

"Who else would give me the arrowhead?"

"That's not the same question."

"No." She closed her eyes, as if thumbing back through mental rather than digital images. "It's him. That's John Running Boy."

Sean pocketed the photo. "I wanted to ask you before I told you what I learned up there. I didn't want anything to color your judgment."

"Now you have me worried."

"Well, there's no need for *you* to be worried, but you might be worried about *him*."

She listened without interrupting, though her concern was easy enough to read.

She looked at him, the obvious question unspoken.

"I'm going to make some coffee," she said. Striking a match against one of the stove burners, she said, "Because he was up at the buffalo jump on the reservation, you think he came down here and had something to do with those bison at the Palisades? I mean, it's three hundred miles from here to there."

"Buffalo aren't the only thing that died, Ida."

"Are you saying John had something to do with that? I thought that man fell to his death. It was an accident."

"I'm only saying that there was an another Indian in that car, and that a young Indian man died at the jump, and that it's hard not to draw the connection."

A silence stretched between them. She handed Sean a cup of coffee and, sitting down, edged to the other side of the bench, so that they were no longer connected by the heat of their skin.

"If I'd known this would get him into trouble," she said, "I wouldn't have hired you."

"I understand that. Look"—he spread his hands on the table—"we haven't found him yet. Let's take it a step at a time."

———

It was a night that could have gone in another direction, Sean thought as he drove back toward Bridger, had the circumstances been different. He couldn't deny his attraction to her. But that's the way they left it, a step at a time, and a step at a time was how he planned to take it at six in the morning, when he hiked down to the military ammunition container that served as his mailbox. He opened the lid—nothing but a note from the mailman imploring him to buy a real mailbox and nail it to a post.

As he smiled, he heard Martha Ettinger's Jeep coming down the canyon road and stuck out his thumb.

She powered down the passenger-side window. "I don't pick up strangers."

"Good morning to you, too, Martha." It was the first he'd seen her since they'd put the cards on the table in her barn, and they regarded each other in more or less comfortable silence. There had been a time, Stranahan recalled, when Martha would walk from her house to his turnoff as the sun rose, collecting his newspaper on her way to undoing the sticks that secured the front flap of the tipi, and then helping him undo whatever buttons he was wearing and unfastening her own. There had been a time when this was almost every morning.

A few seconds passed as he thought of those mornings.

"Where's Choti?" Martha said. "Goldie will need grief counseling if she's gone much longer."

"She's become DIR at the clubhouse. That's what Ken Winston calls her, dog-in-residence. I'll take her back when they drain the pipes and fly to their other lives."

"So where did your case take you? I haven't seen your rig in a few days."

"North."

"Just north?"

"Just north."

"Well, I'm up to something, too, and it's taking me south, so la-de-da." She powered up the window, smiling, keeping the truce, and Sean's eyes followed the Jeep as it got smaller and then turned inward as he went back to thinking about his next step. He checked his phone to see if had a bar, and didn't, and had to walk another hundred yards or so down the road.

He punched in Sam's number.

"Kemosabe." The voice was thick. Was he still in bed?

"Were you still planning to fish Augustine Castilanos tomorrow?"

"Uh, yes. Stop that."

Sean could heard a muffled voice. Then: "You want it? He hired two boats. You guide one, I'll take the other."

"I want it."

"It's yours. No problemo. We've been doing better with the big bugs in the afternoon, so no rush to be first on the water. The plan is to meet up at two, his party's staying at the Cinnamon Creek Guest Ranch, float from MacAtee to Varney. We'll have a shuttle waiting at the bridge."

"Thanks, Sam. Say hi to Molly for me."

Another muffled voice and then, clearly, "Do you think I'm a ten? Sam says I'm only a nine."

"As a mermaid, or as a woman?"

"A woman."

"You're an eleven."

"You hear that, Sam? Sean says I'm an eleven. *Sans scales.*" A pause. In a pooh-pooh voice: "Sam says to hang up the phone."

"Good-bye, Molly."

"Good-bye, Sean."

Sean walked back, examining the dusty strips bordering the road for tracks, the deer last night, the lion before dawn, the hunted and the hunter, a story as old as the earth upon which it was written.

CHAPTER ELEVEN

A Question Chipped in Stone

"You're telling me he cut it off? Jesus, Bob."

Martha Ettinger wasn't squeamish. She'd seen plenty of dead people, among the worst a teenage girl who'd died from exposure after becoming stuck in a chimney, whose eyes had been pecked by crows. The corpse of the twentysomething Native American male lying on the stainless steel examining table wasn't nearly so bad, a point that Doc Hanson, the county medical examiner, brought up after removing the sheet covering the body.

Martha felt her stomach knot as the pulpy bruising around the tear in the man's midsection was revealed, and for a second her eyes lingered on a birthmark a few inches below that. The mark, a Band-Aid color, was shaped like nothing in particular, but a birthmark on a John Doe could be as valuable as dental records to ID a body.

"Of course Wilkerson and company will have the final say," Hanson was saying, "but the end that wasn't caught on the piton is cleanly severed and the knife that you found in his belt sheath has adhered tissue that's being examined in the lab."

"So, he slips trying to descend the cliff face, guts himself like a deer, and then for some reason he can't reach where he's caught on the piton and to free himself he cuts off a piece of his intestine."

"Are you thinking out loud or asking my opinion?"

"Both."

"We've seen this before, if you recall. That bow hunter who fell off his tree stand—"

"Yeah, Harold reminded me. Bummer."

"Bummer?"

"What would you call it?"

Hanson's "ahem" died on the walls. Quietly, he said, "I think the real question is what he was doing there in the first place, but you don't seem eager to tell me about that."

"Can you keep your mouth shut? It's public knowledge that a body's been found, but we're sitting on the details until we have more information."

"What happens in the morgue, dies in the morgue." Hanson shrugged. "Morgue humor. Really, Martha, you have to ask my discretion?"

"No. Sorry. And I appreciate you working the autopsy in this morning."

"It wasn't a busy week for Saint Peter," he said.

"Okay, the scenario we're looking at is that a few people tried to conduct a buffalo jump. We don't have an eyewitness, but it's what the evidence suggests."

"A pishkun?"

"Yes. After Harold and I found the body, we swept the area and came up with five arrows. A couple were broken, like someone had shot them and they'd hit a rock. They look like Indian relics. But they didn't have any blood on them, though I don't know how you miss a buffalo."

"Hmm. That does fit with the evidence." Hanson used a probe to point to a jellylike hematoma that bulged from the upper right thigh. "I initially thought this wound had been made when he fell on a sharp stick, but in fact it was caused by an arrow. The arrow had broken off, leaving the point, which I extracted. It measures approximately six centimeters. To me it looks like obsidian, though you may want to consult a geologist. In any case it's of primitive design."

"And you waited until now to tell me this."

"After that stunt you pulled at the cabin," he said, "you deserve what I give you, when I give it to you."

"I don't remember you calling to complain."

It was the first mention between them of what Martha had come to call her hour of insanity, when she'd played Cupid to bring Bob Hanson, an unhappily but very well married man, together with a woman of dubious reputation at a remote Forest Service rental cabin. What had subsequently transpired between the two she didn't know, but she never saw him, nor raised her eyes to the jagged teeth of the Crazy Mountains where the cabin was situated, without wondering. The silence inched across the marble floor.

"I'm sorry, Bob. It's none of my business."

"Don't be absurd. Of course it's your business. You set me up with her. Or are you going to deny it?"

Martha blew out a breath. How the hell did they get started on this?

The medical examiner's walrus mustache quivered before he spoke. "Ariana Dimitri is a charming young woman and that's all I believe I'll say on the matter."

So it had gone well. *Now the question,* Martha thought, *is am I a matchmaker, or a madam?*

"What's that, Martha?"

"Nothing. Let's have a look at the arrowhead."

He nodded brusquely. "It's above the sinks. Upper right drawer."

Martha carefully unwrapped a square of burgundy jeweler's cloth to reveal the stone point. "Why isn't it in an evidence bag?"

"Because it's been processed. You can touch it."

About an inch of wood arrow shaft was secured to the point by wraps of sinew that had hardened to an amber color.

"This is similar to the points on the arrows that we found," Martha said, turning it in her gloved fingers.

"Do you think somebody shot him?" Hanson asked.

"I don't know. But would it break off like this? Wouldn't you think if it snapped, it would break at the skin level? Then there'd be three or four inches of shaft, not two."

Hanson shrugged. "Perhaps the victim tried to extract it and it snapped off when he pulled on the shaft. I will tell you that had it remained in place until help arrived, the man might still be alive. Wilkerson did some trajectory tests, which indicated the initial position of the head was five centimeters from the femoral artery. About two inches. Her projections indicated that the head moved as the man walked, as the muscles relaxed and contracted. That caused it to continue sawing tissue, eventually lacerating the femoral artery."

"Really? I didn't know a stone point was that sharp."

"Stones shaped by pressure flaking are used as surgical instruments."

"You learn something new every day."

"You're getting that faraway Martha look," Hanson said.

She removed her gloves and scratched a nail under her chin, not registering the comment. What had Sean Stranahan said about his missing person case, that it had a mermaid and an arrowhead? Yes, she was pretty sure that's what he'd said. A mermaid, an arrowhead, and true love.

CHAPTER TWELVE

Martha Knows Best

When part of your job is heading up a search-and-rescue division that performs more searches than any other Montana county, every vista elicits a memory. As Martha Ettinger drove west from Bridger, she caught sight of a basin in the Tobacco Root Range where a back-country skier had become so lost she hooked back into her own trail twice, skiing in circles at twenty below zero and stripping off her clothing a piece at a time in a misguided effort to ski faster. Nearly naked, she was found in the very early stages of rigor, only her eyelids, neck, and lower jaw having stiffened. That one still haunted Martha because Jason Kent's one-ton had bogged down and the hour they spent digging it out of a snowdrift was the hour when the skier had died.

A half hour later, taking the 287 dogleg south out of Ennis, Martha glanced westward to the scene of another search, where a dark triangle in the Bear Creek drainage marked a feeder where she and Walter Hess had found a lost hunter. The hunter was shivering so violently that he'd bitten off the tip of his tongue. They had sandwiched him with their body warmth until help arrived, and on the first anniversary of the rescue Martha received a bottle of apricot moonshine from the hunter with a note: *To keep your blood moving as you kept mine.* She'd drunk a little of it with Stranahan, a little with Harold Little Feather, and a little more with Sheba on her lap and Goldie at her feet, ruing her relationships with all men.

With such recollections to keep her company, the miles passed quickly. It was a little past five when she turned off at the West Fork, crossed the bridge, and snaked down the two-track to the log-and-mortar cabin that served as home base for the Madison River Liars and Fly Tiers Club. Patrick Willoughby and Robin Cowdry rose from wood-slat chairs on the porch, Willoughby rolling his right hand in a flourish as he bowed. Martha's smile was forced. She'd once played poker with "the boys," as she called them, and sat in the very chair Willoughby had risen from, stripped to her bra on a dare. Sam Meslik had never let her forget it, calling her "36C" ever since.

"Gentlemen," she said.

"M'lady," Willoughby said. "I will have Jeeves set another place at the table."

"I'm not staying." She indicated the Land Cruiser on the grassy turnaround. "I just have to talk to Stranahan."

"Nonsense." Willoughby peered over his glasses. "The only further discussion of this matter will concern vintages of the burgundy grape." Martha recalled Stranahan telling her that Willoughby, a former naval officer, had been a hostage negotiator for three presidential administrations. He'd carved a career from his ability to get people to see things his way. It was no use arguing and Martha didn't try.

"He's just up the river with Dorry," Cowdry said. "He's teaching her to cast a fly rod."

Martha found them at a pool of the Madison known as the Looking Glass, Sean bareheaded, his black hair in contrast to the girl's straw mop that peeked from the frayed edges of her hat. He bent to whisper in her ear as Martha approached.

"Sean says to tell you you'll let me see the buffalo."

"Hmm. Have you caught any fish?"

"I caught a whitefish, but he says to tell my uncle it was a rainbow trout."

"He tells people a lot of things, doesn't he? Sean, a word?"

He instructed the girl to keep casting and walked up the bank. "What brings you to the river?"

"Sam said you had a guide day tomorrow and if you were out of cell range, it meant you were bunking at the clubhouse. I had a question that couldn't wait."

"Shoot."

"You said the case you'd taken on involved an arrowhead. Would that be a stone point? Maybe yeay big." She held her thumb and forefinger two inches apart.

"A little smaller."

"You said you were heading north? Would that have been to an Indian reservation?"

"That's two questions."

She gave him a look.

"I went to Browning and to Heart Butte."

Martha blew out a breath, a bubbling sound. She shook her head. "Sometimes I hate being right. Where's this arrowhead now?"

"It's in the glove compartment of the Land Cruiser."

"Tell Dorry it's time to reel up."

———

They carried chairs from the porch, unfolding them on the bank where spring water burbled over an apron of watercress. A kingfisher beat a silver fry against a midriver rock, then turned it in his beak and swallowed it whole, headfirst. The bird repeated the process as Martha filled Sean in on her morning at the morgue and he briefly wrestled with his conscience before deciding that it was in the best interests of his client to bring Martha into his confidence.

She listened, two fingernails drawing white lines down her right cheek.

"I'm just going to think out loud here," she said. She nodded to herself, fingering the arrowhead that Sean had retrieved from his rig. "Okay, here's what we have. We have two Indians and two white men, said to be brothers, visiting a buffalo jump historical site on the Blackfeet Reservation. A week later we have a group with the same makeup seen at a grocery store in West Yellowstone. We have the reenactment of a buffalo jump right here in the Madison Valley, with eleven dead bison and an Indian man killed by an arrow. We have the American Bison Crusade the brothers are reported to be involved with, and we have your mermaid, who a different Indian man from the dead one reached out to in a bar. If, that is, your Ida Evening Star is being completely forthcoming. That's what we have."

She turned the arrowhead Sean had given her. It was smaller than the head Doc Hanson had extracted, but it was flaked from obsidian and was of similar design.

"Do these things have, like, fingerprints?"

"You mean peculiarities that identify the hand of the maker?"

"You took the words out of my mouth."

Sean shook his head. "Brad Amundson might know."

"Buckskin Brad. Yeah, we should run them by him." But she was just saying words.

"All right, what don't we have?" She pursed her lips in and out, a new bad habit that Harold had told her made her look like a carp. She caught Sean looking and stopped.

"We *don't* have the car the men were seen driving, we *don't* have their reason for conducting a buffalo jump, and most of all, we *don't* have a motive for anyone killing the Indian man. We also lack an ID of his body. Which reminds me, I want to take a look at that video, the guy who's supposed to be John Running Boy. I don't have to tell you that he's become a person of interest in this other fellow's death."

Sean nodded. "We can use Ken Winston's laptop." He thought of something. "The guy whose house I slept at, Joseph Brings the Sun, he saw the other Indian man John was with up on the reservation. He didn't get the guy's name, but he could ID the body as being that man. I think he'd come down here if I asked him."

"Good. We can keep that in our back pocket."

They chewed on what they did and didn't have for a while, the river talking it over with them.

"There *is* something else," Sean said at length. "The father of the white kids booked two boats with Sam's guide business for tomorrow afternoon. No guarantee the boys will be part of the fishing party, but if they are, I'll be at the oars of the boat that they're in."

Martha drew her head back, canting it a fraction. "How old are these . . . *boys*?"

"They're college-age, according to Sam."

"Hmm." Again, she caught herself pursing her lips. "Look, Stranny," she said, "I'm not going to tell you this is police business and don't stick your nose in it, but run things by me first."

"That's what I'm doing."

"Yes, and I thank you for that. Listen to me. The only reason this isn't an out-and-out murder investigation is because we can't rule out accidental death. We don't jump to conclusions, and I'll tell you why. When I took on this job, one of my first investigations was a hunter who was killed by an arrow. He was with a buddy who was sleeping with his wife, and they'd fought over her before. I wanted to put a jacket on the buddy—he had motive, opportunity—but Harold, this is when he was freelancing out of Browning, he concluded that the arrow had been lying on the ground with the nock over a deep hoof-print made by an elk. What happened was the man had thrown his bow and arrows into a ground blind, then jumped into the blind after them. His foot came down on the nock, the arrow stood on end and drove into his thigh. His buddy found him down to his last pint and the last thing the hunter told him before dying, so he claimed, was take care of the wife."

"Did he?"

"I heard they married after a decent interval."

"So the moral of the story is don't kill your buddy, if you take him hunting he'll do it himself?"

"No, the moral is, Martha knows best. Reserve judgment, and when in doubt, ask."

They were watching the kingfisher down his third fry when the dinner triangle rang up the hill.

———

Sean could still taste the kongoni steaks that Robin Cowdry cooked on the grill when he helped zip Ida into her tail for her last swim of the evening. He told her about the autopsy while she dusted waterproof glitter across her shoulders and collarbones.

"I just thought you'd like to know that the arrowhead that killed that man was a lot like the one you showed me," he told her. "The sheriff doesn't believe in coincidence. I don't either, for that matter."

"Good for you," she said. From the bar they heard the dolphin chatter that was her cue.

"Sorry for being so abrupt," Ida said. "I'll see you in thirty."

But a half hour later, when she ordered a mineral water and they took seats in the bar, the distance she'd created was still there, stretching across the tabletop. It was in her posture, her chin defiant, her eyes narrow. Her glance darted from her lap to the glazed starfish in the nets suspended from the ceiling, never catching his eyes in the arc. She seemed to have pulled an invisible film across her face. An attempt at small talk stalled, and when she finally got around to looking at him, it was only to thank him for his work and add that he needn't investigate further. Surely he could understand that the last thing she wanted was to be responsible for her childhood friend getting into trouble with white man's law. The adjective, Sean thought, was a clear attempt to emphasize their differences.

We are not the same people after all, her expression said. *It was nice meeting you. Good-bye.*

She stood, her glass, untouched, making a ring on a mermaid coaster. She extended her hand, the palm cool, the green eye and the purple one as opaque as the stones you pocket because their colors are beautiful in the water, only to find that they dry to the color of nothing.

Sean drove the seven miles back to the clubhouse in time to find Martha cutting the cards at the fly-tying table, giving him her dead eyes, dealing him in.

CHAPTER THIRTEEN

The Brothers Fedora

As a trout guide, Sean Stranahan had floated buddies who finished each other's sandwiches, sisters who finished each other's sentences, and, once, memorably, two women attending a romance writers' convention who traded a joint from bow to stern and promised they could finish him off in five minutes tops, if he didn't mind pulling over to the bank and climbing out of his waders. An opportunity declined, not without periodic regret.

But he had never before fished with men who finished each other's casts.

The brothers, cable-muscled and strikingly handsome, were as blond and Aryan to the eye as their father was swarthy and Mediterranean, with a vaguely Asian infusion. The genetic stew, when you added to the pot the mother who advanced each foot as if she was testing the water, and who resembled a Nordic goddess who'd had about half of her blood drained, would have baffled Sean, if Sam hadn't already told him that the boys were stepsons. Sean learned that they had retained their birth father's name, Karlson, while availing themselves of their stepfather's fortune, which he'd made felling balsam trees for pulp mills and then, astutely predicting the decline of the industry with the ascent of electronic media, parceling off his more accessible timberlands for residential development.

The fraternal twins, for such they turned out to be, called Sean "Captain," throwing in mock salutes as they introduced themselves as "Brady and Levi, the Fedora brothers," tipping identical felt Trilbys studded with trout flies. They tumbled into the Land Cruiser, tussling as they fought for shotgun. They wrestled again at the riverbank over the bow seat, then, panting and with their shirts torn, picked the grasses from each other's chest hair, grooming with the absorption one sees of monkeys in a zoo. Brady, the elder by twelve minutes, taller by two inches, and fairer-skinned by half a shade, had won the bow, but less than a mile into the float Levi joined him on the casting deck, where one would make the cast and mend the fly line so that the salmonfly pattern floated freely in the current, then pass the fly rod to the other, who would fish out the drift before making a cast and passing the rod back, and so forth; this, together with a running patter over their relative prowess with the young women at Dartmouth, where they played varsity lacrosse and from which they would graduate the following year, was the way the afternoon began to pass.

Sean didn't know what to make of them. He'd changed the itinerary at the last minute, forgoing a float from MacAtee to Varney for the stretch upriver, putting in at Lyon Bridge, which would pass them into the evening shadow cast by the Palisades. He watched for recognition in their eyes as he imparted the news, but if they were reluctant to visit—or perhaps to *revisit*—the scene of the buffalo jump, he was unable to detect it.

On the water, he pressed the matter by directing them to cast toward the bank under the cliffs.

"A body was found here the day before yesterday," he said. "Up by that big rock. Did you hear about it?" He kept his voice casual.

"We heard this morning," Brady said. "This is where the buffalo fell, is it not?" *Is it not? If you say. Right-o, Captain*—their speech was padded with such supercilious affectation. Clearly, Sean was their employee, or rather their stepfather's, whom they called "Papa-san."

Looking for an excuse to pull over, Sean caught a break when Levi overcast the bank, hooking his fly in a wild rosebush. Sean dropped anchor and walked upriver, reeling in the fly line until he reached the five-petaled flowers that made a splash against the bankside willows.

He snipped off the fly, blood-knotted a new tippet, and tied the fly back on. By the time he turned to go back, the brothers were nowhere in sight. He found them forty yards below the boat, frowning at the cavernous rib cage of a bison. The carcass was swarming with deer flies and yellow jackets. Sean breathed through his mouth to reduce the odor.

"Why didn't they take the meat?" Levi said. "The newspaper said that Indians were going to take the meat."

Two hours into the float they were the first seemingly genuine words either brother had spoken. It was the boy underneath the veneer, his voice higher-pitched; he sounded like a ten-year-old asking a question of his father. There was a tremor in the square-cut chin.

"The ones that died in the fall spoiled," Sean told him. "They could only salvage quarters from the ones that were still alive the next morning. Whoever drove them over the cliff didn't have the guts to finish the job."

It was a shot in the dark. None of the news reports had mentioned the suspicion that the bison had been driven over the cliffs.

"Where did you hear that?" It was Brady speaking.

Sean was finding out that he took the lead in conversation, Levi either riffing off what he said or echoing his meaning with a more self-effacing choice of words.

"The sheriff's a neighbor of mine," Sean said, not looking at him. "She said it was a buffalo jump, there's an Indian term for it . . ." He snapped his fingers, searching for the word and hoping he wasn't overdoing the gesture.

"A pishkun," Levi said, and Sean saw his older brother shoot him a look. "I think that's what it's called," he said, amending his conviction.

Sean nodded. "Yes, that's it."

It was the opening he'd waited for to bring up their involvement with the American Bison Crusade, but the withering look Brady had given his sibling made him reconsider. Sean's information was third-hand, and if they denied it, what would he have gained by putting them on the defensive? Instead, he took the opportunity to plant a seed of doubt.

"The sheriff said they found something that might identify one of the hunters, or maybe it was they knew where to look for something. They're going to come back up here, climb up the cliffs. If we float this stretch again tomorrow, we might run into them."

The walk back to the boat was silent. Sean turned once to see if the brothers were looking up at the cliffs, but they had their eyes on their wading shoes.

Enthusiasm for casting gymnastics waned after that, but as the hours passed and the clouds became limned with the blood of the sunset, the fishing picked up, as did the mood. Sean replaced the salmon flies with elk hair caddis, and when the imitation Brady was fishing disappeared in a swirl, he did most everything wrong, but the fish stayed on. It fought in the air before it fought underwater and was nineteen inches, measured against the net. A big rainbow trout, for fishermen who don't catch them very often, is like a fire in the attic. Those who watch the house burn down are peeled from their skins of personality. Their eyes seem stunned, smells are sharper, sounds more insistent. For a time they'll say anything that comes into their heads, anything at all.

CHAPTER FOURTEEN

The Buffalo Whisperer

When Sean turned under a hazy moon into Martha's drive, he was surprised to see the Suburban that the Liars and Fly Tiers Club leased. She met him at the door of the barn, bringing her finger to her lips. He followed the beam of her flashlight inside, where Robin Hurt Cowdry was sitting on a hay bale by the stall where the young bison lay on its side, the cow a few feet away. Dorry was curled against the bison's back and had fallen asleep with her arm draped over its neck.

Cowdry cocked a finger toward his niece. "The Buffalo Whisperer," he whispered. He unfolded himself from his seat and they went outside, where he fished in his pocket for a vapor cigarette.

"If I hadn't seen it with my own eyes I wouldn't believe it," Martha said. "You recall I told you that the calf had a nervous disposition, wasn't gaining weight? It was bleating like the dickens all evening and then Dorry came and it settled right down, nursed, fell asleep."

"It's innocence, is what it is." Cowdry pulled at the cigarette, its eerie blue light a wink in the night. "Animals have a sense of these things. That little girl in there, she's seen a Rover blown up by a pipe bomb, seen her mother's arm lying on the ground after the explosion. My sister. That little Dorry held her while she died. But she's stayed innocent as snow."

"If only it could last," Martha said.

"Innocence?" Sean asked.

"I'm talking about the bison." She excused herself to Cowdry and pulled Sean aside, keeping her voice low. "Rosco called. It looks like Drake and company feel they have enough law for the court order. It's water-cooler conversation, but that's the word. Maybe by the end of next week. I don't know what to do."

"Call Gail Stocker at the *Star*. Tell her you have a story."

"Obviously you aren't a cop. Not this one, anyway."

"Then I'll do it," Sean said. "It will put pressure on the judge."

"Aren't you the wishful thinker? No, let's let this play out before we do anything we'll regret. I say 'we' because it makes me feel better, but I'm all alone in this. If you'd told me last week that I'd lose my job over a bison calf, I'd have looked at you funny."

When Cowdry left, carrying Dorry, who was asleep in his arms, Sean told Martha what Brady Karlson had said after releasing the trout.

"'That will make you forget about murder on the Madison.'"

"He said that?" Her voice was skeptical.

"'I say, Captain, that will make you forget about murder on the Madison.' Exact words. "There was like this dead silence, and then I said, 'What murder?'"

"'Oh, you know.' He flopped his hand, tried to blow it off as nothing. Then he said, 'I was thinking of the fisherman who was found with a hook in his lip a few years ago.' Cat got his tongue after that and he seemed to go a little bit into himself."

"Just sounds like history to me. There *was* a body with a hook in the lip. You know that better than anyone."

"I know, but it seemed to me he was searching for an explanation. What do you think they'll do?"

"About what?"

"Weren't you listening? I told them that you were going to go there tomorrow and look for more evidence, that you had a lead."

"That's a thin worm to bait a hook with. Did it occur to you that they could have an alibi?"

"Yes, and I asked them where they'd been staying and they said they'd been guests at the ranch for about a week, but their father had only come in over the weekend."

"So they were alone?"

"Not exactly. Their mother was in residence, but the boys are in a separate cabin."

"Do they call her 'Mama-san'?"

"No, they call her 'the white panther.' As in, 'The white panther will be having her first drop of the Irish now.' He affected an Irish accent. "That's their way. They make fun of people. When I asked how they celebrated the Fourth, they said they drove up the valley to see the fireworks, no specifics."

"So, if they do show up at the cliffs, what am I supposed to do, arrest them for walking on public land?"

"I hadn't got that far. And you're right, it's thin. But there's something about these kids, it's like they've drawn a circle around themselves and anyone outside the circle is simply there for their amusement. Brady, he did something that really bothered me. A whitefish took his fly, just a little one, and he grabbed it to unhook it and then squeezed it by the gills it until its eyes popped out. Then he threw it back into the river. I told him that in my boat we treat every fish with respect, and he said, 'Sure, Captain,' gave me his mock salute."

"You can't arrest somebody for cruelty to whitefish," Martha said.

"I know. But the way he did it, the deliberate . . . brutality, I guess. Like his eyes turned red for a second, except not really. Anyway, I thought I'd tell you."

"I'm interested."

He cocked his head. "So the two of us, like old times."

"Like old times," Martha echoed. The last time the two of them had staked out a location, Sean had cajoled her into kissing him and she had, against her better judgment.

"Maybe Harold wouldn't like it, though," he said.

He was pushing her buttons and she knew it, but couldn't help taking the bait. "Harold doesn't tell me where to go or who to go with."

She turned toward the house.

"Where are you going?"

"Get my jacket," she said. "And maybe a wee drop of the Irish for the cold."

Theodore Thackery opened the door wearing a flannel bathrobe buckled in place with a wide leather cartridge belt. He switched a porch light on as he stepped outside. In the sudden light, the steel rims of his glasses and the brass cartridges glinted like different denominations of coin.

"Martha," he said. They'd known each other in a passing-nod kind of way for years. She introduced him to Stranahan and they shook hands. Thackery had a hangdog appearance and dark circles under his eyes. He wiped his glasses against the lapel of his robe and put them back on. Sean noticed that his hands had a tremor.

"What are you packing there?" Martha asked.

"Oh, this?" Thackery gesticulated, his fingers waving in the general vicinity of the cartridge belt. "I got .45-70 rounds for my Sharps. First thing at hand. I don't get many visitors, let alone midnight."

"That's an old buffalo rifle, isn't it? I just saw one of those, belonged to Calvin Barr. He said it was an original."

"Barr," he said. "I don't think I've had the pleasure. My rifle's a replica, made by the C. Sharps Company in Big Timber. I collect weapons from several eras, originals if the price is right. But old Sharps in good condition come pretty dear."

"Sorry about showing up unannounced," Martha said, "but I didn't have your number. Do you have cell reception here?"

"I have a landline inside. Up by the viewing platform, sometimes I can raise a bar."

"Viewing platform?"

"It's about a quarter mile up toward Bobcat Creek. It's a tripod, a log one, like they use in Alaska to keep game meat from bears. I built it so I could get a better vantage of the range. You can scope a lot more country from thirty feet up than you can from the ground."

"Well, sorry again about the interruption."

"No problem at all. What can I do for you?"

"We need to park here for a few hours."

"Be my guest." A short silence, his eyes moving from one to the other, asking a general question. He shrugged. "If that's the way you want it, I won't ask."

"I appreciate that," Martha said.

"You stay out until morning, I'll cook you a proper breakfast."

She said thanks and they left him standing there, looking like a half-dressed tin star investigating a thump in the night.

"He looked sort of like hell," Martha said. "Like he hadn't slept in days."

"Well, it is the middle of the night."

"Strange that he doesn't know Calvin Barr."

"Why's that?"

"Because one shoots buffalo and the other thinks you shouldn't. You'd think they'd have crossed paths by now."

They began the half-mile hike to the escarpment where Harold had found the cairns. It would have been shorter and easier to simply climb the cliffs across from the river access, but that meant leaving a car where the brothers would notice it, if in fact they came.

A badger froze in the beam of Martha's headlamp. It flattened itself out, baring its fangs in the glare. "Harold's grandfather's totem animal," she commented. And to the badger: "Go back about your business." As the moonlight was bright enough to avoid stepping into holes, she switched her light off and they walked on, reaching the open slopes of the escarpment.

"Where do you think we should wait?" Martha said. The lines of authority blurred when she was with Stranahan. Harold, too, for that matter. Introduce people into the landscape, hostility, the need for diplomacy to defuse an escalating situation, and she was the sheriff.

But in the backcountry, she deferred. It didn't mean she liked it, and silently she chastised herself for so quickly asking his opinion.

"Let's go down to the top of the cliffs," Sean said. "If they actually did leave something behind and were going to come after it, it could be below the cliff as well as above."

They eventually decided on an outcrop of ledgerock about six feet back from the precipice, where a banner of orange ribbon tied to a bush marked where the Indian man had fallen and impaled himself on the piton. They sat with their backs against the basalt outcrop, Martha brushing the area first with her hat.

"Rattlesnake country," she said. "Gives me the heebie-jeebies."

"I thought they were only in the lower elevation, down around the Beartrap Canyon."

"Each year they're found a little farther upriver. The district biologist thinks it's global warming. He just can't say it out loud." Her voice rose. "You hear that, Mr. Snake. You get any ideas about warming up next to me, I'll bring back the wrath of winter."

She offered Stranahan a swig from her whiskey flask, then took one of her own. "Ah," she said. "I love getting out of the office, even if it's with my ex-boyfriend."

"The whole drive here you're bitching about it and now you're in a good mood. If Sam was here he'd say, 'Women.'"

"Men who say, 'Women,' don't understand women. But to be honest I don't know why. I've only got a John Doe in the morgue and I'm about four days from losing my job, but other than that, I'm tip-top."

It didn't last. Her mood went from tip-top to this is goddamned uncomfortable to resting her head on Sean's shoulder while a tear tracked down her cheek, all within an hour and without very many words.

"What's wrong, Martha?"

"Oh, nothing. Everything."

"Nice having David for a few weeks."

"Yeah, it was. I never thanked you properly for taking him on that float on the Big Hole. He really looks up to you."

"He's a good kid."

"I just wish I could have been there when he was younger. I thought after the divorce, he'd choose me. How could I have been so naive?"

"He didn't choose his father. His brother did, and David chose not being separated from him."

"I know. That's what I tell myself, but nothing can change what I lost. You can't turn back the clock."

"He's here now. He still needs you."

"You think?"

"I know he does."

"Thanks. That's something I needed to hear." She rubbed her head against his neck. Sean pressed the button to illuminate the LED display on his watch. Two a.m. A bank of cirrus edged across the moon as he began to drift away.

"Why are people always choosing the wrong people?" Martha asked. But Sean was already dozing.

An hour later, he heard rocks clattering and came awake with a start. There it was again, the sound coming from directly below, down by the river. If it was the brothers, why hadn't he seen headlights snaking down the access road? Because they had turned them off, of course. He shook Martha awake and worked the pins and needles out of his shoulder.

"What is it?" she whispered.

"Company."

Lying down, he elbowed to the lip of the cliff and peered down. The clouds had cleared and a shape loomed in the darkness, its silhouette cast on the lambency of the current. It was a bison, moving very slowly along the bank from north to south. Above the undertone of the river, each step the animal took thumped like a heart. The bison stopped and he could swear that a smaller shadow separated from it, though the shadow merged back with that of the larger animal as soon as it had appeared. *A calf?* Sean could feel his own heart beating against the ledgerock.

The bison began to call from deep in its chest. The night had turned chill, and as it called, the steam of its breath enveloped its head. Sean could hear the intakes of breath before each call, could hear his own breath and that of Martha's beside him. The bison began moving again, its moon shadow a ghostly distortion in the ripples of the current. Sean looked for the satellite shadow and again thought he saw it, or was it simply the bison shifting position? The great beast lumbered along the fisherman's trail that followed the bank upriver, until its bulk was engulfed by the darkness. For a few more seconds Sean could make out its shadow where the water was still, then that too was gone. Ten minutes later they heard it call, faintly and from far up the river, and ten minutes after that it called, or maybe not.

Martha and Sean exchanged a glance. Martha shrugged.

They settled back to wait as the night ticked down and false dawn spread its lie on the horizon. Nothing else happened, and when the wind picked itself up, so did they. Back at the game manager's cabin, they said thanks but no thanks to Thackery's offer of breakfast and drove back to Bridger in weary silence. They were turning up the canyon road when Martha mentioned that the department had sprung for a bus ticket for Joseph Brings the Sun. Three-thirty arrival from Great Falls on the following day. Martha asked if Sean could pick him up and take him to the morgue.

Sean said sure as Martha pulled to a stop. He reached for the door handle, hesitated.

"What is it?"

"I'm thinking about visiting the buffalo hippies tomorrow. They can confirm if the brothers were part of their group or not, if nothing else."

"Okay," Martha said. "Thanks for telling me."

"Anything I should know?"

"No, just don't go all starry-eyed and start picketing the capitol dressed up as a bison. You smile, but their leader is charismatic. They call him 'the Great Tatanka'—Lakota for buffalo bull. You know the Nelson Story story? The guy who led the first cattle drive from Texas to Montana back in the 1860s? It's what inspired the book *Lonesome Dove*. Well, Tatanka—his real name is Jackson McKenzie—he's a descendant of one of the men on that cattle drive. Prominent family in the Helena area. It's ironic, because the cattle sounded the death knell for the bison, and McKenzie has devoted his life to trying to bring them back and atone for the sins of his ancestors. Ninety years young and still sharp as a razor. The man's got some get-up. Walt had to arrest him about five years ago for interrupting a Stockmen's Association meeting and fighting with one of the state brand inspectors. McKenzie was putting a whupping on him before they pulled him off."

"I'll try to keep the stars out of my eyes. Hey, this was fun tonight, wasn't it, shivering on a rock ledge. We'll have to do it again sometime."

"Right. Maybe next time we'll see an actual human being."

"We saw a buffalo."

"Yeah, we did. But I've been up all night and I'm done with the subject for a while."

"Later, then," Sean said, but she was driving away. He made it to his cot in time to see sun creep up the tipi walls, setting the canvas aglow, and fell asleep thinking of the bison calling in the night.

CHAPTER FIFTEEN

The Buffalo Shadowers

Sean wasn't entirely surprised when Sam called to say the second guide day had been canceled. Was it because the brothers weren't eager to take another trip down memory lane? He didn't know, and, sipping his morning coffee at two p.m. in his art studio, thought it just as well. He'd had his fill of being called Captain and didn't want to press the brothers on their involvement in the jump until he was sure that they were involved. Standing before his easel, he screwed the cap off a tube of cadmium yellow to line a sunrise on a riverscape, then screwed the cap back on, remembering the impossible colors he'd witnessed only hours ago from the pallet of God. He booted up the cultural center's computer to see what he could learn about the American Bison Crusade before knocking on the door, and found out, among other things, that there was no door to knock on.

The drive to the Hebgen Plateau took ninety minutes. He passed part of it listening to a recorded book by C. J. Box on a boom box— the Land Cruiser didn't have a radio, let alone a CD deck—then switched it off, thinking back to last night. Despite the poor visibility, it had struck him that the bison was a cow; a bull's silhouette would have had more pronounced forequarters. Was it among the handful of survivors that managed to avoid the pishkun? If so, could it be the mother of the baby bison Harold had rescued, walking up and down the river calling for its calf? But then, it already had a calf. Or did it? Sean wasn't sure what he'd seen, and when he'd asked Martha, she said she hadn't seen anything but the one animal.

Stranahan detoured to collect Choti at the clubhouse because he missed her, and not incidentally because he thought he might need an icebreaker. Something told him that he would have more luck driving in late, when the volunteers would likely be gathered at the camp, so he ate a leisurely supper with Pat Willoughby and raided the freezer for a peace offering, selecting a slab of elk round steak. He smiled at the paradox of offering game meat to a group whose express purpose was saving native animals. Well, he'd play that one by ear.

The sun was in steep decline when he found the turnoff that Martha had marked on a map. A half mile up the road he idled down and man and dog put their noses to the wind drifting from the higher elevations. Sean had that feeling of crawfish in his veins that he'd had before, when he sensed that something was about to break. The Palisades where the Indian man had been killed were some twelve miles to the west but he had a gut feeling that this was where the bow was bent and the arrow set to flight. He just had to find out who drew it and why.

Sean put the Land Cruiser in gear. "This is where you earn your keep," he said, regarding Choti's mismatched eyes.

And then for the second time in four days he took a wrong turn, climbing into a gloom of forest before doubling back to find the right road. It didn't lose him a lot of time, but it lost him light so that his first sight of the crusade headquarters was the glimmer of a fire. Sean pulled into the camp, which consisted of a white canvas wall tent set in an old aspen grove, orbited by a motley collection of nylon tents that made domes of color against the monochrome creep of nightfall. A small stream was singing itself to sleep nearby. A drum beat from the campfire—*thump, thump*—like the beat of a heart.

Presently a tall, exceedingly thin young man with a wizard's beard detached from a group obscured by the smoke and raised a hand for Sean to stay inside his vehicle.

"I'm sorry, sir," he said, "but the landowner does not permit us to have dogs in camp, as much as we'd like to."

So much for the icebreaker. Sean cracked the windows for Choti and stepped outside.

"Do you have your application and non-abuse agreement with you, sir? We were not expecting any volunteer arrivals today."

The young man had a southern drawl, the broad vowels of the Gulf. He accepted the hand Sean extended, and Sean found himself looking upward into pale eyes, below the left one a shadow of bruise along the orbital bone.

"I am Isaac," the man said, "I am the volunteer coordinator."

Sean shook a surprisingly strong hand. "I was hoping to speak with Jack McKenzie."

"Is he expecting you?"

"No."

"Then may I ask what your business is?"

"I'm a private investigator who works with the sheriff's office." It wasn't a lie, but as he wasn't under current contract with the department, it wasn't the truth, either.

"Please excuse me," the man told him, bringing his hand to his chest and dropping his head an inch.

He walked toward the wall tent, which was lit up like a harem tent, while Sean wondered whether he'd just been bowed to. A minute later a woman appeared at the door, looked over her shoulder at Sean as she spoke to the young man, and approached, stopping before him with her hands on her hips. She had lank gray hair and a narrow face that added austerity to her expression.

"What do you want with Mr. McKenzie?" It sounded like an accusation.

"It's a personal matter." Sean produced Martha's card. "You can check my credentials with the sheriff. That's her cell number on the back."

"There's no mobile service here."

"There is at the junction. If you will drive with me, you can speak to her." That touched a nerve.

"We obey strict letter of the law here," the woman said in a clipped voice. "We do not condone violence, gender or racial discrimination, or any form of sexual abuse. No drugs. No alcohol. Tensions run high in the field and we must maintain clear heads at all times. Following the herds is demanding work that provides its own high, something you cannot buy from a bottle."

It was a rehearsed speech, words Sean guessed she spoke with little variation for each arrival. She nodded curtly. "Mr. McKenzie will be here shortly. Until then you're welcome to join us."

Sean followed her and offered his smile to the half dozen men and women seated at the fire ring. All were end-of-day tired-looking—the weather-beaten, mile-weary that you see on wilderness trails. Long hair and dreads, beards accented with braids, threadbare flannels, hiking boots caked with mud. Five men and four women, including the woman who'd spoken, whom he'd heard one man call "Mother," which Sean decided not to take literally. The youngest of the women, little more than a girl, had her shirt hiked up and was nursing a baby. Her smile was shy, though she made no effort to conceal her swollen nipples as she passed the baby from one breast to the other. They all seemed deferential, toward Sean as well as Mother. One good thing about edging toward forty, he thought.

Mother explained that the group was the second shift that had recently come in from patrol. McKenzie also was on that shift, which typically ended at sunset, but as there was no activity around the bison they were tracking, he'd sent them back early.

"We call him 'Comes in Last,'" Isaac said.

"I'd heard it was Tatanka."

"He *is* Tatanka—Tatanka who comes in last."

Sean asked where they were from and they were from all over—a Minnesota Frankenstein with a receding hairline; a full-faced black man from Maryland's Eastern Shore who managed to look stylish wearing farmer's overalls; a young Indian man who bore no resemblance at all to the man in the video who might be John Running Boy.

He was the drummer, Bitterroot Salish, he said. The young mother, whose name was Lilly—Sean had yet to hear a surname—was from Hayward, Wisconsin. Isaac was from Whitefish, Montana, but had worked as a naturalist for a wildlife preserve in Jasper County, South Carolina, where he'd picked up the accent.

"What do you do on patrol?" Sean put the question to the group.

Faces turned toward the one called Mother, who said, "Isaac, as you will be taking over my duties next winter, why don't you answer?"

"Yes, brother Isaac," the black man said, "tell the man how much fun it is to step in steaming bison patties all day."

"Well, thank you. I'll choose to ignore that note of sarcasm. All y'all have put me on the spot." He dropped his head to his fist—Rodin's *The Thinker*. "Hmm now, let me see." His fingers twirled the point of his beard. Sean smiled. Whatever he'd expected of these people, it wasn't sly humor.

"Mostly," Isaac said, "we stay with any bison that have left the park—that's why they call us the bison shadowers. We document their movements and video any government or state activities that affect the animals. Things like hazing, hunting by the tribes or white hunters licensed by the state, and capture of bison to be shipped to slaughter."

"We call ourselves the bison shadowers," the young mother said, repeating her fellow volunteer's words. Sean returned her smile. Her guilelessness reminded him of Dorry.

Isaac added, "Any member of the public who witnesses our activities, we explain what we're doing. What the threats to the bison are." Again he tugged the beard. "We don't do anything illegal, like interfering with licensed hunters or driving bison back into the park so they can't be shot. It isn't like the old days, when we'd stand between the buffalo and anyone who intended them harm."

Sean saw several people nod.

"More than one of us has stared down the barrel of a gun." The words came from Mother.

Sean raised his eyebrows, but before he could ask for elaboration, the snapping of the fire was interrupted by the rumble of a motor. Headlights illuminated ghostly swirls of sagebrush. The valley beyond was engulfed in blackness, the sun's last gasp that thinning crust of gold that he'd so often tried to capture with a brushstroke.

A geriatric Sierra Classic ground to a halt, idled, and shut down. Sean heard the door open and shut and saw the silhouette of a man advancing in no particular hurry.

"Ah, the Great Tatanka. Comes in Last comes in *at* last," Isaac said. He rose and bowed deeply. A few of the others also rose, but looking at the faces of those who remained sitting, Sean saw only thin smiles and small headshakes. Evidently, whatever their fearless leader used to inspire with was not fear.

"What's on the spit?"

CHAPTER SIXTEEN

Tatanka

The voice was gruff, but without a trace of rancor. Sean saw a man who was carefully erect despite or perhaps because of his age, and whose hair looked like a nest of rattlesnakes, gray tendrils falling in curls across his shoulders and down his back. He wore a checked wool shirt tucked into wool stovepipe trousers, wide suspenders, and a burgundy silk scarf, knotted at the front, the way cowboys wore them. His profile was an eagle's profile, the face gathered around a hooked beak of a nose with long expressive nostrils. Eyes flashed in the light of the fire. Black eyes with sparkle.

"New meat," he said, nodding his head toward Sean. "Mother radioed your arrival. So, what have you brought me from the United States of America? Something good to eat, I hope."

Sean opened his hands.

The man laughed, a short bark. "Nobody reads the fine print in the agreement clause. I told you, Mother, we'll have to boldface it from now on."

"I have an elk steak in my cooler. But maybe you don't eat game meat?"

"Don't eat game meat! Isaac, what is it that they call us?"

"They call us the bison shadowers, sir."

"No, that other thing."

"The bison shitters, sir."

"Yes, that's the one. It sounds like blasphemy, indeed it does. But our red brethren occasionally stock the larder. We aren't anti-hunting. I'm an elk hunter myself, so are half the volunteers. But our position is that bison shouldn't be hunted until sustainable herds are established on public lands outside the park." He settled on a chair, waving a hand to dismiss the smoke.

"You're here because of those bison that died at the cliffs. Correct me if I'm wrong."

Sean's silence was his answer.

"And you're wondering if we had anything to do with that? Am I on the right track?"

"That's the gist of it."

"Because that's what I'd be wondering if I were you. After all, we're the boots on the ground. Who would better know if the bison were moving and where to find them? And you can make a case for it. We draw attention to the plight of the Indian by honoring his hunting traditions, by killing bison with cliffs and arrows that would have been killed by bullets anyway. At the same time, we draw attention to the state's intolerance for bison migrating onto public lands. Make no mistake, that buffalo Sharps rifle Calvin Barr totes around would have made gut piles of the herd if someone hadn't beat him to the task."

"Better to die at your hands than his."

"Amen."

"So did they—die at your hands?"

"If I'd been a part of it, number one, we'd have finished off the buffalo after driving them over the cliffs. And number two, I sure as hell wouldn't leave a human being to die, though my sentiments would have been with the buffalo. Did they find out who the dead man is?"

"Only that he's Indian. Why do you assume that the bison were driven and didn't just fall? Nothing about a jump has been released in the press."

McKenzie laughed. "You think you got me, huh? Let me tell you, young man, those bison had about as much chance falling over the cliffs as I have falling between the thighs of Scarlett Johansson. I may be just an old smoke jumper, but I know buffalo, and buffalo don't jump."

As a coyote yipped in the lull following his proclamation, McKenzie cleared his throat and sent a howl in rejoinder. It was uncannily accurate, and the song went back and forth, several other coyotes and their human counterparts joining the chorus. The Indian man, Henry, began a song in what Sean guessed was his native language, his wails rising. Soon his song was picked up by the others.

"Sisters of the night," McKenzie said when the racket died down. "Who does a man have to poke to get a cup of tea around here? Please, Isaac, one for our guest, too." From the speed with which the cups were proffered, Sean guessed it was a ritual. "Ah," McKenzie said, taking a sip with an audible slurp, "the smell of sassafras reminds me of summer nights. It warms the cockles of an old man's heart."

He fixed Sean with his cheerful black eyes.

"I'm sorry you aren't getting the answers you'd hoped for. But as you've made the drive, I feel compelled to give you something to take away and chew on—call it a short history of buffalo. Everybody knows that forty million buffalo roamed the plains before the white men started shooting and killed all but a couple hundred. But the story I'm going to tell you starts in the winter of 1988–1989. That's a few years after the great state of Montana, which has been in the back pocket of the livestock industry since my ancestors brought the first cattle over in 1867, decided that there was no place inside its borders for bison. White shooters—I won't dignify their actions by calling them hunters—created a firing line at the Yellowstone Park border, and when the smoke cleared the blood of 569 bison had soaked into the snow. All this while TV cameras rolled. Supporters for bison from as far away as Japan called for a state boycott. Tribal leaders held prayer vigils for the buffalo, while gunshots from the hunters sounded in the distance. Why, it caused such a scandal that the '91 legislature called off the hunt.

"The state and the Park Service were forced to retreat and lick their wounds, and between them they had just enough brain cells to figure out that the best way to lower the decibel level was to bring Indians into the equation. Licensing Indians to shoot bison under treaty rights is more palatable to the public than having it done by park rangers or a goon like Lucien Drake. At the same time it obscures the real reason the bison are being killed. So they throw the red man a bone."

He nodded to himself. "Quite a few bones. Quite a few.

"The way it works today is that the Park Service and the state put their pointy heads together and decide how many bison to murder each winter. The quota this season was more than a thousand. Most are herded into a trap inside the park and shipped to slaughter. A few hundred are shot by tribal hunters and a handful by state-licensed hunters who don't want their pasty faces to be caught on our cameras. Buffalo that migrate beyond the buffer zones where they can't be hazed back in, or that aren't near areas where the hunters are operating, are executed by the Department of Livestock. This has been the story of buffalo for the past twenty-five years.

"Now, let's jump ahead to April last, when thirty-six bison migrated out of the park at the West Yellowstone gate. State employees on horseback drove them back into the park. The bison returned, and what do you know, they were pushed back again, this time with a helicopter. I expected the scenario to repeat itself, because that's the nature of the beast, but the bison did something bison sometimes do, which is be unpredictable. They traveled at night, crossed the park border, and turned west. This caught the DOL in their pajamas, and by the time the sun rose and the dust of their hairy toenails settled, that herd was about a mile and half away from here. Do you know Murdoch Avery?"

"He's the owner of this ranch, isn't he?"

"That's right. Michael Murdoch Avery of Avery Aves Designs in Seattle. They design software for the airline industry. When his ranch manager called him saying he'd caught DOL cowboys on the property who refused to leave, he jumped on his four-wheeler and confronted them at his gate. Told Lucien Drake he'd have him arrested. Drake spat on the ground and quoted state statute MCA 81-2-120, which gives the DOL the right to haze or kill any bison from a disease-infected herd, which is the entire Yellowstone herd, once those bison stray beyond park boundaries and he deems them a threat to cattle.

"Avery told Drake to fuck himself and drew a line in the snow. An actual line. With the toe of his boot. If I'd been there I'd have kissed the hem of his tunic, if he was wearing a tunic. Drake said he'd be back, but a man like Avery doesn't get to own one hundred and seventy thousand acres by standing around waiting. He got the Alliance for the Wild Rockies to file suit, and the district court judge came down in their favor, saying the DOL was harassing a threatened species, grizzly bears, with the chopper racket and issuing a temporary restraining order to cease and desist. I asked for an audience with the man and he gave us permission to camp here and make certain the law's being enforced."

"Were the bison killed at the Palisades part of the herd they were trying to haze?"

McKenzie nodded. "Most surely. When we put the herd to bed last Tuesday night, we counted forty-four head. That includes the calves born on the property in the past month and a half. Usually a mixed herd doesn't move too far after dark, but these bison are led by an old cow with a broken horn who has itchy feet. By eight o'clock Thursday morning we knew the herd had divided and some of the bison had hit the highway and gone up 287 along the Madison River. Wasn't the first time she'd led a splinter group on a sightseeing tour. Bison aren't hard to follow when they're sticking to pavement, it's follow the pies, but we lost them after they crossed to the west side of the river at Raynold's Pass bridge. Nobody saw the herd again until they were on the game range, so they were covering country. I don't need to tell you that after that it was just a matter of time before they were killed, jump or no jump."

"They created an intolerable situation for the state."

"Lucien Drake couldn't put it better himself. Because that's what this is really all about. Tolerance. Sharing a little bit of grassland with a fellow species that was here before we showed up, and that we could coexist with if we tried."

"Is it hopeless to think the situation will change?"

"Not at all. All it takes is some old codgers in the legislature to keel over so that we can pass an interagency plan that shifts bison management from the Department of Livestock back to the state wildlife and parks department, where it belongs. As my old friend Edward Abbey put it, we just have to outlive the bastards."

He threw his head back to implore the sky. "Do you hear me, old man?" And to Stranahan: "As Isaac and Mother have been kind enough to remind me, Cactus Ed didn't outlive the bastards. But they'll find I won't go easily into that good night."

McKenzie picked up his tea and set it back down, seeing the cup was empty. "You'll excuse us for a few minutes," he said. "We need to input today's data and make a game plan for the morning. And Mother has to process applications. We've had more volunteer requests since the news broke than all last winter."

"Forty-one," the woman said, "and I haven't checked the incoming today."

"That must be a windfall," Sean said.

She rolled her eyes. "Look around you. Most of us are too tired to talk by this hour. Volunteers get charged up thinking there's going to be tent hopping and hippie sex, then they find out that animal advocacy is a slog and people call you filthy names and you watch magnificent animals die miserable deaths and the only bathing facility is a creek. We ask volunteers to stay at least two weeks, but most are gone in a few days. And we don't need them now. In the summer the bison stay mostly in the park. When we need bodies is at twenty below zero during the slaughter. We'll see how many show up then."

She stood, which was the signal for the rest, and after Sean shook hands and wished the volunteers good night, he found himself alone. He went to check on Choti. He liked these people, hadn't thought about it but should have known. Sean had decided long ago that liking people was a choice, and he'd always been drawn to the McKenzies of the world, who heard their calling and answered the bell, whose mission broke the heart but who somehow managed to maintain a sense of humor while losing one round after another.

"Let him out if he knows how to stay." It was McKenzie, swinging a lit lantern by its wire handle. Standing next to him, Sean saw that he was almost a head shorter, which surprised him, for the aura was that of a much bigger man.

"Thanks." Sean got the elk steak and a wire grilling basket.

"What cut did you bring me?"

"Top round. A bull, so it's on the tough side."

"That's what your molars are for."

McKenzie sat down by the fire, setting the lantern on a stump. Sean busied himself shifting stones to form a keyhole at the side of the fire ring and scraped some coals into it.

"You didn't really drive all this way just to talk about a few buffalo, did you?' McKenzie said. He tapped the side of his long nose.

"I was waiting until we were alone," Sean said.

"It's just the three of us now." The old man looked deep into Choti's eyes and stroked her head. "Good dog, you're a good dog."

"That Indian man who died," Sean said, "he may have been associated with two young white men, brothers named Karlson. I heard they volunteered for you. They wear felt hats with trout flies sticking out of them, call themselves the Fedora brothers."

McKenzie shook his head. "You're asking me to violate our privacy clause. We have volunteers who would lose their jobs over their association with us. I don't want to be a hard-ass, but you came with a card, not a badge. Try rephrasing your question."

"Fair enough. No need for names. Do you have any brothers volunteering at this time?"

"No."

"Have you had any volunteers who were brothers in the past few months?"

"Yes."

"How long were they here?"

"About a week back in March, during the hazing season. Then they were here last month for a couple weeks after their college semester ended. They left in June, but they were still around last week. We marched in the Ennis parade and I remember seeing them outside the Long Branch and thinking good riddance."

"Good riddance?"

"I had to ask them to leave the camp. Actually, I grabbed one of the lads by the balls and twisted until his eyes popped out of his head. Isaac had caught him in Lilly's tent. Lilly has been a victim of abuse and suffers from low self-esteem, and her reaction to that has been to revert to the personality of a child. She can be persuaded to do what people ask of her, which makes her an easy victim. The man struck Isaac when he tried to drag him off her. When I got there he still had his pants down, and I gave him something to think about for a long time after. His brother had to help him to their truck and they left shouting that we were going to be sued by their father. But I don't expect to hear back. I have a feeling the incident isn't something the old man would want to revisit in a public venue."

"Was Lilly raped?"

"No, it didn't get that far. And the answer to your next question is no, too. I don't have any reason to believe they were involved in the buffalo jump at the Palisades. But at my age there isn't much that surprises you."

"Do you have many Indian volunteers besides Henry?"

"We've had volunteers from all seven reservations in Montana at one time or another. Our cofounder was Margaret Hangs Her Shirt, she's Pend Oreille. But you're thinking of the person who was killed and we haven't had anyone since the hazing season, which ended more than three months ago." He shook his head. "I think you're looking in the wrong place."

Sean had one last question, about the half dozen or more bison that survived the jump, including the one he and Martha had seen the night before. McKenzie stood without a word and led Sean to the tent, which was poorly lit by electric lights that worked off a generator. The main room consisted of a rectangular table, a dozen mismatched chairs, a desk with a computer, and a map that took up half of one wall and was studded with pushpins. He brought the lantern to reflect on the wall and said the pushpins were repositioned twice a day to show where bison were gathered near park borders. He explained that the numbers in the Hebgen Valley hadn't jumped since the herd broke apart, and the bison with the broken horn would have been spotted if it had returned.

"They could be a lot of places," he said. "They could have returned to the park by way of Targhee Pass"—he traced the route with his finger—"or they could still be in the vicinity of the West Fork. A half dozen bison can be hard to spot if they stay in timber."

He showed Sean the woodstove where the camp cook prepared meals and explained the double-layer asbestos cloth that protected the canvas from the chimney pipe. He pulled aside a blanket hanging from a rope to show the partitioned-off room where he slept on a cot. He winked, then drew a bottle of clear liquid that was lumpy with what looked like apricot halves from under the cot.

"Hair of the buffalo. Mother would have a fit if she knew I had it."

They walked back out under the stars.

"How about that elk steak?" McKenzie said. "If you make me wait much longer, we'll be spitting your dog over the coals."

CHAPTER SEVENTEEN

How to Pick Up a Snake

Joseph Brings the Sun tugged his basketball jersey as he looked at his reflection in the window of Sean's Land Cruiser. He ran fingers through his hair.

Sean said, "Dead men don't care how pretty you are."

"I'm just nervous," Joseph said. "We don't have to deal with this shit on the rez. Somebody shows you a body, you just say that's Cuz Michael, and that covers you 'cause you probably have one that's missing."

Their steps echoed on the marble floor of the morgue, Sean leading the way to the room where they donned their PPEs, though with the autopsy completed and potentially hazardous fluids drained from the body, full protective clothing wasn't mandated.

"Is he going to be naked?" Joseph asked, pulling paper slippers over his shoes.

"You'll probably just have to look at his face."

Sean knocked on a door and heard Doc Hanson telling them to come in. "Shit, man," Joseph said.

"It's going to be okay." Sean knew it wouldn't be. The Indian's body would be the third he'd seen in cold storage, and he'd tasted bile in his mouth on each prior occasion.

"You're Joseph Brings the Sun?" Doc Hanson looked at him as if he was a specimen.

Joseph nodded.

"We already signed in at the desk," Sean said.

"There's protocol to follow back here, too."

They followed it, which consisted of another couple signatures, and entered a storage facility that had two doors on each side and was a chilly four degrees Celsius. Hanson opened one of the units, checked the toe tag, and rolled the body out. He pulled the sheet down from the face.

Sean saw Joseph's Adam's apple working.

"It's him."

"State his name."

"I don't know his name. But he's the guy who was with John and the white dudes."

"Are you sure?"

"Yeah, I'm pretty sure."

"Like sixty percent sure?" Hanson said. "Seventy percent? Try to put a figure on it."

"Maybe seventy. It was dark. He was in the backseat and there wasn't like a dome light on."

"Did he have any distinguishing marks or missing teeth, anything that could make you more certain?"

"No, he just sat there. I didn't hear him talk. He never opened his mouth."

"This man has a birthmark on his abdomen."

"What you trying to say? We was getting it on? Hell, man, I never seen him with no shirt off. But it's him, just like I told you."

———

They were back in the Land Cruiser, turning from the pavement onto the gravel of Cottonwood Creek Road. Joseph rolled up the window to keep the dust out.

"Fuck, man, that was just wrong on every level back there. I feel like I need a bath."

Sean drummed his fingers on the steering wheel. He was missing something, it was like a color at the edge of his thought that bled away when you looked at it. He saw a stick on the left-hand side of the road, then, seeing it was a snake, jammed the brake and swerved to the right.

"You do that in Heart Butte, they think you're crazy," Joseph said.

Sean shifted into neutral and set the handbrake.

"Come on, let's see what it is."

"It's a fucking snake."

"But what kind of snake?"

"The kind you run over. White people." But he got out of the car.

The snake, a mature five-foot bullsnake, reared into an S-coil at Sean's approach and hissed loudly. Sean feinted with his left hand, and as the snake struck he reached his right hand around and picked it up, holding it a foot or so in front of its tail. The bullsnake struck once more at Sean's pants leg, then, hanging in shallow S-bends, twisted its muscular body a few times before calming down. Sean paid it out like rope, one hand over the other, the snake's black tongue tasting the hair on his forearm, then tickling at his ear. He explained to Joseph that once the snake started trying to regain its balance, it had forgotten about striking, that that was the way you picked up any snake that threatened to bite. "It wouldn't hurt that much if it did, but if you jerk your hand away, it can hurt the snake's teeth."

"I'll keep it in mind."

"Come on, hold him."

"No way." But Sean shamed him into it, and after admiring the creature they carried it away from the road, where Joseph released it. The bullsnake blended into the leaf litter and grasses so perfectly that it was almost impossible to see, even lying in plain sight. Sean knew then what had eluded him before, the thought he couldn't grasp among the detritus that clogged his memory.

"Your cousin," he said, "from the tribal police—"

"He's my brother-in-law."

"Your brother-in-law, would he have taken down the names of John Running Boy and the others that he ran off the historical site?"

"The pishkun?"

Sean nodded. Joseph shrugged.

"Do you have a phone number for him?"

"My mother does."

Sean unfolded his dumb phone, feeling like an idiot for not think-ing of it earlier.

A minute later Joseph had his brother-in-law on the line. "Whas-sup?" he said. And a few seconds later: "Yeah, they have rivers and trees and all that shit. The Lone Rangers even stop their cars to take snakes out of the road. I'm calling cause, remember those dudes that you run off the pishkun, did you, like, take down their names. They got a body down here and he's an Indian might have been one of them. . . . No, this is legit. You got them? . . . yeah, I got a piece of paper." He took a gas receipt Sean produced and penned a name.

Gary Hixon.

"Not too imaginative," Sean said.

Joseph turned to Sean. "No, a regular name is good. It will make him easier to track. You say 'Running Wolf' in the classroom, half the kids raise their hands."

"How about the names of the white kids?"

Joseph repeated Sean's question over the phone line. He nodded as he listened.

"He says they said Peter and Paul DeCibel. That's what he wrote in the incident book."

"Decibel. Like noise level? Ask him how to pronounce it."

Joseph listened some more. "It's disciple. Peter and Paul Disciple. Like in the Bible."

"Cute," Sean said.

"Yeah," Joseph said into the phone, "sounds like bullshit names . . . No, I'm talking to somebody. Yeah, I'm keeping out of trouble. Tell Mom I'll be back tomorrow."

Sean took the phone and left a message for Martha, who could have somebody work the databases for a Gary Hixon and make calls to the reservation that had enough authority behind them to get answers.

A mile farther down the road stood the cone of Sean's tipi. Sean said that he needed to change his clothes, then they'd head up the Madison Valley, that he wanted Joseph to meet the young woman who had been John Running Boy's childhood sweetheart.

Joseph shook his head as Sean brought the rig to a stop. "I appreciate you putting me up tonight, but I came all the way from Heart Butte to sleep in a lodge? You got to be kidding."

"I told you I lived in a tipi."

"I thought you were bullshitting me."

Sean said he'd perk up after a burger at the mermaid bar.

————

"Kemosabe," Sam said, and kicked out a chair for Sean before noticing that the man following him was Indian. "Oh shit, my bad. I don't mean any disrespect. It's just a thing we have."

"Relax," Joseph said.

"So what's yours?" Sam said.

"Uh, I don't know. A Coke."

"Coke it is."

Sam bought a round for the table as they were joined by Molly Linklatter, whose hair hung in wet curls, making dark spots on her snap-up cowgirl shirt.

"Is Ida swimming tonight?" Sean asked her. He'd looked for her car in the lot, but hadn't seen it.

"As far as I know she's still third shift. I'm a little worried about her. She's been pretty quiet the last two days."

"What do you mean?"

"Distant, distracted. Not anything specific."

Sean saw that Joseph hadn't heard their exchange. His eyes were locked on the tank behind the bar, where the Parmachene Belle was working her tail.

"I got to get off the rez more often," he said, without turning his head.

Sam raised his chin an inch and casually made his right hand a fist, pointing his thumb over his shoulder. Sean got up and followed him outside.

"I got a line on the Fairlane," Sam said. "I put the word out with my clients and someone saw it. At least he thought it could be a Fairlane. It had fins and it wasn't a trout. Guess where?"

"Where?"

"Earthquake Inn. My client said it went up the drive where the trailers are."

"When was this?"

"Yesterday, but he didn't tell me until today because he was embarrassed to admit he was at Jimmy's fly shop. Jimmy's good people but he's a competitor, so the client felt like he was patronizing the enemy."

"That's the trailer court where Ida lives."

"I know that. The plot thickens, or whatever it is you dicks say."

Sean stared at the ridges that lifted like the folds of a fan toward the peaks of the Gravellys. "Thickens" wasn't the word he'd have chosen. Rather, the water had cleared somewhat. So John Running Boy was still in the valley and his car had been seen within a few hundred feet of Ida's trailer. Ida, who had paid Sean to find John Running Boy before having a sudden change of heart. Ida, who was late for her shift.

The bartender, Vic, was taking a cigarette break, and Sean walked over. Vic said Ida had called a half hour ago to say she had a migraine and couldn't make it. Sean asked him to check the number she'd called from. Cell service was a prayer and a wish at the Earthquake Inn.

The bartender looked at his last call. "That's the landline at the trailer court," he said.

"Something's happening," Sean said to Sam.

"I heard. So she's not coming tonight. People get sick."

"No, John's car shows up at her place and next thing she's taking a day off? I'm heading over there. Can you put Joseph up and get him to the bus station tomorrow?"

"What time? I have an a.m. float and the guy's a tipper."

"Forget it. I changed my mind."

He turned toward the bar, leaving Sam itching his chest hair through a hole in a T-shirt that read: *Fishing—For When You Want to Relax and Still Kill Shit.*

"Let's go, Joseph," Sean said.

"I thought we were going to see the Chippewa Nymph."

"She's not swimming. I'll tell you on the road."

It was ten miles to the trailer park and he made it in that many minutes, the Land Cruiser bottoming out at each bump in the road. No Fairlane. A rap at the trailer door greeted by silence.

"What kind of car she drive?" Joseph said.

"Tercel."

Sean walked around to the back, where a folded-up polytarp was pinned to the ground with river stones.

"Hey, man, look at this," Joseph said. He pointed to four spots where the grass was a shade lighter. "That's where the tires were sitting, huh?"

Sean nodded. The spacing clearly showed it had been the Fairlane. The Tercel's wheelbase would have registered tire marks closer together.

"You think it was hidden under the tarp?"

Sean was thinking ahead. Ida had made the call to the bar approximately forty minutes ago. He'd passed the community phone on the way in; it was bolted to the wall of the fly shop. Had she been driving away when she called the bar to say she couldn't make it? If so, then she had a forty-minute lead on him. *They* did, if they were caravanning in two cars.

"Hey, Sean."

Joseph had picked up one of the gnomes by the tomato plants. "It's the trailer key under the gnome trick, except at my mom's it's under a stone frog with its head broken off."

"What are you waiting for?" Sean said.

Joseph turned the key and they stepped into the trailer, where two coffee cups on the sink drew Sean's attention. The cups were rinsed out, but the whistle kettle on the burner was almost hot to the touch. Perhaps she wasn't as far down the road as he'd thought.

Where the gravel drive met Highway 287, he hesitated. Right or left? Right was east, the Hebgen Plateau and Yellowstone Park. Left was north. Ennis was to the north, so was Bridger, she could be heading almost anywhere. Sean turned left, flooring it, driving tight-lipped. Neither spoke what both were thinking, that if you took a compass bearing due north and kept driving, you'd hit the Blackfeet Reservation at first light.

"Is this crazy?" Sean finally said. He eased his foot off the accelerator, bringing the RPMs down where they belonged.

"Not if you're an Indian. We do crazy shit all the time."

"Is it true that Indians are always driving on empty?"

"No, we fill her up, we just do it two gallons at a time. You're thinking we catch up at Ennis, she'd be at the pump? It doesn't take that long to gas up, man."

"No, but someone there would remember if she went inside to pay. Then we'd know if we were on the right road."

"You really are a detective."

Sean smiled. "I'm going to ignore the sarcasm and choose to take that as a compliment, Joseph."

He pressed down on the pedal.

CHAPTER EIGHTEEN

The Indian Way

The convenience store clerk had seen her all right. An Indian caught the attention, especially a woman with different-colored eyes. "Like a heeler," she said. The woman had paid cash to gas two vehicles. The clerk pulled the receipt. They'd been printed at eight twenty-eight, nearly thirty minutes ago. Sean went for the moon, asking if the woman mentioned where she was heading. The clerk shook her head; her dangling earrings were shaped like Idaho, with the hoops attached to the panhandle. "She's pretty," she said. "Very feminine. She said thank you and smiled. Most people don't do that."

Sean waited while she ran his credit card for his fill-up, then had to do it again when Joseph walked up holding bags of chips and soft drinks.

"We're going to need munchies," Joseph said. "You got any tunes? We could buy a CD. Johnny Cash, Merle Haggard. Charley Pride, he's a Montanan. You ever hear him sing 'The Snakes Crawl at Night'?"

"I don't have a deck. You'll have to settle for talking to me."

"Hey, the oral tradition, I dig it," Joseph said.

Sean worked through the gears. Now that he had direction, he considered trying to reach Martha. She'd have the authority to have a trooper stop the Fairlane and hold John Running Boy for a chat. They'd be reaching the I-90 interchange within a half hour and a Fairlane wouldn't be hard to spot. He traced the outline of the phone on his right front pants pocket, then made his decision.

Martha didn't answer, so he speed-dialed the department and reached Judy Woodruff, who patched him through to Undersheriff

Walter Hess. Sean switched the phone to speaker and handed it to Joseph so he could keep his hands on the wheel.

"Gary Hixon, huh? You figure he's the John Doe?"

"That's the name Joseph's brother-in-law took down," Sean said.

"John Running Boy, would he be armed?"

"He'd be more likely to have a bow than a gun."

Silence. Then: "I'll see what I can do about posting a patrolman at the interchange. But it's a short staff week, no promises."

Joseph shook his head. "Shit, man, what are you doing? Making me an accomplice in arresting my own neighbor? You can let me out of this fucking heap right now."

"Nobody's arresting anybody," Sean said. "I just want a chance to talk to him before he does something stupid."

"Like what?"

"Like make himself a fugitive. He isn't going to be able to hide forever. It digs him a hole with the state and makes him look guilty as hell, and the border doesn't mean squat if he's in trouble with somebody else."

"You're trying to make it sound like you're on his side," Joseph said. "But aren't you violating some kind of privacy thing?"

"My contract with Ida expired. And she made it clear she doesn't want me to dig any deeper into the ground. Besides, she found the man she hired me to find, or he found her."

"Then why we laying down all this track? 'Cause you want to know?" The way he said it made it sound absurd. Maybe it was absurd, but they were nearing the crossroads and Sean had other things to think about.

"There's the pig," Joseph said.

The cruiser was parked in the Lucky Lil's Casino adjacent to the overpass. Sean pulled in beside it and the trooper stepped out. He was crew cut, official-looking in his dark greens and Smokey the Bear hat, the new issue, the hats that didn't make them look like cabdrivers.

"Are you Sean Stranahan? County called with your vehicle description."

"I'm Sean."

"Who's your passenger?"

"Joseph Brings the Sun. He came from the Blackfeet Reservation to ID a body."

"The guy who fell over the cliffs. I heard about it."

"Yes. Did you see the Fairlane?"

"No. I parked so I could see if the vehicle turned east or west on the interstate or stayed on the two eight seven. I didn't spot a Tercel, either, but compacts look alike, one could have slipped by."

"If someone wanted to stay out of sight, could he have continued north by bypassing this junction?"

The trooper thought a moment and nodded. "Sure. All you'd have to do is take the Old Town Road a couple miles east of here. Old Town under the overpass to Price, to Hilltop, Salt Gulch, hook back onto the two eight seven on Old Woman's Grave Road. Hidden Montana, there's lots of it just sees tumbleweeds and cattle."

Sean thanked him and the man said sure and be careful. "You know what they say—'Ninety percent boredom, ten percent terror.' You pull somebody over who's on the lam, the ratio goes upside down."

Sean got back on the road, thinking about that. He'd decided to bring Joseph because he thought a friend of John's could act as a conduit if they ever caught up. He saw now that that had been a reckless decision; he had no right to involve an innocent party in what could wind up as a confrontation.

"Hey, man, was that a strip club we passed?"

Sean snapped back to the present.

"Yeah, Puss N Boots."

"Closest I ever been to a strip club was polar bear day at Kipp Lake, watch some overweight white mama break the ice. You ever been inside?"

"Once. A woman hired me because her husband was coming home late every Wednesday and she didn't buy the explanation. I said I'd follow him, but that would cost her my day rate plus expenses, and she wanted me to solve it in my armchair for a flat fifty. So I told her to check the mileage before and after his work next time around, and it's twenty-two miles. I take a compass and make a circle on the map with a radius of eleven miles. The line intercepts the club. They advertise half cover to see the show on Wednesdays, it's a regular ad in the *Star*. By coincidence, the next Wednesday I'm going fishing on the Jefferson and duck in to see if he's there. He's tucking a bill into the G-string of a dancer who's got a balcony you could do Shakespeare from. I snapped a photo for the wife."

"I'm impressed, man," Joseph said. "No, I really mean it. I would have never thought of a compass."

"Don't be too impressed. He threatened to beat me up and she stiffed me the fifty, so how smart was I?"

The urgency of the past two hours was in the rearview now; they'd either find them or they wouldn't. Whatever happened it would be hours down a deserted highway, owls hunting in the headlights, the occasional glimpse of stars in an overcast sky.

"Is that a weasel tail in your braid, Joseph?"

"Yeah, an ermine. It's considered sacred because it changes color with the season, so it symbolizes the cycle of life. My mother weaves it back in every time I wash my hair, says as long as I'm wearing it I'll be safe, keep away the spirits. I got a story, you want to hear it?"

"Sure," Sean said.

"You know about Indian Relay?"

"Tell me."

Joseph claimed that Indian horse racing was North America's first extreme sport, because when you are leaping off one galloping horse and throwing yourself onto the bare back of another for the next lap, shit happens. He'd raced right through his teens until one race where he was acting as the mugger for his older brother. The mugger was responsible for holding on to the horse that the rider had just jumped off, and if he lost control of the reins, the team was disqualified. He'd managed to hold on, even as the thoroughbred reared up and fell over backwards, breaking Joseph's leg when it came down. The tibia had to be plated and pinned in four places.

"I couldn't walk for, like, six months. That's when I started putting on weight. Nothing's sorrier than a fat fucking Indian with a flattop. Anyway, that was the end of Indian Relay."

It was a good story—that was just the bones of it—and it got them to Townsend, to the flat black stain of Canyon Ferry Reservoir, to the outskirts of East Helena. Then Joseph tilted his head back and fell asleep.

———

Sean gassed up again at Augusta, shivering in the dead silence of two in the morning.

"Where are we?" Joseph said. He rubbed at his eye sockets with closed fists.

"Middle of nowhere."

"Looks like Augusta. I was born six miles north of here."

"Really? I didn't think there was anything six miles north of here."

"No, there's the bridge over the Sun River. I wasn't due for another three weeks and my mom was visiting her sister, who was living with some white guy in Helena."

"So is that how you got your name?"

"Yeah. She pulled over to the side of the road when her water broke and got a blanket out of the backseat. She had me on the bank of the river. After I was born she fell asleep, and when she woke up, the sun was on the water. You know how a lot of Indians, their names change as they grow up, but I was always Joseph Brings the Sun."

They drove the six miles and Sean pulled over. Joseph raised his eyes. "Scene of the crime," Sean said, and they walked down to the river upstream of the bridge.

Joseph looked at his feet. "Right here, I think. It was August, so the gravel bar would be more exposed. She used to joke that she should have named me Joseph Brings the Mosquitoes." He shivered in the chill night. "This is only the second time I been here."

They looked at their silhouettes on the moonlit face of the river. Sean was reminded of the bison he and Martha had seen, its image rippled by the current.

"I know you ain't my cuz, like you don't even know me that well, but you're the closest to a white friend I ever had."

Sean was genuinely touched. Joseph was one of those people who are inherently kind, so open, so quick to accept you into their lives that you want to change yourself to be more like them, to reclaim a lost innocence. It made him think of Martinique Carpentras, who had simply opened her arms and whom he had melted into from the start, and who was now out of his life. It also made him think about Vareda Beaudreux, whose brand of attraction was more that of the bullsnake with its forked tongue, beckoning the hapless rat, then encircling it in her coils.

"You're thinking I'm a sentimental Indian, what you got yourself into?"

"No, I was thinking about a couple women I used to know."

Joseph laughed.

Sean said, "You know, I have a friend who's Blackfeet. He's the one lent me the tipi. Right now he's sleeping with a woman I was seeing last year."

"And you're friends with him?"

"I'm friends with both of them."

Joseph shook his head. "You're even more fucked up than I thought you were."

Sean nodded, saw the shadow of his head move on the water.

"You know, a while back there, you asked me what I was doing, paying out of pocket for a goose chase, it got me thinking because it's a question I ask myself all the time. That woman who's with my friend now, she once said that I step into shit even if there's only one horse in the pasture. She meant it as a compliment, but it's not like I have a choice. I have to keep going and see if I can step into shit, even if that means getting beat down along the way and losing faith in mankind, which is all the lesson you get out of it sometimes. But if I don't make the effort, then who will? Maybe nobody will."

Joseph nodded, but Sean wasn't really talking to him anymore.

"There was this guy I used to work with—old Irish ex-cop who did some snooping for my grandfather's law firm. Smelled like Old Spice and hung his shoulder holster on a hat rack. Kind of guy you see in old movies. He told me investigations were like drinking blood, you just kept going until somebody stuck a stake in your heart. I used to think what he meant was that it was the adrenaline, the action. And that was part of it, but there was something else, too. He was saying what you get addicted to is the search. It's like this river. You have to take it upstream to find the source, and you have to follow it downstream to see where it goes. When you take on a case, you're not at the beginning or the end of the river, but somewhere in between, and you don't know which way to go, so you end up going both ways until you figure things out. You go until you know.

"To me, this isn't just about John Running Boy. I want to know who drove those buffalo over the cliffs. I want to know who, and I want to know why, and I want to know about the guy who died there. I want the guilty to pay for their sins. There's a purity in that kind of pursuit. It's black and white." He gave a short laugh. "Unlike the rest of life."

Sean stopped himself there, embarrassed that he'd given voice to the code he lived by, something he'd seldom confessed, even to lovers.

But Joseph was nodding. "No, I understand. The futile gesture. Stepping into shit, getting your ass beat down—that's the Indian way."

CHAPTER NINETEEN

Bird in Flight

Heart Butte, five a.m. A drizzle of rain. A dog walking crooked up a straight street. Sean idled past the house where John Running Boy lived with his mother. All dark.

"What kind of a car does John's mom drive?" He looked up and down the street, the odd vehicle parked here and there.

"Subaru wagon, an old one."

He drove on to Joseph's place. The cat lying on the doorstep stood up and stretched.

"You sure you won't come in? You need sleep, man."

"I know I do. And I'll get some in the rig."

"Why won't you let me come? I can help. John and I go back some."

"We've been through this. I'm not going to put you in a position where something can happen."

"Fuck, man. I'm the one gave you Gary Hixon."

"And I appreciate it. Say hi to your mom for me."

Joseph shook his head, but he opened the door. "I guess I'll be seeing you, then."

"You will."

Sean left him standing in the street, the cat rubbing against his legs. Then he saw him in the rearview, running up.

"Hey, you might need this."

Joseph reached behind his neck and worked his fingers. He handed Sean the ermine tail through the open window. "Keep you safe," he said.

"Don't you need it?"

"Nah, man, I'm okay."

"Thanks, Joseph." Sean tucked the tail into his shirt pocket.

"You bulletproof now, Cuz."

"Maybe, but does it work against arrowheads?"

"Yeah." Joseph laughed. "All kinds of shit."

———

By the time Sean glimpsed the house on the hill, the sun had drawn its highlighter across the horizon. Long lines of birds were backlit on the telephone wires. Above them, to the east, the striated peaks of Glacier Park brooded above a gauze of fog.

Even before raising his binoculars he knew that the sedan parked beside Campbell's old truck was probably Ida's Tercel, and a glance through the glass confirmed it. Sean wondered if they had ditched the Fairlane or perhaps there had been mechanical difficulty. He walked a short length of the road. The surface was damp and he had not gone far before he found what he was looking for. Back at Ida's trailer, he had examined the Fairlane's tread, a repeating W pattern with the left rear worn on the edges from running at too low a pressure. A similar pattern snaked down the left-hand side of the lane, but not the right. So it had gone in this way, but not returned. Maybe it was parked behind the house. The important thing was that the hare had gone to ground.

He got back behind the wheel, having no plan and too tired to formulate one. He slowly motored up the road, scattering magpies that were squabbling over the flattened remains of a gopher. He pulled up behind the Tercel. No sound but the staccato of the straight six. Sean got out and leaned against the hood. He fingered the ermine tail in his pocket as the motor ticked down.

A long minute passed before the turtlelike head of Melvin Campbell appeared at the door. He was hunched nearly horizontal, his unbuttoned flannel shirt draping him like a horse blanket.

"I'm afraid I have company," he said, peering up through forward-hanging strands of his hair.

"I know who's here, Mr. Campbell."

"I'm afraid you're mistaken. I don't want to insist that you go, so I'll ask politely that you respect my privacy."

"It's okay. Tell him to wait where he is." Ida's voice sounded weary and resigned.

Campbell's head craned toward the house. He pivoted on his cane and tapped his way inside as she appeared at the door.

"Don't you look like hell," she said to Sean.

"I could say the same about you."

Her face was shiny, her eyes dimmed, her hair lank and lifeless. She leaned back against the porch railing, hooking one boot over the other as she had the first time he'd met her at the Trout Tails Bar and Grill. She lit a cigarette and dragged the smoke into her lungs.

"I thought you didn't inhale. Sacred medicine and all that."

She blew the smoke out and took another drag. "What did you do, drive all night?"

"About an hour behind you. All three hundred and"—he took a couple steps and looked through the open window at the odometer—"thirty-six miles."

"Congratulations. You found me. You can go back home now."

"Someone died, Ida. We know who it was now, a man named Gary Hixon. I'm not going anywhere until I talk to John about it."

"You don't have a voice here."

"I just want to know what happened. That's all. Where's his car?"

She stubbed out the cigarette. "It's in the garage. You wouldn't believe how much money it cost to drive it here."

"Yes, I would."

She shook her head. "I really did like you. It wasn't easy for me to blow you off. I even thought, before this happened . . . when you were at the trailer. But you kept everything business."

"It was you who kept it business."

"No, sitting with you, I felt guilty because I was supposed to be thinking about a boy I once knew, and here was a man who made me lose my focus."

"So I missed out on seeing the star."

"I wouldn't go that far." It brought the corners of her mouth into a smile.

Sean shrugged. "Bad timing." It was a strange conversation to be having with the world waking up. He yawned, which triggered her to yawn, too.

"When did John show up at your door?" he said.

"The day I told you to call off the dogs, earlier that afternoon. He'd followed me from the day before, so he knew where I lived. I hadn't seen him since we were kids, but somehow he wasn't a stranger. We still had the same shorthand, finishing each other's thoughts."

"How did he know you worked at the bar?"

"He says he didn't. Someone on the reservation told Gary that an Indian girl he'd once known was working at a mermaid bar in the Madison Valley. He walked in and there I was."

"Who walked in, John or Gary? Are you saying you knew Gary Hixon?"

He heard her exhale as she shook her head. "I shouldn't tell you this . . ."

A short silence stretched.

"Tell me what, Ida? How can I help him if I don't know what's going on?"

She stepped off the porch and joined him in the drive.

She lowered her voice. "I knew Gary from when I lived outside Browning. We were all kids together, the three amigos. But like I told you, I moved around a lot. There was a year in high school—this was back on Rocky Boy—Gary was in school there, too. His family had moved to Box Elder and we were in the same year, and he was a big basketball player and that sort of threw us together, because I played on the girls' team. We had something going for a while, but he had something going with another girl, too, and she got pregnant and that was that. Anyway, Gary never told John about us because he knew John thought of me as this idealized person who was stuck in some kind of amber in his mind, the girl who was his first kiss."

"So John doesn't know about you and Gary?"

"He knows we were in school together, he doesn't know what I told you. John's got plenty to worry about without worrying about that. And it doesn't mean anything now. It's only John who matters. I'm his lifeline. That's what he calls me."

"So when you were in my studio, you lied to me."

"No, I told you what I knew *then*. I guess Gary did come into the bar that night, but he had short hair and I didn't recognize him. It was John I saw looking at me, not Gary. I didn't even know that Gary was in the picture until John told me what happened at the jump."

"What happened at the jump?"

"John's going to have to tell you that. He's sleeping now. I don't think he's slept in days." She hesitated. "I wasn't planning to come up here with him, you know. I was just going to give him some money, but he was so alone, you don't know what he went through. It haunts him, not just what happened to Gary. And he wasn't sure the car would make it back, so if I drove, too, then he'd get here one way or other before anything could happen."

"What did he think would happen?"

It was circling the same ground, and before Ida gave him the same answer they heard the determined rapping of the walking stick. The door opened.

"How can an old man eavesdrop when it hurts to stand up?" Campbell said.

As Sean and Ida followed him back into the house, Campbell stretched a sinewy arm toward the love seat.

"I like to see young couples sit together," he said after they had all sat down. "Back in my time there was none of this rampant promiscuity, so you had to make do sitting close and holding hands. It was more romantic."

"We aren't a couple, Melvin."

"So you say."

The ease of their speech made Sean think that Campbell had spent more of the past hour talking with Ida than with John Running Boy, and yet in the custom of country people the world over, the subject that brought them together would be the last to be broached.

Sean had been fighting a buzzing in his head ever since leaving Heart Butte, a back-on-land vertigo that caused him to drift away as Melvin's and Ida's voices receded into background noise. An indeterminate span of time had passed when he felt a draft of air from an open window, then a sudden creaking of steps snapped him back into the room. Seeing Ida's alarmed look, he followed her eyes to a wavering shotgun barrel, the muzzle drawing invisible circles on his chest.

"Is he the one you were talking about? Did you tell him I was coming here?"

The man standing at the bottom of the stairs was shirtless, wearing jeans that sagged from his hips.

Sean tried to keep his voice calm. "I followed her. And I'm here to help you, if you'll let me."

"You don't know anything about me."

"It's okay, John," Ida said. "You can trust him."

John lowered the shotgun to his side, the muzzle only in Sean's vague direction now, though he felt his lungs expanding each time the cavernous bore crossed his body. It was a pump with an exposed hammer, and Sean could see that the hammer was cocked.

"I'll ask you to please put my gun down," Melvin Campbell said. "That old pump has scattered nothing but feathers for eighty years, and that's not going to change now. We do not threaten our fellow man in this house."

"He's a goddamned snowman," John said.

"Regardless of heritage."

Sean saw John's capitulation, his acknowledgment of the one voice of authority that he recognized. An absurd few moments passed as he searched for a place to put the shotgun, settling on propping it in a corner by the bookcase. As John turned his back, Sean let out a held breath and felt Ida's hand close over his wrist. She squeezed it briefly. He looked at Campbell, who was touching his pursed lips to the rim of a coffee cup, the thin hairs at the corners of his mouth searching like a cat's whiskers.

"I'm sorry," John said.

Campbell set down the cup.

"Come sit with us. Ida, would you please bring more coffee? I've had quite enough excitement this morning, so I'll have the decaf; it's the jar with the green lid. And a tablespoon of the condensed. As an old man I drink it rez style."

He turned to Stranahan. "I got the habit back in the days when everybody got the USDA commodities boxes. You'd get the milk and that big block of cheese. John, do you remember that or were you too young?"

"My mother got them," John said. "That was the best cheese."

"It was," Campbell said. "You can't buy it that good in a store."

Campbell's attempt to engage John in small talk left Sean in the wings, from which he took advantage to observe the young man. John was more slightly built than he had supposed he would be, with shoulder-length hair that he presently tucked behind his ears. Ida had been right. He had grown into a strikingly handsome man, his mouth finely drawn under a straight aquiline nose. His chiseled cheeks flexed with an involuntarily tic.

Melvin Campbell assumed his role of authority as Ida returned with the coffee. "John, please sit with Ida. Sean, I'll ask you to bring the chair over from my desk." Turning to John, he said, "We're not here to stand judgment, but we do want to understand what happened."

"What's to stop him from turning me in, having them come get me?" He turned his head in Sean's direction without meeting his eyes.

"He's not here for that purpose," Campbell assured him, "but it wouldn't matter if he was. The state claims an extradition code, but neither our nation nor the Crow recognize the statute. That doesn't prevent a judge from issuing a bench warrant for arrest, and the tribal court can consider the warrant, but in practice such requests are usually denied."

"So I'm safe."

"As long as you are a recognized member of the Blackfeet Nation."

"I got my tribal ID card. I've been here all my life."

"Then we can put that issue behind us."

Campbell took a sip of coffee and turned his gaze upon Sean. "Montana considers our requirements unreasonable. Yet there is no quid pro quo process for tribal authorities to extradite fugitives from outside reservation borders. So it is the old story, the white man demanding the Indian make concessions while offering an empty hand in return."

He rapped the metal tip of his cane on the pockmarked floor. "John, you are among friends. I promise if you unburden yourself, we will be able to offer assistance."

The young man hung his head so that the hair fell forward, and it was with his face half hidden and his right hand gripping Ida's that he began to speak.

"I'm responsible for a terrible thing," he said.

He stopped, the ticcing of his facial muscles wrinkling his cheek. It was trying to begin near the end, and Melvin Campbell gently steered him to that place upriver where the story was easier to start.

He'd first seen the brothers, Brady and Levi Karlson, at the Heart Butte Indian Days the prior summer. They were among few whites who had taken part in the Intertribal dances, shuffling around the oval with everyone from tiny tots wearing doeskin dresses decorated with fake elk teeth to competition grass dancers, their brooches of porcupine hair rippling in the wind.

"I thought they were 'windians'—Indian wannabes. I didn't think about it; they were just there."

John said that he had found himself alone later, sitting on the grass, when the brothers flopped down on either side of him to watch the Crazy Dogs versus Blackfeet Veterans Stick Ball Game. They talked across him, stems of grass bobbing in their teeth, then began to pepper him with questions about the rules. Such was an acquaintance-ship struck, and having nothing better to do, John had taken the brothers up on their offer to drive into Browning and tip back long-necks. They wanted to experience a genuine Indian bar, not a real good idea for a couple of boys with loud voices and blond hair, but the hour was early and John swallowed his misgivings and took them to the Warbonnet, the biggest bar in town. They left when the eyes of several men stared a little too intently in their direction, had a second round at Ick's, got out of that establishment unscathed, and ended up in Charlie's in Babb, the most white-friendly bar on the reservation, where John could breathe easier.

When they dropped him back in Heart Butte, they swore they would keep in touch, the hour and the liquor talking, and of course John didn't hear from them and hadn't expected to. So he'd been surprised when his mother answered a knock three weeks ago and said there were two white men to see him. The brothers told John they were staying with their parents at a ranch in the Madison Valley and thought of him because they'd taken an elective course in Native American history at Dartmouth. They were keen to drive around the reservation and visit museums and historical sites. Would he be their guide?

He took them to the Museum of the Plains Indian in Browning first, where they spent a long time examining a papier-mâché diorama of a pishkun, complete with miniature bison, hunters carrying bows and arrows, even women skinning hides at the bottom of the jump. The diorama was a replica of the famous Head-Smashed-In Buffalo Jump in Alberta, and they asked how long it took to get there. John had only been to Canada once, to visit relatives in the Blood Nation near Lethbridge, and thought the historical sight was near there; it was quite a drive. But there was another site much closer, where the Two Medicine River carved a corridor in the Front Range. Only recently discovered, it encompassed a vast area, tiers of cliffs marching for miles, that had drawn the attention of archaeologists intent on verifying the site as sacred Blackfeet hunting grounds. If they could, it would be a card to play in the future against the trump hands held by the oil companies that had bought up exploration leases years before.

John accompanied them to the area, where they hiked to the top of a U-shaped band of cliffs in time to see the sun set over Moskitsipahpi-istuki, the sacred mountain. Brady told John he had a proposition, but first he would have to take a blood oath of secrecy, and saying that, Brady had pulled a belt knife from its sheath and without hesitation drew it across his palm. He handed John the knife. It was his masculine pride at stake now, and John had done the same, and then Levi had drawn the knife and they were blood brothers, three hands pressed together.

"What are we going to do?" John had asked.

And Brady had spread his hand, dripping blood, to encompass the vista. "We're going to drive buffalo over cliffs like these. We're going to conduct the first buffalo jump since Indians had horses."

He said the idea had come to him while volunteering for the American Bison Crusade, that every evening they would gather around a campfire and listen to the stories told by their leader, whom they called Tatanka. One night Tatanka had related the story of the great buffalo hunt that had taken place in the Dakota Territory in 1883, when a herd estimated at ten thousand moved through the Standing Rock Reservation. The Sioux, who had not seen buffalo on the prairies in years, believed that this was the last herd on earth, and that the buffalo had returned to sacrifice themselves to their Indian brothers, and thus be saved from ignoble death at the hands of the white hunters who were amassing outside the reservation borders. The Indians set fires along the borderline to keep the animals from straying. Then six hundred Lakota mounted their horses, some carrying repeating rifles, others with bows and arrows. When the smoke cleared, the blood of half the herd had seeped into the earth. White hunters quickly finished bison that fled the reservation. One of the commercial hunters, a man by the name of Vic Smith, declared, "When we got through with the hunt there was not a hoof left."

Brady had explained that the bison that left the sanctuary of Yellowstone Park were the walking dead, that their death warrant was signed even as they advanced a foreleg across an invisible border. But that every once in a while a small herd escaped murder for a time, and that as they were speaking this had happened, but that it was only a matter of days before those bison were shot by the Department of Livestock.

He concluded his pitch, saying that by killing the bison they actually would be rescuing them from state hunters, and that the act would shine a light on the injustice of not letting bison roam freely to reclaim their homeland.

John had picked up on his meaning. "They would be sacrificing themselves to us, like the buffalo did in the Dakotas."

"You understand now why we have come to you," Brady said.

A buffalo jump would have a stronger symbolic meaning, Brady claimed, and be more persuasive if it was conducted at least partly by Native Americans. He asked John if he knew any other Blackfeet men who might join them, who were fleet of foot, for he saw the Indians in the hunt as the runners who led the buffalo to the brink. He said he had bought a buffalo skin to make into robes, so that the runners would resemble bison calves. The brothers would conduct the drive and wear wolf skins. John was impressed with the detail of the plan, down to driving climbers' pitons into the cliffs so the runners could suspend themselves safely over the edge while bison tumbled past. John had looked out over the sea of mountains and plain, the people's land, complete but for the one animal that had made it holy, and told Brady he would think about it. But he meant he would think about another runner; he was already sold on the hunt. There were only two catches. You had to know where to find the buffalo, and you had to have cliffs to push them over.

Brady told him that the location would be in the upper Madison Valley, and that he would be informed when the bison showed up.

What would happen after they drove the bison over the cliffs? That was a question that neither of the brothers had addressed. John didn't see how they could get away with it without being caught.

Brady said he'd missed the point. There would be no effort to cover their tracks, or even to leave. They'd be skinning the bison as the television cameras rolled. How else would they get their message to the public? As for the authorities, they would dare them to arrest them.

———

An hour had passed. The coffee was drunk or cold. Sean, listening to John's recitation, felt the hangover of the trip dropping its weight on his skull and thought he'd better get in a question he'd been holding back.

"Brady told you he would be informed about the buffalo. Who would inform him?"

"I don't know," John said. He raised his eyes to Sean; it was the first time he'd looked at him squarely. "He said that the person hadn't committed to taking part in the drive, only to telling them when and where to find the buffalo."

"No names, then?"

"Brady called him the highway man. They would move when they got the highway man's call."

"Does that mean anything to you?"

"No."

"Did you ask him about it?"

"No."

Sean was standing to pour another round of coffee as a flutter of wings made him duck. A bird that had entered one of the open windows was flitting in panic. When it swooped over the coffee table, the hand was so fast Sean didn't see it move. John Running Boy cupped the bird in both hands, allowing its head to peek out, like a fledging peering out from the hole in a birdhouse. He carried the bird to the window and opened his hands.

"Fly away, *poksistki*," he said.

Melvin Campbell lifted his head. "I didn't think you would remember that," he said. He waved his hand to include Ida and Sean. "John, when he was a little one, I taught him some of the language. He had to learn a new word each time I gave him stone. *Poksistki* is 'little bird'—the sparrow, the chickadee."

"So you agreed to take part," Sean said, prompting John to continue.

John nodded. He said that Gary Hixon, a kid he'd known from childhood, had recently returned to the reservation and was up for accompanying him, no questions asked. Plus Gary had a cell phone, and the brothers would need a way to reach them when the time came. John said he'd introduced Hixon to the brothers, and the next day they had gone back to the buffalo jump to practice climbing with pitons. One of the books Melvin Campbell loaned John had a chapter about pishkuns and they read it aloud. That's when Joseph's brother-in-law had reprimanded them for trespass and taken down their names—probably, John thought, just for the chance of scaring a couple white people.

A few days later, John and Gary had driven to the Madison Valley, an all-day affair in the Fairlane, which maxed out at fifty miles an hour. Brady had spotted them gas money, and they had arrived with just enough light in the sky to set up a tent on the West Fork, which was secluded from passing traffic and one of the few camping places in the valley that had cell reception. Brady and Levi had met them there and they had driven to the Palisades the following morning to get the lay of the land.

They decided on the jump site and built the rock cairns to funnel the herd. Three pairs, which was optimistic, for, as far as John could determine, there were only the four of them—the brothers, who would drive the bison, and John and Gary, who'd run ahead of the herd. But Brady had thought of a contingency plan and bought straw scarecrows to stand behind the rock cairns. The brothers had already fixed the pitons, and John and Gary attached ropes to rocks and practiced climbing down to the recess under an overhang.

"How were you supposed to kill the bison that fell over the cliffs and broke their legs?" Sean asked.

John pantomimed pulling a bow. "I brought shafts and a bag of obsidian. That's what we did in camp while we waited for the buffalo. We napped points and fletched arrows and sewed the bison robes. I thought we'd be lucky to get three or four buffalo, so one bow and a few dozen arrows seemed plenty."

"Did the brothers have rifles? Handguns?"

John shook his head. "Brady wanted to keep it primitive. It wouldn't make the right impression if we used white man's weapons."

Sean had done enough research to understand that the chance of four amateurs pulling off a jump that a millennium ago would have included several dozen seasoned hunters should have been doomed to failure.

And possibly it would have been if the animals had not shown up on the one day of the year when thunder and lightning were assured.

———

The call came in early evening. The buffalo were there, fifteen or so, a manageable-sized herd. Brady told them to hurry, that there was just enough light to carry out the plan. Twenty minutes later they rendezvoused at the boat ramp, which at this late hour was deserted. They wasted no time fording the river, John pausing only long enough to stash his bow and his arrow quiver where he could find them later, before climbing the cliffs. Above, on the open ground of the escarpment, the bison appeared as miniature triangles, their humps pitched black tents against the gold of the evening grasses.

The four hunters pressed their hands together a last time, Brady reminding everyone that he would blow a call that resembled the shriek of a red-tailed hawk to begin the drive. John and Gary crouched behind clumps of sage, staying out of sight while the brothers worked through shallow fissures in the escarpment to circle above the herd. The scarecrows they had placed the evening before were gaunt silhouettes, soulless long-haired ghosts recalling legends of cannibal heads that John had read about in Indian folklore.

As the twilight deepened, the first fireworks from the scattered homes along the Madison exploded in umbrellas of color. They would see the long trailing glittersnake of the launch, the pause, then the bright bloom as the thunder rolled up the valley. Like most Indian boys, John had played with sparklers and charcoal snakes sold at the Fourth of July stands on the reservation, but he had never seen real fireworks before and was so mesmerized that the cry of the hawk came as a surprise.

For a time, nothing changed. Then, almost imperceptibly, the black triangles began to move, drawing toward each other like magnetized bits of iron.

"It was going to happen," he said, looking across the coffee table.

Sean saw the dark brown eyes swim out of focus and draw inward, as John Running Boy began to relive the night that would change his life forever.

CHAPTER TWENTY

Falling Through Space

When he heard the hawk call, the fingers of his right hand instinctively reached into his pocket. All his life, John Running Boy had carried arrowheads for luck, so he did not own pants that hadn't been mended with needle and thread as the stone edges wore through the pockets. It had been a standing joke with his aunt, who was always telling him he'd lose his money, John Running Boy, who had never had a nickel to fall from a pocket. Silently he cursed himself for not replacing the point he'd given the bartender.

The arrowhead made him think of her, even as the fireworks lit up the sky. Ida Evening Star was what the schoolboys called cinnamon and sugar, a quarter-white Chippewa Cree from the Rocky Boy Reservation who smelled like cedar shavings. They had fumbled halfway out of their innocence at eleven and twelve, Ida a year older and an inch taller, in the dank gloom of a root cellar, only hours before her parents had driven away with her for a new beginning somewhere else. But the memory that endured went further back, to a day captured by a photograph, the two children crammed onto a slat of wood that made the seat of a swing. The photograph had faded by half, and though it had become increasingly difficult for John Running Boy to imagine the girl's face behind the grain, he could still bring back her scent and in the hollow of his loneliness often did.

Thinking of her, John Running Boy fastened the elk bone buttons on the buffalo skin vest. Had it actually been Ida? He hadn't been certain at first, this vision in blue-tinted water behind a pane of thick glass, nor had Gary been sure. But when John edged to the bar for a closer look, he had seen the eyes that could be no other woman's. And surely she had seen him, too, though her face had not registered obvious recognition. He wondered if the arrowhead he'd handed the bartender was in her pocket now.

Then again he heard the hawk's cry and the invisible chain that had unraveled through the years tightened, and he was pulled back to the present. Stepping from behind the sage, John began prancing about on all fours. He had practiced the bleating sound that calf buffalo made when they were separated from their mothers, and cupped his hands so that the bleat resonated. The herd was still too far away for his antics to register, for a buffalo's eyesight is poor. Their hearing, however, is superb and he could not believe they hadn't heard the bleats. He did not own binoculars, but even in the gloom he could spot two upright figures advancing on the herd from behind, the light wolfskin coats the brothers wore showing as indistinct stains against the veil of darkness. And between them, higher up the slope, was that a third driver? There had been no mention of another. Possibly it was an illusion.

Again, John Running Boy brought his cupped hands to his mouth. Under the hairy robe, his stomach convulsed as he forced the air from his lungs. *"Euuugh!"*

Were the buffalo moving? Yes, they were coming, not running, but the herd had tightened into a knot that was drawing closer. They would see him, see the two of them, and it took all his nerve to remain where he was. It was only when they were almost upon him that he'd run, luring them into a gallop, then the stampede that ended with the fall. John Running Boy turned broadside to the herd, showing himself. He gripped the edges of the robe and flapped the hide. Then he turned and began to move toward the lip of the cliffs in a crouch.

He could hear the howls of the drivers now, in the spaces between the dull, heavy booms of the fireworks. Sparkling cascades of light imprinted against the horizon, held for a heartbeat, and collapsed in colorful tears. He picked up his pace, telling himself not to look back even as he craned his neck, almost tripping on a rock. Forty yards.

Thirty. The buffalo were coming in a ragged V, shoulder to hip to shoulder, like geese flying in a wedge. Twenty yards. Their hooves made a thunder he could feel in his pulse. Ten yards.

A blur of motion as Gary went past him, the figure seeming to stumble, sliding toward the edge of the cliff. John had marked his rope with a bandana tied around a stone and frantically drove his legs toward the edge, even as the cow in the lead drew abreast, pounding by him. He saw her front legs buckle, then she tipped into space. Another buffalo, so close he felt its wind, skidded and fell to avoid going over the edge. He leaped over the stirring hooves, then dove for the rope tied around the rock. Grasping it above a double knot, he swung himself over the precipice, searching for the first piton with his feet. There. Now for the next. Quickly he descended two more, using the pitons like rungs in a ladder, then pulled his body tight to the rock overhang. Below, he could hear the sickening thuds and expelled grunts as the animals smacked the scree at the base of the cliffs.

John Running Boy raised his right hand in a fist and gave his war whoop, but the pleasure that he had anticipated wasn't there. His was not a cry of triumph but of regret, even despair. He heard a drawn-out scream somewhere below and then abruptly, as he lowered his fist and called Gary's name, the rope broke. For a moment his shoes faltered on the metal pitons, then he was falling through space, his eyes registering the upside-down image of a buffalo falling alongside, its iris as wide as a saucer. He hit something that gave under his weight, bounced off it and felt the back of his head smack the stones, and he was out.

Minutes later, or hours, knowing only that the fireworks had stopped and the valley was engulfed in darkness, he came to, his head pounding and a sharp pain in his chest each time he filled his lungs. Something was pinning his legs to the stones. Without turning his head he knew it was a buffalo, its breath sputtering. Each time its ribs accordioned out, the added pressure on his legs made him scream, though no sound came from his mouth.

John tried to drag his leg out from under the buffalo, then fell back, gasping. All around him, animals were dead or dying, steam rising in columns from their nostrils to hang in a fog, their grunts guttural and concussive, like a roaring of rapids. He could smell the blood, the bowels the buffalo had emptied with the impacts, could smell even their fear.

For a moment he thought about Gary, if he had been killed in the fall or managed to survive. He tried to call out, but the pain in his chest was too severe to exhale the breath. He was becoming light-headed. The world began to spin, and to stop it he shut his eyes. At first there was only blackness behind the lids, starshot with ruby points of light. Then an image came into focus, the face of his aunt. The image seemed to pulse, to expand and draw back as another took its place, his mother, as young as his oldest memory of her, then his father's face upside down, a flicker, his presence in life not much more than that anyway, as others crowded past him into the frame. And then without bidding she was there, with her Indian eye and wind-stirred hair, emerging from the photograph to take his hand into the darkness.

———

When he came around for the second time, the weight on his legs had lifted and he was shuddering from cold. From somewhere close a nightjar sang its two-note lament, over and over. The bison that had pinned his legs had rolled off him and was dead now, and John crawled a few yards down the hill to nest against the warmth from its body. All around him rose the sighs of dying animals.

He didn't hear words at first, only the incongruity of human voices. They came from somewhere above and he saw a beam of light paint up and down the cliff face, and then the light and the voices faded out, and then he heard them again, closer, the lights sweeping snarls of undergrowth. It had to be the brothers, searching back and forth for him. He wondered if they'd found Gary, if he was alive or had fallen to his death. John would call out to them, damn the pain, but something in the tone made him hesitate.

Now the voices were closer and he heard, quite clearly, a voice far from sure of itself. "He's got to be here. He's got to be here . . . doesn't he? Or do you think he took the car?"

It was Levi Karlson's voice, John was sure of it.

A second voice: "We'd have heard it. You can't start that thing without two 'shits' and a 'goddamn.'" Brady.

"The highway man's not going to like this." Levi again, his voice rising on the word "like." Lilting.

"Don't talk like a baby."

A sudden incandescence illuminated a limber pine over John's head, lighting it like a Christmas tree. The beam swept across the branches, the men close enough now that John could hear their clothes catching on the thorns, the tearing sounds and their labored breathing. He sipped at air, taking only shallow breaths, willing himself silent.

"I'm going to be sick."

"If you throw up, you're going to eat it. We're not going to leave anything to tie us to this place. No thing and no one. Do you got that? Nothing."

"But he was going to die. What we did, you said, it was the highway man's fault. 'The buck stops with the highway man.' That's what you said."

"It *is* his doing. Let me think."

"But we shouldn't have left him, they're going to find him, we can still—"

"Shut up." Then: "Did you touch the arrow?"

"You got the arrow. The highway man, he's—"

"Not that arrow. Other arrows. Did you touch them? I mean without the gloves on."

"N . . . no."

"Don't cry. No fucking crying. You saw how he was acting. He was a fucking time bomb."

"But—"

"But nothing. If they pin it on anybody it's going to be John."

"But John's gone."

"Think. Do you know how to do that? Because everything here's his. The arrows, they're his. The bow, it's his. Look at me now. Whatever you've got yourself into, I've got you out of it. Like Mary Ellen, remember how worked up you got?

"But you, you wanted . . . that was an accident."

"Trust me. Do you trust me?"

"But if he talks—"

"He won't. If he's alive, he'll make a run for the reservation, mark my words."

"But Dad will—"

"Papa-san won't know. And you and me, we go on like nothing happened. We go to bed, we get up, we eat breakfast like nothing happened. Next week, we drive back up to the rez to fish the lakes like we said we would, like nothing happened. We go back to school next month like . . ." Waiting for the answer. "Like what, Levi?"

"Like nothing happened?"

"Are you crying?"

"I'm not, it's just—"

"Shut up. I say fuck John Running Boy. Let's tear down the cairns and haul our asses out of here."

"But his car?"

"We don't touch the car. The car points to him, not to us. Are you with me on this? Say you're with me."

Silence.

In a small voice: "I'm with you."

"Good. Let's climb back on top."

The light swept over John's head and he saw, imprinted on the trunk of the pine, mottled like the bark, the blurred outline of the nightjar. John tried to become as invisible as it was. Then the light moved on, flashing up at the rock walls. The voices faded, and after a while there was only the river running and the bison dying and the mourning call of the bird.

CHAPTER TWENTY-ONE

Your Money or Your Life

Sean saw John Running Boy's eyes slowly come back into focus.

"Did you actually see Gary Hixon? His body?"

John turned his face away.

"You can tell us," Campbell said. "Whatever you did, or did not do, it is all right. I promise."

Slowly John nodded. He said that after the brothers had left, he got to his feet to go to the river, but that his leg hurt so bad with the added pressure of going downhill that he side-hilled around instead. He said he had to go upstream anyway to find the ford to cross the river. That's when he heard him. He was moaning, and for a long moment he thought it was the dying of another buffalo.

"Where was that?" Sean wanted to see if John's version of the death scene differed from what Martha had told him.

"He was curled up under a big rock with a tree growing out of it."

"What did you do?"

John didn't answer. *A part of him is still back under the cliffs*, Sean thought, *still taking the shallow breaths.*

"I'm sorry," John said. "I was a coward."

"John, please, we are not judging you." Campbell's voice was gentle. "Just talk to me as if no one else is here. Was he alive? Could he speak?"

"I tried to talk to him, but I don't know if he heard me. I just held his hand. He kept taking these long breaths. A hundred times I heard him breathe. It was like this." John drew in a long breath and held it, then slowly let it out. "Each time I thought he would die. Then this sound came out of him, a sort of rattle from his chest. It went on a long time and then it finally stopped. And then like half a breath came out but it was different. I think he was already dead."

John looked at Campbell with tears in his eyes. "I saw him die." He got off the love seat and, kneeling before Campbell, touched the old man's slippered feet.

"I left him. I told myself I would never leave his side, but I was afraid. I am not worthy of forgiveness."

"You do not need to be forgiven. Please sit back down. You were brave to stay with him when he was alive. It is not sin to leave him when he died, to save yourself."

Campbell looked at Sean. "Do you have more questions?"

Sean nodded. "Just a couple. John, did Gary have an arrow in his leg?"

"No. Maybe they took it, I don't know. But there was a lot of blood.

"So then you waded across the river."

"I didn't know how long they'd be up above the cliffs. I felt that I had to get the car and get out of there before they came back down."

"Where did you go?"

"I drove up the West Fork and turned onto some two-track until I was in the trees. I wanted to go farther away in case they came looking, but I didn't have a lot of gas. So I cut some branches to camouflage the car."

"Did you really think they would come after you?"

"You weren't there. Levi, he'd sniffle and talk in a baby voice around his brother, but you'd see him sometimes, he'd get this look, locked in, like a cat looking at a bird. Like he was ready to snap."

"As I'm sure Ida told you, Gary Hixon was killed by an arrowhead. The sheriff says it could have been accidental, but I don't believe that, and I don't think you believe that. Do you think one of the brothers shot him?" Sean was deliberately contradicting what John had intimated earlier.

John shook his head. "I don't know. From what I heard, it sounded like the other guy, that the other guy did it."

Sean led him further along the track of his memory, confirming. "You're talking about the one you saw at the beginning of the drive, up above with the brothers."

"I don't know who else it could be," John said. "But like I told you, there weren't supposed to be any others."

"So this would be who they called the highway man?"

John shook his head. "All I can tell you is what I heard."

Sean changed tack.

"Okay, when you were in the Madison Valley, before the jump, who else did you see the brothers with?"

"No one. We went into town once, but all I remember is some girl with pink hair looking at them, like following with her eyes, and Brady said he'd banged her. But he didn't stop to say hello or anything."

"How about their parents? Did they swing you by the ranch where they were staying?"

"I didn't even know where that was."

Sean was getting nowhere.

"Okay, one of the brothers said the highway man was a time bomb. What was that about?"

"I think he meant Gary, not the highway man. Gary was sort of out there. He used to live in New Mexico, you know, that town where UFOs are supposed to be."

"Roswell."

"That's it. He said he'd written a book about aliens and was going to find a publisher, take a Greyhound to New York City."

"I don't get how that makes him a time bomb."

"Well, he talked about how after that, he was going to write a screenplay about the buffalo jump, that he'd sell it to Hollywood and we'd all get rich. Brady started thinking he'd open his mouth about what we were doing. I didn't see how that was a big deal because the plan wasn't to keep it a secret. We were going to be there skinning the buffalo for the TV people, make our case—that was the whole point.

But Brady, he regretted letting him in on it. He wanted to take all the credit. I think it was an ego thing."

"John, do you really think it was the highway man who killed Gary? Or do you think it was Brady and Levi Karlson?"

John looked down. His voice was all but inaudible. "I think it was them. I think . . ." He paused. Slowly he shook his head, his hair hanging down, hiding his face.

"What, John?" Ida said. Sean saw her squeeze John's hand. "What do you think?"

He took a big breath and let it out. "Everything went to shit," he said. "I don't know if Gary, if he got hurt first or what happened, but I think they knew if he lived, he would talk, and they just wanted to disappear, make like it never happened. I think they killed him. I think, if they found me, they would have killed me, too.

He raised his head. "I think I'd be dead."

No one spoke. Outside, Sean could hear birds.

"John," he said quietly, "would you be willing to come with me to Bridger and tell my friend Martha Ettinger what you just told me? You can trust her."

"No way. They'll know I talked to you."

"You could be in more trouble if you don't. Once they know they're under suspicion, they know that if anything happens to you—"

"No, you're twisting words. That's your snowman's tongue talking."

Sean could see the futility of carrying the argument any further. He said, "All right, John. Think back. Did you tell them about Melvin, about being in this house when you were a kid?"

"I mentioned him. They saw the books he gave me. But I didn't say where he lived."

"Then my advice is stay put. Get word to your mom. No, don't worry about that. I'll have Joseph give her a message when she gets back. But you stay here with Ida. Stay low while I look into this."

Ida shook her head. "I can't give you money I don't have."

Sean waved a hand. "I was in a bad place before I met you. I did something that I was going to see a therapist about. I feel better now because I have a purpose. So you saved me the shrink fee. I should be paying you."

It sounded good. But he'd have to hit Sam up for some guide days soon, if he wasn't to end up like John Running Boy, with no coins to drop through a torn pocket.

They stood to shake hands—if not John's friend, at least Sean was no longer his enemy—and as the warped boards creaked under their combined weight, the shotgun standing in the corner fell, the hammer tripping when the action hit the floor. The explosion was deafening. They froze, stunned.

"Is everyone all right?" Campbell said. His voice sounded like it was echoing from another room.

Sean and John helped the old man to his feet to survey the damage. There was a hole you could kick a soccer ball through on the side of the house. The charge of BB shot had missed the chair where Sean had been sitting by no more than a foot. He felt a prickling sensation, as if a tiny sweat bee had stung the back of his neck.

"You're bleeding," Ida said. She told him to turn around and fingered the collar of his shirt, where a stray BB had torn a hole. She showed him the blood on her finger.

Melvin Campbell was hunched over, probing with his cane through the hole in the wall.

"We better board this up before the mice get in," he said.

———

"Quit squirming."

Martha Ettinger folded his collar down, tut-tutting over the minor wound. "Who patched you up?" she said.

"Ida Nightingale."

Martha frowned. "You just drove six hours with duct tape over a piece of rag."

"It was a lightly worn sock."

"Uh-huh. This is going to hurt like the dickens." She yanked as Sean clamped his teeth. "Now you know what a woman feels like getting ready for a date." She dangled the bloody bandage in his face. "Come on into the bathroom. I'll patch you up, but you need to get dosed with some antibiotics so it doesn't get infected."

"I have amoxicillin from when Choti got into a porcupine. That'll work, right? I don't have health insurance."

"Go to Urgent Care in Bridger. I'll reimburse you."

"Does that mean the county's going to hire me?"

"No. It means you mean enough to me to make me want to make sure you're okay. Promise you'll do it."

He nodded. "I came this close to being killed, but wasn't. How do you react to something like that?"

"You don't. I was elk hunting once, me and Petal up in the Judith, and I was leading her when a Doug fir fell. No wind, no warning. It felt like an earthquake. I looked back and there's Petal on the one side of the trunk and me on the other. Came down smack dab on the lead rope, couldn't have missed either of us by three feet. It was over so quick that Petal forgot to go crazy. I said, 'Petal, that was a close one,' and an hour later I got the elk I was tracking."

"It didn't haunt you?"

"Nope. When I think of that day I remember the hunt."

"Is that the skull and antlers up in the living room, the six-point?"

"That's the one. Life's strange. You never know how you're going to react to a situation until you're in it." Martha rubbed at her throat. "Why are we standing around like this is a cocktail party?" She led him into her office, which was part of the living room, passing a piano that Sean had never heard her play and seemed to be there only for the purpose of displaying old pieces of crockery. She switched on track lighting and they glanced up at the elk mount, hats hanging from its brow tines, and then sat down at the polished slice of stump that served as her desktop.

"What are the chances of getting a warrant for arresting Brady and Levi Karlson?" Sean asked.

"Without a signed statement from John Running Boy?" Martha shook her head. "Zero and zero. And what's the charge, wearing wolf skins and yelling at buffalo?"

"What about murder, or at the very least leaving an injured man to die?"

"What your John Running Boy heard was ambiguous. And if I did start poking around, you better believe the old man would get wind and sew up their mouths with a lawyer."

Sean's nod was grudging. "Martha knows best," he said under his breath.

"What's that?"

"Nothing. Boot up your computer."

He read the question on her face.

"Humor me, as you like to say."

"What do you want to look up?" She pulled her chair over to the desk.

"Highway man. That's what Brady called the man who tipped them off about the buffalo. John mentioned seeing another driver up with the brothers, but he couldn't be sure. I think it was this highway man. I think he could have been the brains of the outfit."

"You say it like it's two words. It's one—highwayman."

"I thought he said it as two. And he might have said highway men, so I'm not sure it's the singular."

"You don't know what a highwayman is? You never heard the song?" She hummed. "'With gun and pistol at my side'?" Johnny Cash recorded it with Willie Nelson. They called themselves the Highwaymen. It's about an outlaw."

"Must have been before my time."

"No. You just don't know music."

Sean shrugged.

"Sometimes I think you're smart and sometimes I'm just not sure. Me, I know a lot about a lot and a little about a lot more. You know a heck of a lot about maybe six subjects and nothing at all about the rest. You have gaps."

"I know that a March brown and a gray drake mayfly don't look alike but are actually the same species, *Mccaffertium vicarium*."

"That and a five-dollar bill will buy you a tater pig at the Sweet Pea Festival."

"Along with a few good trout. Just look up 'highway man.'"

"What do you think I've been doing?" She read aloud. "Highwayman. A horseman who robbed travelers at gunpoint. Often depicted wearing a dark coat and light straw hat. Archetypical 1500 to 1800." She stood up and took a straw cowboy hat off the elk rack, tipped it back on her head, and sat back down. She cocked her thumb and forefinger like a gun. 'Your baubles or your life.' Ring any bells?"

He shook his head. "Go to some other sites. Do you want any more tea?"

"Mm-hmm."

Sean got up to make it, and when he came back, Martha was stroking her chin, looking at the screen.

"What do you have?" He leaned over her shoulder.

"It's a video game called *Highwayman and Bandolero*," she said. "Read the introduction."

The site explained that the Spanish word for highwayman was *bandolero,* and that the English highwayman and the Spanish bandolero were the bad guys that the coachman needed to defeat to stay in the game, because both were attempting to rob the horse-drawn stage with its sacks of shiny coins. The highwayman was depicted as dapper, dressed in black, wearing a tricorn hat and a domino mask. He was armed with twin flintlock pistols. The bandolero wore a brocaded Mexican hat and a long coat. Across his chest were crossed bandoliers that held shiny cartridges, a short sword, a pistol, and a knife. The highwayman rode a black Arabian stallion, the bandolero a buckskin Criollo.

"Remind you of anyone?" Martha said.

"Theodore Thackery was wearing a gun belt over his bathrobe. Put him in a duster and he's ready to rob the rich."

Martha nodded. "While you were boiling water I looked at a few other sites for highwayman. Most of them show a man wearing a gun belt or a cartridge bandolier."

"I should have thought about him earlier," Sean said. "He lives on the range where he can see the bison from his porch. Who else would be better situated to pass on information about the herd?"

Martha dropped her thumb onto her forefinger, shooting the bandolero on the screen.

"Now him, we talk to," she said.

CHAPTER TWENTY-TWO

The Highwayman

They dropped the Land Cruiser at Sean's tipi and he slept in the passenger seat of the Cherokee all the way to the MacAtee Bridge turn-off, jolting awake as the tires crunched gravel.

"Feel better?" Martha said. She pulled the Jeep into the fisherman's access upriver from the bridge. "Wash your face. I'm going to need you to have your faculties."

He splashed water at the river, where the exoskeletons of giant salmonflies clung to the bankside willows. A few of the adult insects flew like biplanes on double sets of wings, and Sean caught one that landed on his sleeve. It looked at him with pinhead eyes.

Martha walked up. "I thought you were a purist. No live bait."

"One can always backslide," Sean said. He opened his hand, and, after the salmonfly flew across the river, told her about John Running Boy catching a bird in flight.

"Barehanded it, you say? And you didn't tell me? Don't you know what the symbolic meaning of that is?"

"I guess not."

Her voice held a note of exasperation. "There *isn't* a meaning. Don't you know irony when you hear it? Get your head in the game, Stranny. Let's concentrate on Theodore Thackery."

"Okay."

"How do you think we should approach him? I'm inclined not to dance around, just tell him straight out that we know he was with Brady and Levi Karlson at the buffalo jump. Catch him off guard.

He's the kind of man I read as basically honest. If he denies it and he's lying, we'll know it right off the bat."

"Are you asking me? Or asking me to agree?"

"Both."

———

Thackery didn't answer the knock.

Martha pointed with her chin. "Is that the same truck that was here last time?"

"The Jimmy? It was night, but I think so."

"Humpff."

She called out, no answer, then turned the handle. Unlocked.

The cabin was homestead-era, logs blackened with a hundred years of soot, the chinking, once white, now a butter color with lighter repairs. A kitchen—small, spick-and-span; a bedroom—spartan; a study with maps on the walls, a file cabinet, a desktop computer backed up by a Remington manual typewriter. The living room was done up in western rustic decor with a rough pine table and slat-back couch with Indian print cushions. A buffalo hide was spread on the floor. An upright piano stood against one wall, a gun case stood against another. Pump 12-gauge, a battered bolt-action Winchester in .300 magnum, a .22, a double-barreled fowling gun with Damascus barrels, a Kentucky squirrel rifle that looked original, with a barrel the length of a broom handle. There were spaces for a couple more guns.

Martha spread her fingers on the piano keys and sunk a chord.

"D minor seventh," she said. She played a jazzy couple of bars, her fingers rippling.

Sean raised his eyes.

"Like I've told you all along, for everything you know about me, there's something you don't. This thing must be hell to keep in tune, set against an outside wall. She fingered one of a dozen framed photographs on top of the piano. A younger version of Theodore Thackery with long hair and a Fu Manchu, standing with his arm around a woman with bangs peeking from a beret. Martha brought the frame to her nose, which briefly wrinkled.

"His wife?" Sean said.

She nodded. "Walt knew him a bit, they both belonged to the Elks. I heard she died of brain cancer and he sold the place in town. He lives here year round now, has to snowmobile in."

"Children?"

"Two. Grown and gone."

"A recluse."

"I don't know if I'd call him that. I used to say good morning to him in church, back when I was tarting for votes and believed there was someone in charge of the planet."

"He keeps the place tidy enough," Sean said.

"That's what worries me. Men who live alone turn feral. The ones who don't have their springs wound too tight."

She was looking at the titles in a bookcase. Tom McGuane, James Welch, A. B. Guthrie, William Kittredge, Ivan Doig, Richard Hugo. A who's who of Montana writers.

"There's more drinking and depression on this shelf than in the whole of Ireland," Martha said.

She bent to look at the next shelf down. Histories of the West, biographies of famous mountain men—Jim Bridger, Hugh Glass, Liver-Eating Johnson. She picked out a book titled *One Rifle, Sixty Million Buffalo*. It was the memoir of a commercial buffalo hunter named Josiah Small, with a grainy photo on the cover of a mustachioed man holding a Sharps rifle, sitting atop a dead bison bull, other dead scattered across the plain. She replaced the book on the shelf.

"I wonder why Thackery's Sharps isn't in the cabinet with the rest of the guns," she said. "And the ammunition belt, I don't see it, either."

"Is this a legal search, Martha?"

"Who's searching? We're making ourselves comfortable until the man comes back from his evening stroll. That reminds me. You being here, that is a violation. I better have you sign a contract as adviser to the department to make things kosher. The last thing you want to do is have evidence tainted because someone inside the ribbon should have been outside."

They walked back onto the porch. A wind had picked up, turning the leaves of the sage. The sun was nailed low above the horizon.

"He didn't tell us how fascinated he was by the era, the buffalo hunting," Sean said. "You gave him an opening as I remember, when you commented on the cartridges in his belt."

"He said he was interested in rifles from several eras. From his gun cabinet I'd say he was telling the truth."

"Where do you think he is?"

"That's a dumb question. Ask a smart one."

"Do you think anything happened to him?"

"Why is that a smart question?"

"Because the truck's here and he isn't, and there's something in the air that's wrong. I have a bad feeling."

"Not every day ends in death." She bent over to tie an unruly shoelace. "Let's take a walk."

They started up a well-worn two-track, heading into the higher elevation. It was nearly half a mile to the forested skirts of the Gravelly Range, stop-and-catch-your-breath country, vistas to all sides. The road kept climbing, climbing, then dipped into a shallow rain wash. Coming up the other side of the wash, they could see the silhouette of the elevated platform from which Thackery said he viewed the game range.

Martha raised her binoculars.

"See anything?" Sean asked.

"No, but it's got some kind of a partial roof. If he's sitting down I wouldn't necessarily see him."

"We could call out."

"Little nervous, are we?"

"A little. I already dodged a charge of buckshot in Browning."

"Take heart. If he's there, that Sharps of his put us in range about a hundred yards back. He wanted us dead, we're already dead."

———

The viewing platform was thirty feet above the ground, built on a scaffolding supported by three stout timbers crossed at the top and wrapped with belts of rusted steel. A ladder comprised of two-by-four sections nailed onto one of the timbers led to an opening on the underside of the platform.

"That would be slippery as hell with a little snow cover," Sean said. He suffered a little vertigo just looking up at it.

"I'll take the honor," Martha said. She unbuckled her utility belt, handed it over, and began to climb. About halfway up, a zephyr of wind took off her hat. Sean chased after it as it flipped over and over, finally trapping it with his shoe. When he picked it up, he noticed that the crown had settled over a bottlenecked cartridge case, mottled and corroded by exposure. He couldn't read the head stamp on the rim, but thought it might be from a Sharps or one of the old rolling block Remingtons of the nineteenth century. Frost heaves unearthed such artifacts all the time, arrowheads as often as cartridge casings, the bloody history of the land written in stone and brass. He idly rolled the case in his fingers.

"You all right up there?" he called out.

No answer. Sean pocketed the case. Ten minutes passed before he saw her descending from the platform. She climbed down, a more sober woman than when she'd climbed up, and she'd been sober then. She buckled her utility belt on and squared the hat.

"Remember what I said? 'Not every day ends in death'? I was wrong."

Sean grimaced.

"It's a pisser being right," Martha said. "You get a premonition about things like this and it's confirmed, you feel like the dead are singling you out to talk to. I've been there. Welcome to the club."

"Suicide?" Sean was looking up at the platform.

"Looks like it. He's got the Sharps and he's wearing the ammo belt. One sock off, like you'd do to work a trigger with your toe. I'm going to go back to the cabin to use the landline. You want to have a look, have one. You know not to touch anything."

The platform was bigger than it had looked to Sean from ground level, long enough for two men to lie down in nose to toe and tall enough to stand in without banging your head on the roof, which was elevated on poles so that there was an open space all around at about sitting eye level. A spotting scope set up on a tripod, a folding chair, a two-by-ten affixed to one wall with braces that made a work surface—it was as tidy as the cabin. A comfortable setup, Sean concluded, though the platform swayed disconcertingly in the wind.

A metal clipboard clamping a stack of papers drew Sean's attention. The top sheet was a photocopy of a topographic map of the game range, scribbled on in pen. Sean recalled Martha saying that Thackery had showed a stack of similar maps to Harold. No personal touches except a campy calendar called "Babes, Boobs and Bait," Miss July wearing hip boots and a smile as dead as the salmon she displayed with her fingers hooked in its gills.

Thackery was dead, too. As dead as the salmon and not as pretty and smelling worse. He was on the floor of the platform, on his side but in a sitting position, his legs hooked around the seat of the chair, which had tipped onto its side. Stranahan only had a partial view of his face, but the eye he could see was bulged out like a hard-boiled egg. He could have seen the back of the head if there'd been a back of the head to see. He was surprised the birds hadn't been at him, but the roof must have shielded the blood from view.

Sean pried his eyes from the carnage. The spotting scope was set up to look south, toward the slope of land where Thackery had talked about seeing the buffalo. If that was his last view of the world, Sean thought, it was a damned good one. His eyes tracked up to the roof, a shaft of sunlight lancing like a sword through a ragged hole the shape of a playing card. Blood spatter on the boards there, bits of matter that might be brains.

When Stranahan climbed down the steps, Martha was grinding up in the Jeep with the hubs locked.

"Harold and Gigi are coming," she said. "Walt, too. And the coroner, just in case he's playing possum. Meanwhile, I got sandwiches and iced tea."

They ate Martha's elk loaf sandwiches in silence, sitting with their backs to the tires and tossing the tea thermos back and forth. When they were done eating, Sean flipped her the old cartridge case.

"That look like the ones in his belt?"

"Could be."

"I found it under your hat."

Martha grunted noncommittally.

"Do you want to talk about it?"

"The guy up the hill? I'd rather not speculate until there's more to speculate with."

"I mean us. Strange, isn't it? Harold's on his way and you and him are together when it should have been you and me."

"Now you bring this up."

"I know. We keep missing each other. Misunderstandings and all."

"I could ask about you and Katie."

"There's skin I can't touch and a mind I can't know. Every time could be the last time and maybe already is."

"Love makes philosophers out of all of us."

She flipped crumbs off the wax paper she'd wrapped her sandwich in and stood up. "Here come the troops."

CHAPTER TWENTY-THREE

Trouble in Paradise

Harold Little Feather leaned against his truck, his arms folded across his chest as Martha talked.

"You met the man," she said. "What's your take on him?"

"Struck me as the kind of a man who lives by a code. Be hard to live with, that kind of man, but strong in his head, you'd know where you stood with him."

"It's the strong who have the guts for suicide."

Harold nodded, looking off. "I'll try to make myself useful, see what there is to see while Gigi's in the treehouse."

When he'd walked away, Martha shook her head. "He never once met my eyes. We're in the doghouse, you and me. Harold's pissed because he wasn't in the loop and you didn't consult him about going to the reservation, and Gigi's got a bug because we climbed to the platform without wearing gloves."

They stood there, feeling chastised, while the sun dropped toward the ridges of the Gravellys. The duly elected death pronouncer, a pathologist named Dirk Stanislaus, arrived in a caravan with Walter Hess. He climbed up, climbed down, handed Martha a piece of paper with the official declaration of death, and said he'd be back in a couple hours to cart the body to the morgue. He had to go see if a woman in Ennis who'd cooked her head in an oven was done medium or medium rare.

"We're not going anywhere," Martha told him, and when he was gone, "That man isn't the least bit funny. I miss Doc. I mean, I see him in the morgue now and then, but I miss him in the field."

"I know what you mean," Walt said. "But the thing about life, Marth, it changes once ever' seven years, I saw it on a show. And Doc, he was in the field about seven years, that's my recollection. So it was time for him to move along."

"Is that right? How many years have you been on the force?"

"Eight."

"You're past due."

Sean heard his name called and spit out the stalk of grass he was chewing. Harold was glassing into the distance and took down his binoculars and handed them over. "Look about three hundred yards across the way, to the right of the little juniper."

Sean raised the ten-powers. "Stack of hay bales."

"That's it. I found these." He handed Sean a pair of peeled sticks bound together near one end with rawhide lacing.

"Shooting sticks?"

Harold nodded. "The kind buffalo hunters used. This was his range. He'd put up targets against the bales and shoot from here. I found three cartridge cases, stamped .45-70. That's Thackery's caliber. You look close, they all have hairline splits at the neck, pressure cracks, so that makes them unsafe to reload. My guess is he pocketed the good ones and left the ones he had no further use for."

Sean placed the cartridge he'd found under Martha's hat alongside the .45-70s. It was close to the size, but a little longer. He told Harold where he'd found it.

"And you figure what?"

"Nothing," Sean said. "It's just an old case."

"Lot of them around."

Harold planted the sticks in a V and knelt behind them, aiming an imaginary weapon. "We okay?" he said without glancing up. "About Martha?"

"Martha makes her own choices."

Harold squeezed the invisible trigger. "Next time," he said, "give me a heads-up before you go to the reservation. You look like you could be half Indian but you aren't. White people don't want to be seen as having prejudice, so they go out of their way to treat Indians like they're anyone else. And that's right about half the time. But there's a fundamentally different outlook, especially with the older generation. I can help you navigate that. Okay?"

"Okay."

"I see Gigi's back on the ground. Let's see what we're dealing with."

———

"So did he eat it or was he force-fed?" Martha drummed her knuckles on the hood of the Jeep. "Don't give me any wait-and-see on this."

"He's what we call a stargazer." Georgeanne Wilkerson pushed two fingers against the soft skin under her jaw. "That's where the muzzle was. Last thing you see is sky."

"So, suicide?"

"All I can say is he didn't have half his head blown off before he reached the top of the steps. Nobody could have got him up there without leaking evidence. The gun, the positioning of the body, the hole in the roof, that could have been arranged."

"I thought I saw powder burns on his face, what I could see of it."

"I saw that, too. I'm not a gun expert, but those old Sharps used black powder, which doesn't burn completely as it passes through the barrel. There's a lot of residue at the site of the wound, which of course is consistent with suicide. And I measured the distance between the muzzle and the trigger of the rifle, and then I measured between his toe and his chin in a sitting position, just to make sure it was possible. That gun's got a really long barrel, but it's short enough for him to have shot himself in that manner."

"Did you bag his mitts?"

"And the foot. But you don't get as much residue on your body from firing a rifle as a handgun. And you can wrap a man's hands around a weapon, or his toe, and get the GSR, so it isn't conclusive."

"All right. What kind of time frame?"

"He's still in rigor, so within the past forty or fifty hours. The facial muscles are starting to soften and the finger joints exhibit secondary laxity, so I'd say the earlier part of that range."

"He was alive Friday morning," Martha said. "Sean and I talked to him."

"Then not too long after that."

"You can have that effect on people," Walt said.

Martha glared at him. "You're overdue for the change, remember? I can facilitate a transfer."

Sean interrupted the testy silence by asking Wilkerson what she'd done with the clipboard. She got it from the backpack she'd carried up into the observation platform, removed it from a Ziploc, and placed it on the hood of the Jeep.

"I saw this the first time I came," Harold said. "He showed me the page where he saw the herd."

"What I'm wondering," Sean said, "is if that was the only time he saw bison here. Okay if I look?" Wilkerson nodded, handing over blue latex gloves.

He started leafing back through the pages. "These are photocopies of a map of the game range," he said. "They're all the same map, but each one has a different date. He marked down where he saw game—species, number, time of day, weather, pretty detailed. See the circles?" He pointed.

"What are you getting at?" Martha said.

"What I'm getting at is that if Thackery was the mastermind behind the jump, he had to have known that the bison were going to show up on the game range. That means he had to have seen them there before. How else would he know where to plan the jump? He was waiting for them to come back and then give the word."

Ettinger nodded that she understood.

Stranahan paused at a map dated three weeks before the jump. The map was marked with three red circles, the larger one with a "7" written inside it and the two smaller ones, nearby, each with a "1."

He read aloud. "June twenty-one. Six a.m. Seven cows, two bulls. One cow with broken left horn."

He leafed back. Another sighting June second—seven bison. Then nothing until way back in April. Five. In all three sightings, there was a cow with a broken horn. Sean pointed out the common thread.

"She's the matriarch," Harold said. "She was leading excursions into her ancestors' territory. When the people hunted buffalo, it was the old cow they killed first. The others would mill around until they shot them, too."

"I wonder why they didn't stay?" Sean said. "They would have been shot if they had stayed, but they didn't know that."

Martha frowned. "Maybe sleeping beauty up on his perch drove them back into the timber, knowing what would happen if he didn't."

"Then turn around and organize a buffalo jump a couple months later?" Walt's expression was skeptical.

"Not so crazy from his point of view, according to what Sean told me," Martha said. "John Running Boy said the bison were sacrificing themselves, that killing them would shine a spotlight on the plight of wild bison trying to return to public lands. It doesn't have to make sense to us if it made sense to them."

She tapped her foot. "We're losing track of the next step," she said. "What do people who commit suicide do before pulling the trigger? What, nobody?"

Walt raised his hand, like a child waiting to be called on by the teacher.

"They leave a note," he said. Walt, who had investigated one hundred eighty-four murders during his tenure as a homicide detective in Chicago. He swallowed his Adam's apple. "I've seen it on TV, Marth."

She could be around him another eight years and never would get his sense of humor.

———

Two hours into their looking for a note, or anything else that could shed light on Thackery's death, the coroner returned for the body. Sean and Harold lowered it from the platform on ropes while Walt shone a flashlight from underneath. The corpse came down stiff, a protective bag over the head, looking like a man sitting in a chair. They watched the taillights ruby their way down the valley, leaving the world engulfed in a vast darkness.

"I could use a brew at Tits and Tails," Walt said. "I don't know about you young-uns, but it would go a ways toward washing out the taste of death."

"Gigi's the one who says when we're done here," Martha pointed out. "Are we done, Gigi?"

"You are. I'm not. But I'll come back in the morning when there's light."

"All right, then." Martha shook her head in disapproval. "But I really don't see what looking at a woman in a goldfish bowl does for a man."

"It lifts his spirits," Walt said.

"Along with another part of his anatomy, if I know men," Gigi said. She giggled, never more than a breath away from revisiting the girl she'd once been.

"Humpff," Martha said.

At the bar twenty minutes later, she put a question to the table: "If it is what it looks like, why did he pull the trigger?" She cleared her throat while several sets of eyes pried themselves away from the Queen of the Waters.

"I'd bang her like a screen door in a lightning storm, and I'm not even bi-curious," Gigi said.

"Thanks for that observation," Martha said. She waited for someone to fill the vacuum.

"I'll give you a couple scenarios," Walt said. "First, the guy felt responsible for what happened at the cliffs. A situation he had a hand in turned south and a man died. Whether he's the fella sent the arrow or it was one of those brothers, doesn't change the outcome. He couldn't go on living knowing he was responsible."

"What's the other scenario?"

"He wasn't the highwayman. You said he had malaria. Maybe it was getting the better of him. Or maybe he was lonely and the animals wouldn't talk back to him. Folks top themselves off for all kinds of reasons."

"Men who live alone are statistically at high risk for suicide," Gigi noted.

Martha set her beer on a bar napkin. "Any reason we should waste our breath talking about murder?" She held up a hand before Wilkerson could respond. "Besides the fact that we don't have enough evidence to rule it out? You still have the table, Walt."

Walt shrugged. "Whoever killed Hixon would be looking to cover his tracks. Thackery was a wit. He'd have a bull's-eye on his back."

"How's it done? She cocked an index finger at Wilkerson.

"Easy. Someone could shoot from the ground when he's in the platform. That accounts for the angle. Then the shooter climbs up, wraps the victim's toe around the trigger, and recreates the same shot, except with the muzzle pressed to the original wound, so that there's GSR and it looks like suicide."

"Wouldn't there have to be a hole in the bottom of the platform from the first shot?"

"Not if the victim was toward the front of it. There could be a clear shot up toward the chin. The killer could have been some distance from the platform."

"Could forensics determine if there were two shots?"

"Maybe. The bullets for the buffalo rifle are lead; they don't have copper jackets. If the autopsy reveals fragments of copper in the body, that's proof of a shot from a second weapon. Or if I find radiation fractures that run the wrong way, or fingerprints that don't match, or blood spatter that's inconsistent with the angle. I'll be able to tell you more tomorrow."

Martha nodded. "When you go back to the cabin, keep looking for a note. I know that a third of suicides don't leave one, but he's a guy who was demoted because he couldn't keep his trap shut. He'd leave a note. And on that note . . ." She crooked her finger toward the waitress. "Another round for whoever wants one. I have to get my beauty sleep. Sean, are you coming?"

"No. I'll bunk with the Liars and Fly Tiers at the clubhouse. I'd like to go back to the scene tomorrow with Gigi, if that's okay, so there's no sense driving all the way back to Bridger."

"Okay with you, Gigi?" Martha said.

Wilkerson said she'd enjoy the company. She offered to give him a ride to the clubhouse, so she'd know where to pick him up in the morning.

"Well, hell, if everybody's leaving," Walt said, and they all walked out under the neon mermaid. Sean saw that Martha and Harold were not walking together and did not exchange words as they climbed into their vehicles. Trouble in paradise? It was late and he was too tired to care.

———

Martha Ettinger stood on the earthen floor of her barn. She was looking at the butt of a hand-rolled cigarette. It was on the ground, in front of the stall for the old milk cow and the baby bison. The stall door was open. So was the double door of the barn. Martha had closed both before leaving, and she'd swept the floor where the cigarette was. She felt a cold rage burn behind her eyes.

"Are you all right, girl?"

Goldie slinked over from where she'd been lying on straw, her hindquarters nearly dragging. Martha held out a hand and the old dog nosed it. Not her normal greeting at all. Martha passed her hands up and down each of Goldie's legs and over her chest and abdomen. "You okay, girl, you okay?"

Martha walked to the house, ushered Goldie inside, and uncased her .30-06, which she kept under her bed. She loaded the magazine and went back outside and got the six-cell Maglite from the Jeep. It had rained while she'd been at the bar, so that the tracks of a truck— it was Drake's truck, one glance at the dragon-tooth tread confirmed it—were clearly visible in the bright circle of the flashlight. She breathed a little easier. There were no narrow treads from a trailer, and the track indicated that the truck had been turned around in a tight radius that would have jackknifed a trailer, had it hauled one.

Martha's fenced land was seventeen acres, about a mile-and-a-half perimeter of three-strand, 16-gauge barbed wire that she began to walk, the rifle over one shoulder, a coiled rope over the other. She could feel her heart thumping, feel the breath fill her lungs and leave her body, feel herself falling victim to an emotion she hated in herself and hadn't felt for a long time.

That son of a bitch.

She spotted the outline of Petal, who trotted right over making little nickers of pleasure, and, followed by the horse, she finally found the cow standing in the northeast corner of the property, showing milkily in the darkness, her outline partly obliterated by the black coal of the little bison. Martha turned the light off and walked up, speaking in her talk-to-the-animals voice, slipped the rope over the neck of the cow and gently coaxed it along, the bison trailing like a shadow. She shut them up in the stall and looked down at the cigarette butt. Lots of Montanans rolled their smokes. For a couple years she had, too, back when her second marriage went to hell and in the process of dumping one bad habit she'd picked up another.

Had he meant to leave it there? She knew damned well he had. It was as conspicuous an act as a wolf leaving scat on the top of a rock. *I'm the alpha here, this is how big I crap, cross me at your peril.*

It was Drake telling her it wasn't over. And if he did get the warrant and Martha tore it up and ordered him off the property at gunpoint, which she could see herself doing? She'd be arrested by the coroner, who, as an elected official, was the only person who had the authority to do so. It would be the end of her career. She walked back to the house and put on her flannel pajamas. Her eyes lingered on the dog-eared copy of *Gone with the Wind* on her nightstand. Scarlett, she thought. What would Scarlett O'Hara do? Scarlett would think about it tomorrow.

"Fuck you, Drake," she said.

She got into bed, placing the loaded rifle within reach.

CHAPTER TWENTY-FOUR

The Thinking Log

"**S**o how did the fishing go last week?" Sean asked. "Get up at dawn and catch that big brown like you threatened to?"

Patrick Willoughby raised his eyes as he served eggs sunny side up with toast and cups of strong coffee. "Shall you tell them, Ken, or shall I?"

"I got up about nine," Winston said. He buttered his toast, his long fingers working as dexterously as if he was figure-eighting the wings of a mayfly pattern. "Patrick beat me to the coffee maker by ten minutes, as I recall."

Willoughby nodded sagely. "As the presiding members of the Madison River Liars and Fly Tiers Cub, we decided that we would rest the old trout for another day."

His eyes twinkled.

"My dear," he said, speaking to Georgeanne Wilkerson, "would you prefer cream or sugar, or both? Not often do we get to enjoy such illustrious and comely company in the same person. Someday you must tell me how you came to be called Ouija Board Gigi."

Wilkerson had spent the night at Willoughby's insistence. Stranahan had invited her in when they saw lights in the cabin, and they had joined Patrick and Ken for a brandy in front of the fireplace as the late hour became one hour later, and she had slept over, as Sean had known all along that she would.

Now she sat at the fly-tying table in crisp khakis—crime scene investigators, she pointed out to him, always carry a change of clothes—and Sean could see she was thoroughly enjoying the attention. Watching her smile for Willoughby, he recalled Winston Churchill's assessment of Franklin Roosevelt. "Meeting him was like opening your first bottle of champagne; knowing him was like drinking it." Willoughby was also the most astute judge of the criminal mind that Sean had ever met, and he found himself confiding in him while drinking his second cup of coffee.

Willoughby nodded encouragingly, not interrupting, and only after Sean had finished asked him to revisit the day he'd guided Brady and Levi Karlson in more detail, along with a few other points of the narrative. As Sean elaborated, Willoughby's eyes became ever more inscrutable under the round lenses of his glasses. He seemed to have pulled back into a place deep within himself. Then he nodded and rose, asking Sean and Gigi to take a walk with him and arming himself with a fly rod. "One must always be prepared," he said with a wink.

The morning was chill enough to don jackets, warm enough to take them off a quarter mile up the river.

"I call this my thinking log," Willoughby said, sitting with his back to the bole of a tree uprooted in a spring flood.

"Is this where matters of state are ruminated?" Wilkerson asked. Sean had sketched in Willoughby's background during their drive to the clubhouse.

"No, my dear. I don't know what nonsense Sean has been whispering in your ear, but this is the place where I divine strategy to outwit the brown trout who lives in the slot near the tail of that island." He pointed with his rod tip. "So far he has had the better of me, though he came up once for my salmonfly. Parting, as Juliet recalled to the fated Romeo, was such sweet sorrow."

"He broke you off?" Sean said.

"No, the fly came out, but not before I saw him. He is five pounds if he is an ounce, though as an angler I may not be entirely impervious to the temptation of exaggeration."

"Fishermen are born honest, but they get over it," Sean said.

"My sentiment exactly."

They listened to the river.

"You didn't ask us here to quote Shakespeare," Sean said. "And I didn't accompany you to quote Ed Zern."

"No. Quite so. I wanted to bring you here because fresh air is the old man's cocaine and also because this problem does not concern Ken, and I did not want to appear rude and ask him to take his coffee elsewhere."

Willoughby ruminated, his hand pinching flesh under his chin, elongating his moonlike face.

"I am at a disadvantage," he said at length, "having not had the opportunity of observing any of the participants in your most fascinating narrative. Nonetheless, I feel confident saying that the officers of your county have underestimated the depth of the situation. They present a plausible motive for suicide, while paying no more than lip service to the possibility of murder, limiting the discussion only to the particulars of its execution. Now, I would not rule out the former, for Thackery does fit a profile—unappreciated in his work, losing a spouse, living alone, etcetera. And I agree with your sheriff that he is the type of victim who would likely leave a note. But whether you return to the cabin this morning and find one is not the most pressing matter before us.

"The crucial elements in this case, in any possible murder case, are opportunity, means, and motive. I speak of Gary Hixon, for his fate precipitated what happened at the cabin, regardless of whether Thackery took his life or it was taken from him. We can agree that those who had the opportunity to kill Hixon on the evening of the buffalo jump include Thackery himself, the Karlson brothers, and John Running Boy. But who among them had the means? According to John's account of the events, the only persons who knew where he had stashed the bow and arrows to finish off the bison, besides himself, were the brothers, Brady and Levi. John's recollection is that Brady implicated Thackery to his brother. But if Thackery shot the arrow, one of the others involved in the jump had to show him where the bow was, or place it in his hands. When trying to reconstruct the events of that night, keep this point in mind."

Willoughby removed his tweed fedora, his wispy gray hair catching the breeze. He picked at a fly stuck in a sheepskin patch on the hat and spoke without looking up.

"We arrive at the question of motive. You describe the brothers as preppy—selfish, privileged, superficially charming. Scott Fitzgerald's careless rich come to mind. But the motive you advance, that Brady, the dominant brother, killed the Indian man because had he lived he would have talked and his story would have reflected badly upon them, cost them the respect of their father, perhaps their chances for admission at a good law school, is, I believe, insufficient reason for murder. Privileged brats do not necessarily murderers make, even those who may benefit from another's death. What stops a person who has motive to kill from following through is his or her basic humanity, which stands as a buffer against the act."

He set his hat beside him on the log and held up a finger. "Impulse control." He raised a second finger. "Moral reasoning." He lifted a third. "The ability to love.

"These are the three defining characteristics of a caring human being. To the degree that a person possesses these traits, he or she is immunized against the antisocial and psychopathic behaviors that precipitate murder. My reading of Theodore Thackery is that he possesses these character traits and therefore we do not need to eliminate motive in order to remove him from the suspect pool. That leaves as possible suspects John Running Boy, who owned the murder weapon and fled the scene"—Willoughby held up his hand as Sean began to protest—"and the brothers. No, let me finish.

"Unless you are withholding a crucial piece of information"—Sean felt himself cringe, remembering his promise to Ida not to mention her relationship with Gary Hixon—"I can see no reason why John would murder his childhood friend. Nor, for that matter, can I ascribe a convincing reason that the Karlson brothers would commit such an act. However, that is not the same as saying that they are innocent. Sean, when I asked you to—" He paused, staring intently toward the island. "Are you seeing—?"

"He's been rising for about five minutes, but I didn't want to interrupt your train of thought."

"Pale morning dun?"

"I'd try a CDC emerger. You'll have to do some fancy mending to get the drift."

Willoughby flipped down the magnifying lenses clipped to the frame of his glasses and busied himself tying on a fly.

"The old naval officer sails to battle," he said, and carefully worked his way out from shore on short sturdy legs, stepping from one rock to another. He got the drift on the third cast, the trout barely dimpling the surface as it sipped in the fly. The trout flipped into the air, its broad pink strip matching the hue that was the horizon's only an hour before. A good fish of about two pounds. Sean saw Wilkerson bring her head back as Willoughby stepped into the shallows to net the trout and slipped the hook to release it.

"The gentleman is impressive," she said, as he sloshed back downstream.

"Luck, my dear, brought on, no doubt, by your presence. As I was about to say"—water streamed from his trousers as he sought a comfortable position on the log—"the lack of obvious motive does not mean that someone has not committed a crime. Back at the cabin, you will recall that I asked you to speak in detail about these two young men. That is because their manner troubled me. The individuals you described appear to lack impulse control and exhibit little remorse for the consequences of their actions. They were deceitful and manipulative of the two young Indian men, and even their behavior toward you, as their guide, shows a sense of entitlement that I would characterize as narcissistic. These are psychopath indicators. The utter callousness with which the more dominant of the brothers tossed aside the whitefish was a red flag as well. It is possible that if you dig into the past, you may find yourself following a trail of dead cats and broken-winged birds."

He paused. "Or worse. In fact, I would predict worse. You mentioned the sexual aggression toward the young mother who works for the American Bison Crusade. Later, you talked about John Running Boy overhearing the brothers talking about a certain Mary Beth, I believe."

Sean nodded. "Mary Ellen."

"The point is that psychopaths can be strongly motivated by sex drive. They enjoy a feeling of power over their conquests that can easily cross the line from a consensual act to rape. The family will have done their best to cover up past indiscretions—the fact that both brothers are in good standing at an Ivy League college suggests they have largely succeeded—but I would bet a boxful of Hendrickson's tied by our late Polly Sorenson that there have been at least a few transgressions involving young women.

"Now, you might wonder what this has to do with Gary Hixon's death. The point I'm making is that these men may not require a threshold level of motive to kill, but could act impulsively. A mouse is found wounded, it is suddenly vulnerable. The cat pounces. And in the process a mouth is shut that might have opened, might have caused trouble. You said John Running Boy is at the house of the tribal elder. Would the Karlson brothers know that location?"

"I don't think so."

Willoughby nodded. "Keep in mind that I could be wrong about this and the young man may in fact be in no danger whatever. Still, it does no harm to err on the side of caution. He is, after Thackery and Hixon, the third mouth that could cause trouble for these men, and the only one who is still able to talk. It might be a wise idea for him to move to a more remote location while the Karlsons are fully investigated. I assume they have been questioned on the matter?"

Sean shook his head. "Martha is afraid if she approaches them, they will deny any involvement and saddle up with a lawyer. She doesn't want the first time she talks to them to be the last."

"I understand her position. But I think it could be a mistake. If she interviews them, they will know that if anything happens to John Running Boy in the future, they will be suspects in the crime. That alone may prove a deterrent to keep them from returning to the reservation."

He got to his feet. "With this cloud cover, I think we may get a hatch that trickles off all morning. I should probably get into my waders so I can fish properly."

They had started for the house when a fox darted from the willows. It was a silver fox, with a black tail tipped with white. It stopped to stare incuriously back, a gopher dripping from its jaws, its nose sharp enough to pen a poem. The fox reminded Sean of a question he had intended to ask Willoughby about the motivation for the buffalo jump. If a psychopath lacked compassion for his fellow human beings, was it still possible to be motivated by the plight of an animal? All Brady's talk about bringing free-ranging bison back to public lands, shining a spotlight on their persecution, was it only an excuse to herd bison over a cliff?

"Psychopaths need excitement," Willoughby explained. "If the highwayman suggested the jump, Brady might jump at the chance to participate, pardon the pun. But genuine sympathy? I think he might be driven more by his distain of the establishment that stands in the path of the bison."

He smiled. "An old Catskill fisherman's two cents," he said.

They arrived at the clubhouse to find Ken Winston in the bunk room with the shades drawn and his head stuck into his wader tops, shining a light to try to locate a hole.

"There's nothing worse than leaky waders," Sean sympathized.

"It's a seam leak at the crotch," Winston said. "I'll not have that river shrinking my cymbals into jelly beans." He pulled his head out of the waders to notice Wilkerson smiling from the doorway. "Mademoiselle must pardon my French."

"Don't you have a backup pair?"

"Last time I looked it was just the two. You need a haircut, Sean."

"I mean the waders."

"Oh. Of course I do. It's the principle. When you purchase waders from a company that charges six hundred dollars for American manufacture, you expect them to keep your boys dry."

They left him tut-tutting about his boys and shook hands with Willoughby in the turnaround.

"Speak to Martha," Willoughby said. "My suggestion of an interview may carry more weight coming from your lips."

CHAPTER TWENTY-FIVE

Straight from the Heart

The chance to talk to Ettinger came sooner than Stranahan expected. It was a few minutes before nine when Sean and Wilkerson drove into view of the game range cabin and spotted Martha's Jeep. They found her in Thackery's office with the wall maps, clattering away at the old Remington manual. She worked the carriage return and placed the piece of paper she'd been typing beside another sheet on the desk blotter.

"Is this what I think it is?" Sean said.

She nodded. "That's his note. I was comparing to make sure it came from this typewriter. The way the H strikes is distinctive because the stem doesn't register, not that there was a question. You don't see these old dinosaurs very often."

Sean felt somewhat crestfallen. That Thackery hadn't been murdered didn't mean the Karlson boys were off the hook for Gary Hixon's demise, or, for that matter, that John Running Boy was cleared of involvement, but it blunted the excitement he'd felt talking with Willoughby, the sense that he was closing in on the truth.

"Where was the note, Martha?"

"You don't sound too happy that I found it. Remember when I played the intro to 'Piano Man'? The D minor seventh chord sounded tinny. It's easier to show you."

They went into the living room, where Martha played the jazzy intro. Then again, more deliberately. "See where my left thumb is? That's C." She pressed it.

"Hear that? It's a clear note. But yesterday it was fuzzy. So was the natural next to it, the D. It's an old piano. I didn't think anything of it at the time. But last night I couldn't sleep, and it came to me that if you placed a piece of paper on the hammers, it would vibrate and make that sound. Remember all the framed photographs on the lid? I pulled down the one of Thackery with his wife? I could smell glass cleaner, but the lid of the piano was dusty. It struck me as odd, like Thackery had taken the photos from somewhere else, cleaned them, and placed them on the piano without buffing the piano top first. Don't ask me why I thought of this, because I don't know, and why he would hide the note rather than leave it where we could see it, I don't know that, either. But like I said, I couldn't sleep. So here I am."

"What's the note say?"

"You can read it for yourself."

They returned to the office, where Sean read aloud with Wilkerson peering over his shoulder.

> *My Jeremy and my Catherine, whom I love, know that what I do now does not reflect on you in any way.*
>
> *It has been my mission in life to work toward a future balance of nature, that one day the land that rises from our state's great rivers would be home to the bison that grazed here by the millions once, and that could again if extended the opportunity, for the ancient trails are ingrained in their bloodstreams and they know the way.*
>
> *It has been my conviction that man's future, his very survival, depends upon his tolerance for other forms of life. To the degree that we work toward the preservation of our environment and its animal denizens, we show the humanity and resource that can save our planet. To the degree that we harden our hearts and meet the struggles of our wild brothers with bullets and barbed wire, we diminish our humanity, show that we are with neither mercy nor understanding, and draw the circle of our wagons until the world outside*

the walls can no longer be seen as breathing and in need of our succor. In such direction lies the end of our tenure on earth. For if we cannot make the small, reasonable sacrifices to save those who share our planet, how can we possibly make the larger, more difficult ones to save ourselves?

Is it any surprise that such unpopular opinions have banished me to these hinterlands, where my voice is heard only by those who have no votes in their futures?

Some may find it incongruous, even mad, that I chose a course of violence in driving a herd of bison to their deaths last week. In my defense, I would say that these bison would have been summarily executed by the state, probably the next day and with as little fanfare as possible, and that by taking the matter into my own hands, and in turn placing it in the hands of a few of the like-minded, I could give the bison a voice that would have otherwise been suppressed, and to some extent direct the discussion that followed their demise.

In this effort, which was from the heart and well intended, I failed. I failed because in driving bison over the cliffs a man fell with them. Although a relapse of malaria made me return to my bed before seeing the drive to its conclusion, I have no reason to disbelieve the accounts of those who were there, that the man fell on an arrow that had been intended for buffalo. Nor is it my place to point a finger by revealing the identities of the brothers who carried out the drive. As the pishkun was initially my idea, I alone accept the full responsibility for the accident and the death that it caused.

The question I face today is not if life is worth living, but am I worth living life? My wife, your blessed mother, rests in the arms of Jesus, and though I speak to her every day, it is growing harder to bring back the sound of her voice. It's no secret that my remaining time on the earth is limited by my health, and that while I am still hale and sound of mind the

*choice to end my life on my terms, and not to become a
burden on you, is an easy one.*

*My only regret is that my last breath will be drawn on a
landscape that should tremble under the hooves of bison
and ring with the songs of wolves, and instead carries only
the whisper of wind. It is my last wish that someday those
who pass this way will not know such silence, but with senses
filled place ear to ground, and hear there the rumble of the
coming of the herd.*

> *Your loving father,*
> *Thack*

Martha exhaled a breath. "I've read suicide notes as simple as 'farewell,' but they never fail to move me."

Wilkerson shook her head. "I don't get it. You leave a note so somebody finds it, you don't hide it. And what's he mean by brothers? Is he talking about the Karlsons?"

"Maybe it's generic," Sean said, "like brothers in arms, or brothers of the buffalo."

"Maybe," Martha said. "But I'm not sure it was hidden as much as placed somewhere it would take a bit of digging to find. I mean, we'd find it eventually, or someone would. He makes a point about taking responsibility, not revealing the names of the others, about the Indian boy dying as an accident—it sounds to me like he was trying to convince himself. I mean, falling on an arrow? It can happen, but it had to have crossed Thackery's mind that something wasn't kosher. We really don't know how well he knew Brady and Levi Karlson, or how he got together with them in the first place. But common sense tells me that somewhere between the plan being hatched and the night in question, Thackery would have figured out that these guys were hinky. Sean, you were with them only a few hours and had doubts right off the bat."

"That's a lot of surmising, Martha, from someone who hasn't met them."

Martha took the pencil from behind her right ear and twirled it in her fingers. "I'm not surmising. I'm thinking out loud. If you were Thackery and somebody reported back to you about someone falling on an arrow, wouldn't you be skeptical? He was a smart guy. He would have known he was a loose end."

She scratched the underside of her chin with the eraser tip. "I think it's time we have a sit-down with the parties in question."

"We, as in me, too?"

She nodded, her lips tight together. "You have the advantage of having met them and heard John Running Boy's account of the jump. Gigi, you don't really need us here this morning, do you?"

"No. It's a clusterfuck when you have to keep telling people what not to touch."

"Gee, you'd think I might have done this once or twice."

Martha excused herself to use Thackery's bathroom and Wilkerson fluttered her eyes. "That woman never has liked me." She affected a man's voice. "'For someone who hasn't met them.' That was pretty slick. I was wondering how you were going to bring up Willoughby's suggestion. Looks like now you don't have to."

"There's smart, and then there's smart like that fox we saw on the river," Sean said. But he couldn't shake the thought that he'd missed something, that it was there in front of him yet out of sight, like the note under the lid of the piano.

CHAPTER TWENTY-SIX

Turning Over Tombstones

Melissa Castilanos, the former Melissa Karlson, smoked the way sirens smoked on the silver screen, making theater of it, her head thrown back, the cigarette between her first and second fingers. Her face was bone china under a silver Stetson with a rattlesnake band that was as faded as the gray of her eyes. She exhaled and the smoke drifted down the valley.

"Two a day," she said. "One before riding, one when I step off the horse. Three if I have a brandy after dinner."

Stranahan, under his smile, took her as one who seldom missed that brandy after dinner. They stood on the porch of one of the two cabins the manager of the ranch had directed them to as being registered under the name Castilanos. Melissa had told them the 'boys' weren't around—she had pointed to the adjacent cabin, and without further prompting added her husband to the missing. He'd flown to Tacoma on business and would be gone several days.

"Tell me again why you want to speak with my sons," she said.

Stranahan knew she was buying time, and he watched her face as she bought it and Martha rephrased her question.

"We think they might have known one or several of the people involved in the buffalo jump last week. We'd like to ask them about these people. Do you know where they are so that I might ask them a few questions?"

"'These people' being who, exactly? I heard about the Indian boy, that was a sad business, but I didn't know anything about others."

"I can't tell you anyone specifically until we have more information. That's why we want to talk to Brady and Levi."

"I can assure you they had nothing to do with that . . . affair. They
loved buffalo. They even volunteered for that American Bison Crusade, took their whole spring break in the mud and the snow when
they could have gone to Cabo with us. Wait, that's why you're asking,
isn't it? It has something to do with them."

"We don't know that."

"I told them not to have anything to do with that bunch. It's just
ne'er-do-wells and unwashed hippies. But if you tell them that they
can't, that's like withholding catnip, isn't it? Being a mother who
hasn't learned anything in twenty years, I told them they couldn't,
and guess what they did anyway?"

"Mrs. Karlson, do you know when they might come back?"

"My name is Castilanos now." She dragged at her cigarette. She was
a handsome woman on her way to not being one. The smoking
showed in her face the way a low sun shows on a parched riverbed,
mercilessly emphasizing the cracks.

"You're about a day late," she said. "They went on a fishing trip up
to the Blackfeet Reservation, some lake or other."

"Do you know what lake?"

"Like a glove maybe."

"Mitten?" Sean asked. He'd never fished the reservation, but Sam
had mentioned several of the better-known lakes.

"That's it. That was one of them. There was another with an animal name." She shrugged. "Small something. I can't think of it."

"What kind of car did they drive?"

She looked thoughtfully at the cigarette, then stubbed it out against
the porch rail.

"You're not accusing them of anything, but you want to know
where they went and what car they drove. You can't wait until they
come back. You know what I think? I think the next time you want
to talk to my sons you can talk to my lawyer."

Her eyes meant it, and Sean could feel them burning into his back as he and Martha walked to the Jeep. When he looked back, she had lit another cigarette.

"She's going to exceed her quota," he said.

Martha shook her head. "I handled that like a greenhorn. Now I won't get a thing out of those kids." She took a card from her wallet, her personal number, and tucked it under the windshield wiper of the dove-colored BMW parked in front of the cabin. "You never know," she said. "They don't want to talk to you, and then they grow a conscience."

"I think you were damned if you didn't and damned if you did," Sean said, "if it makes you feel any better."

"It doesn't." She shook her head. "She strikes me as somebody who has a snifter of blood and steps out of the coffin every night. Men like that kind of woman. I don't see the attraction."

They climbed into the Cherokee and Martha asked Sean to call Walt back in Bridger, his cell phone, not the office. He got through and pressed the speaker button as they drove out the ranch road.

"Walt, I'd like you to have somebody do a Crime Information Center check for Brady and Levi Karlson. Tell them I'll be back in the office in an hour and expect to be pleased."

"I can put Hunt on the NCIC. You want him to turn over tombstones?"

"And smaller rocks. Even if it's just complaints of loud music."

Sean folded the phone and she fingered her chin. "I'd like to have somebody see if the rig they drove is actually at that lake," she said. "What about your buddy, Raises the Sun, whatever you call him?"

"Joseph Brings the Sun."

"Was there a vehicle parked by the cabin the day you took them fishing?" She twirled her pencil.

"A Highlander. Montana plates and a grille plastered with blue-winged olives. I can't remember the color. Maybe black?"

"You recall what kind of mayflies are smashed on the hood, but the car is *maybe* black?"

She shook her head, but it didn't really matter. The manager of the ranch should have the color and plate number and did. He handed Martha the registration copy with his lower lip clamped on the hairs of his mustache. Guests like Augustine Castilanos kept the place in horses, and he'd prefer this didn't get back to him. Martha told him it wouldn't and passed the sheet to Stranahan with an arched eyebrow. The license plate was a vanity—TSR TROUT.

"TSR?"

"Trouser Trout," Sean said. "It's Internet shorthand."

"Everybody's a comedian," the manager said.

———

Sean hadn't been to Ettinger's office at Law and Justice since the calendar page on her wall had twice flipped, the leopard on the acacia branch replaced by baboons replaced by a gaboon viper patterned like autumn leaves. He leaned over her shoulder and stared at the computer screen showing a map of Blackfeet country, searching in vain for Mitten Lake.

"This is useless," Martha said after a minute, and called down to the main office for someone to rustle up a travel plan map of the county. She'd take a large-scale paper map over a digital one anytime; screens were just too small to cram in the details.

They waited for the map in silence, Martha with her hands laced behind her head, Sean running his eyes around the room before settling on the snake.

"Gaboon vipers have the longest fangs of any snake in the world," he commented.

"Really?" Martha said. "I thought that title would go to one of your old girlfriends."

There was a knock at the door and a young woman entered, carrying the map. Martha said thank you and told her to send up Hunt-singer in fifteen minutes. She unrolled the rubber bands and spread the map on a light table, pinning the corners with chunks of petrified wood. She tapped a forefinger, naming the lakes as she found them on the map.

"Mitten, Dog Gun, that's an animal, Mission, Duck . . . Here we go, Minnie White Horse Lake."

"They could be at any of a couple dozen lakes," Sean said. "Fisher-men don't stay put."

"If that's what they're doing, fishing, then maybe there's nothing to worry about." She shook her head. "Still, I think it's worth a try if your buddy's game." She indicated her phone and Sean put through a call to the landline at Joseph's house. He picked up and Sean ex-plained the situation. He waited for Joseph to get a piece of paper to write on and repeated the lake names and the letters of the vanity plate.

"Now repeat what else I just told you," Sean said.

"I see if it's at the lake. I leave. I go to the next lake. I leave. I don't get out of the car unless I got to take a whiz."

"This is serious, Joseph." He hesitated. "Would the Karlson broth-ers know your car?"

"Yeah, they seen it. Everybody knows the Pinto. But you gotta four-wheel into those lakes. I been under the hood of Jerry's truck a bunch of times. He owes me. I could borrow it."

"Then take his truck. I don't think it's a good idea to drive anything they'd recognize."

"I got you covered. I'll get up there this afternoon."

"Call me either way and fill up the tank for Jerry. I'll see that you get reimbursed for your time, too."

"Now I'm like your sidekick, huh?"

"Joseph, this isn't—"

"I'm just messing with you."

Sean replaced the phone on the cradle, shrugged. "Worth a shot, I guess."

There was the expected knock and Martha told the pink-shaven Deputy Huntsinger to take a seat and tell her about the Karlson brothers and make it good.

"Oh, it's good," he said.

CHAPTER TWENTY-SEVEN

The Purple Panty Murder

Brady and Levi Karlson had been born into a rough-and-tumble logging family in Kelso, Washington, in the shadow of Mount St. Helens, the infamous volcano that claimed fifty-seven victims when it erupted in 1980. Their grandfather, Quincy Karlson, was included in the tally, albeit indirectly; he'd collapsed from a heart attack while shoveling two feet of ash off the roof of his carport. His son, the boys' father, also Quincy, called "Squint" for his hooded eyes, had died some twenty years later, while working as a chain setter for Weyerhaeuser. When a cable slipped, a log crushed his pelvis, and his last words to the feller who tried to comfort him were to tell Melissa he loved her and that she should remarry for the sake of their sons, who were five, and to never let them cut a tree as long as they lived.

The first part of the promise she kept, tying the knot with Augustine Castilanos, a timberlands baron whom she'd been rumored to have been having an affair with for years. The second part had gone by the wayside, as the boys had worked out of logging camps their summers off from high school, cutting pulp from hemlock stands on the western slopes of the Olympic Peninsula. The foreman of the camp hired girls to shake the bark off his crew—the prostitutes were known as Hoh River Hohs, as the camp was on the upper Hoh River—and Brady and Levi had lost what little innocence they may have had to high school dropouts and meth addicts from Hoquiam and Aberdeen.

One such young woman, Twyla Jane Curry, who called herself TJ

Spice, a stripper from Hoquiam with a half dozen arrests for solicitation, had been discovered by hunters about six miles from the lumber camp. Or what was found was what was left of her. Her body had been dug up from a shallow grave by a black bear, which the hunters shot as it stood over the remains. An autopsy found semen in the victim's vagina, though it was too degraded to provide DNA for comparison. That it was a homicide there was no doubt; the woman's skull had been caved in by a heavy piece of wood that had shed splinters into the wound. Proximity dictated that the half dozen workers at the camp were questioned, and three months after the murder Augustine Castilanos, who may have harbored reservations of his sons' involvement, reached into his pocket to place the boys in a military academy in Massachusetts, thus getting them away from the relatively short arm of the law's investigation. The fact was that the bear had generated more ink than the deceased. The woman's underclothes were revealed in a nearby pile of scat, a detail one of the hunters leaked to a reporter who had traveled from Olympia for his scoop; the headline in the *Olympian* read "The Purple Panty Murder."

At this point in the deputy's narrative, Ettinger, who had been sitting back with her hands cupped behind her head, leaned forward and fixed Huntsinger with skeptical eyes and an upside-down smile.

"I heard about this case," she said. "It came up when we had a grizzly bear unearth a couple bodies in the Madison Range. I seem to recall that it was solved."

"It was and it wasn't," Huntsinger said. "A bridge gnome copped to it, but he'd copped to other crimes where he admitted he was just looking for a way to get indoors for the winter."

"A bum who sleeps under the overpasses cops to murder? If he wanted a pass to the pen, wouldn't you think he'd pick a lesser crime?"

"I know. It doesn't compute, but boozers like him, they can piss on a match and start a forest fire. We're talking zombie IQ here."

"Did he retract his confession?"

"No, but he said he committed the murder with a two-by-four, and the slivers of wood found inside the skull were red alder. Two-by-fours are made from all kinds of spruce and pine, but not from alder. So the thinking is he made it up. Anyway, they cut him loose."

"And this is all you have, those boys being a few miles from a murder scene four years ago?"

"Well, they were questioned about a roof fire in Kelso."

"Why was that?"

"It was the home of the quarterback of the football team, who had beaten out Brady Karlson for the position."

"Arrested?"

"No. Nobody talked and there wasn't sufficient evidence."

"Anything else?"

"Not really. Fighting with players from a rival team. Game violation for jacklighting deer. Your usual country bumpkin bullshit."

"Okay, what about after they left town?"

"I was getting to that." Huntsinger rifled through his papers. He said that enrollment records showed they had indeed attended the military academy, where their grades were good and their lacrosse, which they'd only played at a club level in Washington, head-turning. At least it turned the head of the coach of the Dartmouth team far enough around to recruit them.

"From Gomers to Ivy League gods," Martha commented.

Huntsinger nodded. "Their names popped up in the school newspaper a few times. Brady made all Ivy League second team as a sophomore. Coverpoint position, whatever that is."

"No black marks? Panty raids? Sneaking into a girls' dorm after midnight?"

"The only thing they got into trouble for was throwing snowballs."

He said a student had suffered a detached retina during the "On the Green Snowball Fight," an annual event that happens on the night of the first snowfall. The Karlson twins were among several boys mentioned in the incident. For which the coach benched them for the season opener against Sacred Heart. After which they had kept their heads down for the remainder of their junior year. Which brought them up to the summer and the present time.

Huntsinger spread his thick fingers across his too-many-sweet-buns stomach. He shrugged. "That's all I found. But you got to admit, a bear is sort of quirky."

Martha thanked him and dismissed him. "He's going to shrug himself right out of a job," she said after the door had shut behind him. "We're missing something here, aren't we?" She propped her chin on her fist.

Stranahan did the same on the other side of the desk.

"Don't," Martha said.

"Mary Ellen," Sean said.

"Mary Ellen?" Her jaw bobbed on her fist.

Sean nodded. "John Running Boy overheard one of the brothers say something about a Mary Ellen. Something about Brady getting Levi out of trouble—Remember what happened with Mary Ellen."

"Ellen as a last name?"

"Or middle, I don't know. But what if 'Mary Ellen' happened sometime during their three years at Dartmouth? She could be a student."

Martha tapped keys on her computer.

Sean walked around the desk to look over her shoulder. *Mary Ellen Dartmouth,* she had Googled. Nothing popped up worth tapping a key.

"Eliminate her name. Add missing and murder."

She did. Nothing.

"Eliminate Dartmouth and put in Vermont and New Hampshire," Sean said.

"Quit your backstreet driving." But she typed it in and shook her head as the possibilities popped up. "I all but fired Hunt in my head and now I need him. He can work the Web as well as anyone in the department." She scrolled down the list of sites and stopped.

UMass Women's Crew Team
Member Found Dead

The article, from the *Hanover Evening Sun,* was dated November 5 of the Karlsons' junior year, some eight months previously.

Martha read aloud:

> "Mary Ellis, a member of the UMass Minutewomen's crew team who was reported missing November 2nd after participating in the Green Monster Invitational in Hanover, was found dead yesterday in the Connecticut River. Chief Deputy John Hirvela of the Hanover County Sheriff's Department said Ellis's body was reported by a man walking his dog in the early morning hours on the New Hampshire bank of the river, about a mile east of the starting line for Saturday's race. Hirvela said an autopsy is pending and would not confirm a cause of death.
>
> "Ellis, 20, of Pittsfield, Massachusetts, and a junior at UMass, was a sweep rower in the Minutewomen's eight crew 'A' boat entered in Saturday's race . . ."

Martha continued moving her mouth, reading the rest of the article in silence. She read a follow-up story biting her lower lip and sat back in her chair.

"If Mary Ellen turns out to be this Mary Ellis, it gets interestinger, I give you that," she said.

"It doesn't say who was at the party," Sean said. The follow-up had reported that Ellis was last seen at an after-race party of fifty or more people on the Green at the Dartmouth campus, but had not returned to her room at the Courtyard Marriott, where the team was overnighting. Her roommate said that Mary was having a "good time" when she'd seen her around nine p.m., that Mary said she could get a ride and had a key to the room. She didn't report Mary as missing until the team gathered in the lobby after breakfast to board the bus. She had assumed Mary had spent the night elsewhere and didn't want to get her in trouble for missing curfew. No, she hadn't remembered anyone from the party with whom Mary had been fraternizing.

Martha looked up the Hanover County sheriff's office and made a direct call and asked to speak with Chief Deputy Hirvela. And got him, mouthing "small miracles" to Sean, who had sat back in his chair. She spoke into the phone, listened, scribbled notes.

Stranahan looked at the walls until she hung up. "Well?"

"Open unsolved. She drowned. They're working it on the theory that she was raped and then jumped into the river and drowned, or that after the rape someone forced her head under the water. Or she was killed before the rape. They can't rule that out. Just when you think you've found something that men aren't capable of, it turns out they are. That's a working assumption I've found useful in this occupation."

She shook her head. "Tears in the vaginal walls pointed to forcible sex, but the rapist was apparently wearing a raincoat because no semen was recovered. Hirvela said there were bruises on her arms and throat consistent with being held down or pinned against the ground. Forty-seven people who were on the Green the evening of the party were questioned. Levi Karlson was among them, but so were a lot of other athletes. Karlson admitted speaking to Ellis in a group setting, but said he left the party alone at ten o'clock, and she was seen after that by other people."

"Did anything point to him?"

"No, but Hirvela spoke to a lot of people that night and Karlson was one of two or three that stuck out. Nothing solid, just a vibe. But enough to make him contact Levi's roommate to verify the story that he'd gone home at ten p.m. Guess who the roommate was?"

"His brother."

"You got it. But there was nothing to tie him to the girl, and Hirvela only spoke to him the one time."

"Mary Ellen was the name John Running Boy remembered."

"So you said." Martha's eyebrows ran together. "Ellis was the number four seat on the boat. Hirvela spoke to the crew coach, who said the numbers three through six seats are the boiler room, where the most powerful sweep rowers sit. Mary Ellis was five ten, a hundred fifty pounds. The coach told Hirvela she was the strongest woman on the team, that she could choke out an Adirondack bear if she got an arm around its neck. Not an easy person to rape unless she was drunk or somebody slipped her a roofie, but the toxicology report was negative. She'd had a few beers, but over the course of the evening. She was sober enough to resist."

"They were two strong boys. Psychopaths can treat something like this as a challenge. They're not after sexual gratification so much as prevailing in the challenge."

"I'm aware of the theory." Martha's expression made it clear it wasn't necessarily hers. "You do realize, Sean, that this is circumstantial. At best. There isn't any direct evidence linking them to either the death of the prostitute, the crew woman, or, for that matter, Theodore Thackery."

"Don't forget Gary Hixon," Sean said. "The fact that someone died at the Buffalo Jump seems to have got lost in the shuffle."

"Or him. All this"—she gathered invisible wool from the air by wiggling her fingers—"it's just speculating with some words overheard by a fugitive from the law who refuses to give a statement saying he overheard the words."

"They're skaters," Sean said. "They've been protected by money and influence their whole lives."

"Which gets us nowhere. Me, anyway. I have no clout where they've gone. But I promise you, I will put them through the interview process when they come back to the valley."

"Let's just hope nothing happens in the meantime," Sean said. "I mean to anyone else."

He watched as Martha's fingers went to her carotid and subconsciously brought his own to scratch at the ermine tail wound in his pocket. And felt a slight creeping sensation at the back of his neck. Joseph had worn the tail at his mother's insistence. She had woven it into his hair so that it would keep him safe, repel the spirits. But the tail's magic wasn't doing him any good in Sean's pocket, and less than an hour before, Sean had deliberately asked Joseph to check on the whereabouts of two men who might have reason to look suspiciously on his presence.

"I can't send him out there," he said, and before Martha could respond, he had punched the recall on his phone.

"Hello?" It was Joseph's mother.

"Hello, Darleen. This is Sean. Is Joseph around?"

"No, he went out somewhere with Jerry."

"Is Jerry's truck still on the street." Joseph had said that Jerry lived practically next door.

"Hold on." She was back. "No, it's gone."

"You said *with* Jerry. Not just borrowing his truck."

"He said he was going fishing with Jerry. I don't know where."

At least he wasn't alone. But that was small comfort.

"Please have him call me as soon as he gets back."

She said she would, and told Sean that it was good to hear his voice, that she was looking forward to cooking for him again, that she'd make her venison stew with parsnips and juniper berries. He flipped the phone shut, feeling like he'd betrayed her family, that she would turn her head the other way seeing him walking down the street if she'd known what he'd done.

"If you feel like you have to go up there, I won't stand in your way," Martha said. "But be careful." She shook her head. "I sound like my mother."

"I can't go without a car."

"Yeah, you keep bumming rides off women. I'll have somebody drive you back to your place."

"Can you spare Huntsinger for that? He might remember something else useful."

"I doubt it, but sure. See if you can get anything more than a shrug out of him."

Sean stood, hesitated.

"What now?"

"Money. I'm not working for Ida anymore and I've been turning away guide days that pay the bills."

"You're on the county dole until I say you aren't. I thought I'd told you that." She pushed back her chair. "You're what I call a Montana Renaissance man. You have about five different jobs and still you have to stick a hose down a gas tank to siphon up enough fuel to get to the store."

"That's the fate of the artist," Sean said.

"No, what it is, is pathetic. You own land, you've poured a foundation for a house, but three years later you're still living in a tipi and showering at your studio." Her voice softened. "Look, Sean, I care about you. I *worry* about you."

"Not enough to leave the light on."

"This isn't about us. It's about you."

"Just ring down for Hunt."

"Sure. Whatever you say."

When he shut the door, her shoulders fell. She looked at the ceiling and let out a long breath. He was halfway down the hall when she caught up to him and dragged him into a stairwell. "Hold me," she said. "Don't say anything, just hold me."

"No kiss?"

"Shut up." She kissed him.

"I'm sorry," Sean said.

"Sorry for what, being you? I'm sorry for being me every day."

She tucked her chin into the hollow of his shoulder. "Don't you dare die on me. Don't you dare do anything stupid up there and die on me."

"I'm the one with the ermine tail, Martha."

She pushed him back and fingered the tail out of his pocket. She didn't believe in magic. She didn't believe in fate, either. Or coincidence. And God was just the wish to never die. But she believed in the wisdom of the past, and the Indians had been here long before her people. She kissed the black tip and tucked the tail back into his pocket and buttoned the flap.

"Get out of here," she said.

CHAPTER TWENTY-EIGHT

Talking Dirty

Martha had been right. Huntsinger had given Sean little more to chew on before dropping him at the tipi, although at Sean's probing he'd revisited a point he'd mentioned earlier, about the semen found inside the body of the prostitute.

"You said it was too degraded for a DNA match with the perpetrator of the crime," Sean said.

Huntsinger said that's what he'd been told.

How long did it typically take for that to happen?

The deputy had shrugged. It wasn't his area of expertise.

It was Georgeanne Wilkerson's area of expertise, however, and the newly constructed crime lab that shared quarters with the Fish, Wildlife, and Parks lab in a metal Quonset hut on the outskirts of Bridger was Sean's first stop after fueling the Land Cruiser. Wilkerson had returned from the game ranger's cabin in the valley a couple hours before and met him in the lot, where she was retrieving her lunchbox from her truck.

"You can't stay away from me," she told him. To which he replied, "I want to talk about semen."

"You've found the right girl," she said.

He sketched in the reason for his visit as they entered the lab and she ushered him into her office, such as it was, a metal desk against a curved interior wall with one personal touch, a framed photograph of Wilkerson standing on a rocky beach with a bearded man about twice her size, both wearing wetsuits, a sea kayak pulled up on shore.

"That was in the Aleutians," she said. "Last August."

"Your paramour?"

"My fiancé. We're getting married next month at his parents' ranch up the Boulder." She looked down, embarrassed. "It's just family. I couldn't invite all the people I work with."

"I understand. Congratulations."

"Thanks." She took a laboratory coat from a plastic garment bag hanging from a peg on the wall and shrugged into it. "So the man wants to know about semen," she said.

"I do, but did you find anything interesting this morning?"

"Yes, but you first. Why do you want to know about jizz?"

He explained the circumstances of the prostitute's murder in Washington. Wilkerson's eyes widened behind her glasses at the mention of the bear.

"That's way cool," she said. "That's a case I'd liked to have worked on." She paused. "Semen's all over the map when you're talking DNA. I mean, nothing could be more important than semen carrying sperm and sperm carrying DNA, right? The future of the species depends on it. But when the all-knower made the human body, he made a few mistakes, especially with reproduction. Here you've got the clitoris where it can't receive direct stimulation during coitus— that's what makes you figure the creator had to be a man. Then, a lot of females have an allergic reaction to their mate's semen. I mean, come on. We're the only mammal allergic to our own reproductive juices? Really? And finally, when the semen actually does get where it can do some good, the sperm stop swimming and die. From a forensic perspective, the problem with semen is it degrades quickest in a warm, moist environment like the vagina, which of course is exactly where you'd want it to persist. The ability to identify DNA from semen deposited in the vagina drops like a stone after about twelve hours, and after forty-eight hours you typically can't build a useful profile to compare with the genetic markers of a suspected donor."

Sean wanted to ask a question, but Wilkerson was warming to her subject.

"Now, dried semen," she said, "that's tougher stuff. It retains identifiable DNA practically forever. I mean, if you could find semen on the petrified skin of a Tyrannosaurus, you could build yourself a Tyrannosaurus. That's why when I go to a scene, I'm looking for stains on clothing or a film of semen dried on the thighs or caught in pubic hair, because that stuff's gold. And it's a pet peeve of mine that so many women are waxing off their hair, because the semen stays in hair long after it's washed away or rubbed off the skin. I'm like, 'Sister, grow your 'fro. Give me a comb and I'll send him to Rome'—Rome like being where men have sex with each other."

"I get it. But it's still really dumb, right, to rape without a condom?"

"Major league. Serial rapists learn to put a papa-stopper on it if they don't want to get caught. You mentioned two victims. I'm guessing the second one there isn't any semen, so you're wondering if it's a different MO, does that mean it's not the same perp?"

Sean nodded. "I don't want to delude myself into thinking there's a connection between these two if there isn't."

"So these Karlson brothers, I take it they were proximate to this crime as well as the Hoh River murder?" He explained the circumstances of the second death.

Wilkerson nodded. "I wouldn't put too much emphasis on semen versus no semen. What we're finding out about rape is that for a significant percentage of the perps, it isn't a once-or-twice deal. Serials are the norm, not the exception, and there's a learning curve. The pro in Washington might have been their first and they didn't start covering it up until they went Ivy League."

She cocked her head. "You want to know what I think?"

"Yes."

"I think you're on the right track. Come here, I want to show you something. I really didn't find much of interest after you and Martha left, but I did have time to work up a fingerprint analysis for the suicide note."

"And . . ."

"And now I'm not so sure as I was."

She retrieved an acid-free plastic sheath from a filing cabinet. "It can be hard lifting latents from copy paper, but disulfur dinitride usually does the trick. See here, the purple partial at the very edge? This ridge pattern is what you'd find on the edge of the thumb, like you were barely pinching the paper between the thumb and your forefinger. It's too incomplete to provide enough points of similarity to prove a match, but it's complete enough to eliminate whose fingerprint it isn't. And it isn't Thackery's. These"—she tapped a half dozen other prints, partials and completes exposed by the disulfur dinitride—"*are* Thackery's."

"So that means the note's genuine."

She nodded. "The signature at the bottom matches others I found on business correspondence in his study. That, together with the prints on the paper, are, in my opinion, conclusive proof of originality."

"Yet someone besides Thackery handled the note."

"Well, someone handled the paper. I can't absolutely rule out that the dissimilar print was made before the note was written." She peered up at him with her magnified eyes.

"So what do you make of it, Gigi?"

"Well, if you read the note, it says that there are brothers involved in the buffalo jump. At the same time it says that Gary Hixon's death was accidental. So what if they, Brady and Levi, went up to the cabin to off Thackery. But they were too late and he'd already killed himself. They see a suicide note that places brothers at the scene. That could mean people in a brotherhood, could mean this, could mean that, but it could mean them. At the same time, the note exonerates these brothers"—she scrolled quote marks with her fingers—"from culpability for the fatality. At least Thackery takes the blame."

"Puts them in a bind," Sean said.

Wilkerson nodded. "It makes them think. If they just leave it lying about, then maybe somebody with a badge comes knocking at the door. Who knows, there could have been people who saw them with

Thackery before the jump, and this would confirm their participation and put them at the scenes of two deaths. But if they destroy the note, there goes Thackery taking the blame. So they go about it half-assed. They put it where it might not be discovered for days or even weeks. That way, if the department comes up with evidence down the road that paints them as perps, they can tell somebody where to find the note, which is their get-out-of-jail pass. They can say that they hid it because they didn't want to be associated with the jump."

"They admit to the lesser crime."

"If running buffalo is a crime at all."

"It's complicated," Sean said, "but it fits. Gigi, I think you've missed your true calling."

"Nah." But she blushed anyway.

"So, does this mean that it was definitely suicide?"

"No, it could still have been murder and made to look that way. But if that was the case, Thackery had already written the note. They just beat him to the knockout punch."

Sean nodded. "I gotta run. Will you pass this on to Martha, all of it, including your deductions?"

"I can't guarantee she'll listen."

"I think you're wrong about that. Tell her I'm heading back up to the reservation."

"You're a man on a mission and here I thought all you wanted to do was talk dirty."

"Next time, I promise." He thanked her and congratulated her again on her engagement.

She smiled and frowned in the same breath. "It will be interesting. He can do biceps curls holding me like a barbell, but he can't stand the sight of blood."

"True love knows not logic nor lust, but the synchronized beating of hearts."

"Is that Shakespeare?"

"Sean Stranahan. When you live in a tipi with a dog, you think deep thoughts."

———

Deep thoughts took him from Bridger to Three Forks, from Three Forks to Helena, from Helena to Augusta, where Sean once more found himself stretching his back muscles where Joseph was born, this time at a little past four, with the Sun River living up to its name. He'd been in and out of cell range for the past five hours, mostly out, and had no way of knowing if Joseph had tried to contact him. He surprised himself by picking up a bar and made the call to Heart Butte. Joseph's mother didn't answer and that was just as well. If he'd got through and she asked why he kept calling, he wouldn't know what to say.

You're the closest to a white friend I ever had, Joseph had said, standing on the exact spot where Sean's shoes dented the damp gravel. Sean climbed back into the Land Cruiser and continued north, his face grim.

Clouds with a sickly yellowish tinge had been building to the west, and he drove under them and then into them, entering Heart Butte with raindrops staggering down the windshield. The brittle-whiskered cat meowed to be let in as he knocked on the door. The Pinto was parked on the street. No other car. No answer. He tried the knob. The door opened and the cat darted past him into the living room.

"Joseph?"

It was a small house. If he wasn't in the living area or kitchen, he was behind the closed door to his bedroom. Sean knocked on the door, a feeling like motion sickness in his belly.

"Joseph, you there?" Louder, reaching for the knob: "Joseph?"

"That you, Cuz?"

Sean took a deep breath and felt his ribs collapse as he let it out. "It's me. You had me scared to death."

"You pound on the door I'm taking a nap, you think I'm not scared?"

Sean entered the room. Joseph was dressed in boxers and a Daffy Duck T-shirt. He held a lever-action carbine at port arms and set it down onto the rumpled sheets on the bed.

"My grandfather's," he said, sheepishness in his voice. "See all the brass tacks in the stock? There's twenty-seven, one for every white settler *his* grandfather shot with it."

"Really?"

"Nah, he was just telling stories. Maybe one for every deer if he was lucky. I only got a few cartridges that came to me with the rifle, after he died. Must be about a hundred years old. They'd be like a dud firecracker now or blow up the rifle."

"You never shot it?"

"No, but I pointed it at a BFI who was threatening my mom with a Coke bottle, like about something she didn't know anything about, some grudge against her sister or something."

"BFI?"

"Big Fucking Indian."

"What happened?"

"He took it from me and slapped my face. I was, like, eight. That's the rez giving you an update, keeping it real, case you forget."

"You want me to make some coffee?"

"Sure, I'll get dressed."

He got around to it halfway through the first cup. He and Jerry had driven to the lakes on the list Sean had given him, and hadn't seen a black Highlander at any of them. The last lake they visited was Mitten, where a couple men were bait fishing, waiting for a flat to be inflated by an act of God, their words. They had seen two white men fishing the lake in a pontoon boat, and yes, they were driving a black SUV. The white guys fit Joseph's description, and the men said that the boys had helped them change their first flat before leaving. Then, like idiots—again their words—they had kept fishing as the spare deflated, instead of getting the hell out to the pavement. They gave Joseph a number to call so a friend could bring them another tire. The friend might not make it until tomorrow—did Joseph have any food? He had Spam and baked beans. He and Jerry ended up eating with the two guys, using the hood of Jerry's truck for a dinner table, that's why he was so late getting back.

Sean asked him if the brothers told the fishermen where they might be heading. Joseph said they hadn't.

"You're going up to the house, right? Where John is." The old cat had jumped into Joseph's lap and was rubbing its face against his knuckles. "You ever think that you call, somebody might answer?"

Sean dialed the landline number that Melvin Campbell had given him on his first trip to the house. It rang. No answering machine.

"I'm going with you," Joseph said.

"No way. I practically had a heart attack worrying about you on the drive. That reminds me." Sean placed the ermine tail on the table. "I'm not leaving this house until you take it."

Joseph picked it up. "But I'm still going," he said.

"Joseph." Making his tone reasonable and hating the implication. A grown-up talking to a child, or worse.

"What am I, your fucking Tonto?"

"No, it's that—"

"Ain't no 'no.' How long you known John? Like for an hour? I've know him ten years. Besides, you don't even have a gun. What are you going to do if those bad boys are there? Throw Whisker Bill here at them? He'd just lick their face."

CHAPTER TWENTY-NINE

Blood Brothers

If Harold Little Feather was with them, he'd have followed the clues like the teardrops of a blood trail. Invisible, perhaps, but there all the same and, Sean knew now, had been all along. He'd allowed himself to be sidetracked by Ida's past with Gary Hixon, had for a time even entertained the idea that Gary had told John about his relationship with Ida, or that John had deduced it, and that he had used the cover of the night to kill Hixon in a jealous rage. But John's recollection of finding Gary's body had matched Martha's down to the details of the rock that served as his headstone, and if he'd been intent on covering something up, Sean would have guessed that John would have maintained that he'd never seen Hixon at all after he fell off the cliff.

More important, to believe John was a killer meant that Sean had to overlook the basic humanity and honesty he'd read in the young man, to believe that was simply a front that he presented. Sean was better at reading people than putting together puzzles of deception, and he knew in his heart that John was no more a killer than Theodore Thackery was.

No, it was not John who had brought him here. Brady and Levi Karlson had laid down the trail before him, and the question wasn't what they would do when they caught up with John Running Boy, but whether Sean was too late to stop it. Buying a tribal license, hitting a few lakes, that was just a cover story if anyone questioned their presence on the reservation.

"You scared, bro?"

Joseph had been uncharacteristically quiet during the drive from Heart Butte.

"Nothing wrong with being afraid," Sean said. "Are you?"

"A little, I guess."

They parked at the dirt track turnoff and Sean raised his binoculars. The Highlander wasn't there. Nor were either of the cars that John and Ida had driven up from the Madison Valley.

"Campbell's truck is gone," Sean said. He had handed over the binoculars and noticed that Joseph's fingers were making them shake.

"You think he's in there?" Joseph said. "Maybe they're all there. Or—"

"Listen to me, Joseph. Are you listening?" Joseph's lower jaw was vibrating. "Stay here with the rig. If the good guys are home I'll give you a high sign. If you don't see me back on the porch in fifteen minutes, call your brother-in-law. No, make that thirty."

"I'm coming with you."

"Smarter if one person stays with the rig." Giving him the out.

"Yeah, man, it's just . . . I'm fuckin' shaking."

"Stay here. Here's the phone."

"Oh, man, I'm sorry." Joseph was squeezing his hands, his knuckles bled white.

"Nothing to be sorry about."

Relieved that he'd have only his own neck to protect, Sean unwrapped Joseph's grandfather's rifle from a blanket in the backseat. It was a Marlin Model 95, .32-20 caliber engraved on the half-octagonal barrel. Back at the house, Sean had tied a length of monofilament to a twist-on lead weight used to sink your fly leader—*Good thing I'm not a dry fly purist,* he'd thought—and knotted the other end around a piece of cloth, makeshifting a bore cleaner. He'd jacked open the lever, dropped the twist-on down the chamber, and pulled the monofilament out through the muzzle. The cloth came out black and he'd repeated the process until a cloth came out clean. The cartridges were of more concern, the brass so old it was mottled like lichen. He had only four, fed them into the magazine and chambered one. He raised the hammer block safety and started walking up the road, not glancing back at Joseph. He felt his hands sweating on the rifle.

Two hundred yards from the house, he left the road for a ribbon of tree cover. Walking on the exposed stones of a dried-up creek bed, he came up on the house from the back side, spotting Ida's Tercel, which was parked behind the detached garage. Three windows on the ground floor of the house, two on the second. No curtains and nothing to be done about the exposure he'd risk unless he waited until dark, which he had no intention of doing. He worked to the edge of the trees, felt himself breathing, then ran, bent over, across open ground until he reached the detached garage. He raised to his toes to peer in a smeared window and saw John Running Boy's Fairlane. So, maybe they were home and had simply been keeping the vehicles out of sight, as Sean had advised them to do. But if they were here, why hadn't they answered the phone? Another twenty yards to the house, down on hands and knees to stay under line of sight from the ground-floor windows. He put his ear to the crack around the back door. He heard no sounds from within and waited for his heart to come back into his chest. He wiped the sweat off his palms and brought the hammer to full cock.

The knob turned and the door pushed open. Sean had a sense of déjà vu. Little more than an hour ago, he'd felt a queasiness in his stomach entering Joseph's house. Not fear so much as anxiety, dread. A wanting to get it over with. He felt that again, felt his gut clenching like a fist. *Just breathe*, he told himself.

It took less than a minute to check the ground floor—living area, kitchen, the bathroom, well-thumbed *Reader's Digest*s and issues of *Indian Country News* in a rack. Melvin Campbell's bedroom door was closed, but the staircase to the second floor beckoned and he decided to clear the rooms up there first, not liking the possibility of someone being above him. He peered into the small bedroom where

Campbell kept his journals. John Running Boy's clothes were heaped on the bedcovers, but no John Running Boy. He checked the upstairs bathroom, then opened the door to the second bedroom and was surprised to see Ida's backpack zippered open. He would have expected them to be sharing a bed, but apparently not. He shook the thought from his mind, the distraction of any thought, and went back down the stairs.

He stopped at the bottom step.

On the floor of the living room was Campbell's gnarled walking stick, half protruding from under the sofa. Sean had never seen Campbell without that stick within reach of his hand. His eyes moved to the closed bedroom door. He came up to one side of it, reached out a hand to turn the knob, and pushed the door open with the muzzle of the rifle. Nothing happened and he edged to where he could peer inside. He could smell the tang of urine mixed with musty old man smell before he saw him.

Melvin Campbell was lying spread-eagled on the bed. He was dressed in the same black-and-white checked flannel shirt Sean had seen him wearing on his first visit. The shirt had been ripped open, the buttons torn from it and scattered across the floor. A bruise colored the exposed part of his sternum, and the left half of his face was swollen and purpled. A film of blood on his upper lip swelled into a half bubble, collapsed, then swelled again.

Sean felt for the pulse. A thread of metronome under his fingertips, the chest rising and falling with an irregular stutter.

He could hear the Land Cruiser coming up the drive, its harsh idle, then, jarring in the silence, the trill of a red-winged blackbird from the strip of dried watercourse.

"You here, Cuz?"

Joseph was standing inside the front door, holding Sean's metal fly rod case in a batter's crouch. Sean had completely forgotten about Joseph.

"Call 911," he said.

———

Courage, true courage and not the semblance that is the absence of fear, is an earned commodity. Sean knew a little about this, for he was one of those people who opened the door without taking stock of consequences, who failed to consult the barometer of fear that others rely on to give pause. True, he'd entered Campbell's house with a rifle in his hand, but he would have opened the door with nothing but the change in his pocket if it had come to that. Lack of discretion was the missing chip in his armor.

Joseph's fear was more rational. He'd been nearly paralyzed by it only a half hour before, and the courage it had taken to drive up when Sean had failed to signal, to expect the worst and walk through the door with only a rod case for protection, was a triumph of will, leaving Sean no doubt about who had been the truly brave man.

While they waited for the EMTs, Melvin Campbell reached out with a livered hand, clamping his fingers over Sean's forearm as he attempted to speak. But his voice was more a feathering of breath than an utterance, and it was Joseph who discerned that he was asking for paper. In belabored scrawl, the veined hand shaking, he had produced a single illegible word, then, after a pause, attempted a second word before his strength failed him and he dropped the pen. Campbell brought his forefinger to his face, which Sean had wiped with a washcloth although he was bleeding again from his nose, and then used the dripping finger to scrawl haphazard lines in blood, some straight, others jagged like lightning bolts, the lines tipped with triangles. He brought the hand back to his face and rubbed at the blood, then with an effort faced his palm, pushing it toward Sean.

"High five," Joseph said. "He's telling you he wants a high five."

Sean opened his hand and they pressed palms. The effort seemed to exhaust Campbell and he sank back in his bed. A minute of labored breathing later, he had reeled back into a state of unconsciousness.

"We need some fucking *Grey's Anatomy* here," Joseph said, his voice a half octave higher with panic.

"He's going to be all right, Joseph. His breathing is already stronger than when I found him. Look at this. What's he trying to say?"

Bllod Brot

—> <——> <——>—> <—>

"They look like fucking arrows, man, I don't know."

"What about the words? Could it be 'Bold'?

Joseph nodded. "Yeah, maybe."

"'Brot,'" Sean said. "'Brothers,' maybe." His mind leafed through pages of his memory, something sliding along the edge of thought. "'Blood Brothers,'" he said. "Not bold brothers, blood brothers. He couldn't write it so he used his hand. He made me his blood brother."

Sean hadn't told Joseph about the pact that John Running Boy had made with the Karlson twins.

"They were at the pishkun," Sean said. "They cut their hands and pressed them together. The arrows here mean the pishkun. The Indians finished off the buffalo with arrows. Melvin's telling us that's where they are."

"You mean on the Madison River?" Joseph said.

"No, here on the reservation. The buffalo jump on the Two Medicine, where they were when your brother-in-law told them to leave. Melvin's telling us that's where they've taken John and Ida."

CHAPTER THIRTY

Good Guy or Bad?

Forty miles down the road, following the directions on a map that Joseph had scribbled on the back of the bloody paper, Sean wasn't so sure. He'd waited until the ambulance pulled up before leaving, telling Joseph to stay with Campbell in case he regained consciousness and could better explain himself. Now he wondered if he should have done the same instead of blindly forging ahead through unfamiliar country, the day in decline, knowing neither what to expect nor what to do once he got there. "There" being vague enough, a series of cliffs that John Running Boy had said stretched at least several miles. Now Sean wished he'd questioned him more closely, for the only detail he could recall was that from the top they had seen a sacred mountain with an unpronounceable name. Which was next to meaningless. The horizon was jagged with mountains, their crags still stippled with snow.

Coming up a long rise in third, Sean pulled to the side before the road crested and climbed on foot the remaining distance to the top. He sat down and rested his elbows on his thighs to steady his binoculars. This was where Joseph's map had taken him, where the ink ended. Below him the sun glanced off bends of the Two Medicine as it snaked through an amphitheater of grasslands with bands of cliff showing chalk white, separating the green basin from the paler sage color of the upper elevations. Beyond and farther to the west, the sheer faces of the Front Range made a solid wall.

Sean mentally separated the field of view into quadrants bisected by the road, which arrowed into the distance before disappearing behind a peninsula of land. It took him ten minutes of glassing, but he found what he was looking for in the far northwest quadrant, a glint like a fishing spoon winking from the depths of a river. Above him the clouds looked solid enough for angels to dance on, casting enormous moving shadows so that he lost the glint almost as soon as he'd marked it. Three miles away, maybe four, near the base of an isolated butte. It was a car, although he couldn't eliminate a piece of old ranch machinery. In any case it was metallic, and as the only vehicles Sean had seen in twenty miles were two Depression-era trucks tipped into an outside bank of the Two Medicine River, some rancher's idea of erosion control, he thought there was a good chance it was the Highlander.

He fought the impulse to drive closer. This was no time to ride in with guns blazing. Especially not with a saddle rifle that hadn't earned a brass tack in close to a century. He walked back to the Land Cruiser and rummaged around, finding a length of parachute cord that he cut a few feet from to makeshift a carrying strap for the rifle. He put the rest of the cord into a belt pack, along with a liter of water and a tin of sardines, then remembered his bear spray and looked for it for five minutes before recalling that he'd lent it to Katie Sparrow in June, when she was riding horseback patrol in Yellowstone Park and wanted a backup.

He slipped the rifle over his shoulder, then abruptly shrugged it off and covered it with a blanket in the backseat. A vehicle was lifting a trail of dust as it crested the hill he'd just walked down from. It was a flatbed truck, its shot leaf springs shuddering on the washboard road surface. The driver's side window came down as the truck idled to a stop. The driver gave Sean a once-over and raised his eyes. He had a big impassive face alligatored by weather. He removed a hat with a feed store logo to reveal a two-toned forehead.

"Are you a good guy or a bad guy?" he said.

"I'm a good guy."

He nodded as if it was the answer he'd expected. "Reason I ask is back the way I came, I give a fella some water for his radiator and damned if he didn't say he was a good guy, too. That's about your month's quota, this part of the country."

"The rest are bad guys?"

"I wouldn't call *them* bad guys. But the outfit they work for, there ought to be a hunting season ever' day but Christmas. You got to respect a man's religion." The stone face cracked into a smile, though not an inclusive one that stretched as far as Stranahan.

"I was just going to take a hike," Sean said. "See if I can find any cairns where they used to have the buffalo jumps."

"That's the same thing the other guy told me, close enough. I'll tell you what I told him. This is tribal land and about three miles west it becomes Forest Service. I can't stop you from walking on either one, but I'll ask you not to disturb anything. Reason I'm here is I have a contract with the council to identify the pishkuns and place GPS waypoints on spots where I think we should dig. Last few years we've had two digs about four miles southwest of here, found buffalo bones compacted thirty foot deep. Deepest layers a thousand years old. Scapulas arranged like Stonehenge, even some bits of bone carved into toys for tiny tots."

He opened his glove compartment and handed Sean a carved turtle the size of a skipping stone.

"There's a war going on here, 'case you didn't know it. Been going on in the Badger Two Medicine for thirty years, ever since the BLM and Forest Service issued oil leases without consulting the tribal council. Inadequate EIS. Direct violation of Endangered Species Act. You look out from the top there, far as you can see there's evidence of traditional hunting. One campsite alone, six hundred tipi rings. Six hundred *and one*. Drive lines, piled-up rocks, go on for *miles*. These were some of the biggest mass-scale hunts for buffalo in North America. This is where you weep tears for your fathers, where they wept tears for their fathers and their fathers for their fathers. Sacred land. But the man wants to dig it, frack it, could give a shit. And all we got to fight them is our National Indian Congress and Pearl Jam, bunch of Indians looking like white men and half a dozen longhairs wishing they were Indians. Myself, I see a rig out here isn't part of the archaeological groups, it's either a rock climber or it's the man. Now, I can tell you aren't the man, just as I could with the other one. My guess is maybe you're looking for him, or you're looking for what he's looking for. Agitated young fella, didn't speak a single word of truth. And him an Indian, disrespecting his elder like that. You want to tell me? 'Cause I can't even guess."

"Was he driving a red truck with a grille like a cow catcher?"

His lack of answer was affirmation. "Like I said, you want to tell me?"

"If I told you, then I'd be making up a story. It's a private matter. There's a woman involved."

The man drummed the fingers of his left hand on the truck door, his big arm hanging outside the window. He slowly nodded. "That's the one thing you could have told me I'd believe."

He cocked his head. "Here's my problem. This young man, he had a shotgun in the rig. You, I come up over the top, I thought I might have seen you put a rifle back in your vehicle. If this is some cowboy-Indian shit, you're about a hundred and thirty years too late. You kill our people with pieces of paper now, been happening a long time."

"We're on the same side," Sean said.

"Same side of what?"

Sean didn't answer.

The man drummed his fingers. "Lester, this is none of your business," he said under his breath.

"I give you my word," Sean said.

"You and that boy, you straighten it out, I'm the ranch you passed about four miles back down the road. Stop by and we'll talk buffalo, won't even mention the female of the species. Put my mind to rest that you're all right. Otherwise I'll be up worrying about people I don't even know."

"I'll do that," Sean said, and turned back to his truck.

"Aren't you forgetting something?"

Sean felt the turtle in his hand and handed it back.

"You and that other fella, you're like young people in the city, all of you preoccupied, walking around with your head down, pecking at your phone. It's called 'not being present in the moment.'"

"That's what women can do to you," Sean said.

The stone face cracked again, the smile better this time, reaching farther.

CHAPTER THIRTY-ONE

Blood Never Dies

Trackless ground: sage, thornbushes, cheatgrass. In May you pick the ticks off and in June you watch out for snakes. In July, you look for snakes, too, but mostly you just sweat.

Sean had assumed that the glint was the Karlson brothers' Highlander, but that was before he'd talked to the rancher, who'd said that an Indian man had run into overheating problems two miles farther down the road. Sean had been tempted to drive down the road and see if Campbell's truck was there, but what if it wasn't, or what if it was and John Running Boy was gone? He'd have exposed himself to anyone looking down from the cliffs and lose the advantage of surprise. But then, what if the brothers were holding Ida captive and Sean sat on his hands and something happened to her? You could "what if" yourself into the ground over it.

Sean tied his bandana around his forehead to keep the salt out of his eyes and began to hike, four miles becoming three, becoming two. The land that had appeared flat from the vantage of the road was cut up by rain washes, and he kept to them as much as possible, trying to stay out of sight from anyone on top of the cliffs. When he judged that he was no more than a few hundred yards from the butte, he climbed on all fours to a pinnacle of rock and raised the binoculars. He could feel his stomach muscles crawling against the ground. It was all real now; the ten-power glasses brought the Highlander so close that he could practically make out the vanity plate. From this perspective it was clear that the SUV wasn't at the foot of the butte, but parked a quarter mile or so to the near side, where a two-track ended at a coulee carved by flooding. The butte wasn't as it had first appeared, either. It wasn't actually a butte, isolated from the plain around it, but rather a broad beavertail plateau that dropped away on three sides in a series of striated cliffs. The bands of sandstone no longer danced in the heat haze but dripped with gold, gone molten in the gunsight of the dropping sun.

This must have been where the bison were driven to their deaths a millennium ago, Sean thought, but how the hell had the hunters gained the top of the cliffs? Sean hated heights and the smile he forced was grim. He began to pull himself backwards with his toes, then, hunched over, scrabbled back to the base of the hill, out of sight from anyone on the cliffs.

He sat down with a stunted piñon tree for back support and picked prickly pear spines out of his knees. He ate his sardines and tried to get some rest, knowing it would be at least a couple of hours before darkness became his friend and he could move without fear of being discovered. But he had no more than shut his eyes before an image of Martha Ettinger wormed to the front of his mind. He felt her Chap-Sticked lips sliding along his in the stairwell, her arms drawing him close.

Don't you dare die on me. Don't you dare do anything stupid up there and die on me.

"I'll do my best," he said out loud.

A few feet away, a glittering thread of ants emerged from a crack in a rock outcropping to find refuge in another crack. Sean, watching the ants, heard a muffled cough and whirled round. John Running Boy held Melvin Campbell's shotgun at port arms, and for the second time in a week he felt his insides draw tight as the muzzle drew circles on his abdomen.

"What are you going to do," he said, "shoot the one friend out here you have?" The sensible, conversational tone he tried for made it to the word "shoot." His voice was thick and he had to clear his throat, but at least John lowered the muzzle of the shotgun.

"I was just trying to get your attention."

"You got it."

"What are you doing here? Did you follow me?"

"From where I'm standing, you're the one following me."

"I saw you, I thought maybe you were one of them."

"I found this place because Melvin Campbell told me where you'd gone."

"That's a lie. He's dead."

"He's in bad shape. He isn't dead. A friend of mine's at the hospital in Browning with him right now. Joseph Brings the Sun. You know him. He's the one who told me how to find this place."

Sean read the relief on John's face, replaced almost immediately by skepticism. "But they shot him," he said. "I heard the shot."

"He's alive, John. I need to know what we're up against. Are they up on the cliffs? Do they have Ida? You've got to tell me what happened."

Finally, John set down the shotgun and drew his legs under him, sitting cross-legged. "Do you have any water? Some guy gave me water for the radiator, but he said it was from a stock tank. I haven't had a drink since the house."

Sean handed him his water bottle.

———

It was the middle of the night and he hadn't heard them drive up. Later, the brothers would say that it was because they'd put the hybrid in EV mode, the battery operating as soundlessly as the wings of a moth. They called it the Death Star. But all John knew then was that the door to the room where Ida was sleeping had creaked open, and he'd heard her go down the stairs in her bare feet, presumably to the bathroom because the plumbing was broken on the second floor. Time had passed and he'd risen to find out why she hadn't returned.

She was sitting on the sofa beside Brady Karlson, who had a smile on his face that grew wider, like a dog welcoming home his master.

"Ssshh," he said, bringing his finger to his lips. John noticed he was wearing blue plastic gloves, like nurses do in a hospital. "I was just having a chat with this young woman. Please, won't you join us?"

It was when he beckoned to him that John had seen the pistol, Brady casually displaying it with a gloved forefinger inside the trigger guard. He said .380 ACP was a 'pissant' caliber, but if you put the barrel in someone's ear, the bullet would find the brain, no trouble at all. He'd demonstrated, pulling back Ida's hair from her ear. Ida was sitting very still with her knees pressed together and her hands clasped like prayer against her chest. Brady told John they needed to have a conversation, directed him to sit in the chair, and again urged him to speak quietly. He said that Levi was with the old man in the bedroom, watching him sleep, and that if he woke up they were going to have to kill him. In fact John needn't speak at all beyond answering a few questions, starting with why he'd disappeared the night of the buffalo jump.

John had lied, telling him that he had fallen over the cliff and stumbled around before passing out, and that when he awoke he was alone, that he'd called out for help and nobody had answered, and then after a long time he'd left and got back into his car.

And he hadn't seen or heard anything?

He'd heard the moans of the bison. If there were any other sounds, it had drowned them out.

"You didn't hear us searching for you? We were so worried."

No, he hadn't.

And what had he done after, for the next several days? John said he'd laid low because he'd heard that Gary Hixon was dead and that the police were looking for him. That's why he'd come up to the reservation, where they couldn't get to him.

"And who is your tasty treat?" Brady said. He'd rubbed the muzzle of the handgun in a caressing gesture, circling Ida's ear.

She was Melvin's niece, John said. She was visiting. He barely knew her.

"I'd like to get to know her," Brady had said. And again the smile.

Here's what would happen. They were all going to take a drive together, back to where they had become blood brothers, and they were
going to renew their vows. They were going to make another pact,
this one of silence. And if John swore the oath, Brady in return would
take his word, all hard feelings would be erased.

John had not been fooled into thinking that anything of the sort
would happen. He thought that the brothers would push him off the
cliff, or him and Ida both, maybe carving their hands first to make it
look like a suicide pact. His only choice was to fight, to somehow
overpower Brady and take the gun before his brother arrived, making
it two against one. He was trying to formulate a plan when Brady
jerked the barrel up and told John to walk outside onto the porch.
John pushed the screen door open and stepped out, Brady following
with the pistol at Ida's ear. As the door shut behind them, there was
a crashing sound from inside the house and John heard voices raised,
then a sickening thunk like an ax striking punky wood. Brady swiveled the upper part of his body toward the sound, and as the barrel
of the gun veered away from Ida, John leapt forward and tackled him
by the knees. They went careening off the porch into the yard, John
feeling a white heat as his forehead cracked against stones. He remembered climbing Brady's back like he was a tree, trying to work
his arm around the corded neck to choke him. Then he felt a jolt of
pain as his head jerked violently backwards, lights pulsing behind his
eyes. He must have passed out and when he came to he was spitting
blood.

"You almost killed him," he heard Brady say.

"I only hit him twice. He's just unconscious."

"Not the old man. Him. John. He doesn't die here, you idiot. Now
he's got blood all over him. That shit doesn't come out. What do I
always tell you? Come on, what?"

"Blood never dies."

"That's right. Blood never dies. And I got it on me, too. That's okay,
though. I have other clothes. We can dump the ones I'm wearing."

"What about the old man? You want me to—"

"Shut up. I need to think." John, still curled into a ball on the ground, could see Ida's feet dangling as Brady bear-hugged her from behind, lifting her off the ground.

"If you don't stop kicking, I'll make it so you can't breathe," Brady said. "Like this. You want this. Or maybe this." The feet stabbed out ineffectually and then went rigid. Brady released his grip and she folded up on the porch a few feet away from John. Brady handed his brother the gun. "Put it on them," he said. "Don't let him get any of his blood on her. I have to think about this."

John shut his eyes to the pain in his head and heard Brady's footfalls moving away, then coming back. His voice was low, calm. "This is the deal. You're going to take the gun and finish the old man. A shot to the body, not the head. I don't want any blood spatter on you."

"He's lying like he's on a cross."

"Then step onto a chair so you can shoot down and get the angle. But from the doorway. No closer."

"I don't want to. We studied that stuff, remember? If you don't get the spirits out of the body before it dies, they haunt you."

"What do you want us to do, burn sweetgrass and chant? The old man heard us talking, he was only pretending to be asleep. That's what you told me, so end of discussion. After you do him, go upstairs and bring down some clothes and shoes for pretty what's-her-name. Much as I like to see a girl in her panties, she needs to be dressed. What did you say your name was, darling? Some kind of star, wasn't it?"

He didn't receive an answer and Levi spelled the silence.

"Do I get clothes for him, too?"

"No. He stays here. Change of plan."

"You mean alive?"

"I mean alive."

"But why would we do that?"

"What did you just tell me? Think."

"Blood never dies?"

"That's right. He gets into the car, it's a fucking DNA-mobile. There's going to be nothing that ties him to this car, and there's going to be nothing that ties us to this house. That's why we wore the gloves. If we were never here, who do you think is going to go down for the old man's murder? John will, maybe her, too. They were living with him, maybe they wanted to rob him. Maybe it was some Indian voodoo shit. It went south and they split."

John had seen the shoe coming and braced his stomach muscles against the impact. "Where's he keep his money, John? We have to make it look good."

"He has a money clip under his mattress." He was telling the truth, seeing that there was a window now, that he might still have a chance to save Ida.

"He'll just go to the police," John heard Levi say.

"Levi, Levi, Levi." Brady's voice was weary. "Even you ought to be able to see why he won't do that. If he goes to the police, he might as well have shot her himself. Because if anyone shows up besides him, she'll be dead. And he knows that. See, we're giving him a chance to be the man on the horse. He's going to follow us to the buffalo jump, try to be the hero. We're going to give him until nightfall to show up. No, let's make it at least an hour before nightfall, so we can see that he's alone. You'll be alone, won't you, John?"

"I'll be alone," John said.

"See, Levi, he'll come alone."

"But he hardly knows her. He said—"

"He's in love with her. I know that's outside the realm of your emotional landscape, but trust me, he is. He doesn't care about his own life, only hers. We've found his weakness. But how will he get there? Not in that Motor City eggbeater. You need clearance—"

"I can drive the truck," John said.

"It will get there?"

"Melvin drives it into town. It's just slow."

Brady nodded. "Thank you, John. I think you've solved the problem. Slow is good. I don't want you trying to catch up, play road chicken. And it will look like you stole it. All right, then, that's settled. Just be sure you're there a couple hours before dark, say eight o'clock. You go about this on Indian time, you know what happens to Ida. Or maybe you don't. In fact, I don't think you'd want to know."

John heard Brady clapping, as if congratulating his brilliance.

"I do believe we have a plan. Now we're just waiting on you, Levi. Go on, get on with it."

"I've never done anything like this."

"There's a first time for everything, isn't that what they say?"

John felt a stinging sensation as blood from a cut forehead ran into his eyes. He shut them, and listened for the shot.

———

As John spoke, the shadow of the butte engulfed them. He kept glancing at the sun and picking distractedly at a scab on his elbow.

"I better get moving," he said. Then, sudden resignation in his voice: "Shit, they're going to kill her anyway."

"Don't think like that," Sean said.

"How you want me to think?"

"Positively. Did you write a note before you left the house, make any calls?"

"No, I was just worried about getting here in time. I should have. That was dumb."

"Forget about it. All that matters is now, what we do now."

"You can't come with me. If they see you with me, they'll kill her."

"They'll kill you if they see you carrying that Winchester. Did you think about that?"

"It's a Model 97, it breaks down. I can stuff it into the pack." He rotated the magazine tube and unscrewed the barrel, putting both halves in his pack, from which they protruded only a couple inches. "Did you think I'd bring a bow and arrow?"

"I guess I don't know my shotguns," Sean admitted. "Okay, I'll wait until dark to follow you. Your job is to stay alive until I get there. You'll have to use your wits, play off what you know about them, anything to get an edge."

"Brady's arrogant. He thinks he's right about everything."

"Then use that to your advantage. Keep in mind that this is a game to them. They were stupid letting you go like that. They will do something else stupid."

John nodded.

"You'll think of something," Sean said. "I have faith in you. Now how do I get to the top?"

"You walk around the cliffs until you get to the back side. There's a game trail to the top, but I don't know if you'll be able to find it in the dark."

"Won't they be looking to see if anyone followed you? Isn't that the logical place to watch?"

"Yeah, I guess."

"There's no other way up?"

"There's the pitons we practiced with. When we got run off, we left them in the rock. It's pretty scary, though, unless you have a rope."

Sean had a rope. He thought about it.

"I'd better get moving," Joseph said.

"What about weapons? Did you see anything besides the handgun?"

John shook his head. Sean saw him looking at the rifle with the brass tacks in the stock.

"That's Joseph's grandfather's gun, isn't it?" John said. "He told me his father shot white people with it, or maybe it was his grandfather who shot them. I told him it didn't look like it was good for anything but collecting spiders."

Sean smiled. When he'd jacked open the action back in Heart Butte, he'd had to remove a crust of fossilized insect larvae from the chamber before using the bore cleaner.

"So what's the plan?" John said.

"If I make it up there, I'll either shoot or do something else to cause a distraction. You have to know what you're going to do when that happens. If you can get the brothers into a position where I might be able to crawl close by sticking to some cover, do that. The moon's in its last quarter, so it will come up around midnight. I'll make a move sooner than later, to take advantage of the dark."

"Were you like a policeman before you became a detective?"

"Do you mean, 'Do I know what I'm talking about?'"

"Yeah."

"I'm a watercolor artist."

CHAPTER THIRTY-TWO

Bison Were Her Weakness

Martha Ettinger leaned against the stall divider.

"You're nothing but trouble," she said to the sleeping calf. "And here I thought cowboys were my weakness." She shook her head and muttered, "Humpff." Cowboys, a cattle auctioneer, an artist, a certain Native American man—they had all been her weakness at one time or another.

The word had come from the horse's mouth just before her quitting time, the horse's mouth being Judge Arthur Orenko Sanchez, who had told Rosco Needermire, who had called Martha with a sigh in his voice. Lucien Drake, acting as agent for the Department of Livestock, had petitioned Judge Sanchez for a bench warrant to confiscate the bison on Martha's property on three grounds: One, bison management was the domain of the Department of Livestock, not private individuals; two, Martha Ettinger was in possession of wildlife in violation of state statute; three, her property did not meet requirements for quarantine. That she had promised to keep the calf inside her barn until quarantine standards were met did not, Drake had argued, constitute cause for denial of the warrant. In fact, any delay in granting the warrant would put cattle in the area at risk for disease transferred by the bison.

The last had elicited a roll of the venerable judge's eyes. Everyone in Montana knew that there hadn't been a single instance of bison transferring brucellosis to cattle, and that a bull calf posed no risk whatsoever. Still, he was inclined to grant the warrant, but had told Drake he would need to rewrite it, clearing up the inherent contradiction of the first two grounds for cause. If bison were state-owned wildlife, what provision of law gave the DOL the right to manage them as livestock, rather than the Department of Fish, Wildlife, and Parks, which managed all other wildlife species? He needed that point clarified to his satisfaction.

According to Rosco, Sanchez also let Drake know that the warrant was not a high priority and he need not be bothered with it during nonbusiness hours. Drake had in fact presented Sanchez with his petition for warrant while his highness was on the first tee of the Riverside Country Club, and Sanchez had blamed his errant drive, a wicked slice that shattered a plastic hummingbird feeder on the clubhouse porch, on the intrusion.

That had been earlier today, late Monday afternoon, and Sanchez was taking the next two days off work due to trial cancellations. Which meant Martha had at least until Thursday before Drake pulled up with a horse trailer, which for all intents and purposes would serve as a hearse.

"Don't you dare let them take you and die on me," she said to the bison, only a slight revision of the words with which she'd admonished Sean, could it have only been this morning? She could shut her eyes and still feel the kiss. He'd kissed her back; at least he'd done her the courtesy of losing himself to the moment. What if he'd pulled away?

"Don't you dare do anything stupid up there like die on me," she said, her voice a harsh whisper.

She climbed over the divider and kissed the little bison on the top of his head, and, straightening up with his scent in her nostrils, not wiping her tears nor knowing for whom or for what they were shed, she walked back to her house as the moon drew the upper lip of a smile on the horizon.

CHAPTER THIRTY-THREE

At the Count of Three

Sean was a spider on the cliff wall when he heard the voices. Indistinct, carrying from somewhere on the plateau above him. He stopped climbing and threaded the parachute cord through the rope hole in the uppermost piton he could reach. He was no mountaineer and didn't really know what he was doing, but the cord around his waist, knotted off short to the piton, gave him some feeling of security. One thing about climbing at night, at least you couldn't see where you'd fall if you slipped, though at this point he was so far from the ground that the point of impact was an academic concern.

Sean tried to smear himself against the rock face. Again, he heard a murmur, a rising and ebbing of sound like a wave. Was it a voice? He tried to put it out of his mind and remember the basics of rock climbing he'd learned as part of his search-and-rescue training.

"Use your legs to climb, your hands and arms for balance," he recalled the instructor saying. "Nose over toes. Place your foot, shift your weight onto your foot, stand on your foot. Pick up your trailing foot only when there is no longer any weight on it. Repeat."

It wasn't so bad. There were lots of hand- and footholds. The real danger wasn't slipping but the stone crumbling. The sandstone was "bad rock" in climbing lingo, about as stable as peanut brittle.

Sean searched for another foothold. *Place, shift, stand. Repeat.* And the spider climbed the wall.

Two hours had passed since John left him with a handshake. Sean had watched his progress through his binoculars, his heart beating against the ground, trying to squeeze his ears shut to the sound of a shot. The last words John had spoken before walking into the open were that he'd see Sean on the top. "I think they'll let me live at least until I get there," he'd said.

And maybe they had. At least no shot had been fired as the figure worked around and out of sight, and Sean had waited for darkness, keeping his eyes on the sky as the sun caught on the horizon, bled while the twilight purpled, and then sank behind the mountains.

Only one piton to go now. He had a flash of panic as he lost a hand-hold and foothold at the same moment and swung out from the cliff face like a barn door, feeling the chasm yawning below him. Then, getting a grip mentally, he used all his strength to bring himself back to the wall. Another heaving effort and he'd drawn himself onto the ledge that formed the lip of the drop-off. He lay there, two hundred feet above the floor of the basin, feeling his chest rise and fall. For a time his mind couldn't seem to focus, his thoughts fleeting, like shards of broken glass. It took awhile before he came back into himself, felt the rough rock under his hands.

The plateau, what he could see of it in the darkness, was studded with outcropping of rock, sage clumps, and dwarf piñons. He crawled on hands and knees to the nearest tree, where he sheltered and took stock. He hadn't heard any sounds for the last part of the climb and could hear nothing beyond the cool sifting of the downdraft. The moon was still behind the shoulders of the mountains and the darkness was nearly complete, as the big moving clouds had covered up Mars and the few early stars. The only light was some distance up the plateau, a reddish-orange glow.

A lantern? The gleam of a campfire? Nights set in cold in the mountains, and this was no exception, though the rocks were still warm to the touch. If it was a fire, then all to the good. Staring at fire made you night blind and he'd be able to approach with less caution.

Stooping low, he zigged from one tree to another, closing the gap. The darkness made the fire—it was a fire, he was catching glimpses of flame intermittently—look farther away than it actually was. In the direction of the flames he heard a voice, the words indistinct. But the tone struck Sean as cordial, even friendly.

A few minutes later he'd reached the last tree that afforded cover. It was still a long sixty yards to the fire, a belly-to-ground sixty yards if he didn't want to be seen. He shrugged the rifle off his shoulder and stuck a twig down the barrel to make sure the bore hadn't clogged with dirt. He'd removed the cartridge from the chamber before climbing the cliff and been so relieved after gaining the top that he had forgot to rechamber it. Lever-action rifles have complicated mechanisms, making a sequence of metallic clicks as the lever is operated, and he thought about retreating a distance before reloading. As a fisherman, he knew how far noises carried across water at night, but was less sure how they carried across land. But the rifle was old and well worn, and he had oiled the lever back at Joseph's house, and so he took the chance, working it open and shut with his shirt stuffed over the action to muffle the sound. He adjusted the carrying cord to snug the rifle across his back and started to crawl.

Fifty yards, forty. Again Sean could hear voices, but they were low voices, still unintelligible.

He stopped, determined to think things through before crawling closer. His hands and forearms burned with a hundred tiny cuts. What stung the worst were the spines of prickly pear cactus that had pierced his gloves to imbed into his palms, yet this pain, too, paled in comparison to his heightened sensitivity to the sound and feeling of his breath. Sean had heard hunters talk about going inside themselves when the rifle was lifted and the sights aligned, finding that calm, detached center that was the place from which they killed. When the moment came, he would try to will himself into that impersonal darkness.

But he would have to get closer yet to be sure of the target, let alone to trust the accuracy of his aim. He took the rifle off his shoulder and held it in his right hand, using only the heel of that hand to crawl forward.

Thirty yards from the fire a saddle-shaped rock with a twist of tree root growing over it blocked his advance and he stopped in its scant cover. He could see the figures now, the slight silhouette of Ida, the men not so clearly differentiated. One sat next to Ida; the other two were side by side with their backs to Sean, on the near side of the fire.

"Are you sure you wouldn't like a s'more?"

Sean recognized Brady's voice, his supercilious mocking tone, the words taunting.

"I had a girlfriend, she liked a glass of wine before sex. Myself, I like a toke and a good s'more. Do I not like a good s'more, Levi?"

There was no answer.

"Levi is quite serious tonight, aren't you, dear brother? He gets this way. I used to think it was the moon, but I've seen him do things of a certain nature at all the lunar phases. Are you sure you don't want one, my dear? You with your contradictory eyes? Oh, come now. No need to cry. It will be over so quickly. Only an hour, even Levi can't go for more than an hour."

Sean saw Ida's silhouette begin to sway.

"Really, you disappoint. I thought you'd be a firebrand, a raging squaw about it. I—and I speak for my brother, do I not, Levi?—had hoped for a little more . . . spunk."

"Just kill us. Get it over with." It was John, his voice thick. He was the one sitting beside Ida. He seemed to be listing to one side. Sean wondered if he'd been beaten or his hands tied behind his back. Regardless, it *was* him, and if John was on the same side of the fire as Ida, then Sean was looking at the backs of the brothers. Brady was a little taller than Levi, but sitting down negated the difference. Who was who here? Who held the pistol that John had seen back at Melvin Campbell's house? And what about the shotgun John had carried in his backpack? They had obviously taken it from him, but where was it?

Again, Brady's voice: "Don't you want a turn before we play 'Blood Brother'? Surely, John, if one has to die, die satisfied, I say. Don't you agree, Levi?"

"I've got to pee," Sean heard Levi say. He was sure it was Levi, and as one of the two figures with his back to Sean stood up, Sean immediately saw that both hands were empty. That meant Brady must be in possession of the weapons, Brady, still sitting, whose broad back offered a target even a hundred-year-old rifle could find. But what if the bullet passed through him to strike John or Ida on the far side of the fire?

Move away. Move just a few inches away. Sean tried to squeeze the thought out, to emit it as a low-frequency wave, and then heard, in a mutter, "Goddamned smoke." And the figure shifted a foot to the right.

Sean rested the rifle on the saddle-shaped rock, avoiding the root, and lowered his cheek to the stock. He caught a slight blur of motion as the root slipped over the rock. Even before it disappeared, Sean knew what it was. A brief pause, the spit and crackle of the fire against the silence of the night, then the abrupt whir of a rattlesnake.

Sean saw Brady launch himself over the fire at Ida, heard the impact of bodies and then the harsh voice. A command. "Show yourself. Right now! Count of three and she dies. One, two—"

A shot sounded. Sean heard the bullet richochet off a rock ten or fifteen feet away. He froze. The rattlesnake's buzzing seemed to be coming from directly underneath his chest. It must have slid into a hole under the rock.

"Drop your weapon or I'll shoot again."

Sean willed himself silent. The whirring intensified as the snake shifted its position. Sean could feel it under him, their bodies separated by inches, the vibration in his heart.

"You got him all riled up. Careful now, those things bite." An edge of nervousness had crept into the voice, an uncertainty. Sean wondered if the man only had the cartridges remaining in the pistol, that that was why he held his fire.

He gripped the rifle, his thumb on the hammer. Instinct told him to stay perfectly still.

"Get back over here, little brother. Pick up the shotgun. It's on the ground where we were sitting. And turn on your goddamned flashlight so I know where you are."

Brady stood, dragging Ida up beside him. Sean could see the pistol in his left hand, raised to Ida's ear. The light of the flames licked up and down their bodies. Brady's right arm was around her, was squeezing her against his side, like he was presenting her at prom. *She's mine, isn't she pretty?*

"That Levi," Brady said, the bluster back in his voice, "he drinks too much beer."

Sean saw Ida sag against him, her head lolling. Her right hand, dangling at her side, looked translucent in the firelight, possessing a silver finger. Sean stared at the glint, something about it, thinking back.

"See," Brady said. He seemed to be speaking to Sean, or at least in his direction? "No fight at all. No *spunk*. No *juice*. It will be like fucking a bag of peanut shells."

He squeezed her more tightly, his right arm around her back, the hand cupping her breast. "Feels like you've got a natural pair, darling. I'm a breast man, myself. Levi, though, niceties of the flesh don't matter to him so much. He's got a one-track mind, don't you, Levi?" Shouting now. "Get over here and pick up the goddamned shotgun. I'll tell you what I told that bastard out there with the snake. You've got to the count of three or you don't get another s'more."

Then pouting, affecting indignation. "See what I have to put up with? It's like hunting with a dog who doesn't come when you blow the whistle."

At the periphery of his vision, Sean saw the shape of Levi Karlson extract itself from the darkness. He switched on a flashlight , its sudden beam illuminating his brother standing beside Ida. Sean saw the silver finger in her hand reflect in the firelight.

"One, two . . . two and a half."

Sean saw Brady turn his head toward his brother, and in that moment Ida's right hand jerked upward, trailing a glitter like a shooting star. Sean heard Brady cough.

Ida's fist was to his throat and he coughed, wetly. The pistol fell as he reached both hands to his throat. She was now supporting him, and as she pulled away he looked around, as if he was seeking a place to sit. He sat down. His hands scrabbled at his throat, the blade black with blood as he drew it out. He looked at it, the knife that Sean had first seen when Ida had stuck the point into his desktop.

"Brady," his brother said. "Brady, are you all right?"

Sean reached for the flashlight in his pants pocket and swiveled the barrel, turning it on, keeping its beam covered with his hand.

"Goddamn you!" Levi shouted in Sean's direction, his voice hysterical and wild.

Sean threw the flashlight to his right, its beam winking bright, pulsing as it turned over before sparking against the ground. He saw Levi grab at the ground and come up with the shotgun, heard its explosion, and in the vacuum of its echo a scream like a banshee wail, inhuman, piercing.

Sean ran toward the fire, the rifle in his hand but afraid to fire for fear of hitting Ida. He fully expected his charge to be met with another blast from the shotgun. But there were only Levi's sobbing wails, and Sean found the man on his knees, bent over, clamping his hands tightly. Firelight glinted off the shotgun lying on the ground a few feet away.

Ida had the handgun Brady had dropped and was holding it out toward Levi, her arm shaking.

"Don't." Sean opened her fingers, feeling the tremor of muscles in her forearm. He took the pistol and held it on Levi as the man staggered to his feet and moved closer to the fire, where his brother lay curled on his side. Levi pulled him to a sitting position and knelt beside him, his cheeks glistening in the light. Brady's eyes were swimming as the blood pulsed from his neck, and Levi shadowed over him with his arms wide, the way Sean had seen hawks mantle over a kill, spreading their wings to hide it from eagles.

Sean turned his attention back to Ida, who had picked up the blade where it had fallen from Brady's fingers. "It's to cut the cord," she said. "They've got John all tied up with baling twine." Her voice was steady. She walked toward the shadow of John Running Boy. "You listen to me, John," Sean heard her say. "I don't want you trying to stand up. Once I cut you loose, you lie there and we'll figure out what's wrong. No, don't try to speak." A pause. "You're going to be fine."

Sean removed the parachute cord from his belt pack. Levi looked up at him, the flames of the fire dancing in his pupils. The words he was speaking were gibberish. The only word Sean recognized was 'Papa-san.'

"Papa-san isn't here," Sean said. "Lie down. Put your hands behind your back."

Levi was Sean's size, younger, stronger, and had nearly killed Melvin Campbell with his fists only a few hours before. But he slowly relinquished his hold on his brother, whose eyes were unseeing now, and let him slip to the ground. He lay down beside him and brought his arms behind his back.

At first, Sean thought the blood on Levi's hands was from his brother, then he saw where two fingers were missing. Sean looked over at the shotgun, which had burst apart where the action met the back of the barrel. It had exploded when Levi pulled the trigger, the hot metal shearing off his fingers. Sean realized that if the gun had fired without exploding, he would probably be dead now.

He called Ida over and had her cover him with the handgun while he tied Levi up. He had never tied anyone up before, but forty feet of paracord did the job, even if the only knots he knew were fisherman's knots.

He sat back. He felt lightheaded but strangely laden, too, as the adrenaline began to flush out of his system and an ache settled into his bones. He became aware of the whirring of the rattlesnake and wondered if it had been rattling all along and he'd blanked it out. It made a white noise behind Ida's voice, which rose and fell, telling John it was all okay now, her words a mantra. It rattled off and on for a time after she stopped talking and sat cradling John's head in her lap. Then there were just the odd sparks snapping out of the fire.

CHAPTER THIRTY-FOUR

The Girl Who Couldn't Ice Skate

At the Blackfeet Community Hospital in Browning, Sean found Joseph asleep in the ICU waiting room, his head lolled back, breathing with his mouth open.

Sean stirred him awake, briefly told him what had happened, and asked about Melvin Campbell's condition. Joseph said he was going to make it, that the doctors had been able to relieve the pressure on his brain caused by the hematoma.

"They took like a Black and Decker to his skull," he told Sean.

"Wasn't he shot?" Sean said.

"No, man, it was the blow." He made a fist. "But I found a hole in the headboard that looked like a bullet hole. I don't see how anybody could have missed, though. It's a tiny room."

"I don't think anybody missed." Sean told him what John had said about Brady ordering his brother to shoot the old man and Levi hesitating because he was afraid of spirits.

"A white guy misses on purpose because of ghosts? On a rez? That's like irony or something, huh?"

"Something like that," Sean said. He was thinking down the road, as he had been since they'd marched Levi Karlson down from the cliffs. It had taken them a long hour to reach the Highlander, because with his hands tied behind his back, Levi kept falling, and John Running Boy needed Ida's support. The baling twine had cut off the circulation below his ankles for so long that he had to hobble, his feet feeling like blocks of wood as they struck the earth.

The rancher who had promised Sean a conversation about buffalo was not too pleased with the one they had on his porch about a dead man and a knife. That was an understatement. But he made the call to the tribal police, and it was in his living room that Joseph's brother-in-law and another officer named Laboeuff had taken their statements, after which they had taken Levi Karlson into custody. How long he'd stay in custody was the question Sean turned over.

To start with there was a jurisdiction issue. Levi had committed battery on Melvin Campbell and abetted in the kidnapping of Ida Evening Star on tribal land, but the plateau above the cliffs where he was apprehended straddled the border between the reservation and the Lewis and Clark National Forest.

Another problem was that the only eyewitness to the assault charge was the victim, who was lying in a barbiturate-induced coma to prevent his brain from swelling. And what else really did they have on Levi Karlson? Kidnapping? That was the word of a Blackfeet Indian who was avoiding state extradition, along with a private detective who had no standing on the reservation, and a quarter-white Chippewa Cree woman who waved a tail for a living. Against their word was an Ivy League lacrosse player in good standing with the law, whose father owned enough pulp timber to print the *Times of India*. Sean's pessimism had been ingrained by the master, Martha Ettinger, who had seen too many "assholes," her blanket description for nearly all criminals—"training wheel assholes" or "TWAs" encompassing the rest—walk.

Sean reached her at four in the morning, after the doctor on night shift upgraded Campbell's condition from critical but stable to serious.

"Is he conscious?" Martha asked.

"They took him off the coma drugs, but I don't think they'll let anyone talk to him for a few more hours. And it happened at night. He might not be able to identify his attacker even when he comes out of it."

"And you're calling me why?"

"For advice. Joseph's brother-in-law seems to be the one in charge, but he's not being very forthcoming about the situation. All I get is what I get from Joseph."

"The sit . . . u . . . a . . . tion," Martha said, emphasizing each sylla-ble, "is there's going to be an investigation. If they run their ship like we run ours, they have forty-eight hours to charge him with a crime or they have to cut him loose; that depends on the investigation and if he cops. Has he been interviewed?"

"He gave a statement after the doctors worked on his hand, but not much of one. I don't think he admitted to a damn thing. Joseph says he used his phone call to call his dad, who sent a lawyer out from Seattle. He'll be here tomorrow, I mean today. Four, five hours from now."

"So he's not cooperating. Tell you what. Stay in cell range and I'll get back to you. I've got no idea what protocol they follow up there as to lawyer visits, detention policy, any of it. I'll talk to Harold. He'll at least know a good Indian lawyer. You might need one."

Sean couldn't help wondering if talking to Harold was just waking him up from the other side of the bed.

"Bet he's pissed at me, huh?"

"I think Harold's mood is the least of your problems. Papa-san's lawyer is going to try to paint the three amigos as the bad guys, you can bet the farm on it. All of you gave statements, right?"

"We did. I just told John and Ida to tell the truth."

"And the truth shall set you free? Keep dreaming. But for your sake, I hope that's true."

———

Sean had gone outside to talk, had wandered under the stars a ways, and turned around to see John and Ida sitting on a bench near the emergency room entrance. John was lying on his back while Ida mas-saged his feet. Sean sat down on the grass and asked how John's an-kles were doing.

"They said another hour and I'd have lost my feet," John said.

"Levi hit him in the chest pretty hard, so they were worried about his heart swelling, but they don't think there's any internal bleeding," Ida said.

"What happened before I got there?"

"You mean, where did they jump me?"

Sean nodded.

"Brady had his gun on me before I got to the top. I was just going to put the shotgun together when he got the drop. He told me to hand over the pack and then got all mad because he couldn't figure out how to assemble the gun. He took the shells out and told me if I didn't put it together for him, he'd have Levi do things to Ida. It was dark enough that he couldn't see my hands, so I dropped the buttstock on purpose and grabbed a stone off the ground when I picked it up. I wedged it up into the barrel before I attached the action. I figured if he shot it, the stone would at least throw off the shot. But I didn't really think it was going to blow up."

"What happened after Brady took it from you?"

"He marched me over to the fire and Levi hit me a few times. When he hits you, it's like you can't breathe. It's like he's a grizzly bear or something, gets this rage in his eyes. But Brady was the scary one. He talked like there was an invisible person beside him. He scared the hell out of me."

"Well, your stone worked," Sean said. "It saved my ass."

"Yeah, maybe, but if it wasn't for Ida we'd all be dead. She only acted like she was afraid. Tell him what you told me."

Ida pulled at a cigarette and looked off into the night.

"I'll tell him," John said. "Her mother knew this story about Indians kidnapping a white girl to make her a slave. It was in a magazine."

"She wasn't a slave," Ida said. She flicked the ash of the cigarette. "They took her so they could adopt her into the tribe. I'll tell it."

She passed the cigarette to John as Sean listened to her story, how Indian boys had raided a white settlement and stolen some ice skates.

When the river where they were camping froze over, the boys put the skates on and fell on the ice. Then they let the girl have a turn and she stumbled around, too, falling on her face, and everybody laughed. After that, they had no reason to hide the skates from her, and one night after everyone had gone to bed, she put them on and skated away down the river. She'd known how to skate all along. She was just lulling them into complacency, waiting for the right moment to escape.

She shrugged. "For some reason I remembered that story when Levi got the jeans for me. He didn't check the pockets, so he didn't know I had a knife. I decided to act like I was a coward and wasn't any threat and waited for the right moment." She looked down at her hands, her body looking lost in the work shirt Sean had given her after the policemen took her bloodstained shirt into evidence. Again she looked off. Maybe it was beginning to sink in, killing a person. Sean wanted to tell her it would get worse before it got better, but it would get better. At least that was what he told himself.

"This is where you guys are." It was Joseph, walking out of the floodlit entrance of the emergency room. "Man, I've been looking all over for you."

"You found us," John said. "Do you know when we can go home?"

"Yeah, that's why I was looking. My brother-in-law says we can all go home, but nobody can leave the rez. Looks like you and Mr. Whiskers are going to share the couch," he said to Sean.

"How long do you think it will take to straighten this out?" John said.

"What? You have a bad day and you aren't an Indian no more? All of a sudden you're worried about time? It takes what it takes."

Ida struck a match and lit another cigarette. She pressed it to John's lips. Joseph took it and put it under his heel. "I thought you was quitting."

"Don't you know that smoking's traditional?" John's voice went up on "traditional," making a question of the word.

"You see how it is," Joseph said. "You want to do something that's bad for you, you just say, 'It's traditional,' and that makes it okay."

"Fuck you, Joseph," John said.

Sean saw Ida staring off to the east, where a smear of lavender made an inroad on the horizon. A good fishing hour, an even better one for the comfort of a couch and a brittle-whiskered cat.

CHAPTER THIRTY-FIVE

White Flag

It took four days to straighten it out, at least to the extent that Sean was granted release from the reservation—Joseph convincing his brother-in-law that if Sean was requested to come back to answer more questions or provide testimony, he would. He also managed to wiggle off the hook with the state of Montana, after an off-duty game warden hiked up to the jump with a GPS and determined that Sean's involvement in the events was restricted to the reservation.

Melvin Campbell's condition improved sufficiently for him to make a statement identifying his attacker as being a man. But it was dark in the house and his eyesight without his glasses bordered on blindness, so he couldn't identify Levi Karlson, or even if his attacker had been white. That left the preponderance of evidence against Levi being the sworn statements of Sean, John Running Boy, and Ida Evening Star, and though their stories concurred, Levi's recounting of events was equally plausible—a classic "he said, she said" dispute, or in this case "he said, they said."

The surviving brother admitted knowing John Running Boy from a prior visit to the reservation, said they had become friendly and decided to drive to the buffalo jump to sit around a campfire and pass a bottle, Ida and Sean tagging along for fun. An argument had ensued between Brady and John, who both fancied Ida, and when the argument threatened to turn violent, Ida had produced a concealed weapon and stabbed Brady in the throat. Levi had wrestled with John over the shotgun, which had exploded and injured his hand.

Levi's story provided no explanation for the injuries on John's ankles, nor did he admit to ever being in Campbell's house, let alone firing a handgun in his bedroom. The bullet might have linked him to the assault on Campbell if it could be proven that the .380 ACP belonged to the Karlsons, not to Ida Evening Star. But the jacketed bullet from the "pipsqueak" caliber passed through a weak spot in the wall and was never found, expending its energy somewhere along the 49th parallel.

Taking his lawyer's advice not to add to his statement or answer any questions about the discrepancies in his story while the lawyer threw his weight around, Levi stayed mute, and after spending two nights in the Browning jail he was released pending further investigation. As tribal authorities had no extradition agreement with the state and vice versa, it meant that in all likelihood he would neither be arrested nor papered to provide testimony as to the particulars of the death of his brother.

Sean was less concerned with Levi walking than he was with Ida being charged with second-degree murder. Self-defense was difficult to claim when no one had assaulted her, and a verbalized threat of rape, even if supported by corroborating recollections of others at the scene, was not in itself sufficient justification for stabbing a man in the neck. But Sean and John had both heard the click as Brady drew back the hammer of the pistol before inserting it in her ear. That was a lie Sean could live with and John could go along with, if it ensured her release, and along with Brady's prints on the gun, it did. There was still the possibility of the FBI becoming involved, especially as Karlson was non-Indian and his death was being investigated as a major crime, a combination that gave the bureau authority. But federal gears turned reluctantly when it came to reservation matters, and when Sean visited Melvin Campbell's house to say his good-byes, the legal entanglements that clouded their futures had lifted, if not cleared.

———

Sean heard the tapping of the stick on the floorboards and steeled himself as the knob turned. He hadn't seen Melvin Campbell since his release from the hospital and expected the old man to be more stooped and turtlelike than ever. He was shocked when Campbell greeted him with eyes that reached the level of his own.

"I thought I was growing in reverse, but apparently that was coyote playing a trick on me."

Campbell said that a physical therapist had introduced him to the McKenzie method of back extensions, coaxing the protruding disks in his lower spine back where they belonged, and enabling him to stand fully erect for the first time in almost thirty years. "A Blackfeet elder with a yoga mat, what would our grandfathers think?" He offered Sean coffee, and when Sean went to make it, tugged his sleeve. "Good for me to move around," he said.

They had their coffee in the living room, which had been thoroughly cleaned and really was a living room now, not simply the place to park yourself that it had been on prior visits. Campbell said that Ida and John had agreed to move in for the rest of the summer, to help him get a handle on his papers. The curator of the Museum of the Plains Indian had been by, had oohed and ahhed over his collection of verbal histories, but then detailed the considerable transcription work that needed to be done before they were suitable to archive.

"For posterity," Campbell said. "So this old wind talker will be a voice on the wind after his spirit has departed."

Sean asked him where the "kids" were, and Campbell smiled.

"That Ida, she's a serious one. I think she's the influence that young man needs. When she goes back for the fall semester I'm hoping that will make John want to follow. He never got his diploma, but I got him enrolled in a summer program to earn the credits. He'll have them if she has anything to say about it. Young man in love isn't too hard to steer."

"I didn't think they were that way," Sean said.

Campbell smiled. "I saw how you looked at her, but there's no fu-

ture there. The only reason they're in separate bedrooms is to ap-
pease my antiquated notions of propriety. But I know every board in
this house, and they don't squeak under the feet of my wife's spirit. I
don't let on that I know."

He rose to shake Sean's hand. He said that Ida and John were down
at the trailer, that his tenant had moved and he had put John to work
renovating the property while it was vacant. "I'm sure they'll want to
see you," he said.

It was a fine morning, the Precambrian thrust of the mountains
gold and the valley green, and Sean decided to walk the lane that
connected the properties, to breathe some fresh air before spending
the next six hours behind the wheel. Lupine had grown up in the
fields and on the strip of grass dividing the lane, and where the ruts
bent around a copse of trees he caught a glimpse of the trailer, and
saw that John and Ida were sitting on the seat of the swing set in the
yard. The set was repainted red and the one lopsided seat had been
replaced by a board that swung level. John was dragging a toe to
make the seat twist as they swung, Ida to his left as she had been in
the old photos. Sean remembered that John liked her to sit on that
side so that the eye in which he saw his reflection was the one with
the purple iris. Sean also remembered Ida telling him that that was
where they had first kissed. He had a feeling that if he stayed they
might revisit the moment and that he would feel like an interloper in
someone else's story. He'd been a part of it for a while. Now, he realized, he wasn't.

"You never were going to see that birthmark," he said, exhaling a
breath. His voice was greeted by the snorting of a whitetail buck,
which bounded away through the aspens, waving his white flag. He
walked back the way he had come. It was still a fine day and the old
country lane was something out of a poem and he was free to walk
it. After a while, he whistled.

CHAPTER THIRTY-SIX

Friends, No Benefits

Martha answered the door wearing an apron. Sean had never seen her wearing an apron. He had never seen her cook.

"I'm baking a Flathead cherry pie," she said, in what he took as a defensive tone of voice.

"What's the occasion?"

"David's coming for the weekend. The roads up in the breaks turned to gumbo, so the dig's on hiatus until the weather improves. He says he's bringing someone to meet me."

"A girl?"

"It better be. I want grandkids someday." She led him back to the polished stump that served as her desk. "Take a look at today's flyswatter."

It was the morning edition of the *Bridger Mountain Star*, the headline above the fold: "Ivy League Athelete Haunted by Buffalo Jump Killing," the subhead, "Seeks Solace on Madison River." The reporter, Gail Stocker, had managed to weasel the stern seat on Peachy Morris's pink ribbon driftboat for a float from Lyon Bridge to MacAtee Bridge, a trip that passed directly under the shadow of the Palisades.

"Imagine what it must have been like," Levi Karlson was quoted as saying. "Runners leading the bison to the brink, the hunting cries of warriors wearing wolf skins. Imagine what it could be today if bison were free to roam on public lands."

"He doesn't give a damn about buffalo," Sean muttered.

"Keep reading."

Sean read aloud:

"Karlson, 21, said that he continues to be haunted by his brother's death on July 15 at the Two Medicine Buffalo Jump on the Blackfeet Indian Reservation. He said that those responsible will pay for their crimes.

"'They can't hide up there forever,' he said.

"Karlson said he was unable to comment as to the identity of those he considered responsible for his brother's death, as the investigation by the Blackfeet Tribal Police remains open, or to provide further details on the recommendation of his lawyer. A spokesman for the Blackfeet Tribal Police said that the investigation into Karlson's death is ongoing, but would not confirm rumors that they had been contacted by the Federal Bureau of Investigation."

The rest of the article recapped the known events concerning Brady's death, which was week-old news at this point, then switched gears to paint a portrait of a grieving young man who had retreated to the river to find a little solace, albeit, as Sean pointed out, at four hundred and fifty dollars a day paid to Sam Meslik's outfitting business, for which Peachy Morris guided. A photo of Karlson showing off a rainbow trout, his right hand bandaged, Peachy with the net, illustrated the article.

"Nothing like rubbing it in your face," Martha commented.

"I doubt Papa-san is amused," Sean said. "The last thing he wants is for his stepson's name to keep coming up in the news."

"Take this as a lesson, Stranny. Money talks. Assholes walk. The second that lawyer stepped off the airplane, the chances of Levi Karlson going down for assault or anything else became about as good as my chance for reelection."

"Ah," Sean said. "I was going to ask about that. How's your little guy doing?"

"My 'little guy' doesn't live here anymore. When Lucien Drake came with his warrant, I made sure he was somewhere else. The less you know about that, the better."

"He's with Harold?"

"Like I said, the less you know."

"What did you tell Drake?"

"I told him exactly what he told us after Harold brought the calf across in the boat. 'Sometimes, animals just disappear. It's a fact of nature.' You should have seen his face. It was red as a roadcut on the Musselshell."

"Where was Harold when this happened?"

"Right beside me. I thought they were going to drop the gloves and go at it then and there, but Drake just turned around and whistled up his lackey, Calvin Barr, like he was some dog you wanted to jump into the truck. I shot him the finger, I'm not proud of it. But it's just a reprieve. The law's on his side and you can't hide a bison calf and a milk cow forever. Even in a county the size of Hyalite."

Sean couldn't help himself. "About Harold," he said.

"About Harold, what? You want to know where we stand, it's on the same rung of the ladder where we always are. Nothing so high you can't live if you fell. Same as you and Katie. Same old, same old."

"I'm not with Katie."

"Does she know that?"

"Martha." Sean shook his head. "It doesn't have to be like this."

"Yes it does. At least for the time being. Let's just see how things play out. I am—look at me—I am very, *very* thankful that you are still in one piece. You're going to stay for dinner and tell me about it. Friends?" She stuck out her hand and he took it.

"No benefits?" He smiled.

So they were back to sparring and innuendo, back on that safe familiar ground.

Sean was helping with the dishes when Martha's cell phone buzzed once, then fell silent. She wiped her hands on a dishtowel.

"This is odd," she said.

"What?"

"Nothing. I don't know the number. Mine isn't something I just give out." She worked her chin with her fingers.

"Just call it, Martha."

She did, raised her eyes, and turned to Sean with her mouth making a shape. "Remember when I left my card under the windshield wiper of Melissa Castilanos's car? Well, that was her voicemail."

"Do you think her son is staying at the guest ranch?"

"You read the paper. He's in the valley. I'm sure he's still sponging off Papa-san. But why is she calling me at this hour?" She drew the right side of her face up in concentration. "I'm going to call the manager, have him check to make sure everything's okay." She did. It went to voicemail as well.

She tapped her fingers on the sink counter. Then she walked to the mudroom where her dirty belt hung from a ten-penny nail.

CHAPTER THIRTY-SEVEN

Souvenirs

The stars had been out two hours when Martha cut the headlights. The old farmhouse that served as the ranch headquarters was silhouetted against the rise of land behind it, all the windows dark, although the guest cabins that fronted Cinnamon Creek showed a few rectangles of lamplight.

"That's the Highlander," Sean said. He could make out its boxy shape on an apron of grass in front of the cabin that the brothers had shared. No light in that cabin, or in the one rented to the parents. But the BMW with the Washington plates where Martha had tucked her card was there.

Martha placed a hand on the hood, shook her head to indicate it was cool, walked up and knocked on the door.

"Are you home, Mrs. Castilanos? This is Sheriff Ettinger." No answer. "Your door is unlocked. We're going to come in, we just want to check that you're okay. Are you okay?"

She caught Sean's eye, held up a finger, two fingers . . .

Sean pushed the door open. Martha stepped in front of him with the Ruger in both hands.

"I'm over here," she said.

She was sitting in the dark, her brandy after dinner voice coming from a sofa facing an unlit fireplace. From where Sean and Martha stood they could see only the back of her head. "I'd really prefer that you not turn on the light," she said. "I find it easier to talk in the dark. It's like you're talking to yourself. You'll say things you wouldn't if you thought that people were listening."

"Mrs. Castilanos, are you okay?" Martha said.

"Am I okay?" Out of the silence an audible scratch and the sudden flame of a match. The sound of her inhalation, then the exhalation through her nose and the acrid odor of smoke. "That's a question everybody says yes to. 'Sure. I'm fine, and how are you? Are *you* okay?'"

Another exhalation. "No, I'm not okay. I haven't been okay since I buried my first husband, since he was alive, I mean. The man who was with him when he died, he said the last thing Squint said was that I should remarry for the boys' sake. That they would need a father. Do you know where I was when he said that? I was having my hair done so I would look attractive to the man I was cheating on him with. That's where *I* was."

The shadow of her head changed as she looked over her shoulder at them. She dragged at the cigarette. "Sit. Anywhere. I mean, please, don't just stand there."

"Why did you call me, Mrs. Castilanos?" Martha said.

"I wanted to talk to someone. But I couldn't seem to breathe, so I hung up. I'll quit talking now if you don't put that gun away. I'm not dangerous. Come sit with me. Here, I'll light a candle." Another match flared, its circle of light dipping, and then the soft illumination of the candle on the coffee table beside her. "These antler candelabras are a nice touch. I bought three of them for gifts at the Blue Heron in Ennis. They went out of business last summer. A pity."

The two chairs were set at an angle to the couch, so that when Martha and Sean sat down, Melissa Castilanos's face was in profile. She smoked, tilting her head back, gazing at the ceiling. "I'm sorry, I should have offered you a drink. I'm out of cognac but there's a fifth of Macallan on the kitchen counter. 'Mi casa es su casa,' as they say in Uruguay."

"We're fine," Martha said. "You mentioned your first husband."

"Yes, that I was cheating on him. I cheated on him with a *lot* of men. I guess because I could. I liked the thrill of it and being able to make men want me. A place like Kelso, there wasn't a hell of a lot of distraction. Do you know what Squint's idea of a romantic weekend was? It was to go off in the truck camper and troll for coho. What was I supposed to do, just sit inside that tin can and listen to the rain? I was from Seattle. I wanted a *life*.

"But don't get the wrong idea. Squint was a good husband and he was a good father. He was a better husband and father than I was a wife and mother. I used to think that if that chain hadn't slipped, if he'd lived longer, at least until they got through high school, that he could have made a difference in their lives. I've thought about it a lot. It's funny how you think about what you can't change. Sad, really."

She tapped the cigarette out in an ashtray and lit another. She dragged at it, waved it.

"But who am I kidding? Those kids made their own world."

Sean saw her smile, the kind of smile that isn't. "I'm one of those women who grew up looking in the mirror, because her looks were the sum total of her worth. She's not so pretty anymore, is the fair maiden?"

The smile vanished.

They waited in silence for her to go on, which presently she did.

"Squint wanted to name them Peter and Paul, after the apostles. Thank God I talked him out of it. The only thing those boys ever worshipped was themselves. Anyway, I was about to say something and I've lost the thread. No, I remember. When the twins would misbehave, get rambunctious, Squint would press his forefinger to his lips. His right forefinger. 'Now boys,' he'd say. 'It's time to settle down. Your mother needs her peace and quiet.' And I'd catch them mimicking him behind his back, putting a finger to each other's lips. 'Now boys,' they would say. 'Now boys.'"

She looked critically at her cigarette and set it down beside the butt. "I haven't smoked this much in months. *Months*."

"Mrs. Castilanos," Sean said, and saw Martha glare at him, the minute shake of her head. *Don't interrupt.* But the woman was looking toward the ceiling again and hadn't seemed to hear. Advancing headlights glanced off the windows of the cabin as a truck slowly idled past. When they could no longer hear the motor, she went on.

"When they arranged him in the casket, the mortician's assistant made it so that his hands were folded for the viewing, so that his left hand covered his right hand. That was so the mourners couldn't see that the first two fingers were mangled. I found the pruning shears in the station wagon. What happened, what I imagine happened, because they were good little liars even then, was that the shears were in the station wagon and they didn't get the idea until they saw them. The casket had been brought out for the viewing the night before, and I'd brought the boys along because I couldn't just leave them alone at home. I was busy with the preacher talking about the memorial service and they were running around the funeral home, like kids do. I didn't think it had sunk in, his death. It wasn't until Morticia, that's what I called her, went to do the makeup the next morning that we saw what they'd done. I mean, I hope that it was spontaneous, that they *found* the shears. They could have sneaked them into the car. That would have been even worse."

She nodded to herself. "You tell yourself what you have to. 'Kids, you know.' Their brains haven't formed; they're only seven. They'll grow out of this stage and I didn't want them to be . . . traumatized by it, by the memory. So I didn't make a big deal out of it. I just told them that they shouldn't desecrate a body that way. Is that the right word, 'desecrate'? Anyway, do you know what Brady said? He said, 'But he couldn't feel it. He was already dead.' He said that they had taken turns, that they had tried to cut off the fingers but it was too hard going through the bone, so all they got was about half an inch of the tips. I tried telling them that this was wrong another way, but they couldn't seem to grasp what I was saying. After the burial, I asked them where they put the fingers, and they took me into the basement. They'd put them in a jar of formaldehyde with some frogs they'd pickled. Don't think I didn't think of that when Levi came back here with his fingers blown off. Poetic justice, but I doubt he saw it that way. Anyway, I think that was the first act, how it started."

She looked directly at Sean and Martha. "Would somebody have a drink with me, *please*?" She held out her glass. Sean took it and poured one for himself while he was at the counter. He cut it with a little water from the faucet without asking.

She took the glass from his hand, looked him up and down. "You're the fishing guide who took the boys out, aren't you?"

Sean said he was.

"They liked you. They went around calling each other 'Captain' all the next day. What are you, like her sidekick?"

Martha spoke for only the second time since they'd sat down. "Mrs. Castilanos, we're here to listen and to help you in any way that we can."

She snorted. "Don't be disingenuous. You're here because you think I'll say something to incriminate my sons. Well, you're too late for that, aren't you? None of that matters now. I thought you'd be interested to know how it started, how I *knew*."

She swallowed her drink.

"I knew as soon as you danced around the subject last week that they were involved in that buffalo jump fiasco, what happened here in the valley. They called that Indian boy's death an accident, that he fell off the cliffs. As a mother, you give your children the benefit of the doubt. But it has an expiration date. Now, my husband, he can't see even with his eyes open. He acts like there's nothing wrong, that anytime the boys are where something bad's happened, that it must be a coincidence. He has that quality of not being able to see people for who they really are. Other men who wanted me, they saw right through those boys and decided to find their milk and honey somewhere else."

"Where is he now, Mrs. Castilanos?"

"Auggie? He was here a few days after we heard about . . . up on the reservation." Her voice caught. Her fingers found the cigarette in the ashtray. She knocked off the long coal and dragged at it and then shook her head. "He's back in Washington on business. He left me to deal with the cremation. What a legal quagmire *that* turned out to be. But then that's Auggie for you. He retreats into his fishing and his work and leaves the messes to be cleaned up by other people. He compartmentalizes, something I've never been able to do. At least that's what a shrink told me. I saw one for a while this winter, after something happened back east when they were in school, and I was trying to rationalize it away."

"What happened back east, Mrs. Castilanos?" Martha said.

"Call me Melissa. We're all friends here, or would be if someone would have a drink with me. I mean for Chrissakes."

Sean lifted his glass, drained it, and poured two more for the table.

"Straight up, please," she said.

"That's better," she said. "I do like liquor. I find it a requirement for someone in my circumstances." Her voice was thick. "Where was I?"

"Something happened back east."

"Yes, the rower. A girl from a crew team was raped and drowned in the Connecticut River. You see, by then, the mere fact that they were in school there, that they were in the same *state,* was enough to make me suspicious. I said, 'Melissa, be reasonable.' And when I mentioned it to Auggie, he laughed it away. But then a month or so later, the parents of the girl finally talked to some reporter—oh, yeah, I kept an eye on the news—and they said the girl's oar was missing, a detail that the police hadn't released. She'd built the oar, I guess, or turned it on a lathe, or however you make one. Her mother said she'd carved her name on it. And I knew. Just like that, I knew.

"Because they took souvenirs, you see. They wouldn't fly an oar back home on a plane—they weren't stupid—but I'm sure it's back in the woods somewhere where they could visit it. And I'd bet if you looked hard, you'd find *their* initials on it, too, except they'd be in some kind of a code. That's because it was always a game to them. Before, the other times when I thought, 'It can't be them, that can't be my flesh and blood that did this horrible thing,' I would never know for certain until something was reported missing. An oar, a violin bow, sunglasses. *Something.* Because that's what they did. That's how I knew they were involved in that Indian boy's death the night the buffalo died, when I heard that arrows had been found, but that the bow was missing. Then this thing last week on the reservation, I knew it had to be related. So when Levi was being held up in Browning, I went to the manager and got the key. Their cabin is just like this one except it's got a moose skull instead of this elk, and there's an old rifle over the mantel instead of these snowshoes. It's like something from the Civil War. That's where the arrow was, down the barrel. It was just an arrow with a broken tip, no point or anything. I had to make a little hook doohickey with a clothes hanger to pull it out. I'm sure they did something with the bow, hid it somewhere, but think of the arrogance, keeping a murder weapon in a rental cabin."

"Melissa, how do you know it was a murder weapon?"

She canted her head, regarding Martha as if she was a curiosity. "It had blood on it. I took it as a clue."

She looked back up at the mantelpiece. "So I showed it to him," she said. "All these years, it's the first time I ever had the courage to confront him like that, either of them. I mean, I knew, but as long as they didn't tell me, there was the possibility I was wrong. Or at least I could go on trying to lie to myself."

"When was this?" Sean said.

"Last night, when he came back here after feeding that reporter woman a pack of lies. She gave him a ride because his battery was dead and wouldn't jump. Pretty little thing. Someone should tell her there's other colors in the wardrobe besides brown.

Anyway, I thought maybe with Brady dead, if I brought it out into the open, Levi would confess what they'd done. Because Brady was the ringleader and Levi wouldn't be as strong with him gone. But that was only generally true. They fed off each other, built themselves into more than they could be by themselves. They could even trade personalities. There were times I'd hear them talking and *I* didn't know who was who, and I was their *mother.*"

She shifted her focus from the mantel to Stranahan. "Are you an Indian?"

"No ma'am, I'm not."

"*Ma'am?* Why, you're a gentleman? I'm not sure I've ever met a gentleman."

"Would you like me to freshen your drink, Melissa?"

"Please. Why couldn't my sons have grown up like you?"

Sean got her whisky, and she made a point of touching his hand when she took it. Her fingers were ice cold.

"How did your son react when you showed him the arrow?" Martha asked.

"Oh, he said something about winning it playing pool. He made it into a story, how he was in a reservation bar and he thought he was going to have to fight his way out of there, and then the guy handed him the arrow and they broke the point off and clasped hands around it, like it was some totem and they were brothers. Everything he says, he has to decorate. He learned that from Brady.

"I said, 'Then you wouldn't mind if I turned it over to the police so they can check the DNA.' *That* got his attention."

"What did he do?"

"Flew into a rage. Hit me in the face, knocked me down onto the floor. Back there, by the kitchen. Here, I'll show you." She struck another match and lit the other two candles on the antler candelabra. She brought the piece up to illuminate her face, which was blotched and red. Then she reached her hand behind her head and pulled on her hair. "He dragged me by this, like it was a mop head, and then he just glowered over me like some jungle cat, like he was waiting for me to move and when I did, he'd swat me with his paw. I've never seen eyes like that before. But then that passed and he was petting me and looking around like he didn't know how I got on the floor. He wasn't contrite, he didn't apologize or anything. It was like he wasn't aware what had happened. He helped me up and I said I needed to go use the bathroom. Told him to make us a drink and I'd be right back.

"That twenty feet to the door, that was the longest walk of my life. Any second I thought he might just, I don't know, pounce. But I went into the bathroom and he was still standing there, so I shut the door and turned the water on. And then I opened the other door that goes into the bedroom and found the pistol Auggie keeps between the mattresses. I put a pillow over it because I didn't know if cocking it would make a noise. I could hear him talking to himself in the kitchen. 'We were just going to have a little fun. It's not our fault he got his guts ripped out.' And I starting thinking about the other times they had fun, like the girl being raped and holding her head under the water. So much *fun.* So I walked back into the room and he had this smile on his face. I'd tucked the gun down the back of my pants and I could feel my skin sweating under the barrel. I asked him what happened to the boy on the cliff. He said he'd got caught on a piton and they were telling him to cut it off, cut it off, like daring him to cut off his intestine, and then he said the boy was going to die anyway, so they took turns shooting at him with the arrows until Brady hit him and he fell.

"They were just having a little fun, you see."

She turned her gaze to Sean. "I brought the gun out and he lifted his shoulders, like, *Really, you'd do that to me?* I just shot him."

Out of the corner of his eye, Sean saw Martha's hand move to her holster.

"You don't have to do that. Like I told you, I'm not dangerous."

"Where's the gun, Melissa?" Sean said.

"It's down in the crack of the seat. Right here." She started to reach down with her right hand.

"I'll get it, if that's okay, ma'am," Sean said.

He placed his hand over her forearm and reached down with his other hand and felt the steel. He pulled out a thin, long-barreled pistol. He pressed the magazine catch and detached the magazine and checked to make sure there wasn't a bullet in the chamber.

"It's just a twenty-two," she said. "That's why nobody came around afterwards, because it didn't make much noise. And there was hardly any blood. I cleaned it up, but it was only a few teaspoons."

"Where is your son?" Martha said.

"He's in his cabin the last time I looked. I shot him in the arm once and in the stomach. Twice, I think. That's all the bullets that were in the gun. When he walked outside, he was holding his stomach. I followed him and he had a hard time getting the door open and he went in and sat down on the couch. He asked me to get him a glass of water, so I got it for him. He told me to call 911. I got out my cell phone and acted like I did. Gave the address and everything, quite the little actress I was. I told him the ambulance would be here in twenty minutes. I said I'd go outside and wait for it. He was making sounds, strange sounds. I kissed him on the head, I don't know why I did that. Maybe it's because despite everything, he's still my son. Then I walked outside and called you, but I was having a hard time getting my breath, so I hung up."

Martha and Sean were moving toward the door.

"You have to understand." Her voice had a quaver in it. "I couldn't let it go on any longer. It had to stop. *He* had to stop. *They* had to stop."

He had stopped all right. He had got off the couch and was lying facedown dead on the living room floor.

CHAPTER THIRTY-EIGHT

Something to Talk About

"He got a warrant to search Harold's sister's place," Martha said.

"Drake?"

"The devil himself."

"So that's where the little buffalo's been."

She leaned back in her office chair. "I assume that's where Harold's been hiding him. I have deniability."

Sean saw brightness at the corners of her eyes—her posture, fingers linked behind her head, her voice, professional, only thinly masking her emotion.

"Don't beat yourself up. You did all you could," Sean said.

"Did I? Why don't I feel like I did?" She made a helpless gesture. "Nowhere to roam. Nobody willing to share just a little piece of earth with him."

"Change takes time. Like that man they call Tatanka told me, 'We just have to outlive the bastards.'"

"That doesn't do him any good." She shook her head. "I let him into my heart. You'd think I would have learned my lesson with men."

Sean reached across her desk and took her hand. "You did what you could."

"Sure."

They moved on to other subjects before getting around to Levi Karlson, or rather his mother, Melissa, who had changed her story twice since being arrested. She'd amended her initial statement to claim that her son had asked to be shot, had sung about it to Gail

Stocker like a meadowlark in May, the *Star*'s story running under the headline "Solace Seeker Sought Death."

Two days later, presumably with the prodding of her attorney, she'd remembered that Levi had advanced upon her in a threatening manner after she'd emerged from the bedroom with the gun, strengthening a claim of self-defense that started with the bruising on her face.

"As far as I care, she can walk out of jail tomorrow," Martha said. "She'll do the taxpayers a favor by saving us a trial."

"Do you think he would have been convicted?"

"Levi? You mean if his mother had turned over the arrow? Hard to say. If the shaft could be matched to the arrowhead found in Gary Hixon's body and the fingerprints in the blood on the arrow could be matched to Levi, I think Rosco would have gone to bat with it. Especially if he had the mother's testimony to back it up. But I don't care how many cases he's won wearing a *Jaws* T-shirt, he'd have gone up against a damned good attorney who could make a case that Levi was helping to pull out an arrow that Hixon had accidentally impaled himself with. It wouldn't have looked good, leaving him there to die, but it wouldn't be murder. Something interesting, though, we found boots in the boys' cabin that matched a print Harold found above the cliffs. It had a missing cleat. That would have put him at the scene, put one of them there, anyway."

She lifted her hands from her desk. "Tell you what, let's not talk about anybody named Karlson for the next five minutes."

"Okay, what do you want to talk about?"

"David drove in last night. There was more rain up at the dig, so they're on another break."

"Did he bring his girlfriend?"

"Yes, and she didn't come last week like I thought she would, so I just met her."

"And . . ?"

"Tall and tan. Young and lovely. One of those California blondes who pulls her legs up under her when she sits down. Except she's from New Mexico. David says all the girls sit that way when they're sorting dirt for dinosaur bones."

"What do you think of her?"

"I don't know yet. She's polite, but not shy. Her hands are rougher even than mine. Walked in and took over the kitchen and made spaghetti. We all had some wine and they went to bed in what used to be David's old room, the one in the loft."

"Modern Martha."

"Wishful thinking Martha. I'd buy her some little bit of nothing to wear if I thought it would get me a grandchild. I turned on the noise machine so I wouldn't hear them at their rituals."

"Where are they this morning?"

"They took my johnboat to float the Madison."

"I'm headed up the valley myself. Sam asked me to trailer the Adirondack guide boat to Wade Lake. He says he has a new method of finding fish, but he won't tell me what it is. He says I'll want to see for myself."

"You ever fix the bullet holes under that gunwale?"

"Not yet."

"Nostalgia, huh? The good ol' days."

"Not if you were the one getting shot at."

"You have a point. So what's on your mind, or did you just drop by to interrupt a busy woman for no good reason?"

"I figure if l skulk around the vicinity of a stairwell long enough, sooner or later you'll drag me into it again."

"Keep dreaming."

He leaned across the desk, put his palms on either side of her face, and kissed her on the mouth. "I'll do that."

She flushed, then struggled to muster her composure. "Go on, get out of here," she said. She didn't let her game face fall until he'd shut the door behind him.

CHAPTER THIRTY-NINE

How to Find Fish

The Queen of the Waters surfaced, her hair waving like turtle grass. She stood on her tail and kicked around until she saw the boat.

"Over here," she shouted.

Sean saw the bobbing of her head and pulled at the long, thin-bladed oars.

"How deep?" Sam asked.

"About twenty-five feet. There's about a dozen suspended over the bottom."

Sam marked the spot on his GPS.

"You want me to find another school?"

"One more, Molly," Sam said.

"Okay." She dove down and they watched her tail undulate as she swam away.

It was the fifth location Sam had marked inside an hour. The next time Molly found fish, after collecting her, they'd go back and fish the hot spots in rotation, starting with the first she'd found, just off the point of the bay, giving the trout plenty of time to settle down after the intrusion. Though, as Molly had pointed out, they really didn't shy away. In fact, sometimes two or three trout would break away from a school and swim over to check her out. Sean didn't blame them. She was quite a sight, Molly Linklatter, wearing nothing but water drops and her emerald tail, her bare breasts buoyed up each time she surfaced.

"I got some more," they heard her call.

"Are you sure this isn't illegal?" Sean said.

Sam laughed. "If it isn't, it should be. Anything this fun you figure FWP would get a stick up their butt about."

They marked the spot and Molly swam into shallow water where they could jump out and hold the boat steady for her to climb aboard. Sam unzipped her and she peeled out of the tail, revealing her bikini bottom. She began to towel off with a flannel shirt.

"That's right," she said, catching Sean's appraising glance. "Get a good look at them. This body isn't going to look like this for very much longer."

"What do you mean?"

"What she means is Sam's salmon know how to swim." Sam smiled, revealing the grooves in his teeth.

"There was a malfunction," Molly said. "They got past the dam, so to speak."

"You're pregnant?"

She pulled the shirt around her. "It's a boy," she said. "And I'm just thrilled. I've never been so happy in my life."

"Well, this is great news. Congratulations are in order." The words were easier to get out than he thought they'd be. He really was happy for them, but already he felt a sense of loss, not that he'd lose Sam, but that his essential loneliness had just become that much more pronounced.

"We're going to have the wedding in the grove of cottonwoods behind the shop," Sam was saying. "August tenth. Guess who's best man?" He cocked a finger at Sean.

"Hey." He shrugged, the slabs of heavy muscle shifting across his shoulders. "It was time. I have name recognition now. They call me the Jerry Garcia of fly fishing on the forums. Guys want to fish with me. They want to buy gear from me. They want to be *insulted* by me. So with the mail order and some off-season guiding in the Keys and Cuba, if that gig in Las Salinas comes through, I can provide. And even I couldn't go around being a screwup forever."

"He's going to be a great dad," Molly said.

"You will," Sean said. "I know you will."

"I just have to stop swearing for a while. I can't have the first words out of his mouth be, 'Where the fuck is my Tonka truck?'"

The trout cooperated, deep fishing with chironomid pupae, not Sean's kind of fishing but fishing nonetheless. Then they didn't cooperate, perhaps sensing the barometer drop. All morning, anvil-shaped thunderheads had been grumbling with each other, and now they let loose with a torrent. Sean rowed to shore, where they flipped the boat over on a gravel bar and propped it up so they could shelter underneath to eat their lunch.

"Is this the life or what?" Sam said.

It really was and Sean started to feel better about it. This part of it, the fishing, the camaraderie, a life lived largely outside walls, it wouldn't change. It couldn't change, could it? But then he looked at Sam, who was holding Molly's hand and whispering something, the two of them forming their own world and soon to be three, and he knew it had changed already.

By the time they rowed back to the dock it was evening, the clouds scattered and lilac-tinged, swallows dipping for mayflies as they crisscrossed over the water. Sean offered to buy them dinner at the Trout Tails Bar and Grill to celebrate.

"Thanks," Sam said, "but they serve beer and I'm trying to be a team player. If Molly has to stop, I'm going to do my damnedest to support her. We'll just have a quiet night at home." He held out his hand for Sean to give him his keys and hiked up the hill to get the rig.

"They're going to be shorthanded for mermaids," Molly said. She picked up a stone to skip it across the lake. "I turned in my notice and Ida isn't coming back, at least not this summer. It's a job with a lot of turnover." She smiled at him. "That's what you call a mermaid joke," she said. Already, he noticed, she was radiant.

"But can it still be a mermaid bar if you don't have mermaids?"

"Well, there's the Parmachene Belle, and I'm sure someone else will fill the tails."

"No one can fill your tail, Molly."

She laughed. "I've been told that before, but it's nice of you to say so. But I don't know. Maybe I'm getting out just under the wire. They finally hired a piano player and she's got a get-away face. All the men give her the look. When you're a mermaid and the stool warmers swivel to drool over a woman in a dress, that's the writing on the wall."

"Yeah," said Sean, "but can she find fish?"

CHAPTER FORTY

Twist of Fate

Sean found Kenneth Winston standing outside the bar, sharp in his Levi's Slim Fit Boot Cuts, working a toothpick. One lizardskin Tony Lama rested on the bottom rung of the porch rail. He tipped the brim of his black Stetson in Sean's direction.

"Hey, Ken, are Pat or any of the other guys inside?" Sean asked.

"No, just me loitering, practicing my mid-distance stare. Nothing put a Montana bar out of business faster than a black man on the stoop. I figure if I loiter in front of every bar between West Yellowstone and Ennis, I can put the whole valley out of business in a month. Then we can have all the good fishing to ourselves."

"Come on in. I'll buy you a French 75."

"Can't. I got a date with Lois Lane. That reporter for the *Star* wants to do a story, 'Hot Hands Winston, world-famous fly tier, graces Madison Valley.' Won't say I don't deserve it. She's going to meet me here and caravan back to the clubhouse for dinner with the gang. You're invited. Robin's defrosting some of those eland steaks he brought from Africa."

"Maybe I'll be by later," Sean said.

Ken's nod was a fraction of an inch. "Partner," he said, and tipped his hat, his eyes reassuming their mid-distance stare.

————

The parrot clock on the wall read seven p.m., bar time. Fishermen coming off the water were just beginning to trickle in.

Sean took an end stool and ordered a Moose Drool. The bartender with the sleeve tattoos asked after Ida, if she was still up on the rez. Sean was surprised that he knew. The names associated with Brady Karlson's death hadn't been released by the tribal police, at least to his knowledge.

"Oh, this time of summer there are a lot of birds in the valley," he said. "You tell her Uncle Vic says hi, that everybody here's thinking about her."

It was only a big valley in a geographical sense. Sean should have known the news would get around.

A splash followed by a fizz of bubbles, a vision in crimson and white spinning like a barber pole, changed the subject. The Parmachene Belle knew how to make an entrance, and Sean's eyes swirled with the colors.

Behind him, he heard fingers pressing on piano keys. He didn't turn around, even with the first glissade when he thought it might be her, even after the first stanza when he knew that it wasn't, when relief was tinged with a measure of regret. He'd always suspected that she would sing her way back into his life someday, Vareda Beaudreux with her scent like oranges and lips the color of old blood. But this was someone else, a woman with chestnut hair and a voice that was as lush and as warm as the Montana evening. A frayed alto that took you back, singing songs written for whiskey and dark bars. "Sweet Love," "Unbreak My Heart," "Simple Twist of Fate."

He lifted a finger and told the bartender to take a Johnnie Walker Black to the piano player, his compliments. He looked at his reflection in the bar mirror as she sang about a couple in a park, the evening growing dark, a one-night stand that would haunt a man forever. Sean emptied his glass and thought about unlit porch lights and empty stairwells, about skin that couldn't be kissed and phones that rang without answer. All the emptiness of a life lived alone coming to bear, even as the Parmachene Belle beckoned him with her expressive fingers. Only later, when he swam out of the depths of his own dark water, would he realize that this was where the story had started, with a woman behind glass seeing a vision from her past. A twist of fate to be sure, but far from simple.

When the set ended Sean walked out the door and stood under the early stars. He caught the scent of caramel and spice as the steps came up behind him.

"What are you, some kind of no-hat cowboy? My mother told me they were the worst kind." A smile in the voice, a hint of mischief in the eyes as Sean turned to face her.

He smiled. People up here were never who you thought they were, even if they were from somewhere else.

"I'm not going to have to do all the talking, am I? You're not that kind of a cowboy."

"I'm not a cowboy at all."

"No? So if you aren't a cowboy, then who am I thanking for the drink?"

"I'm a private detective," Sean said.

"Really?"

"Sort of," he said.

Epilogue

The ranger manning the entrance booth didn't return Harold's hello when he handed over his season pass. It was ten-thirty at night, no time for pleasantries.

"Do you need a map?" she asked.

"I didn't think you kept the booths open this late," Harold said.

"You do when you have tourists coming in who are driving rental Winnebagos for the first time."

"Well, I just need a campsite," Harold said. "Are there still sites open at Madison Junction?"

She said there were. After the Fourth, the campground rarely filled up during weekdays. He thanked her and had put the truck camper in gear when she asked if he could answer a couple questions. The park was conducting a survey about congestion at the entrance gates and wanted visitor input.

"Sure," said Harold, pressing down the clutch. He felt the hot ice of sweat bead at his temples under the band of his hat.

His right hand came up to his cheek. It had been two weeks since Lucien Drake had served him with the warrant at his sister's place, and, whistling to Calvin Barr to start the truck, not having found the baby bison on the property, had swung on Harold, a sucker punch that sent him sprawling. The eggplant bruising had finally faded, but the scabbing where Drake ground his cheek into the gravel was still scabbed over and he was glad the driver's side window was on the left, so he could offer the attendant the acceptable half of his smile.

"Shoot," Harold said.

A couple of questions turned into five. How often did Harold visit the park? When was the last time he was caught in a queue that caused delay? Had the inconvenience ever caused him to change his travel plans? What did he think about the addition of an automated machine that could scan park passes and facilitate faster entry? Would he be willing to pay a surcharge for the use of such a lane?

"Anything to move along," Harold said. He found that he was swallowing and that his mouth was dry.

"Thank you," the ranger said, but Harold was already rolling the camper forward. He let out a long breath, cursing himself for not doing his homework. Had he known that the booths were attended so late, he'd have waited another hour. All it would take was a little bit of noise from the camper and she'd have asked what cargo he was hauling. Then what would he have said?

Harold's fingers itched at the scabbing as he thought back.

Lucien Drake. He should have been ready. Instead, he'd got lucky. If Drake had connected solidly, Harold would have been out cold. As it was, he'd seen the world swim away before a vision flashed through the pain, a vision of the boy a father had made fun of by giving him a girl's name. That boy had been knocked down, too, and had always got up. Harold had got up, seen Drake, his tombstone teeth milky in the moonlight, beckoning with a hand, the worms under the skin of his chin crawling. "You want some more, Chief?" Drake said.

Harold had beat him senseless and was straddling him, trading hands, digging at the liver with the left, when Barr pulled him off. "Jesus, Harold, you'll have a lawsuit on your hands."

"He's an asshole. How the hell can you work for that son of a bitch?"

Barr, wiry and bowlegged, his breath smelling of chewing tobacco, circled Harold's chest with his orangutan arms and dragged him away from the man curled on the ground.

Barr's voice was a raspy whisper. "Do you know Jackson McKenzie, the one they call Tatanka?"

"What does that have—"

"Answer me. Do you or don't you?"

"I've met him. It's been awhile."

"Do you know where the camp is? Keep your voice down."

"Not exactly. What are you getting at?"

Harold turned to look at Drake, who was whimpering, making dog noises. He broke away from Barr and walked over. Harold put the heel of his boot on Drake's right hand, the one that had beckoned to him when he thought he was the better man. "You stay until I tell you you can get up," Harold said. "Not until, you got it?"

He ground the heel. Drake pulled his hand under his body and groaned.

The truck with the horse-and-cattle emblem was parked up the drive. Barr found a pad and a pencil in the glove compartment and drew Harold a map. "You come day after tomorrow, couple hours before dark, make sure you got the passenger. No horse trailer, something else, something enclosed."

Barr looked at him, his face, all cracks and crannies, illuminated by the dome light. "You understand what I'm telling you?"

Harold nodded. He was looking at the Sharps on the truck's gun rack, the two bandoliers of paper-patched cartridges, each the size of a small cigar.

Something tugged at his brain.

He looked back at Drake, a lump on the ground thirty yards away.

Said to Barr, "You're the highwayman. The way I heard it, that was Theodore Thackery."

"They called both of us highwaymen, 'cause of the cartridge belts. We gave them the idea for the jump, and I'll go to the grave regretting it. But I wasn't there that night. I never met those Indians, never knew they existed. I give no thought a'tall to those fellas carrying through."

"Those fellas, the Karlson brothers?"

"I didn't even catch their names."

"How did you meet them?"

"That doesn't matter."

"Tell me."

Barr shrugged. "They came to see the mermaids. Everybody saw them girls; it was the talk of the valley. Even a couple old pokes like me and Thack. I recognized the boys 'cause they worked for the crusade a few weeks. They bought a bottle of scotch and we took it outside the bar. I don't care what they say, that stuff all tastes like soap to me. Buffalo came up, it was what we had in common, guys on either side of the issue, finding out you aren't enemies after all."

"Just who the fuck are you, Calvin? You part of the bison crusade? You pass on information about what the state's up to, where the buffalo are so they can haze them away from the guns? Are you like a spy for them?"

"More like tell them where to put the cameras. We share a vision of the future, we're just getting there different ways."

"Why the hell didn't you go to the sheriff?"

"And say what? That I met a couple college boys and we talked about Indian hunting customs? State didn't have a damned bit of evidence, there was nothing a DA could do. And I never saw what happened. I wasn't no party to it."

"Somebody told those kids when the buffalo were coming, where they could find them."

"Why do you s'pose Thack killed himself?"

"Did he kill himself? Personally, I don't think that he did. I think those boys made it look that way."

The man looked hard at Harold. "It ain't here nor there who pulled the trigger. I told you what I told you. You want to foller through, make something right that the man yonder says is wrong, you be there when I said."

"Okay," Harold said.

"Now hit me." Barr tapped his eye. "You don't have to kill me, but hit me. All this talking's going to make him suspicious."

———

Harold rubbed his knuckles, still sore, as he drove his sister's truck camper past the turnoff to Madison Junction Campground. He turned south, the road dipping to cross the Gibbon River near its junction with the Firehole, where the two currents bled together to form the Madison, and then he was following the gunmetal thread of the Firehole River upstream. A glare on the water where the headlights dipped as he crossed the bridge over Nez Perce Creek, following the road that dead-ended at the trail to Ojo Caliente Hot Spring. He idled along, big broad meanders of the Firehole to the south, looking for the pullout marked on the handwritten map. The openings in the flared forests trembled with a breeze, the long grasses flowing in waves like bear hair. He found the pullout. Across the river was where Tatanka had told him the herd would be, when he'd visited the camp of the American Bison Crusade a couple hours earlier.

Tatanka—buffalo bull. An old man, a white man, but a chief all the same. Plain enough to see. He told Harold that the bison that had survived the buffalo jump, that had veered from the cliff edge just in time, must have stayed in cover, moving only at night, before finally returning to the national park, where one of his field workers had recognized the cow with the broken horn. Because the cow had had twins, a very rare occurrence for bison, and campaign volunteers had seen her often with two calves, and because she was accompanied by only one now, he thought there was a better than even chance that the bull calf Harold had rescued was her offspring. The cow was still in milk, that was the crucial consideration. The calf was only forty days old and it wouldn't be weaned until six months.

"It's just one buffalo," Tatanka said. "But he's got his mother's blood. Buffalo will need leaders when the time comes that their hooves aren't hobbled. It will warm the cockles of this old man's heart to see it, God provide I'm around." He'd nodded toward the truck camper. "How are you going to keep him quiet when you go through the gate?"

"Got a plan," Harold said.

"Then I won't ask."

He'd shaken Harold's hand. "I'm not going to give you any of this 'brother of the buffalo' crap," he said. "But I will say a prayer to the gods we share and hope that you fare well."

The old man had gone back to the fire. Harold heard him say, "What's on the spit?" to the ragtag group of followers who stood to welcome him.

———

Harold turned into the pullout and stepped out of the truck. He lifted the ten-power marine binoculars. Twilight's curtain had drawn, but the sky was clear with a half moon that cast more than enough light, even to recognize a bison with a broken horn. Sweeping the openings on the far side of the river, he didn't see any bison, but that didn't mean they weren't there, back in the trees. Bison often grazed at dusk and in the hour or two after dark, and Harold felt sure that sooner or later they would come out into the open to feed on the lush grasses. That is, if they were still in the vicinty.

He unbolted the spare tire and found the coil of orange hose designed to bleed air from one tire into another. Set them by the right front. A cover story if he needed one, a curious park ranger driving up and asking what he was still doing there after dark.

He didn't have long to wait. The first bison, a cow, moved along the dark wall of the pines, then broke free from shadow to stand in the moonlight. More followed, cows with calves, a couple younger bulls, spreading out as they came onto an apron of grass in the bend of the river. And the cow with the broken horn was with them, her calf close, moving in and out of her silhouette.

Harold walked to the back of the camper and opened the door with a key. "It's time," he said.

She smiled, her head sticking above the little humped shoulder. Straw covered the floor of the camper and her hair was matted, with bits of it sticking out.

"You did a great job back there, Dorry."

"Are the buffalo here?" She hugged the bison's neck, which came up past her waist, the calf having grown a half foot taller in the weeks since Harold had found it.

"They're across the river."

"I was afraid he was going to bawl when that lady was asking you the questions. He doesn't like it when anything changes, like when the truck stopped."

"How did you keep him quiet?"

"I fed him with the bottle and talked to him. He likes it when I whisper."

She moved past the calf in the narrow corridor and stepped outside. Harold put up the ramp he'd made from two-by-tens and the girl led the bison down it, coaxing him along.

"See them?" Harold pointed.

"I see them."

They could hear them, the low rumblings of a contented herd.

He took her hand and they walked toward the riverbank, the calf trailing. With only the span of the current separating them from the bison, one of the bulls turned to face them, then the other bull, followed by the cows, the calves indifferent. The herd began to move away and had gone a few yards when the bull calf bleated. Immediately the cow with the broken horn stopped, the rest continuing to move, not alarmed, just creating space. The cow called to the calf. Dorry whispered, her mouth close to the calf's ear. Harold didn't hear what she said and would never ask her. He took her hand and they backed slowly away, the calf staying behind on the bank, bleating. A few short steps and he was in the river, his legs plunging as he was swept downstream. The cow followed him, keeping pace on the far bank. The calf's head bobbed, a moving dot in the middle of the river.

"We've got to help him," Dorry said. Harold could hear the catch in her voice.

"No, he'll make it. River's not fast here."

Even as he tried to assure her, the calf rose out of the current, formed a silhouette. He had gained the shallow water on the far side and stepped up onto the shore. He fell, his hooves slipping as he tried to climb the bank where the earth had sloughed off into the river. The cow bison stood farther up the bank, calling. The calf tried half a dozen more times, struggling, wobbling, falling back.

Harold could feel the girl's hand tighten.

"He's got a big heart, Dorry, he'll make it."

Finally the calf made it to the top, where he was engulfed by the larger bison's shadow.

"Where did he go?"

"He's there."

Harold handed her the binoculars. "Do you see him?"

She nodded, the heavy binoculars wavering. "He's up under her. I think he's nursing."

"Good."

The other calf had been edging along the river and it now joined the cow, the cow walking up the bank to rejoin the herd, trailed by the calves trotting to keep up.

"I don't know which one he is now," the girl said.

"That's okay," Harold said. "That's what we wanted."

"Are we going to go camp? You told my uncle we were going to set up a tent."

"The tent's in the truck."

"You said you'd give me an Indian name if I helped you."

"I did, didn't I?"

"What is it?"

"I'm thinking," Harold said. The night was setting in cold and he put his arm around her shoulder. She smelled like a little girl who had lain in straw and hugged a buffalo.

"Hanata," he said.

"That's pretty. What's it mean?"

"Peace," Harold said.

The river shone now with moonlight. It didn't appear to move, and together with the shadows of the bison on the silvered grasses it seemed timeless, as close to a portrait of Eden as any of Harold's grandfather's grandfathers had ever known. But the river moved, it was always moving, and Harold knew that in time the bison would again follow the current down into their past, into their uncertain future.

"Peace," he said again. "Like right here. Peace like a bend in a river."

Afterword

I sent the finished draft of *Buffalo Jump Blues* to Kathryn Court and Victoria Savanh, my wise editors at Viking Penguin, last July 15th, before driving to West Yellowstone, Montana, for a book reading. Like most writers who have sent in a book—one might as well have mailed in one's heart—I was worried. There was, of course, the concern that they wouldn't like it. But regardless of its reception, I worried that I had misrepresented or overstated the plight of the American bison, the subject around which my story is told.

After the reading that evening, I drove over Targhee Pass into Idaho. As I crested the pass on Route 20, I caught sight of a lone bull bison plodding along at the side of the road. I stopped and took a few photos as he came abreast the WELCOME TO IDAHO sign. One of the photos is posted on my Facebook author Web page (Keith McCafferty) dated July 17, 2015. Take a look at that photo, for the story of that bison is the story of my novel.

The irony of the situation struck home immediately. This icon of the West was not welcome in Idaho, any more than he was welcome in Montana. In fact, by straying outside a narrowly drawn buffer zone surrounding Yellowstone Park, he had signed his death warrant, although he was on public land and posed no danger to livestock in the area (in the form of transference of disease), or to private property, or to human beings. I drove off reluctantly, knowing his fate. In fact, he would be shot by officials of the Idaho Department of Livestock the next day and loaded onto a truck, then quickly covered with a tarp to keep the shame of his demise from the critical eye of the public, though not from volunteers of the Buffalo Field Campaign, who posted a video of his execution on their Web site.

No, this was not fiction. No, I had not been guilty of overstatement.

If you are concerned about the future of bison, you may be interested to know that an environmental impact statement is being drafted for an Interagency Bison Management Plan, jointly being prepared by the National Park Service, Montana Fish, Wildlife & Parks, and other state and federal agencies. Updates on the progress of the plan, including information on public comment periods, can be found at fwp.mt.gov.

As of this writing, as many as a thousand wild Yellowstone bison are killed each winter to reduce herd size in the Park and to prevent them from recolonizing their historical ranges. Attempts to establish unfenced herds on Indian reservations and vast tracts of sparsely inhabited public lands are met with stout resistance by the state. These practices will change only if people raise their pens as well as their voices.

It was not my intention to write a political novel with *Buffalo Jump Blues*. I hoped only to tell a good story, and if that story casts light on a subject that has been deliberately obfuscated and kept from the public eye, so much the better. You will be the judge of the novel. As far as maintaining my neutrality about bison, which once freely roamed the breadth of the continent in tens of millions, and today, reduced to a few thousand head, are by and large treated as unruly cattle to be fenced and sent to slaughter, I admit my failure.

Bozeman, Montana
February 19, 2016

Keith McCafferty's sixth novel in
the Sean Stranahan mystery series
is available now.

Read on for the first two chapters of . . .

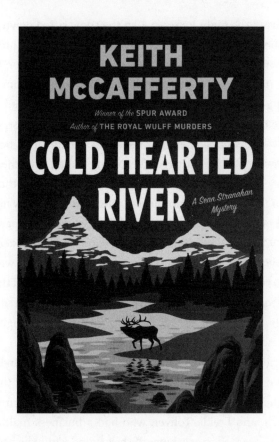

CHAPTER ONE

The Aphrodisiac Graveyard

It had started the night before, when the snow sifted down onto the carcass of his horse and there was no sound beyond the intermittent release of its gases and no stars to wish upon. That's when he began to "What if" it to death, going back to the morning, kissing her face and feeling the flutter of her eyelashes that, as he'd helped her from the saddle two hours later, were already icicling with frost.

What if he'd stopped before three kisses became four, before four became more? But he hadn't, and too long in bed gave them a slow start, their breakfast hurried, the Sunday edition of the *Bridger Mountain Star* outside the mudroom where the paperboy had tossed it. If he'd picked it up he would have checked the back page for the weather. What kind of Montanan were you if you didn't keep an eye on the sky? But he had a pannier in each hand and they were in too much of a rush to get to the property where they pastured the horses, and then to the trailhead with dawn breaking, a sifting of snowflakes she caught on her tongue, but dead calm, just cold enough that the horses blew steam from their nostrils.

It was called the Aphrodisiac Graveyard, a series of wind-scoured openings on a south-facing slope some few miles west of the wilderness boundary. Here the bulls shed their great antlers in February and March, and Freida Toliver, who had a business making antler chandeliers, wanted to get them off the ground while the beams were still that rich dark mahogany and the tines ivory tipped, before porcupines gnawed them and the weather blanched them of their value.

That was before the fairytale snowfall turned into stinging shards of ice and the temperature dropped thirty degrees in an hour, and any thought of collecting elk antlers was long forgotten.

He couldn't really say where they made the first wrong turn. Like most people who become lost, he thought that he knew where they were for some time after he didn't. It wasn't just the visibility, which had dropped from twenty miles to as many yards, but the wind blew the snow into a sea of scallops, dulling colors and swallowing landmarks to the point where it might have been a different country, or, rather, no country at all. A trail that he remembered as crossing a low saddle seemed to have vanished, along with the saddle, and so they took another trail—"This is it, right, Freida?"—and she shook her head yes, feeding into his confidence, willing it to be so. An hour of lying to themselves later, it became obvious that it wasn't.

"I thought you were an Indian," he said, trying for a smile, and failing. *Where the hell are we?*

It was a gamble, giving the horses their heads, trusting that they would find their way back to the pack trail. And their hearts lifted when they thought they had found it, only to discover that it was an elk trail that branched like a strong man's forearm veins, some bleeding back into each other, others not. The horses followed one of those veins down into a creek bottom, and it was there, in the dark heart of the mountain, and no longer sure even which mountain, that he'd made the first attempt to build a fire. But the pack of bar matches he found in a pants pocket were damp, the heads only smearing against the chemical strip.

What if I hadn't given up smoking and had my lighter, he'd think. *What if?*

"I might have some in my fishing vest," she'd said. It seemed absurd now, the notion that they might do a little fishing in one of the high-altitude tarns. "It's in the saddlebag," she told him. But her hands shook so badly she couldn't undo the buckle.

"Here, let me." He rummaged through the vest.

"Try the inside zipper pocket, the one with my license."

"I did."

He lifted his shoulders and let them fall. She looked at him, and did exactly the same. Like she was his echo. That's what they were to each other. He even called her that, Little Echo. She was Northern Cheyenne and had taken to it. Told people it was her tribal name.

He bent down and hugged her. He felt the frost of her eyebrows melt against his cheek and thought of the morning, holding her close, feeling her heart beat.

"I don't want to die," she said.

He looked at her, a small woman made smaller by the immensity of the country that was felt rather than seen and the fourteen hands of her horse that stood nearby, its empty saddle already frosting with snow.

"Nobody's going to die, Freida. Don't even think it."

It was the way they had together, one strong, then the other.

I could start a fire with the gun, he thought. It was something he'd read about, possibly in the same issue of an outdoor magazine where he'd read about a hunter who'd survived a night of thirty below zero by crawling inside the carcass of a moose.

He pulled the handgun from the holster, the single-action Ruger Blackhawk that was her birthday present to him when he'd turned fifty. Five cylinders loaded, the chamber under the hammer empty. He tried to recall the procedure. You formed a tinder nest with cloth, dried grasses, anything that was flammable. Then you pulled the bullet from a cartridge case, dumped half of the powder and stuffed a piece of cotton cloth over the remaining charge, and fired it into the tinder nest. The idea was that the smoldering cloth would catch the tinder aglow, and you could lift up the nest and coax it into flame with your breath. In the illustration, it had looked like the man was praying, lifting his hands to heaven, exhaling fire.

He had a multi-tool in one of his saddlebags, fifty feet of parachute cord and a roll of duct tape in the other. A Montanan's holy trinity. You could do anything with a kit like that—mend fence, haul a deer out to the road, splint a broken arm. Maybe even start a fire.

He broke a handful of the tiny branches that quilled the lower trunk of a pine tree and collected some larger wood to feed in later. Tinder took more thought, and she was the one who suggested that he unravel wool threads from the tops of his socks. He wadded up the threads as she searched her pockets and came up empty.

"Did I see you put on the panties with the hearts?"

She nodded, too cold to frown at the question.

"Oh, right," she said, the shoe dropping. Nothing burned like cotton.

"I'd use mine, but they're poly."

She said okay, but her hands were so numb she couldn't trust them. "I might stab myself," she said. She had bitten through her tongue from the shuddering of her jaws and her voice was thick with the blood in her mouth.

"I'll do it," he told her.

He worked her zipper and carefully cut a patch of cloth from the top of the panties. Under his fingertips, he could feel her abdominal muscles crawl from the ice of his touch.

"We're going to laugh about this someday," he told her.

She nodded, but didn't speak. The cold had started with her hands and feet. Then it had crawled up her arms and legs. Now it had settled like a pick in her chest. Even the drawing of breath was an effort. She turned away and spit blood onto the snow.

"This is going to do the trick," he said.

He tore thin strips from the cloth and wove them into the tinder nest. Pulling a bullet wasn't easy—the hard-cast .41 Magnum loads were crimped into the case necks so they wouldn't shift during recoil—but by rapping on the neck to expand the brass and twisting the bullet with the pliers on his multi-tool, he managed. He placed the nest at the base of a big pine so it wouldn't be blown over by the gas escaping from the barrel.

The first shot from the heavy revolver resulted in a brief glow in the center of the nest, but it went black before he could pick it up.

A little more powder? The second try was better, producing an orange-limned marble of smoldering tinder that died slowly enough to give them heart, but died all the same.

"What about the flies?"

"What are you talking about?"

"You can shave off the hair and the feathers. It will burn."

"Trout flies, you mean?"

She nodded. "I packed my vest in the pannier. Those big dries, the golden stones and the salmon flies, they have lots of wing material."

"You know, that's a really good idea," he said. "I knew I married you for some reason."

It looked like modern art, a softball-sized bird's nest of dried grasses, rusted pine needles, bits of cloth with pink and purple hearts, all of it woven together with ginger neck hackles, bucktail and marabou stork fibers dyed in a half dozen hues.

"That ought to catch fire just looking at it," he said.

Then the .41 spoke and for a time there was a new color on the mountain, a molten candle of hope. The matchstick-sized sticks caught fire and the flames licked up as they used their hands for wind blocks. But the ground was cold and it sapped the fire even as they fed it.

Come on. Come on. They blew on the struggling licks of flame.

"Not so hard. You're blowing it out. This needs a woman's touch."

That's my girl, he thought.

But it was like the CPR he'd once performed on a victim of lightning strike. You kept pressing the breastbone and sharing your breaths, even after the heart under your hands grew cold.

She had been waving her hat to coax the flames and pushed the frozen clumps of her hair out of her face.

"Éoseetonéto," she said. "It's really cold." And in English, "I'm freezing."

He knew soon as she went to the people's language that he'd lost her. She never did that unless she was at wit's end.

"Maybe he was right," she said.

"Who was right?"

"The man, the one I told you about. With the cat. He said that April was the best month to die."

"He's just a crazy old loon. You said so yourself."

"Yeah, I guess."

But that's when it had really sunk in, and looking down at her—she was in the dark, the fire was out—he had a thought. *This is how it ends. You wake up with the woman you've searched all your life to find, who changed her name for you and who you can't think of going on without, and that night you lie down with her and die. There are no premonitions. You're just another victim of nature's impersonal calculus.*

He told himself to stop it. After all, there were still two bullets in the Ruger. He tipped out the cylinder to double-check. And thought of the horses. They were Rocky Mountain horses, not the biggest of their breed, but just as big as a moose.

He shook the cartridges into the palm of his left glove to show them to her; sensed, rather than saw, the recognition take shape in her face.

The brass gleamed in the light of his headlamp.

"Time to decide," he said. He meant they could try again to start fire or—the unthinkable. The unthinkable that had started as a half-hearted joke only an hour before, but was far from it now.

"I don't think I can do it."

"What? Shoot old Henry? You always said he was nothing but a mule with short ears."

"Either of them. They're our family."

He looked at her, her eyes squinted up against the cold, the frozen creeks of tears that ended in beads of ice.

"I'm sorry it's come to this," he said. "It's sure enough my fault."

"I'm the one with the damned business. I'm the reason we're here."

True, but little solace.

"I know what you're thinking and you can just stop it right now, Mister J. C. Toliver."

The paisley scarf she'd pulled up over her mouth was frosted from the exhalations of her breath and her voice shuddered, but the words held out a note of hope. "I thought maybe if we could just get them to lie down, we could snuggle up between them."

"You know they won't lie down in this kind of weather. Hell, old Henry barely lies down ever. And when's the last time you saw Annabel off her feet? It's the only way. If we can ride out this storm, we can walk off this mountain tomorrow morning."

"I know." For a moment the wind that swirled in the treetops died and they listened to the horses blow.

"All right," she said. A harder edge to the voice, another woman speaking now, the one he was counting on.

"If we're going to do this, let's do it while it's still light enough to see. But I'm not shooting my own horse. We're shooting each other's. Down in that little witch's heart." She gestured toward a patch of tangled timber. "If you can pull the trigger, I guess I can, too."

"All right then." And again: "It's the only way."

"I just need a minute, that's all. Just a minute with her. Go down there and wait for me."

"We don't have long."

"I won't be long. I just have to say goodbye."

He'd never seen her after that. He'd called out for her. He'd gone looking. He still had the gun and the two bullets. After a while, he used one of them.

The Witch's Heart

It was fourteen degrees with the second cup of coffee growing cold on the counter when Martha Ettinger got the call. No number she knew; a snowbird, she found out, just opening up the summer house in the Madison Valley. He'd been shoveling out his driveway when a truck pulled up, an empty two-stall horse trailer clattering in tow. The driver apologized for his appearance and assured the man it wasn't his blood, then asked if he could use the landline to call the sheriff. His name was J. C. Toliver, and Martha knew him as well as you know anyone you see twice a year who only has one subject. Chuck, that's what he went by, shoed Martha's horses; you could go right down the ranch directory for three counties and he could tell you half the horses' names and bore you with the bloodlines.

His voice was hoarse, the message terse. He told her to get a hasty team up the Johnny Gulch Road to the Specimen Ridge trail access where he'd meet them, that his wife was dying up there and for Christ sakes hurry, and the line had gone dead.

She'd hit the redial and the snowbird picked up, told her that Toliver had lurched out the door. "Like a zombie," the man said. "Like on that FX." Martha asked him to describe Toliver's condition. Did it smell like he'd been drinking? Was he coherent? Was he driving straight when he drove away?

No, he smelled like a slaughterhouse. To the other questions, yes, and yes.

Martha had taken the man's name and thanked him. She'd waited a beat as the snowbird cleared his throat. "Ah . . ." A note of hesitancy was in his voice. "You think you could thank me to the tune of a couple thousand bucks? He left gore all over a double diamond Navajo rug."

"Are you joking?"

"Not funny, is it? I'm one of those people doesn't know what to say sometimes and it comes out inappropriate. I mean no disrespect. Please call me when you get his wife out. I'd sure like to see a happy ending to this. It's the kind of thing that can ruin a man's summer."

Like most Montanans, Martha owned two Carhartt jackets: an older one for hunting and farmwork, another for town and to wear with the badge. She remembered what the snowbird had said as he ruminated about a ruined summer. She zipped into the old jacket. She'd meet Toliver with open arms, and she knew that whatever she was wearing, she might be able to get the smell out of it, but the blood would be another matter.

———

At the trailhead there was no time for introductions, just the sounds of the horses being unloaded, high whinnies, a "Come on, Trudy, settle down, now, the blanket doesn't bite." Matter-of-fact voices that didn't register circumstance, weather, or even fellow man. The masculine undertone that was the soundtrack of Martha's life.

Well, except for Katie Sparrow, who spoke mostly to Lothar, her Class III search dog, in what was a separate language altogether.

Martha called them over and they gathered around the warm hood of her truck, where she'd pinned down the corners of a topographic quad map. Walter Hess, her undersheriff, raised his eyebrows at one of the paperweights, a loaded clip from Martha's backup 10-millimeter. Hess was all angles and had a Chicago pallor that nine years in Montana hadn't changed much. He also had a sense of humor that Martha wouldn't get if she lived to be a hundred.

"Is that a Glock in your pocket or are you happy to see me?" he said, looking at the clip.

"Walt, that doesn't even make any sense."

"It's a metaphorical reference, Marth. That means—"

"I know what a metaphor is. Here's the deal." Her eyes went from Katie Sparrow to Harold Little Feather, her former deputy with whom she had shared more than the job on occasion, and who had recently climbed the rung to Criminal Investigations agent for the state office out of Helena. "Remember those hunters who got lost in a snowstorm and shot their horses so they could crawl inside them? Up in the Bear Paws? Well, that's what we got here, except one walked out this morning after a night in the carcass, and one couldn't pull the trigger when the time came and ran off with the other horse."

She gestured toward Toliver, who was standing by his pickup, changing into a spare set of clothes that Harold had had the foresight to bring when he got the call.

"Some of you know Chuck Toliver," she said. "It's his wife, Freida, that we're looking for."

"She have a gun?" Walt asked.

"Chuck says no."

No one looked at anyone else, to affirm in another's eyes what they were thinking. With no bullet waiting for a change of heart, Freida Toliver's chances of having survived the night were almost nothing.

Katie Sparrow had a face a blind person could read, and Martha watched a cloud come over it. No change of expression from Harold, not that she expected it. Words were just white noise to him. Part of him was already up the mountain, his mind working out the trail.

"Any chance she could start a fire?" Katie said.

Martha shook her head. "Not without divine intervention."

———

They were single file up the trail—Harold on his big paint, then Martha riding Petal, her Appaloosa, followed by Hess on a quarter horse Martha pastured named Big Mike, with Katie Sparrow bringing up the rear on her Rocky Mountain mare. Everyone in a line except for Lothar, who strayed here and there to hike a leg and proclaim his canine supremacy, which ended abruptly where a wolf track crossed the trail. After that, the shepherd kept his nose on the tail of his handler's horse.

It was a skeleton crew to be generous, which brought two of Martha's fingertips to the artery in her throat, a tip-off of her worry. But there was nothing to be done about it. The spring storm had dropped a blanket of trouble over the entire county, leaving more than three dozen motorists stranded, this in a place where people didn't swap out their snow tires until Memorial Day. The priority were two lost bear hunters—in any case that's what they'd told their wives they were hunting. As that call came in first, the search-and-rescue hasty team had responded, leaving the county closet more or less bare.

Martha called ahead to Harold to let the horses have a blow and crooked a gloved finger for Toliver to pull his mount up alongside.

"Can't be too much farther, huh, Chuck?"

He didn't look so bad now, in the change of clothes. He'd washed his face with snow and his blood-caked hair was covered by a hat, so except for his eyes, which had a glazed-over appearance and looked at nothing, and his gloved hands, which ran a tremor and shook the reins, Martha might have been talking to a normal person.

"I dunno," Toliver said. His red nose held a drop of moisture in suspense.

"I know you told me once, but tell me again just what happened this morning. You followed the trail she laid down when she left you, am I right about that?"

"I tried to, but it had snowed so much they were just pocks. I couldn't be sure it was the trail we made coming in, or the one she made going out. So I just started walking in circles, hoping I'd cut a fresh track if she was still moving, but I was all wet and cramping up and figured I better get back inside the horse. But by then the danged carcass was up a pretty steep slope and I didn't have the energy to climb up to it. I just couldn't get her done. So I told myself I better get on out while I could still walk a little bit."

He turned in the saddle, looking away. Martha could see his back heave, saw him roughly scrub at his face with the back of his glove. "That woman a' mine . . ." He shook his head. "She was so softhearted she couldn't even hunt anymore. Just stalked elk and counted coup. I'm the one had to fill the freezer. I should've known she'd never shoot her horse."

"We're going to get her, Chuck," Martha said. But she was looking at the depressions in the snow that were much shallower now that they'd climbed, the backtrail Toliver had made hiking out already indistinct where the wind had its way.

"Look," she said, lowering her voice. "You take as much time as you need. We'll leave when you're ready."

"I'm fine."

She watched Toliver turn his horse without touching the reins. A horse that the man hadn't set eyes on until two hours past. He was that kind of horseman. Something was off about him, though, and it took her a moment to realize what it was. With the day warming, Toliver had unzipped his jacket to expose the snap-up denim work shirt that Harold had lent him. It was a shirt that Martha had seen Harold wear a hundred times. Her favorite shirt of his, one she'd had occasion to unsnap before things went the way they did.

She chased the thought from her mind.

"Chuck, I want to ride up ahead with Harold. You hang back now with Walt and Katie."

Toliver touched the brim of his hat in acknowledgment, one in his catalog of country manners that were automatic. Martha rode to catch up with Harold, who was keeping to one side of the nearly blown trail, hanging his head to see past the withers of the horse. He called it reading the white book, deciphering the tracks in the snow.

"Can you still see that? I can hardly see it anymore."

"Plain as the sun," Harold said.

Martha could have said, "What sun?" But didn't.

———

He lost the trail a mile farther along. Or rather it was obliterated. Sometime after Toliver had walked away from the carcass of his horse, a herd of elk had wandered across the face of the ridge, churning the snow with their hooves. If the herd had walked single file, as elk typically do in deep snow, it would have been easy enough to see where Toliver's track strayed from it. But the elk had spread out to nip clumps of fescue peeking through the snow cover, the bulls that had yet to shed their antlers minding their headgear, circling from the main group to walk around trees with low-hanging branches.

"Are we fucked?" Martha said.

"No, I can work it out, but it's going to take awhile."

It cost them nearly an hour, the herd easy to follow but the going slow on the steep face of the ridge. Finally Harold found where Toliver's backtrack emerged from the maze of hoofprints to cross a saddle and head east. From this point the trail zigged down the face of the ridge, Harold twice pointing out places where Toliver had fallen, something he hadn't mentioned to Martha.

"I'm getting the heebie-jeebies about this," she said.

When the rest caught up to them, Martha pointed out the depressions in the snow. "You fell here, Chuck? Do you remember that?"

He nodded. Ice beads clung to the hairs in his nostrils. "I think it's just over the next rise, there's an elk wallow with a little creek running out of it. It's in a patch of timber there. Freida called it a witch's heart."

Suddenly he called out. "Freida! Can you hear me, Freida!" His voice echoed away.

"That'll do, Chuck. We don't want her struggling or doing anything that could get her hurt because she hears us. We'll backtrack to the carcass and go on from there. Any trace of her trail is left, Harold can follow it or the dog will smell it." She made her voice casual. "I see you're still carrying your piece. I thought the bullet you shot your horse with was the last one you had."

"It was. It's just, I don't know, rightly. I just feel naked without that weight on my hip."

"I'm on the same page with you," Martha said, patting the grips of her Ruger. And let out a breath, feeling relieved. She knew if they came up that rise and found a dead woman, her husband might well draw his revolver and put a bullet in his brain.

"Why don't you let me carry it anyway?" she said.

"Sure, if that's what you want."

"Yeah, I got plenty of room in the panniers."

Toliver pulled the handgun and nudged his mount over so he could lift the flap on Martha's pannier. "That satisfy you, Sheriff? Now if you don't mind, I want to find my wife."

They didn't. At least she hadn't made her way back to the little hollow. Toliver's horse was there, his skyward eye opaque and drawing back into the socket, his purpled intestines spilled out, the dark loaf of his liver and pink lungs pulled out. The flanks sagged hollow over the empty abdominal cavity. Bloody snow all around. Martha couldn't help but think he'd done a neat job of it, cutting through the diaphragm so it all came out in a piece, as he would an elk he'd shot.

"Field dressed to a tee," Walt commented.

"Old Henry," Toliver said. "He weren't the best horse, but he was a trusting animal and I killed him, and he saved me. How do you get your head around something like that?"

"You didn't have a choice," Martha said.

They moved upwind and out of sight of the carnage, where they dismounted. Martha edged away with Katie and Harold for a brief council.

"This is your show," she said. "Katie, does Lothar have enough to go on?"

Katie nodded. "They had extra clothes in the truck. He can isolate her scent, but eyes before nose. If Harold can see tracks, I'll hold Lothar back."

Harold nodded. "No sense having paw prints muck up the trail if there's one to follow. Give me twenty minutes. I can't find her, Katie and the dog take over. She's hypothermic. She isn't going to have made it far."

Martha looked past them. "Won't be an easy thing, telling him that we wait behind."

"You'll find a way. Like I said, she won't have gone far."

She hadn't, or at least her horse hadn't. Fifteen minutes later Martha saw Harold riding back through the timber, Freida Toliver's saddleless quarter horse shadowing his paint.

"You find her? You find . . . my Freida? You . . . tell me you found her."

Toliver rushed past Harold to the following horse. "Where is she, Annabel? Where's our Freida?" Then to Martha: "You tell me she's all right. You got to tell me she's all right." He dropped to his knees, all the cowboy gone out of him, just a man hanging his head, shaking, wavering back and forth in a personal wind. The tears came now, even before the news.

"You couldn't hear it?" Harold said. "She found her way into a bear den, no more than a quarter mile. I got upwind, that bear, it put up a hell of a ruckus. I'm guessing a sow with her newborns. All of us, we might be able to shoo her out long enough to see if Freida's alive in there. Human tracks going in. I didn't see any coming out."

"Take the horses or leave them?" Martha said.

Harold shook his head. "Ground tie them here. And Katie stays behind with the dog. He gets his hackles up, starts barking, he'll bring mama griz down on us like a bad wind."

Only Walter Hess had brought a rifle, his elk gun, a .300 Winchester Magnum. He took the lead as a quarter mile was halved, and halved again.

"That dark spot, that's the den entrance?" Martha asked.

Harold nodded. "Her tracks went right up to the entrance."

"A body would have to be desperate . . ." Hess's voice trailed away.

"You there, bear?" Harold called out.

No sound beyond the muffled plopping of snow as it melted from the laden pine boughs.

"Hey there, bear!"

Suddenly a chopping sound from outside the den in the trees up the slope, the sound of a bear clashing its teeth. Grunting roars reverberated in the confined space of the thicket.

"Cover me," Harold said.

As Harold and Walt moved forward, Toliver rose to follow them. Martha grabbed his coat. "Let them do their job."

The bear's roaring had become continuous. Up the slope from the den, Martha could see a tree whipping as if in a storm, its branches dropping heavy burdens of snow as the bear bristled up against the trunk.

Then there was the crash of Walt's big Magnum, the muzzle pointed up into the air.

"She's coming, Harold," Martha called out.

She could see her now, the bear rushing side to side, glimpses of her grizzled coat; could hear the menace of her popping teeth.

Harold was halfway back out of the den, dragging something heavy, then scooping it up into his arms and running with Walt trailing, all of them in retreat as the bear came bursting out of the pines and charged down the hill.

Another shot from Walt's rifle, the bullet kicking up the snow ahead of the bear. The bear stopped. She shook her huge head back and forth, then stood, leaning forward, snuffing at the air. She turned to peer at them, her poor eyesight unsure, then at the den behind her.

She dropped to all fours and moved toward the den. A last look around. The threat gone, she ducked her head and was gone from sight.

They didn't stop moving for another hundred yards.

"This is far enough," Martha said. "Bear's not coming."

Harold sat in the snow with Freida Toliver's body curled in his lap.

"Is she alive?" Toliver reached tentatively.

Martha felt for the pulse. She was alive.

"Let me." Toliver clutched the body against his chest.

Let him, Martha told herself. *It's his wife.*

Staggering under the weight, Toliver carried her back to the witch's heart. Martha hurriedly unsaddled her horse and spread the horse blanket on the snow to help insulate the motionless body. She could feel Freida's heart beating, making a thread of pulse as Harold went about building a fire, beating when Walt pulled the cord on the chainsaw they'd packed to clear a landing space for the helicopter that he'd called on the satellite phone.

Her heart was beating until it didn't and they all knew it, and nobody would admit it but the man who'd felt her eyelashes flutter against his lips the morning before. He lunged for the revolver in Martha's pannier, having one last cartridge in his revolver after all.